THE WIMBOURNE BOOK OF VICTORIAN
GHOST STORIES
Volume 11

Alastair Gunn is a writer, musician and professional astrophysicist based in the UK. Alastair writes a regular column for *BBC Science Focus* magazine, has written for *The Daily Telegraph*, *The Independent* and *The Guardian* and is a contributor to many astronomy magazines including *Astronomy Now* and *BBC Sky at Night Magazine*. His fiction includes a collection of supernatural stories called *Ballymoon* and his debut novel, *The Bergamese Sect*. He is the editor of the successful anthology series entitled *The Wimbourne Book of Victorian Ghost Stories*.

By Alastair Gunn

BALLYMOON
THE BERGAMESE SECT
THE WIMBOURNE BOOK OF VICTORIAN GHOST STORIES

THE WIMBOURNE BOOK OF

Victorian Ghost Stories

Volume 11

Edited and with an Introduction by

ALASTAIR GUNN

Wimbourne Books 2022

THE WIMBOURNE BOOK OF
VICTORIAN GHOST STORIES
(Volume 11)

First Publication Worldwide
Published by Wimbourne Books 2022

Copyright © Wimbourne Books 2022

ISBN 978-1-8382689-3-0

A CIP catalogue record for this book is available from the British Library.

Cover illustration: A portrait of American author Harriet Beecher Stowe (1811-1896) by Alanson Fisher (1807-1884) [National Portrait Gallery, Smithsonian Institution].

Typeset in Palatino Linotype by Wimbourne Books, UK.

Contents

THE WIMBOURNE BOOK OF

Victorian Ghost Stories

Volume 11

Wimbourne Books 2022

Introduction

Alastair Gunn

We have now reached *Volume 11* in the series entitled *The Wimbourne Book of Victorian Ghost Stories*. In this edition I have chosen to celebrate (again) not only the contribution of female authors to the genre, but also that of American authors, who are often overlooked in compilations of Victorian supernatural fiction.

As mentioned in previous volumes, it is possible that, of all the ghost stories published in the Victorian era in British and American magazines, about 70% were by women. In an era when women were far from emancipated it is important to consider why ghostly fiction attracted female writers. It was previously suggested that the draw was often monetary — that widowed, educated women could easily support themselves and their families financially because of the demand for short supernatural fiction. But this is a gross oversimplification.

Author Michael Cox contends that the supernatural genre allowed women the freedom to explore ideas and concepts beyond the normal social constraints of the time — indeed, darker, more intimate and even erotic overtones would be less likely frowned upon in the supernatural setting. Hence, female authors are often found exploring thoughts of love, death, marriage and even sexuality in the pages of Victorian periodicals — conversations that would clearly be shocking if expounded at the dinner table.

Another factor is perhaps that Victorian rationality itself promoted the female as an authority on the quasi-scientific, or, as one writer says, as 'repositories of residual instincts and intuitions'. Women were also held in esteem (mostly) as upholders of the moral high-ground and thus permitted to explore the themes of retribution, betrayal and misguided avarice — themes which appear often in the ghostly tale. But the female-penned ghost story also reveals some of the frustrations of the author and often deals with pre-suffrage themes such as dispossession of property, the patriarchal society, unhappy marriage, the dominant father-figure and economic bondage — as well as the common resentments and anxieties of the Victorian woman. There is no doubt also that many of their stories continue the tradition of the Victorian 'sensation fiction' — a genre more often than not dominated by women writers. In many ways, then, Victorian women writers used the traditional ghost story, like the sensation novel, to highlight the cultural inequalities of the era.

Of course, male American authors rightly appear alongside those masters of the supernatural genre from Europe and elsewhere; such as Nathaniel Hawthorne, Washington Irving, Edgar Allan Poe, Fitz-James O'Brien, Frank Richard Stockton, Ambrose Bierce, Henry James, Ralph Adams Cram and William Chambers Morrow. But women too are extremely well represented, if not dominant, in the arena of American macabre literature during the Victorian era. Although the most prolific in the field were probably Madeleine Vinton Dahlgren and Mary E. Wilkins Freeman (and later Edith Wharton), I have chosen for this volume stories which are either by lesser known authors or authors not predominantly known for their supernatural tales. So, here I present another twenty excellent ghost stories from the American presses; ordered chronologically, spanning the years 1846 to 1901.

Just as in previous volumes, I have not been too strict on the definition of a 'ghost story'; they are all stories of the supernatural that present or imply a force or apparition beyond our common perception. I should also point out that I have rarely edited the following texts to reflect modern spelling or usage — they appear as they do in the original publications (with the exception of a few obvious typographical errors). However, certain Victorian peculiarities *have* been changed, for example the hyphenation of 'to-day' and 'to-night', and the propensity of Victorians to separate words like 'everyone', 'anyone', 'sometimes', 'everywhere', etc., into their component parts. These corrections are simply because the originals tend to trip up the modern eye.

Following the tradition begun in *Volume 4*, I hereby include a contemporary Victorian essay on the theme of ghostly fiction, this time from an American journal. The article is entitled simply *Ghost Stories* and was published anonymously in the periodical *Flag of Our Union* in March 1861. This essay welcomes the perceived return of the traditional ghost story remembered from the author's youth —

"Fashions in literature, like fashion in dress, revolve in a circle. It is unsafe to ridicule the costumes of our great-grandfathers and great-grandmothers, for they may come up again in our own time. Not so very long ago, we were laughing at high-heeled shoes and hooped skirts for ladies; lo and behold! both these abominations were not long after adopted in Europe and America. We gentlemen may come to powdered hair and satin coats and knee-breeches, and ruffles round the hand, and small swords and three-cornered hats for aught we know. So in this ever-recurring repetition of the past, we are come again to the genuine ghost story — the tale of horror calculated to freeze the blood of youth, to set the hair on end, and to make the flesh creep. Not your Mrs. Radcliff ghost story — where, after shuddering through two volumes of midnight apparitions, mysterious noises, blue lights and magic music, at the close of the third everything is explained on natural principles, and the ghosts shown to be flesh and blood, the blue lights phosphorus, and the magic music the sounds of a hurdy-gurdy rendered romantic by distance. No such humbug as that; but real spiritual visitants — criminals repeating the evil deeds of their lives in the scene of their earthly enormity — gibbeted assassins coming down from the gallows to walk the earth — genuine grand-fathers resuscitated for the purpose of pointing out secret drawers where their last will and testaments lie concealed, and all that sort of thing. Fitz-James O'Brien does a little of this — Bulwer has lately tried his hand — anonymous writers are beginning to pile up the horrors at so much per folio.

"This revived taste carries us back to the childish days when every literary dish palled upon our appetite that was not well spiced with horrors. We well remember how the German story of 'Der Freischutz: or, The Magic Bullet,' thrilled our marrow; how reluctant we were to go down cellar after wood in the evening when we had been reading the 'Spectre of the Hartz Forest,' or 'Raymond and Agnes: or, The Bleeding Nun.' The going to bed after 'supping full of horrors' was a very trying performance. There were a couple of dark closets that had to be explored, the doors being opened in the full expectation of seeing a skeleton snugly ensconced behind each of them. The old armchair had to be lifted out of place, to be sure that it did not conceal the cowering form of a vampyre, or a ghoul, or a wehr-wolf. After the lamp was extinguished, some time was passed under the bed clothes in fearful expectation that the clothes would be pulled down by a bony hand, and that we should be compelled to look a moist, unpleasant gentleman, divested of his flesh and muscles, and taking a genteel airing in his bones, full in the face. All of us boys revelled in ghost stories, but we are not aware that they materially affected our nerves or unfitted us for the realities of life. We certainly consumed a very fair allowance of beef, bread and potatoes, enjoyed marbles, peg-tops, football and kite-flying, and indulged in pugilistic encounters much after the fashion of youngsters of the present day. We don't recollect a single authentic instance of a boy being actually 'frightened out of his wits' by a ghost story. And, what was very curious, amateurs as we were of ghosts, and desirous of making their acquaintance, not one of us ever succeeded in seeing a ghost. We have laid wait for them in their favorite haunts, old burying grounds, lonely groves, in the woods, deserted houses, but never caught them at it.

"The new crop of ghosts is very different from the old run of the same article; they are more refined, metaphysical, ethereal gentlemen and ladies. Some of them are too attenuated to be cognizable by mortal vision, though they manifest their presence by good round thumps on solid mahogany tables and bedsteads. Sometimes a cold hand passes over your face. Sometimes, as in one of Bulwer's stories, the spectre steals your watch as adroitly as Dummie Dunnaker would have done. Sometimes they regale your ears with music, not even disdaining the humble banjo as an instrument. On the whole, they are an improvement on their predecessors, and it is refreshing to know that the advance of the age has not been without its influence on those who no longer have their portion in the world we live in, but revisit it at intervals. Seriously, we think these ghost stories will have a moderate run, culminate in ridiculous exaggerations, then die out, giving way to a different phase in fiction, to be again resuscitated for the delectation of some future generation."

As usual, before we delve into the realms of the ghosts themselves, I present some basic biographical and bibliographical details for each of our authors in this volume.

The career and body of work of writer and poet Elizabeth Fries Lummis Ellet (1818-1877) is perhaps marred by a tendency to emphasise her notoriety for 'jealousy or a taste for scandal-mongering'. Her name is often associated with gossip surrounding the alleged liaison between author Edgar Allan Poe (1809-1849) and poet Frances Sargent Osgood (1811-1850). These two, both married, appeared to be engaged in a flirtatious relationship within the pages of Poe's magazine *The Broadway Journal*. Ellet was apparently witness to indiscreet letters from Osgood to Poe, possessed by Poe's wife Virginia, and on Ellet's suggestion Anne Lynch (Botta), author and hostess of New York's best known literary salon, and Margaret Fuller, journalist and critic, visited the Poe household to retrieve the letters that might harm Osgood's reputation. This interference infuriated Poe so much that he forever afterwards spoke of Ellet in extremely negative terms. Osgood's husband also threatened to sue Ellet unless she gave a formal retraction of the allegations. This she did but she appears to have held a grudge against Poe that has since negatively tinged her twentieth-century reputation. This is a shame because she is otherwise regarded as an important contributor to the American literary scene of her day, an early pioneer of feminist scholarship and a significant recorder of women's history during the American Revolutionary War. Ellet was born in Sodus Point, New York, in 1818 to a prosperous physician, William Nixon Lummis and his wife Sarah. Educated at a female-only seminary in Aurora, New York, she began publishing at only sixteen. She soon after married William Henry Ellet and moved to South Carolina where her husband had been offered several academic appointments. Elizabeth continued to make contributions to local, regional and national publications, primarily of poetry, but also translations and criticism of Italian and German writers.

Between 1845 and 1850, when her husband returned from South Carolina, Elizabeth lived separately from her husband in New York, in order to advance her literary career. Throughout a long and distinguished career Elizabeth directed her skills toward many genres; from poetry, fiction, tragedy, and stories for children, to essays, criticism, biography and history. She is certainly not known for supernatural leanings but it is an honour to include in this volume her ghostly tale entitled *The Haunted House in Georgia*, which first appeared in *The Columbian Lady's and Gentleman's Magazine* in November 1846.

Little is known about author Nancy Thorning Munroe (1820-1883) other than that she was from Charlestown, Massachusetts, was the daughter of John Thorning, a Boston flour and grain merchant, and his wife Fanny, and may have been a vague associate of journalist and abolitionist Mary Livermore (1820-1905). Nancy married Edward Munroe (1812-1868) in 1839 in Charlestown and appears to have been very active, along with several other members of her extended family, in the Universalist movement in the Boston area. For example, she is known to have sung a hymn at the laying of the cornerstone for what is now Tufts University in Somerville, originally called the Universalist College. She and her family were also active in the puritanical press in the Boston area. Writing as 'Mrs. N. T. Munroe', and before her marriage as 'Miss N. Thorning', she contributed many poems, hymns, short stories and articles to the local Universalist press in the late 1830s, 1840s and 1850s; mainly in titles such as *The Lily of the Valley*, the *Universalist and Ladies' Repository*, the *Evangelical Magazine and Gospel Advocate* and *The Rose of Sharon*. She also wrote a substantial number of pieces for several national periodicals published in Boston; namely *Flag of Our Union, Ballou's Dollar Monthly Magazine* and *Ballou's Pictorial Drawing-Room Companion*. In 1846 she published an unreserved Universalist reformation manifesto, thinly veiled as evangelical fiction, called *Is It a Small Thing?* In *Volume 11* of *The Wimbourne Book of Victorian Ghost Stories* I have included Nancy's only known supernatural tale, *The Haunted House*, which was published in *Flag of Our Union* in April 1854. Nancy Thorning Munroe is buried in the Mount Auburn Cemetery, Cambridge, Massachusetts.

Rose Terry Cooke (1827-1892) was an American author mostly known for her romances of rustic life in New England — her style presaging what became known as the 'local-color' movement. Born into a well-off family in West Hartford, Connecticut, and well-known to the more famous author Harriet Beecher Stowe (see below), Cooke was a somewhat sickly but extremely intelligent and accomplished child. She graduated from the Hartford Female Seminary in 1843 before becoming a teacher at a Presbyterian school in Burlington, New Jersey, and then a governess in the family of the clergyman William Van Rensselaer. But she soon returned to Hartford and began a literary career with poetry submitted to the *New York Daily Tribune*, *Graham's Magazine* and the *Atlantic Monthly*. In 1873 Rose married Rollin S. Cooke who, enamoured by her poetry, had pursued her with something of an obsession for several years. Although a successful poet it was really her short stories which made her name; these were collected in several collections — *Somebody's Neighbors* (1881), *The Deacon's Week* (1885), *Root-Bound and Other Sketches* (1885), *The Sphinx's Children and Other People's* (1886) and *Huckleberries Gathered from New England Hills* (1891). I have included here Rose's tale called *My Visitation* which appeared in *Harper's New Monthly Magazine* in July 1858, but does not appear to have been later anthologised.

Born in Worcester, Massachusetts, (Mary) Jane Goodwin Austin (1831-1894) was a direct descendent of the Plymouth Pilgrims. Her father, Isaac Goodwin, who died when she was just two years old, reputedly left an enormous archive of historical and legal documents pertaining to the Pilgrims, the location of which is still a mystery today. After receiving an excellent private education, Jane married Loring Henry Austin (1819-1892) in 1850 and spent her life in Cambridge, Concord and Roxbury. She had four children: Lillian (1851), LeBaron (1853), Isabella (1854), who died in infancy, and Rose Standish (1860). Although publishing children's fantasy as early as 1859, it would be the 1880s before Jane became a reasonably successful author of novels and short stories, and that success was born out of her imaginative and well-researched Pilgrim novels (*A Nameless Nobleman*, 1881; *Standish of Standish*, 1889; *The*

Dr. Le Baron and his Daughters, 1890; *Betty Alden* 1891), although Jane is known to have wildly exaggerated the underlying facts of these 'historical' stories. Her other works include *Fairy Dreams* (1860), *Moonfolk* (1874), *Mrs. Beauchamp Brown* (1880), *The Desmond Hundred* (1882) and *Nantucket Scraps* (1882). Jane was apparently close friends with other Massachusetts authors Nathaniel Hawthorne, Ralph Waldo Emerson, Ellen Louise Chandler Moulton (see below) and Louisa May Alcott and was highly regarded amongst the literary circles of Boston and New York. This volume includes Jane's ghostly tale called *The Deserted Hut: A Ghost Story*, which appeared in *Flag of Our Union* in November 1865 (and also, in the UK, in *Reynold's Miscellany* for December 1865).

Elizabeth Stuart Phelps Ward (1844-1911), born Mary Gray Phelps, was the daughter of a clergyman and educator, Austin Phelps, and his wife Elizabeth Wooster Stuart Phelps (1815-1852). After her mother's early death, Mary, then aged only eight, asked to be renamed after her mother. She subsequently dropped 'Gray' and substituted both her mother's Christian and maiden names. She also took the name of her husband, Herbert Dickinson Ward, when she married in 1888. Born in Andover, Massachusetts, Elizabeth kept house for her father, who became the President of Andover Theological Seminary, from a young age. She had a passion for writing, apparently inherited from both her mother and father. Her father's works became standard textbooks for Christian theological study and her mother wrote the 'Kitty Brown' series of girls' books under the pen name of H. Trusta. Elizabeth's first published work appeared in the *Youth's Companion* when she was just thirteen and she began her novel-writing career with a series of children's books (which she continued into the 1880s). But her first adult novel was the sentimental and spiritualist-influenced tale called *The Gates Ajar* (1868). Concerning the bereaved sister of a Civil War casualty, who imagines their reunion in a utopian afterlife, the book became very popular on both sides of the Atlantic, even though it controversially rejected the traditional Calvinist view of Heaven. Elizabeth would go on to write on themes that sailed close to the wind in Victorian American society, such as the domestic status of women, labour relations and antivivisectionism. She is recognised as an important early feminist writer who constantly challenged the traditional and conservative view of women in society. Her most important works are *The Silent Partner* (1871), *The Story of Avis* (1877), *Beyond the Gates* (1883), *The Gates Between* (1887) and *Trixy* (1904). Elizabeth wrote a number of supernatural tales during her long career; most of them contained in her early collection titled *Men, Women and Ghosts* (1869) or the later title *The Empty House and Other Stories* (1910). The tale included here is called *Kentucky's Ghost* and appeared in the former collection, but first saw the light of day in the November 1868 edition of *The Atlantic Monthly*.

Harriet Elizabeth Prescott Spofford (1835-1921), a prolific author of Gothic romantic fiction, poetry and essays, was much esteemed by such fellow writers as Harriet Beecher Stowe, Rose Terry Cooke, Mary Wilkins Freeman, and William Dean Howell. Born in Calais, Maine, to a well-to-do seafaring family, Harriet spent most of her life in Newburyport, Massachusetts. The daughter of Joseph N. Prescott (who was first a lumber merchant, then lawyer and finally gold prospector), and his wife Sarah née Bridges, Harriet showed an early aptitude for language and received a very good education. This put her in good stead as the senior bread-winner of the household after her father's business interests failed and both her parents became invalids. She turned to writing as a source of income, writing over one hundred tales in little more than three years, most of which, being published only in the local press, are now lost. However, Harriet achieved a good measure of success after the inclusion of her story *In a Cellar* in the prestigious and widely-circulated periodical the *Atlantic Monthly* in 1858. Her first novel, *Sir Rohan's Ghost*, appeared in 1859. Although her career spanned more than sixty years, she is mostly forgotten today — her most important works are the two collections of short stories (*The Amber Gods and Other Stories*, 1863; *A Scarlet Poppy and Other Stories*, 1894) and the novels *The Thief in the Night* (1872), *Marquis of Carabas* (1872), *Hester Stanley at St. Mark's* (1883) and *The Servant Girl Question* (1884). It was her short stories that received the most acclaim (*In a Cellar*, *Circumstance*) and she was quite accomplished in the macabre genre, stemming from her love of the Gothic. Harriet's tale included here is *The Strange Passengers*, which appeared in *Lippincott's Magazine* for June 1868, but which does not appear to have been later anthologised.

Author Harriet Beecher Stowe (1811-1896) was famous for her anti-slavery novel *Uncle Tom's Cabin*, first published in 1852 and still in print today. It was (and still is) a bastion of the abolitionist agenda and broke all publishing records of the time. She wrote over thirty books, some novels, but others including advice on housekeeping, travel memoirs, religious studies and biographies. Harriet was born in 1811 in Lichfield, Connecticut, the sixth of eleven children, all of whom became ministers or were active in education or women's rights. Harriet started writing at an early age; her first publication being a textbook on geography for children. In 1832 the family moved to Cincinnati and there she met Calvin Stowe, a widower who was a professor at the local seminary, and they married in January 1836. The couple later moved to Brunswick, Maine, where Calvin was appointed a lecturer at Bowdoin College. Harriet and Calvin had seven children together. It was the death of one of these, Samuel Charles Stowe, of cholera, at only eighteen months of age, which inspired Harriet to begin the novel which made her famous. She later explained: 'Having experienced losing someone so close to me, I can sympathize with all the poor, powerless slaves at the unjust auctions'. With the financial security that *Uncle Tom's Cabin* brought her, Harriet embarked on a literary career that lasted over fifty years. Other notable works include *The Minister's Wooing* (1859), *The American Woman's Home* (1869, co-authored with her sister Catharine), *Lady Byron Vindicated* (1871) and *Pogunuc People* (1878). Harriet produced some excellent ghostly fiction in short-story form, including *The Ghost in the Cap'n Brown House* and *The Ghost in the Mill*, most appearing in the collection *Sam Lawson's Oldtown Fireside Stories* (1870). The tale reproduced here, *Tom Toothacre's Ghost Story*, is also from that collection.

Even though widely regarded as one of the first 'realist' writers in America, and as an important social historian, and despite having published over 500 works, Rebecca Blaine Harding Davis (1831-1910) is today a largely neglected nineteenth-century author. Her works have variously tackled social issues such as (what today would be called) post-traumatic stress disorder, female emancipation, the oppression of immigrants, the negative results of capitalism, and corruption, greed, and racism in all their forms; and all in a style that is intrinsically 'American'. Her short story *Life in the Iron Mills*, published in the *Atlantic Monthly* in 1861, is a seminal attack on both capitalism, oppression of the labouring classes and female bondage, and garnered Davis the devotion of several important writers of her day; including Nathaniel Hawthorne, Louisa May Alcott and Ralph Waldo Emerson. Born in Washington, Pennsylvania, but growing up in Wheeling, West Virginia, Davis was initially home-schooled before attending the Washington Female Seminary, graduating valedictorian in 1848. She then rejoined her family in Wheeling where she worked in obscurity as a journalist (and sometime editor) for the local newspaper, *The Intelligencer*, for more than a decade until *Life in the Iron Mills* catapulted her to relative notoriety. She went on to become an editor of the *New York Tribune* and published regularly and successfully throughout the 1870s and 1880s, but by the time of her death in 1910 had been largely forgotten. It is not surprising to find, in such a large body of work as Davis's, one or two supernaturally-themed stories. One of these, included here, is the excellent *The Story of a Shadow*, which first appeared in the periodical *Galaxy* for April 1872.

Clara Florida Guernsey (1836-1893) was born in Pittsford, in upstate New York, and lived all her life near Rochester, N.Y. From her father, businessman and philanthropist James T. Guernsey, Clara inherited a close link with the Iroquoian-speaking Seneca tribe who would stop at the Guernsey home during their travels east. Later in life, Clara would write about the Seneca peoples often and was eventually adopted as a tribe member. Clara's elder sister was Lucy Ellen Guernsey (1826-1899) who was a very successful author, producing over sixty novels. Although not hugely successful, and unfortunately much forgotten today, Clara penned upwards of thirty volumes herself, including various collections of fairy-tales (*Christmas Greens*, 1865; *The Merman and the Figure Head*, 1871), adventure stories (*The Silver Rifle*, 1871; *The Shawnee Prisoner*, 1877) and domestic romances (*Aunt Priscilla's Story*, 1867; *Elmira's Ambitions*, 1875). She wrote articles and short stories for *Gleason's Pictorial*, *Godey's Lady's Book and Magazine*, *Atlantic Monthly*, *Lippincott's Magazine*, *Appleton's Journal*, *The Aldine* and *The Cosmopolitan*; several of her short stories were of a ghostly nature. In this volume Clara's tale *The Walking Boy* is included — it was first published in *Harper's New Monthly Magazine* for January 1873.

Another 'Clara', Clara Le Clerc, was actually a pseudonym of Henrietta Clay Ligon Gorman (1844-1919), a woman originally from Alabama, but who became an important artistic and literary figure, and shameless self-promoter, in Fort Worth, Texas. Henrie (as she was known) received an M. A. degree in 1862 from College Temple, a women's college located in Newnan, Georgia, before marrying, in 1870, Francis Alexander Stephen Gorman. The couple moved to Fort Worth in 1873, and Henrie quickly established herself in a fledgling literary community in the town, eventually becoming, for a time, the society columnist for the *Fort Worth Gazette*. She also opened her home as an unofficial public library and established a literary club, called 'The Nest', which promoted 'self-improvement, mutual benefit and development of Southern literature'. Based on the style and function of a college magazine on which she had worked, in 1899 Henrie founded a quarterly literary magazine called *The Bohemian* which contained essays, critiques, poems, and short stories (mostly by Southern authors, including Henrie herself), as well as plentiful photographs of Fort Worth and its environs. Having published her first short story at age fifteen in the *Temperance Crusader* (Atlanta), she went on to write sporadically throughout her life. She published, under the Le Clerc pen name, a collection of short stories entitled *Uncle Plenty*, in 1892, and apparently another (now lost) volume entitled *Aunt Clara's Friday Afternoon Stories*. The tale included in this volume appears to be Henrie's only tale submitted to the mainstream periodicals of the time. It is called *The Haunted House by the Mill: A Texas Story* and appeared in *Ballou's Monthly Magazine* for December 1875.

Lucretia Peabody Hale (1820-1900) was born in Boston to Nathan Hale (1784-1863), lawyer and owner/editor of the *Boston Daily Advertiser*, and his wife Sarah Preston Hale (née Everett). From a family with connections (her father was the nephew and namesake of American Revolutionary War hero Nathan Hale, and her mother was the sister of politician and diplomat Edward Everett), Lucretia had a comfortable life socialising within the suburbs of Boston's literary scene. Two of Lucretia's younger brothers (Edward Everett Hale, 1822-1909, and Charles Hale, 1831-1882) both became writers; Lucretia's first literary endeavour was the joint authorship, with Edward, of a novel entitled *Margaret Percival in America* (1850). She later published a substantial number of books, both fiction (mainly romances) and non-fiction (needlework manuals, board games, religious works); her most important are *The Struggle for Life* (1861), *The Service of Sorrow* (1867), *Six of One by Half a Dozen of the Other* (1872), *The Wolf at the Door* (1877), *Fagots for the Fireside* (1888) and *The New Harry and Lucy* (1892). Lucretia was probably most successful during her day with her popular whimsical short stories of the Peterkin family that adorned the pages of periodicals *Our Young Folks* and then *St. Nicholas* for almost a decade. These were later collected in *The Peterkin Papers* (1880) and *The Last of the Peterkins* (1886), both still considered classics of children's humorous and nonsensical literature. In *Volume 11* of *The Wimbourne Book of Victorian Ghost Stories* I have included Lucretia's story called *The American Ghost*. This first appeared in *Swinton's Story-Teller*, published in December 1883, but almost simultaneously featured in both the *Boston Daily Globe* and the *Washington Post*.

Ellen Louise Chandler Moulton (1835-1908) overcame a lonely childhood, repressed by the radical Calvinist views of her parents, to become a significant figure in the New England literary scene. She was born in Pomfret, Connecticut, the only child of Lucius Lemuel Chandler and Louisa Rebecca Chandler (née Clark), and received a very conservative education, first in Pomfret and later at Troy Female Seminary (now the Emma Willard School) in Troy, New York. She married, aged twenty, William Upham Moulton, who had been the publisher of Ellen's first forays into literature in the Boston periodical *True Flag*.

Those early works, mostly poetry, but including song lyrics and prose pieces, were highly regarded — many were collected in *This, That and the Other* (1854), published when Ellen was just eighteen, and selling over twenty-thousand copies. After two further books (*Juno Clifford*, 1855; *My Third Book*, 1859) Ellen's fiction output was somewhat curtailed by the American Civil War, but she had in the meantime fostered a career writing reviews, critiques and literary news for the *New York Tribune*. In 1876 she undertook a lengthy tour of Europe, taking in London, Paris, Rome, Florence and Venice, and came in contact with many of the premier literary figures of the day, including Robert Browning, George Eliot, Thomas Hardy and Algernon Charles Swinburne. On her return to America her reputation, mainly as a poet, continued to grow; her lyrical and verse skills were even compared to Milton, Wordsworth and Rossetti. She produced volumes of poetry (*Swallow-Flights and Other Poems*, 1878; *In the Garden of Dreams*, 1889), children's stories (*Bedtime Stories*, 1873), travelogues (*Random Rambles*, 1881; *Lazy Tours in Spain and Elsewhere*, 1896) and collections of short fiction (*Miss Eyre from Boston, and Others*, 1889) throughout the latter decades of the nineteenth century, although many of her periodical publications were never collected. Ellen produced the occasional ghostly tale, most of these being collected in *Miss Eyre from Boston, and Others*. For this volume I have selected the tale *On the Stroke of the Clock* which appeared in that collection but first appeared in *The Continent Weekly Magazine* in August 1884.

Like Rose Terry Cooke (see above), (Theodora) Sarah Orne Jewett (1849-1909) is recognised as a leading writer in the 'local color' or 'regionalist' genre of American literature. She was born in South Berwick, Maine, and drew on her experiences of New England coastal life to create realistic and homely vignettes of rustic small town society. Her work was highly praised by the literati, including William Dean Howells, Willa Sibert Cather (see below) and Henry James. Afflicted with severe arthritis, Sarah was encouraged to spend long hours walking and would often accompany her father (a doctor) on his travels, giving her the key experiences that informed her writing. She wrote only three novels; *A Country Doctor* (1884), *A Marsh Island* (1885) and *The Tory Lover* (1901), as most of her output was in the short-story form. She published these in a wide range of local and national periodicals; from the *Atlantic Monthly* and *Harper's Bazaar*, through *The Cosmopolitan* and *Century Illustrated Magazine*, to *McClure's Magazine* and *The Ladies' Home Journal*. Many of these were collected in her numerous anthologies, the most important of which are *Deephaven* (1877), *The White Heron and Other Stories* (1886), *The Country of the Pointed Firs* (1896) and *The Queen's Twin and Other Stories* (1899). The tale included here is *The Gray Man* which appeared in *A White Heron and Other Stories*. Sarah never married and in later life lived with fellow-writer Annie Adams Fields (1834-1915) in a relationship which today is sometimes referred to as a 'Boston marriage'; although there is no evidence that the two women were romantically involved. In 1902 Sarah was severely injured in a carriage accident that left her unable to write. She died from a stroke in June 1909.

Remembered today chiefly for her powerful, semi-autobiographical story depicting the mental breakdown of an emotionally abused young wife, *The Yellow Wallpaper*, Charlotte Perkins Gilman (1860-1935) endured a childhood of poverty and a life of depression to become an important humanist, feminist, lecturer and author. Born in Hartford, Connecticut, Charlotte was an intelligent child interested in literature and science but did not do well at school. Her father, Frederic Beecher Perkins, a writer, editor and librarian from the prominent Beecher dynasty, abandoned his wife, Mary Fitch née Westcott, and children, when Charlotte was young. Although this caused the family untold hardship, and although they were never fully reconciled, Charlotte recognised the influence of her father's family heritage, saying that her "Beecher wit and gift of words" was owed to him. During this impoverished childhood, in which Charlotte was also emotionally shunned by her mother, she was often found in the company of important literary figures; she was a grand-niece of Harriet Beecher Stowe (1811-1896) and a niece (by marriage) of Lucretia Peabody Hale (1820-1900), both of whom are featured in this volume. In 1884 Charlotte married artist Charles Walter Stetson (1858-1911), but after the birth of their only child, Katharine Beecher Stetson, in 1885, Charlotte suffered from serious post-natal depression in

15

what was to become the start of a long battle with mental illness. The pair separated in 1888 and officially divorced in 1894, although they generally remained on amicable terms, particularly where their daughter was concerned. After removing to Pasadena for five years, Charlotte returned to New York to remarry, to her first cousin, Houghton Gilman, before returning to California in 1934 after Houghton's death. Diagnosed with inoperable breast cancer, Charlotte took her own life in August 1935. During an interesting, and sometimes tragic life, Charlotte developed an enviable literary and intellectual reputation. She began writing poems and stories for various periodicals after relocating to California, eventually carving out a niche for herself as a vocal and reasoned feminist. Her *Women and Economics* (1898) was a hugely popular manifesto for the economic independence of women. She further explored the role of women and domestic politics in works such as *Concerning Children* (1900) and *The Home* (1903). In her influential novel *Herland* (1915) she would crystallise her feminist thesis in a fictional, utopian setting. She also became a popular and well-travelled lecturer on the reformation of the institute of marriage, the duties and responsibilities of parenthood and labour ethics. Although her seminal works were in feminist theory, Charlotte was also an accomplished fiction author, producing numerous poems, about 186 short stories and nine novels; much of her fiction output appearing in her own magazine, *The Forerunner*. The occasional story by Charlotte had a supernatural theme; from these I have chosen to include the excellent tale called *The Giant Wistaria*, which was published in the *New England Magazine* for June 1891, under Charlotte's first husband's surname of Stetson.

Mollie Evelyn Moore Davis (1844-1909), a 'Southern Lady of charm and grace', was born in Talladega, Alabama. Her father, John Moore, originally trained as a physician in New England but later moved into iron production whilst in Alabama. In 1858 Moore relocated the family to Texas to set up a cotton plantation, eventually settling near the town of Tyler. Mollie Evelyn (who was actually christened 'Mary Evalina') received a private education at their country estate, Sylvan Dell, and showed an early aptitude for poetry. She began publishing at age fourteen in the *Tyler Reporter*, and after the family moved to Galveston, in the *Galveston News*. She eventually came to the attention of Edward H. Cushing of the *Houston Telegraph* who published her first poetry collection, *Minding the Gap and Other Poems*, in 1867. In 1874 Mollie married Thomas E. Davis, who in 1879 joined the staff of the *New Orleans Times*. Taking her already substantial reputation with her, Mollie moved to New Orleans, eventually becoming a significant figure in the city's social and literary field; her home in the French Quarter becoming a 'literary salon'. She went on to produce another twelve volumes, including novels (e.g. *In War Times at La Rose Blanche*, 1888; *Under the Man-Fig*, 1896; *The Wire Cutters*, 1899; *The Little Chevalier*, 1903; *The Price of Silence*, 1907), a history of Texas (*Under Six Flags*, 1897), short story collections (*An Elephant's Track and Other Stories*, 1897) and plays (*A Bunch of Roses and Other Parlor Plays*, 1903). Mollie was both a patriotic Texan and a devoted student of the Creole culture of New Orleans. She wrote for both adults and children, across a diverse range of themes, in prose and poetry, but it was her short fiction that brought her most recognition. Although retaining a love of Texas, and locating much of her literary output in that State, Mollie remained in New Orleans until her death in 1909, aged only fifty-eight. In this edition of *The Wimbourne Book of Victorian Ghost Stories* I have included Mollie's atmospheric Gulf Coast tale of spirits inhabiting a forgotten cemetery. *The Soul of Rose Dédé* first appeared in *Harper's New Monthly Magazine* in July 1892 and was later included in the collection *An Elephant's Track and Other Stories*.

Amongst all the authors in this volume, Willa Sibert Cather (1873-1947) was perhaps the most accomplished. She won the 1923 Pulitzer Prize for her World War One novel *One of Ours* (1922) and has been inducted in both the *National Women's Hall of Fame* and the *New York Writer's Hall of Fame*. She was born at her father's farm in Virginia but moved aged nine with her family to Nebraska where her father would eventually run an insurance and real estate business. Willa was well-read as a child and entered the University of Nebraska with the intention of studying medicine but soon found her calling was in literature. She changed her University major to English and began contributing articles to the *Nebraska State Journal*, the *Lincoln Courier* and eventually became the editor of the University paper *The Hesperian*. In 1894 Willa moved to Pittsburgh, Pennsylvania, and took up roles with women's magazine *Home Monthly* and the *Pittsburgh Leader*, whilst also teaching and publishing her own work. Her first collection of stories, *The Troll Garden*, appeared in 1905. The following year she moved to New York for a position on the editorial staff of *McClure's Magazine*; that periodical serialised her first novel, *Alexander's Bridge*, in 1912. She followed this with a trilogy of novels set on the American prairie; *O Pioneers!* (1913), *The Song of the Lark* (1915) and *My Ántonia* (1918). These works cemented her reputation as one of the most important writers of the early twentieth century. Her depiction of the hardships of life on the frontier, culled from her passion for Nebraska and her experiences with the Bohemian and Scandinavian immigrants of her home town, won her great renown. In later years she moved away from the prairie setting but explored themes such as warfare (*One of Ours*, 1922), materialism (*A Lost Lady*, 1923), the coming-of-age (*The Professor's House*, 1925), missionaries (*Death Comes for the Archbishop*, 1927) and Catholicism (*Shadows on the Rock*, 1931). Willa never married but lived with Editor Edith Lewis in her New York apartment for the last thirty-nine years of her life. She died in New York in 1947 and is interred in the Old Burying Ground, Jaffrey, New Hampshire. During a long and accomplished career, Willa wrote only a couple of pieces that have a supernatural theme. One of these, *The Fear that Walks by Noonday* was published in her Junior Class Yearbook, called *The Sombrero*, whilst at the University of Nebraska, in 1895. Although the story was credited to both Willa Cather and Dorothy Canfield, Willa later stated that her associate's input was minimal; the story is therefore often solely ascribed to Willa Cather. It is an excellent tale of the spirit of a deceased football player returning to his distraught team-mates.

Another author commonly included in the 'local color' genre of American literature, in which idiosyncratic characterisation often identifies location, is Annie Trumbull Slosson (1838-1926). Annie (who appears to have been christened 'Anna') was the daughter of merchant and local politician Gurdon Trumbull

(1790-1875) and Sarah Ann Trumbull (née Swan) of Stonington, Connecticut. The family later moved to Hartford, Connecticut where Annie attended the Hartford Female Seminary, originally set up by Harriet Beecher Stowe's sister, Catherine Beecher (1800-1878). Although mostly ignored today, Annie made her name as a short story writer during the 1880s and 1890s, publishing often in *Harper's Bazaar* and the *Atlantic Monthly*. Although she started her literary career with a quaint novel called *The China Hunter's Club* (1878), her most important works, in which she reached the pinnacle of her descriptive and vernacular style, are the short story collections *Seven Dreamers* (1890) and *Dumb Foxglove and Other Stories* (1898). Her later books included *White Christopher* (1901), *Aunt Abby's Neighbors* (1902), *A Dissatisfied Soul* (1908), *A Little Shepherd of Bethlehem* (1913) and *Puzzled Souls* (1915). As her popularity as an author waned at the turn of the nineteenth century, Annie began to concentrate more on her life-long passion of entomology. She published regularly in the entomological journals of the time and over one-hundred insects bear the taxonomic suffix 'slossonii' in her honour. This volume includes Annie's 'local color' ghostly tale called *A Transient* which was first published in *Harper's New Monthly Magazine* of December 1898 and also made an appearance in *Dumb Foxglove and Other Stories*.

Elia Wilkinson Peattie (1862-1935) was an author and critic, originally from Kalamazoo, Michigan. She married a journalist and began submitting work to newspapers, eventually being employed as the first female reporter for the *Chicago Tribune* and *Chicago Daily News*. After relocating to Omaha with her husband, Elia rose to become the chief editorial writer for the *Omaha World-Herald*, and became a prolific writer on issues ranging from frontier life to politics, socialism to prostitution. She wrote a history of America, an Alaskan travelogue, as well as numerous novels and short stories. Her tale *The Shape of Fear*, included here, was first published in Elia's collection of thirteen supernatural stories called *The Shape of Fear and Other Ghostly Tales* (1898). That collection, original copies of which are now impossible to find, is widely (and rightly) regarded as a classic of the genre.

Marie Louise van Vorst (1867-1936) was born in New York City, the daughter of a Superior Court judge and member of a wealthy and prominent New York family. She was privately educated at home then at a school in New Jersey and decided on a career in letters at a very young age. With both French and Dutch heritage, Marie felt an affinity with France that later led her to travel extensively in Europe, eventually settle in France, and, after marrying an Italian Count, Gaetano Cagiati, live out her days in Italy. Her most enduring family friendship was with her widowed sister-in-law, Bessie McGinnis van Vorst, with whom she often collaborated on novels and articles (e.g. *Bagsby's Daughter*, 1901). After spending some time living together in France, the two women returned to America and took on the guise of working class labourers; Marie engaged at a shoe factory and cotton mill, Bessie at a pickle factory and later a clothing mill. Based on these experiences they wrote *The Woman Who Toils* (1903) to highlight the discriminatory and derogatory plight of women and child labourers in America. Prefaced by President Theodore Roosevelt, the book is widely regarded as a milestone in social investigation. Marie's other novels, many of them dealing with the struggles of the poor, include *Philip Longstreth* (1902), *Amanda of the Mill* (1905), *The Sin of George Warrener* (1906), *The Girl from His Town* (1910) and *Big Tremaine* (1914). A commission by *Harper's Monthly Magazine* to provide a series of articles on rivers saw Marie travelling continental Europe from 1906 to 1909. By the onset of World War One she was living again in France and volunteered for service with the Red Cross and the American Ambulance. Her wartime experiences, attending the injured in field stations across France, formed the basis of her volume *War Letters of an American Woman* (1916). She returned occasionally to America to lecture and campaign on France's behalf, but remained domiciled in Europe until her death in 1936 in Florence. Her later novels (*Mary Moreland*, 1915; *Fairfax and His Pride*, 1920; *Tradition*, 1921; *The Queen of Karmania*, 1922) were not particularly well-received. In this volume of *The Wimbourne Book of Victorian Ghost Stories* I have included Marie's very first published short story, entitled *The Path of the Storm*, which appeared in *Harper's New Monthly Magazine* in November 1899.

Originally from Milwaukee, Wisconsin, Elizabeth Garver Jordan (1867-1947) was a prominent journalist, author and suffragist, and the elder of two daughters of William Frank Jordan and Margaretta Garver. She initially trained as a shorthand typist but secured a position as editor of the women's pages of *Peck's Sun*, a local Milwaukee newspaper, before reporting for the *St. Paul Globe* and the *Chicago Tribune*. In 1890 Elizabeth joined the staff of *The New York World*, in New York, becoming a highly-regarded reporter; some of her articles on the deprivation of inner city accommodation being collected as *The Submerged Tenth* (1893). She followed this with a short fiction collection, *Tales of the City Room* (1895), also mainly concerning the conditions of New York tenements. She moved to *Harper's Bazaar* in 1901 as editor, in which role she remained until 1913, and remained on the Harper's staff as a literary advisor until 1918. During her time at Harper's she published novels (e.g. *May Iverson, Her Book*, 1904) and short story collections (e.g. *Tales of Destiny*, 1902). Elizabeth is often remembered for the two collaborative novels she instigated; *The Whole Family* (1908), including chapters by, amongst others, Henry James and William Dean Howells and *The Sturdy Oak* (1917), including chapters by, amongst others, Fannie Hurst, Dorothy Canfield Fisher, Alice Duer Miller, Ethel Watts Mumford and William Allen White. She continued to publish right up to her death in New York in 1947. Her most important collection for the supernatural aficionado is *Tales of the Cloister* (1901), from which the story included here, *The Ordeal of Sister Cuthbert*, is taken. This excellent tale, finishing off the present volume, begs the question of whether a person need be dead for the soul to leave the body.

After reading this collection of twenty tales of the ghostly I hope the reader can appreciate their diversity, their obvious 'Americanness', their skill of construction, and indeed, their femininity. In this volume we have the full gamut of the diverse and fascinating cultures that combine in the nation's collective history; from American-Irish to African-American, from the Anglo-Saxon to the Creole. In these stories we hear all their voices, their quirks and rhythms of language that place them firmly in time and location. We can often see down to the root of their spiritual beliefs, the legends of their ethnic heritage, and yes, the history of their suffering. The subjects and objects of these macabre stories are diverse too; we have ghosts on land, ghosts at sea, invisible ghosts, ghosts that are merely shapes, ghosts of children, ghosts of parents, and of course, family curses. But, here is not just the voice of America. Perhaps most compelling of all, we hear the voice of woman; subtle, delicate, emotional and intelligent — and at the same time powerful, resourceful, commanding and eloquent — occasionally subjugated, but always clambering forwards towards the hope of emancipation. These are frankly some of the best supernatural tales told by the best American authors of the Victorian age. I hope you enjoy them!

The Haunted House in Georgia

Elizabeth Fries Lummis Ellet

> "Can such things be
> And overcome us like a Summer cloud,
> Without our special wonder?"

No traveler to Savannah is allowed by the citizen of that pretty southern city to leave it without being pressed to visit Buonaventure. This is a remarkable spot, seven or eight miles distant from the town. It is reached by a drive over sandy roads, through a country pleasingly diversified with hill and valley, winding streams, and glimpses occasionally of the broad expanse of one of the arms of the sea, here called the "salt," in contradistinction to the fresh waters of the river. The country hereabouts presents an agreeable variety to the low, flat region bordering the Savannah, and affording rich and extensive rice and cotton plantations. The woods are close and extensive; the foliage luxuriant and varied in character, such as enchants the eye unaccustomed to the beauty of southern forests. Here in Spring the queen magnolia spreads her snowy flowers diffusing fragrance through the air, and the yellow jessamine flings its golden shower of blossoms, delicious in perfume, over the saplings and bushes. The wild rose clambers over the myrtle trees, and the bay and calico flowers decorate the borders of the streams. Evergreens are numerous; the live oak, almost unknown in the upper country, is abundant; and in the swampy spots, the trees are covered with the long "trailing garments" of moss, so wonderful and beautiful to the Northern visitor.

These majestic vales become more frequent as you proceed, mingled with the wildest and richest profusion of deciduous foliage. The traveler, after a few turns in the road finds himself in a spot of singular beauty. On every side stretch broad, extensive avenues, perfectly straight, as far as the eye can reach. These are bordered and enclosed by live oaks of immense size, their gloomy foliage draperied by the floating gray moss, that waves like a shroud in the wind, and droops almost to the ground. These avenues cross each other at right angles and are carpeted by a smooth green sward. The trees were planted many generations since, by the ancient proprietor of the soil. It is impossible to describe, so as to do them justice, these stately, sweeping avenues. The antiquated, solemn appearance of the live oaks — proud monarchs of the forest — with their dark verdure and streaming drapery, the dense woods in the distance, and the air of romance, seclusion and solitude that impresses the mind — give a unique effect to the scene. The heart is filled with a calm awe. There is more here than the mere beauty of scenery, or a combination of those objects that in a landscape give pleasure to the eye. It would scarce need a poet's fancy to imagine these the lengthened aisles of some mighty cathedral, roofed by the blue sky and walled in by wooded hills. "The organ's solemn influence," would here be appropriate. As the sun descends, a religious gloom fills this sanctuary of nature; and the wanderer, escaped awhile from the busy stir of town-life, finds in the solitude and silence around him the truest aids to devotion.

It is this effect, and the singular character of the scenery, that has made Buonaventure so celebrated a spot. Some of the Georgians imagine it as great a curiosity as Niagara. They quote a saying of a noted English traveler — that to see it was alone worth crossing the Atlantic.

"A drive to Buonaventure" is the favorite afternoon recreation of the citizens of Savannah, so long as cool weather permits. But with the sunny season of May this resort becomes dangerous. The "country fever" — that most alarming of all diseases — the scourge of the low countries, prevails throughout this region. Only the town and the dry and elevated portions of country are safe from its ravages. The hanging moss, beautiful as it is, that grows so luxuriantly in the moist lands, is a certain token of the insalubriousness of the climate. It is a kind of banner of death. This place, in consequence, is forsaken in the Summer months or only visited early in the day; for with the evening comes the miasma. This circumstance imparts to it an additional interest, by deepening the sense of loneliness. The solemn grandeur of the scene is marred by no habitation of man. The fear of pestilence guards the gates of this spacious temple, that the sellers and money-changers come not therein. Peace, the peace of prayer, seems here to have its appropriate dwelling.

About a quarter of a mile from one of the avenues there stood, a few years since, a large and strongly built house, much defaced by time, that had been for a long while uninhabited. The wild pigeons made nests in the chimneys, and some of the stones had fallen out; but on the whole the building was in good repair, though its court was overgrown with weeds, and wild vines clambered over the windows. It was removed, and a neat, small mansion erected not far from its site, where the owner of this estate occasionally resides. In his absence it is kept in order by an old negro who serves as castellan, and who lives with his wife in a hut on the premises.

It was toward the end of April 184— that I visited Buonaventure, in company with a party of friends, most of them strangers to the locality. An individual from Savannah, who kindly accompanied us as guide, was extremely communicative in regard to the different persons who had been, from the period reached by tradition, owners of the ground. One of the party observed that such a domain in England would be a princely fortune; and even here, where it had comparatively little pecuniary value, it was one which no man, who knew how to value so noble a possession, would ever part with.

"Aye," answered our guide, "when it could he held with a safe conscience. The proprietor is a most worthy and excellent man; none can speak a word against his right; but that could hardly be said of the dwelling-house that used to stand yonder."

"The one we see there?"

"No! that was built lately by the owner of this property and is occupied when he visits the place, as Buonaventure is too sickly to live in. I mean the house which was taken away."

"Did not that, also, belong to the estate?"

"No; it never was a part of it. It was built they say more than a hundred years ago."

"Was there anything remarkable about it?"

"Why, nothing that one could speak of, at least in its outward appearance. It was a gloomy looking building enough, with old-fashioned windows, and the broken down wall you see yonder surrounding it. But it was not inhabited, though it had a fine garden and grounds attached for five or six years before it was removed. To speak plainly, it had the reputation of being haunted."

All laughed at the idea of a haunted house in Georgia at this day.

"You may laugh if you will but it was true nevertheless. I know many who would not have passed a night there for any reward. And why should not ghosts appear nowadays, I wonder, as well as in old times, when there is occasion for them?"

"If you can show that there is occasion," said one of our party.

"Well, there are several things that might render their appearance proper. For instance — a murder unpunished, or the innocent suffering for the guilty."

"Was any story of this sort connected with the house?"

"Not that I knew of; I never heard of anybody being murdered there. But there *was* a tale — I heard it from my father — who heard it from his — of the rightful owner of the property being turned out of house and home with his family and left to die in poverty, while another took possession of his inheritance."

Of course we all inquired concerning the particulars.

"I can tell nothing but what I have heard;" continued the narrator; "and hearsay knowledge is apt to be uncertain. Many years ago — as perhaps you may be aware — a house and plantation were worth far more than at present. Those were the times when the Southern planters were like princes; and each as independent as a duke in his own castle. Then — I remember it well — the house I speak of was occupied by a worthy man; he had no children, however, and all the grounds were in excellent preservation. That wall enclosed the court yard; and the trees within were in full vigor. There was a double row of orange trees just in front, that were as beautiful to the sight, as valuable for their fruit. The garden, I recollect, was full of choice flowers. In short, the place had everything about it desirable for a rural residence. The mansion was well furnished also, though the furniture was old-fashioned. And yet the person who lived there, though, as I said, a most upright man, seemed to be never altogether comfortable. He did not rest till he had sold the plantation and removed."

"Perhaps on account of the unhealthy climate?"

"That could not be, for this spot is dry and salubrious. As I told you, rumor said there were appearances in the house that could not be accounted for. The old story was revived about the transfer of the inheritance. There was a law-suit concerning it in my grandfather's time; but the person whose father had held the property could not make good his claim, by reason of his failing to produce the documents that secured his title. So his opponent gained the cause; though almost everyone thought his claim an unjust one."

"And what became of the former proprietor?"

"He left the state, with his children; it was reported that he died of the fever, in Alabama."

"A hard lot, if unjustly deprived of his property."

"Precisely; and that brings me to the wonderful part of my story; which proves that Providence does, indeed, watch over human affairs. I shall tell it, notwithstanding you may ridicule what I say."

"Impossible, my good friend;" said Mr. — "Pray, let us hear the rest."

"My father," continued our guide, "has often told this to me; and I know him to be incapable of any departure from truth. He was not married at the time it happened, and was a stranger in this part of the country. He was hunting, in February, in the woods with a party of friends. It was after dark before they were ready to return, and you know what a tedious ride it is now, because of the sand, between here and Savannah. The road was then difficult to find for one unaccustomed to the forest, and my father proposed asking the hospitality of the gentleman who lived in the house I have been describing for a night's lodging. The others refused, alleging as a reason the rumors they had heard. My father was as incredulous as yourselves, and with a laugh protested that he feared neither ghosts nor devils enough to take a long ride through the woods, on an uncertain road on their account.

"The others were not of his mind; and so my father begged an introduction to the gentleman of the house, from one of the hunters, and they all rode up to the gate. The proprietor was an open-hearted man, of courteous and obliging disposition, as almost all our Southern landholders are. He received the whole party with a cordial welcome, invited them to remain all night, and insisted at least on their staying to supper. His excellent wine caused the guests to be very communicative, and in the course of conversation, all that had passed between my father and the others came out. The host smiled as he heard it; but some thought his smile a forced one. At all events, when my father asked leave to stay till next morning, and his companions begged that he might be put into the haunted chamber if there was one, he promised to satisfy them to the extent of his power. The whole party made an engagement to meet next day at dinner in the hotel then standing at the corner of Monument Square, in Savannah, that they might hear all that had passed. The host accepted an invitation to join them. Then, as it was late, the hunters had their horses brought to the gate, and departed. My father remained alone and conversed with his new acquaintance, who seemed a man of much intelligence and information, till bed-time. That hour came earlier in former times, as you know, than at present.

"As the host conducted my father to his chamber he observed with a smile, that he was sorry he had no haunted room for his reception, which might afford him an adventure, and a subject for their dinner's discussion. "But I will give you," he said, "the old library apartment, that was formerly occupied by my father, both as study and bed-room. There are some curious volumes in it; they will give you plenty of stories of apparitions, if you choose to consult them. For my part, I am inclined to think such things exploded at the present day."

"It was a large, old-fashioned room into which my father was shown; with several shelves, on which were old leathern-bound volumes, some in folio. He examined several that excited his curiosity, and found them valuable relics of past ages — illuminated manuscripts, ornamented with rare and curious paintings. The owner of the house had a fine taste in such things. The room was also hung with several portraits of members of the family. The paintings were fine, though much soiled by smoke and dust: and had in the candle-light quite a life-like appearance. It was late when, after examining them, for he had a great fondness for pictures, my father retired to rest.

"He was awakened from a profound slumber by the clock striking. It struck three. He was surprised to find it so late. The moon was shining faintly in at the windows, and fell in a line of silver on the polished floor. Every object in the room was visible, though not directly in the light, the long table, with the candlesticks, the books, the massive oaken chairs, and a marble urn that stood in the corner.

"In a few moments, to the surprise of my father, the clock struck one; it had struck three quarters before. At the same time he thought he heard a rustling in the apartment, as of someone moving behind the curtains of his bed. He partly rose from the pillow, and looked around. Gradually, as vision returns to one who has been dreaming, he became conscious of seeing a figure seated in a large leathern chair, just beneath one of the portraits. It was that of a man, dressed in regimentals, as the portrait had been, and with a face so exactly similar, that my father involuntarily glanced at the picture. What was his astonishment to see the frame empty!

"The other portrait frames that hung around the room were empty also! At the same time he perceived other figures moving about, or seated in the chairs. One was that of an old lady in a stiff brocade, that rustled as she moved; another a younger female, with a bridal veil upon her head; another a middle-aged man, with a roll in his hand. Between these moved a number of other figures, less distinctly seen, their faces being hid in the shadow, and their forms, as it were, blended together. There was no noise of footsteps; but my father could hear voices whispering, and even distinguish some of the words they uttered. He thought he heard one lady, who had seated herself near the bed, say to another, "Are we to have no music, or dancing, anymore?"

"The military-looking man seemed the superior among them. Almost everyone looked to him with an expression of deference; but he appeared regardless of them, and his face exhibited both concern and melancholy. He walked to and fro, my father said, with unequal steps, now stopping short, now pushing forward through the crowd, as if intent on something the rest knew nothing about. Once he came close to the bed-side; and my father saw that his features were noble and expressive, though the countenance was overcast with sadness.

"Suddenly he went up to the middle-aged man, who was standing motionless in the middle of the room, and attempted to take the roll from his hand, saying something, of which my father could only distinguish the words, 'My children,' and 'The papers,' spoken rapidly and in seeming agitation.

"So great was the interest my father felt in this scene, that he forgot his fear of supernatural appearances, and watched with intense curiosity the face of the military man. This personage, after taking a few turns, in apparent perplexity, through the apartment, again went up to the middle-aged man, and said, in a low voice, but distinctly, 'Be just — be just! yield up what is not your own! Let not the innocent suffer.'

"The other shook his head slowly; the military man turned his face so that the faint light fell upon it; and my father saw that it was distorted and dark with contending passions. The face of no living human being could have expressed so much, with such wild and terrific energy. The sight was a fearful one; my father closed his eyes shudderingly; and the next moment the whole scene faded away. The outlines of the figures first became tremulous and indistinct; then they seemed to melt into one another; and at length all was dark, for the moon went down behind the hills. A strange drowsiness, or rather exhaustion, overcame my father and he fell into a deep slumber, from which he did not wake till late in the morning, at the entrance of a negro servant to inquire his commands. My father's first glance was at the portraits. They were all in their frames as he had seen them the preceding evening; and the picture of the military man hung directly opposite him.

"The host was particular in his inquiries as to how he had rested; but my father, for many reasons of his own, chose to say nothing of what he had seen. He expressed, however, some curiosity about the portraits, which the gentleman of the house was very willing to gratify. Some of them were ancestors of his own; and the man in military dress he described as having been an officer in the old war, to whom the estate had originally belonged. His right had been disputed, after his death, by another branch of the family, who succeeded in establishing their claim and obtaining possession after the tedious lawsuit I have mentioned.

"My father said nothing to all this; nor did he relate to the company he met at dinner, the least of what had occurred. There seemed, he said, a sort of sacredness in this confidence of the dead; besides, how could he have convinced them it was not all a dream, or a delusion of his imagination?"

"It were most reasonable to suppose it such, indeed," answered the spokesman of our party

"Nay," said the other; "my father might have thought so, *himself* — but for a singular occurrence. Many years later, some workmen employed in digging a well — there, you may see where it has been filled up — near the house, found a half mouldered piece of parchment, on which the writing was nearly defaced. It was one of the documents so long lost; and though insufficient, without others that could not be found, to establish the right of those who had been deprived of the property, yet it proved such writings to have been once in existence. But the wronged heirs were no longer to be found: the estate had been dismembered and was greatly diminished in value; and nothing was ever done with the recovered parchment. It was sufficient, however, to convince my father that what he had seen was no dream."

A smile of incredulity was the only comment.

"Since then," concluded the narrator, "to the day of his death, he could never look on a portrait of the size of life, without a sort of horror."

There was no use in attempting to shake the belief of our friend in his marvelous tale; so no further attempt was made. We only thanked him for his narration; and thought the wild and solemn scene before us a fitting one for the enactment of a ghost story.

The Haunted House

Nancy Thorning Munroe

"So you don't believe in ghosts?"

"Believe in ghosts? No! They are among the things that were, and have no place in this enlightened age. We never hear of them now excepting in some old nurse's tale, or among the emigrants from the Emerald Isle."

"Though I am neither an old nurse, nor yet an Irishman, yet there are some things I cannot account for. I will tell you a short story — a story of my own experience."

"Well, go on, I am all attention."

"It was in the year 18—, that I was engaged driving an express wagon from London down to C——. My first trip was on a cold day of the last of autumn, or the first of winter, I forget which, but I know it was a dismal day enough, for the north wind blew keen across the plain, and once in a while came gusts of sleet or snow; and glad was I when I descried through the fast falling darkness the large, fine looking house where I was to spend the night.

"As I drove into the yard, it was so near dark a servant came out with a lantern to assist me in taking care of my horses. This work lasted for some time; my assistant seemed to be of a taciturn disposition, — this being contrary to my inclinations, as you well know, I endeavored to draw him into conversation.

"'Fine house, here,' said I, to him.

"'The house looks well enough,' replied he, as I thought, rather shortly.

"I was not to be discouraged.

"'What's the name of the gentleman who owns the establishment?'

"'Benton,' replied he.

"'That span of black horses belongs to him?' said I, pointing to a couple of fine looking animals who stood eating their supper, showing by their fat, sleek sides that they were well cared for.

"'Yes, they are his; fine beasts they are, too,' going up to them and smoothing their coats; 'never drove better, sir,' he continued, as I came towards them, to examine them more closely; 'kind and gentle as lambs, but spirited, too, and fast, I can tell you. I'd back Jim or Bill against any horse in England, sir.'

"'Does Mr. Benton, your landlord, drive them much?'

"'Drive them! Lord bless you, sir; drive them like a man possessed. Sometimes they'll be harnessed into the carriage, and I must drive him to London, and if I drive a bit slow, just up hill, or when I come to a bad place in the road, just so sure he pops his head out of the carriage window and says, "Drive faster, Joe; why do you mope along the road?" Well, sir, the horses hear him, and away they go like birds. And sometimes Jim, for that is the one he always takes for the saddle, sometimes Jim is ordered to be brought to the door in the wildest storm that ever you see, and out he will come muffled up to the eyes, mount the beast, and away they will go as if Satan himself were after them, and I verily believe—'

"And here his voice sank to a low, muttering tone, and I lost the remainder of the sentence.

"Our work was done, and we went into the house, the inside of which was in keeping with its outward appearance, large, spacious, and comfortable. There was a blazing fire in the kitchen, and two or three maids were busy preparing supper, and there was a savory smell of meat cooking, potatoes boiling, and tea and coffee, which, to a man who had rode all day in the face of a north wind was peculiarly gratifying.

"In a room adjoining the kitchen stood a large table ready laid for the evening meal, and here too a large, cheerful fire was burning in the grate. After washing my face and hands I came into this room, which was called the breakfast room, and sat down by the blazing fire. While I was thus seated the door opened, and a thin, pale, stern looking man entered. He started on seeing me. I rose, and slightly bowed, for I knew not what to do.

"'Who are you,' said he, 'and why are you here?'

"'My name is Craft,' said I, 'and I drive the express from London down, and I believe my predecessor always stopped at this house on his way, overnight, and I intended doing the same.'

"'O, yes, yes,' said he, as if relieved. 'I understand, a new driver; excuse me for speaking to you thus; but one who keeps a public house cannot be too careful whom he allows to enter!'

"So saying, he passed through the room into the kitchen, and I heard him say:

"'Joe, have Jim brought round to the door in a quarter of an hour. I must ride tonight; d'ye hear?'

"'Yes sir; but it storms very badly, sir.'

"'And what of that? I didn't ask you for the state of the weather. I merely told you to bring the horse.'

"He turned on his heel and was gone from the room. I passed out into the kitchen just as Joe had started to execute his master's orders. He looked towards me with a peculiar expression, as much as to say, 'Didn't I tell you so?' Soon my supper was ready on the table, hot and smoking. Delicious ham and eggs, glorious coffee, the whitest of bread, the sweetest butter. 'They keep a nice table here,' thought I; 'no scrimping hand presides.' While I was at my meal I heard the tramp of horses' hoofs, and soon after Joe entered, muttering between his teeth. The housemaids looked at him, and one remarked:

"'I knew he'd be going as soon as I heard the wind rise, and the storm coming on.'

"'Yes,' replied Joe; 'all I hope is he won't be the death of the horse; the evil one will be sure to take care of his own, so he is safe.'

"All the evening the wind howled, and the storm beat against the windows in a frightful manner. We sat around the blazing fire telling stories, some merry and more gloomy, as befitting the time. I made the remark that it was just the night for ghost stories, and as I spoke, I noticed a look of intelligence pass around the party, though I paid no attention to it at the time, but went on with the tale that was in my mind, which chanced to be a ghost story of the most frightful nature, and seemed to have a great effect upon my audience, who cast furtive glances into the dark corners of the room, and at each other, all of which, I enjoyed very much, for I had no faith in ghost stories then.

"'I tell you what,' said Joe, when I had finished, 'don't tell another story of that sort; if you do I shan't sleep a wink.'

"I laughed outright.

"'You may laugh,' said he, 'but I fancy you never saw, or heard a ghost.'

"'Not I. I don't believe in the animal.'

"Now I observed a curious smile pass from one to the other, and Joe shook his head.

"'Well, I hope you never will see, or hear anything to make you change your belief, that's all.'

"It was now growing late, and feeling very weary, I expressed a wish to retire. Accordingly Joe taking with him two lighted lamps, said he would show me to my chamber. Here he very kindly bade me good-night, and said, in what was meant to be a jocular tone, but which was, in truth, half serious, 'I hope you will rest well, and hear nothing of ghosts.' Taking one of the lamps, and leaving the other, he went downstairs.

"I was soon in bed, and sound asleep, notwithstanding the violence of the storm without. I had slept, as I thought, some time, though I had no means of knowing, as I had extinguished my light when I went to bed, when I was awakened by a noise, though I could not tell what it resembled, not being fully awake.

"It is the landlord returned, thought I, to myself, and turned over to go to sleep again, remarking that the storm was still raging. Just as I was beginning to doze again, another noise, as of the falling of a heavy body. I started bolt upright in bed, and was just upon the point of crying out and alarming the family, when I heard more noises, — the shutting of doors, and the tramping of feet.

"The house is astir, thought I; perhaps someone is sick. I was confirmed in my opinion, for just then I heard groans from the chamber adjoining.

"If I can be of any assistance, thought I, they'll not hesitate to call me; but I think I had better not go unless called, as my presence may be considered an intrusion. So I lay down again, and tried to sleep. But it was impossible. Still the noises continued, — the slamming of doors, the hurrying of feet by my door, the groans from the next chamber; and once, yes, once or twice I heard something which sounded like the clanking of chains, but no sound of the human voice; had I heard but the faintest whisper I should have felt assured. I lay there till I got quite nervous, and at last could stand it no longer. I jumped out of bed, opened my door and peeped out. All was pitchy darkness. Surely there is no one astir — there is no glimmering of light from the chamber door — all is dark, and at the moment still as the house of death. I stood a while expecting to hear something. I did not have to wait long. A door slammed far off, then I felt a rushing as of a hurrying body going by me, a stifled scream — the door next mine was opened, and slammed to with violence — a groan, a clanking of chains, and then a deathly stillness, but all darkness, — Egyptian darkness.

"I closed my door — bolted it — crawled into bed, and covered my head with the clothes. I remained thus a few moments; then thought I, to myself, 'what a coward, what am I afraid of? I should have called and ascertained the cause of this alarm. Someone is in distress. I will lay here no longer.'

"I rose again, — again I opened the door — again peered into the dark, dark passageway, but all was still. I stole softly out, and crept along to the next chamber, tried the door, — it was fastened. I put my ear to the key-hole — not a breath was to be heard. Strange! I merely heard the door bolt violently. That might be, too, and be fastened on the inside. But everything was now quiet as death itself; from whence had proceeded the groans, and the noise of chains, I could not tell. Again I crept back to my bed, where I lay till morning, and was no more disturbed by strange noises, but I did not go to sleep again.

"At the first dawn of day I rose and dressed myself. During the night the storm had abated, and the morning promised to be fair. I crept to the door of the mysterious chamber, and applied my eye to the key-hole to see if the key was on the inside. It was not. To be sure it might have been removed after fastening the door, yet there was a mystery about the whole affair. I went back to my chamber and waited till I heard the family stirring. As I was about leaving my room I heard the tramping of horses' hoofs, and looking from my window, saw the landlord upon his coal black steed ride into the yard. The horse was white with foam, as if he had travelled fast and far, and the rider was spattered with mud. He flung the bridle to Joe, who stood ready to take the animal, and who was examining him very carefully. I went downstairs, and in passing through the hall door met Mr. Benton. He looked as if he had had a hard night of it, and his brow was dark and sullen, though when he saw me and recognized me, he tried to smile and speak cheerfully.

"'We have had a stormy night, sir,' said he.

"'A hard storm, which you seem to have suffered from;' I replied.

"'Yes, I was obliged to ride last night, but I hope you were more comfortable in the house?'

"I fancied he looked at me anxiously. I cared not to tell him the night's adventure, and merely answered, carelessly:

"'One need not fear the storm in a good house.'

"'Just so,' said he, and passed on.

"I went out to the stable to look after my horses. Here I found Joe rubbing down the horse who had been out in the storm, and to whom he was talking as if he had been a human being.

"'Good morning,' said he, when he saw me, 'I hope you rested comfortably.'

"'Is anybody sick in the house, Joe?'

"'Sick! no,' said he, bursting into a laugh, 'what made you think there was anybody sick?'

"'Why, I heard a great deal of opening and shutting of doors, and concluded somebody was sick.'

"'You did! well, I haven't heard of anybody being sick, and as to opening and shutting doors, you may hear that most any night. But did you not hear nothing else?' said he, pausing in his work, and looking sharply at me.

"'Yes, I heard what I thought the groans of someone in distress.'

"'No doubt, no doubt; anything more?'

"'I thought I heard, too, the sound of chains.'

"'Quite likely,' returned he, not at all surprised.

"'But did you hear nothing?' said I.

"He nodded his head, still looking at me.

"'From whence came the groans and noise?'

"He still looked at me, and I saw the corners of his mouth begin to twitch, and his eyes to sparkle, and at last he burst into a loud laugh. I knew not what to make of this, for I saw nothing very laughable in the occurrence, and told him so.

"'You don't believe in ghosts?' said he, going to work again upon the horse.

"'I confess the thought of a ghost had crossed my mind in the night, especially when I looked out into the dark, felt the rushing by me, and heard the slamming door. You don't pretend to say that all this noise was caused by a ghost?'

"'I do, though,' said he, working away very diligently.

"'And do you hear those noises every night?'

"'Not every night; mostly when it storms.'

"'The house is haunted, then?'

"'Just so,' said he, 'you guessed right the first time.'

"'Can you tell me?'

"'Can't tell you anything,' said he, interrupting me. 'I haven't told you anything, — 'twas you who told me. Don't say I told you anything.'

"'No, no; but why do you stay in such a place?' said I. He put his hand in his pocket, and jingling some silver, gave me to understand that he had extra pay for his services. 'But what does your master say about it?'

"'I told you,' said he, shortly, 'that I shouldn't tell you anything more about it. Master leaves the house stormy nights. Why do you suppose he leaves it? He prefers the storm outside to the storm within, and why? ah, why, that's the question.'

"'Well,' said I, turning to leave him, 'I don't think I shall stop overnight here again.'

"'Ha, ha; O, you don't believe in ghosts. I thought last night you would alter your tune before morning.'

"After I had attended to my horses, I went into the kitchen. All eyes were directed to me, and inquiries were made as to how I had passed the night. I answered them carelessly as I could, and sat down to breakfast as if nothing had happened. I took my meal alone in the breakfast room, and just as I had finished, the door opened and a woman entered. A woman of middle age, very handsome, and handsomely dressed, and extremely lady-like. She walked across the room with the grace of a queen, and came close to me where I was standing.

"'I am afraid,' said she, 'that your slumbers were disturbed last night; if so, be kind enough to forget the annoyance, speak to no one of it, but come again in your regular course, — you will find it will not be for your disadvantage.'

"The tones of her voice were very sweet and musical, yet sad, and she held out to me a purse, well-filled, which she motioned me to accept.

"'I thank you, madam,' said I, 'but had rather not accept your money; indeed, I know not why you offer it me. I will not deceive you; my rest last night was disturbed — the cause is to me unknown — to you perhaps not. I know nothing to your disadvantage; but that there is a mystery about the whole affair is very true.'

"She seemed dissatisfied with my reply.

"'You have been treated well, have you not? have you aught of which to complain?'

"'Nothing.'

"'Well, don't, then, because there is a mystery about the house that I cannot disclose, stand thus in your own light.'

"'It is no use talking, madam,' said I, very bluntly, for, to tell the truth, I was afraid to talk with her long, lest I should yield, there was something so bewitching about her. 'It's no use talking, I can't take your money, neither can I sleep in this house again; on these two things I am decided.'

"I fancied I saw a flush of anger cross her face; if so, it was gone in a moment, and she said:

"'I am very sorry to hear you say so, and you are acting very much against your own interest.' So saying, she left the room as gracefully as she entered.

"Well, I left the house immediately, after vowing I'd not stop there again, and I did not; for the next time down I stopped at a small public house about a mile farther on. This house was kept by a very pleasant couple, and although it did not speak of wealth, everything was pleasant and comfortable. As we sat around the fire, for it was again a stormy night, and there happened to be no one there but myself, I thought I would ask concerning the Bentons. They knew them well; indeed, Mrs. Carey, my hostess, had formerly lived with them as chambermaid.

"'Indeed,' said I, 'I stopped there overnight on my last trip, and perhaps you may be able to give me some light concerning some mysterious circumstance connected with the family.' She said nothing, but waited for me to proceed.

"'During the night,' said I, 'I was awakened by strange noises, and thought at first someone was sick. Then I heard groans, and sounds of hurrying feet and shutting of doors. I opened my own door, but could see nothing. On making inquiries in the morning, I was told that the house was haunted. I know not how that may be, but I determined I would not stay there another night.'

"'Was it a stormy night?' said she.

"'It was,' I replied.

"'Where was Mr. Benton?'

"'He went away at nightfall, and did not return till morning.'

"The husband and wife looked at each other, and at last the former said:

"'It will do no harm; tell him, Fanny.'

"Accordingly, Mrs. Carey told me the following story, which I relate in her own words.

"'Mr. Benton was once a poor man, — poor and proud, and his wife was also a very ambitious woman, and very handsome, and exercised a great influence over her husband, who was very fond of her.

"'They commenced keeping a public house, but did not get along well at all. He did not like to work, neither did she. She seemed to have a natural turn for a great lady, and I used to think, many times when I lived there, which was when they were poor, it was a thousand pities she was not a countess, or at least a rich gentleman's wife. Well, after a while Mr. Benton had a brother come from the Indies, or somewhere over the seas, and they said he was very rich. Indeed, one might judge he was, for he wore a gold chain nearly as big as your finger, and a monstrous gold watch, and gold rings on his fingers, and was, withal, very lavish with his money, and used often to make us handsome presents, and also to give his sister-in-law a great deal of money, and jewelry, and seemed very fond of her.

"'Soon I noticed that Mr. Benton, our master, grew sullen, and said scarce anything, but his brother was always lively and chatty, always near Mrs. Benton, making her some presents, or carrying her to ride, and seeming, in truth, to admire her very much, and she seemed rather to encourage him in it, as I used to think. I thought in the first place her husband was jealous of his brother's attentions, then after a while the husband and wife, between whom there seemed to have been some coldness, appeared to have a mutual understanding, and so for a while things went on.

"'Well, one day I saw that my mistress had on a splendid gold chain — she said it was a present from her brother-in-law.

"'"I took it," said she, "because we must indulge him in his whims."

"'I did not know exactly what she meant.

"'"He is not," said she, "just right. Don't you notice how lavishly he spends his money? No, poor George is a little flighty, and we fear that he may sometime be really deranged. It is a dreadful thing," and I think the tears stood in her eyes.

"'"Why," said I, "I am sure I never thought anything of the kind."

"'"Well, I hope I am mistaken, but I fear it is too true."

"'And here is a mystery I cannot explain; ere long George Benton was, in truth, a raving maniac. They were obliged to chain him in his room, and no one had any control over him but Mrs. Benton; with her he was as gentle as a lamb, but the moment he set eyes on his brother, his eyes would flash with rage, and he would gnash his teeth like a wild beast. Well, sir, it was a sad time, a dreadful time, when he was so bad. We could not sleep in the house nights, because of his cries and shouts, which were enough to terrify one. The servants would all have left, but they pitied their poor mistress, who said she would give them any wages if they would but stay.

"'Well, it did not last long; in a short time he died. That was a dreadful stormy night; the wind howled and roared — I never remember such a night; and in the morning the poor man was found dead in his chamber. He had been left chained the night before, as he was always left, so that he could move but a short distance, and we heard no noise from him during the night, — or if we had, the noise of the storm drowned all other noises, and in the morning, as I said before, he was dead.

"'We could not mourn much, still it was very awful to think of his dying all alone, no one knew how. My mistress wept, and my master shut himself up for days, and did not look upon the face of his brother again. They had a coroner's inquest upon the body, and it was also examined by physicians, and I believe they thought he must have died in a fit, but I think they knew nothing at all about it. There were no marks of violence upon the body, that was certain.

"'Well, they had a great funeral, and when the will was opened, it was found that all his property, which was immense, was left to his brother, and brother's wife; indeed, he had no other heirs, for he was a single man.

"'Now our master was poor no longer. He constantly enlarged the house, kept his own carriage, and a splendid pair of horses. My lady had as many servants as she wished to do her bidding, and no need of lifting her finger to do a bit of work; but, O, I had rather be poor, and beg my bread from door to door, than live in that house, — for on stormy nights the dreadful noises which one hears are enough to make one mad. But all this you know. I lived there but a short time after the poor man's death, for I could not endure it. Mrs. Benton tried to tempt me with money, but money was no temptation; I left, and have not entered the house since.'

"'And this is all you know about it?'

"'Yes, this is all.'

"'But, why,' said I, 'if the poor man died in his bed, as you say, why does his spirit still haunt the house, as you seem to believe, and as I myself can hardly help thinking.'

"'Ah, that is it,' said she, 'if he died in his bed.'

"'But you say there was no suspicion?'

"'No, I did not say that; I said nothing was proved. He was dead in the morning, that is certain, — how he died no one as yet have been able to tell. Dead men tell no tales, they say.'

"''Tis very strange,' said I.

"'It is, indeed,' said she.

"And that is my story."

My Visitation

Rose Terry Cooke

"Is not this she of whom,
When first she came, all flushed you said to me,

Now could you share your thought; now should men see
Two women faster welded in one love
Than pairs of wedlock?" — *The Princess.*

If this story is incoherent — arranged rather for the writer's thought than for the reader's eye — it is because the brain which dictated it reeled with the sharp assaults of memory, that living anguish that abides while earth passes away into silence; and because the hand that wrote it trembled with electric thrills from a past that cannot die, forever fresh in the soul it tested and tortured — powerful after the flight of years as in its first agony, to fill the dim eye with tears, and throb the languid pulses with fresh fever and passion.

Take, then, the record as it stands, and ask not from a cry of mortal pain the liquid cadence and accurate noting of an operatic bravura.

The first time *It* came was in broad day. I was ill, unable to rise; the day was cold; autumnal sunshine, pure and still, streamed through the house and came in at both the south windows of my room, the curtains drawn wide to receive it, for the ague of sickness is worse to me than its pain, and not yet had my preparations for winter enabled me to have a fire. Everything was clear and chill; Aunt Mary, downstairs in the parlor, sat and knitted, as it was her custom to do of an afternoon; Uncle Seth was not at home; the servant had gone to mass, for it was some feast-day of her Church — no sound or echo disturbed the solitude.

There is something peculiar in a silent day of autumn; melancholy pierces its fine sting through the rays of sunshine; sadness cries in the cricket's monotonous voice; separation and death symbolize in the slow leaves that quit the bough reluctantly, and lie down in dust to be over-trodden — to rot. I can endure any silence better than this hush of decay; it fills me with preternatural horror; it is as if a tomb opened and breathed out its dank, morbid breath across the murmur of life, to paralyze and to chill.

But that day I had taken refuge from the awe and foreboding, the ticking of the clock, the dust-motes floating on light, the startling crack that now and then a springing board or an ill-hung window made. I had taken a book. I was deep in Shirley; it excited, it affected me; it is always to me like a brief and voluntary brain-fever to read that book. Jane Eyre is insanity for the time. Villette is like the scarlet fever; it possesses, it chokes, flushes, racks you; it leaves you weak and in vague pain, apprehensive of some bad result; but it was Shirley I read, so forgetting everything. I am not lonely usually, yet I know when I am alone; there is an indescribable freedom in the sense of solitude, no alien sphere crosses and disturbs mine, no intrusive influence distorts the orbit; I am myself — or I was, then. Presently, as I lay there, the clock struck three. I was to take some potion at that hour. I must rise and get it. I set one foot on the floor, and was putting a shoe upon the other cautiously, when it occurred to me, why was I so careful? and I remembered that it had seemed to me something was on the bed when I moved — my kitten perhaps. I looked, there was nothing there; but I was not alone in the room — there was something else I could not see. I did not hear, but I knew it.

A horror of flesh and sense crept over me; but I was ashamed; I treated it with contempt. Shivering, I walked to the shelf, reached the cup, swallowed my nauseous dose — now tasteless — and went back to bed. It is not worth denying that I trembled. I am a coward. I am always afraid, even when I face the fear; so, shaking, I lay down. My throat was parched, my lips beaded with a sweat of terror, but the consciousness of solitude returned in time to save me from faintness. *It* had gone. And that was the first time.

Here, perhaps, it is best to interpolate my own story, as much of it as is needful to the understanding of this visitation. I was an orphan, living in the family of my guardian and uncle by marriage, Mr. Van Alstyne. I was not an orphan till fifteen years of happy life at home had fitted me to feel the whole force of such a bereavement. My parents had died within a year of each other, and at the time my story begins I had been ten years under my uncle's roof. He was kind, gentle, generous, and good; all that he could be, not being my father.

It is not necessary to say that I grieved long and deeply over my loss; my nature is intense as well as excitable, and I had no mother. What that brief sentence expresses many will feel; many, more blessed, cannot imagine. It is to all meaning enough to define my longing for what I had not, my solitude in all that I had, my eager effort to escape from both longing and solitude.

After I had been a year under my guardian's care, Eleanor Wyse, a far-off cousin of Mr. Van Alstyne, came to board at the house and go to school with me. She was fifteen, I sixteen, but she was far the oldest. In the same family as we were, in the same classes, there were but two ways for us to take, either rivalry or friendship; between two girls of so much individuality there was no neutral ground, and within a month I had decided the matter by falling passionately in love with Eleanor Wyse.

I speak advisedly in the use of that term; no other phrase expresses the blind, irrational, all-enduring devotion I gave to her; no less vivid word belongs to that madness. If I had not been in love with her I should have seen her as I can now — as what she really was; for I believe in physiognomy. I believe that God writes the inner man upon the outer as a restraint upon society; what the moulding of feature lacks, expression, subtle traitor, supplies; and it is only years of repression, of training, of diplomacy, that put the flesh totally in the power of the spirit, and enable man or woman to seem what they are not, what they would be thought.

Eleanor's face was very beautiful; its Greek outline, straight and clear, cut to a perfect contour; the white brow; the long, melancholy eye, with curved, inky lashes; the statuesque head, its undulant, glittering hair bound in a knot of classic severity; the proud, serene mouth, full of carved beauty, opening its scarlet lips to reveal tiny pearl-grains of teeth of that rare delicacy and brilliance that carry a fatal warning; the soft, oval cheek, colorless but not pale, opaque and smooth, betraying

Southern blood; the delicate throat, shown whiter under the sweeping shadow and coil of her black-brown tresses; the erect, stately, perfect figure, slight as became her years, but full of strength and promise; all these captivated my intense adoration of beauty. I did not see the label of the sculptor; I did not perceive in that cold, strict chiseling the assertion that its material was marble. I believed the interpretation of its hieroglyphic legend would have run thus: "This is the head of young Pallas; power, intellect, purity are her ægis; the daughter of Jove has not yet tasted passion; virgin, stainless, strong for sacrifice and victory, let the ardent and restless hearts of women seek her to be calmed and taught. *Evoe Athena!*" Nor did I like to see the goddess moved; expression did not become her; the soul that pierced those deep eyes was eager, unquiet, despotic; nothing divine, indeed, yet, in my eyes, it was the unresting, hasting meteor that flashed and faded through mists of earth toward its rest — where I knew not, but its flickering seemed to me atmospheric, not intrinsic.

I looked up to Eleanor with respect as well as fervor. She was full of noble theories. To hear her speak you would have been inwardly shamed by the great and pure thoughts she expressed, the high standard by which she measured all. Truth, disinterestedness, honor, purity, humility, found in her a priestess garmented in candor. If I thought an evil thought, I was thereafter ashamed to see her; if I was indolent or selfish, her presence reproached me; her will, irresistible and mighty, awoke me; if she was kind in speech or act if she spoke to me caressingly — if she put her warm lips upon my cheek — I was thrilled with joy; her presence affected me, as sunshine does, with a sense of warm life and delight; when we rode, walked, or talked together, I wished the hour eternal; and when she fell into some passion, and burned me with bitter words, stinging me into retort by their injustice, their hard cruelty, it was I who repented — I who humiliated myself — I who, with abundant tears, asked her pardon, worked, plead, prayed to obtain it; and if some spasmodic conscientiousness roused her to excuse herself — to say she had been wrong — my hand closed her lips: I could not hear that: the fault was mine, mine only. I was glad to be clay as long as she was queen and deity.

I do not think this passion of mine moved Eleanor much. She liked to talk with me; our minds mated, our tastes were alike. I had no need to explain my phrases to her, or to do more than indicate my thoughts; she was receptive and appreciative of thought, not of emotion. Me she never knew. I had no reserve in my nature — none of what is commonly called pride; what I felt I said, to the startling of good usual persons; and because I said it, Eleanor did not think I felt it. To her organization utterance and simplicity were denied; she could not speak her emotions if she would; she would not if she could; and she had no faith in words from others. My demonstrations annoyed her; she could not return them; they could not be ignored; there was a certain spice of life and passion in them that asserted itself poignantly and disturbed her. My services she liked better; yet there was in her the masculine contempt for spaniels; she despised a creature that would endure a blow, mental or physical, without revenging itself; and from her I endured almost any repulse, and forgot it.

She was with us in the house three years, and in that time she learned to love me after a fashion of her own, and I, still blind, adored her more. She found in me a receptivity that suited her, and a useful power of patient endurance. Her will made me a potent instrument. What she wanted she must have, and her want was my law. No time, no pains, no patience were wanting in me to fulfil her ends. I served her truly, and I look back upon it with no regret; futile or fertile, such devotion widens and ripens the soul that it inhabits. No after-shock of anguish can contract the space or undo the maturity; and even in my deepest humiliation before her sublime theories and superhuman ideals I unconsciously grew better myself. A capacity for worship implies much, and results in much.

Yet I think I loved her without much selfishness. I desired nothing better than to see her appreciated and admired. It was inexplicable to me when she was not; and I charged the coolness with which she was spoken of, and the want of enthusiasm for her person and character in general society, to her own starry height above common people, and their infinite distance from her nature.

So these years passed by. We went to school; we finished our school-days; we came out into the world; for, in the meantime, her mother had died, and her father removed to Bangor. She liked the place as a residence, and it had become home to her of late. I hoped it was pleasanter for her to be near me. When Eleanor was about twenty a nephew of Uncle Van Alstyne's came to make us a visit; he was no new acquaintance; he had come often in his boyhood, but since we grew up he had been in college, at the seminary, last in Germany for two years' study, and we did not know him well in his maturer character until this time. Herman Van Alstyne was quiet and plain, but of great capacity; I saw him much, and liked him. Love did not look at us. I was absorbed in Eleanor; so was he; but to her he was of no interest. I think she respected him, but her manner was careless and cold, even neglectful. Herman perceived the repulsion. At first he had taken pains to interest her — to mould her traits — to develop some inner nature in which he had faith; but the stone was intractable; neither ductile nor docile was Pallas; her soul yielded no more to him than the strong sea yields place or submission to the winged wind that smites it in passing.

He was with us three months waiting for a call he said, but stricter chains held him till he broke them with one blow and went to a Western parish.

He had not offered himself to Eleanor and been refused. Wisely he refrained from bringing the matter to a foreknown crisis: he spared himself the pain and Eleanor the regret of a refusal that he regarded truly as certain. I was sorry for the whole affair, for I believed she would scarcely know a better man, but it passed away; I promised to write him when his mother found the correspondence wearying, and we interchanged a few letters at irregular intervals till we met again, letters into which Eleanor's name found no entrance.

Three years after he left I went, early in July, to spend some weeks at the seaside, for I was not strong; in the last few years my health had failed slowly, but progressively, till I was alarmingly weak, and ordered to breathe salt air and use sea-bathing as the best hope of restoration. I do not know why I should reserve the cause of this long languor and sinking: it was nothing wrong in me that I owed it to the breaking of a brief engagement. A young girl, totally inexperienced, I had loved a man and been taught by himself to despise him — a tragedy both trite and sharp; one that is daily reacted, noted, and forgotten by observers, to find a cold record in marble or the catalogues of insane asylums, another perhaps in the eternal calendar of the heavens above. I was too strong in nature to grace either of these mortal lists, and I loved Eleanor too well. I had always loved her more than that man; and when the episode was over, I discovered in myself that I never could have loved any man as I did her, and I went out into the world in this conviction, finding that life had not lost all its charms — that so long as she lived for me I should neither die nor craze. But the shock and excitement of the affair shattered my nervous system and undermined my health, and the listless, aimless life of a young lady offered no reactive agency to help me: so I went from home to new scenes and fresh atmosphere.

The air of Gloucester Beach strengthened me day by day. The exquisite scenery was a pleasure endless and pure. I asked nothing better than to sit upon some tide-washed rock and watch the creeping waves slide back in half-articulate murmur from the repelling shore, or, eager with the strength of flood, fling themselves, in mock anger, against cliff and crag, only to break in wreaths of silver spray and foam-bells — to glitter and fall in a leap of futile mirth, then rustling in the shingle and seaweed with vague whispers, that

"Song half asleep or speech half awake,"

which has lulled so many restless hearts to a momentary quiet, singing them the long lullaby that preludes a longer slumber.

It was excitement enough to walk alone upon the beach when a hot cloudy night drooped over land and sea; when the soft trance and enchantment of summer lulled cloud and wave into stillness absolute and cherishing, when the sole guide I had in that warm gloom was the white edge of surf, and the only sound that smote the quiet, the still-recurring, apprehensive dash, as wave after wave raced, leaped, panted, and hissed after its forerunner.

The Beach House was almost empty at that early season, and I enjoyed all this alone, not without constant yearnings for

Eleanor; wanting her, even this scenery lost a charm, and I gave it but faint admiration since I could not see it with her eyes. It must be a very pure love of nature that can exist alone, and without flaw, in the absence of association. The austere soul of the great mother offers no sympathy to the petulant passion or irrational grief of her children. It is only to the heart that has proved itself strong and lofty that her potent and life-giving traits reveal themselves. In this love, as in all others, save only the love of God, the return that is yielded is measured by the power of the adorer, not his want. Truly,

> "Nature never did betray
> The heart that loved her;"

but she has many and many a time betrayed the partial love — scoffed at the divided worship.

After I had been a fortnight at the Beach, I was joined by Herman Van Alstyne. He had come on from the West to recruit his own health, suffering from a long intermittent fever, by sea-air; and hearing I was at Gloucester, had come there, and asked my leave to remain, gladly accorded to him. We had always been good friends, and my unspoken sympathy with his liking for, and loss of, Eleanor had established a permanent bond between us. In the constant association into which we were now thrown I learned daily to like him better. He was very weak indeed, quite unable to walk or drive far, and the connection of our families was a sufficient excuse to others for our intimacy. I delighted to offer him any kindness or service in my power, and he repaid me well by the charm of his society.

We spent our mornings always together in some niche of the lofty cliff that towered from the tide below in bare grandeur, reflecting the sun from its abrupt brown crags till every fibre of grass rooted in their crevices grew blanched, and the solitary streamer of bramble or wild creeper became crisp long ere autumn. But this heat was my element; the slow blood quickened in my veins under its vital glow; I felt life stealing back to its deserted and chilly conduits; I basked like a cactus or a lizard into brighter tints and a gayer existence.

There we often sat till noon, talking or silent as we would; for though there was a peculiar charm in the appreciative, thoughtful conversation of Herman Van Alstyne, a better and a rarer trait he possessed in full measure — the power of "a thousand silences."

Or, perhaps, under the old cedars that shed aromatic scents upon the sun-thrilled air, and strewed bits of dry, sturdy leaves upon the short grass that carpeted the summit of the cliff, we preferred shadow to sunshine; and while I rested against some ragged bole, and inhaled all odor and health, he read to me some quaint German story, some incredibly exquisite bit of Tennyson, some sensitively musical passage of Kingsley, or, better and more apt, a song or a poem of Shelley's — vivid, spiritual, supernatural; the ideal of poetry; the leaping flame-tongue of lonely genius hanging in mid-air, self-poised, self-containing, glorious, and unattainable.

I have never known so delicate an apprehension as Mr. Van Alstyne possessed; his nobler traits I was afterward to know — to feel; but now it suited me thoroughly to be so well understood — to feel that I might utter the wildest imagination, or the most unexpected peculiarity of opinion, and never once be asked to explain what I meant — to reduce into social formulas that which was not social but my own. If there is one rest above another to a weary mind it is this freedom from shackles, this consciousness of true response. Never did I perceive a charm in the landscape that he had not noticed before or simultaneously with me; the same felicity of diction or of thought in what we read struck us as with one stroke; we liked the same people, read the same books, agreed in opinion so far as to disagree on and discuss many points without a shadow of impatience or an uncandid expression. We talked together as few men talk — perhaps no women —

> "Talked at large of worldly fate,
> And drew truly every trait"

— but we never spoke of Eleanor.

And so the summer wore on. I perceived a gradual change creep over Herman's manner in its process; he watched me continually. I felt his eyes fixed on me whenever I sat sewing or reading; I never looked up without meeting them. He grew absent and fitful. I did not know what had happened. I accused myself of having pained him. I feared he was ill. I never once thought of the true trouble; and one day it came — he asked me to marry him.

Never was any woman more surprised. I had not thought of the thing. I could not speak at first. I drew from him the hand he attempted to grasp. I did not collect my stricken and ashamed thoughts till, looking up, I saw him perfectly pale, his eyes dark with emotion, waiting, in rigid self-control, for my answer.

I could not, in justice to him or to myself, be less than utterly candid. I told him how much I liked him; how grieved I was that I could have mistaken his feeling for me so entirely; and then I said what I then believed — that I could not marry him — for I had but the lesser part of a heart to give any man. I loved a woman too well to love or to marry. A deep flush of relief crossed his brow.

"Is that the only objection you offer to me?" asked he, calmly.

"It is enough," said I. "If you think that past misery of mine interferes against you, you are in the wrong. I know now that I never loved that man as a woman should love the man she marries, and had I done so, the utter want of respect or trust I feel for him now would have silenced the love forever."

"I did not think of that," said he. "I needed but one assurance — that, except for Miss Wyse, you might have loved me; is it so?"

I could not tell him — I did not know. The one present and all-absorbing passion of my soul was Eleanor; beside her, no rival could enter. I shuddered at the possibility of loving a man so utterly, and then placing myself at his mercy for life. I felt that my safety lay in my freedom from any such tie to Eleanor. She made me miserable often enough as it was; what might she not do were I in her power always? Yet this face of the subject I did not suggest to Mr. Van Alstyne; it was painful enough to be kept to myself. I told him plainly that I could not love another as I did her; that I would not if I could.

He looked at me, not all unmoved, though silently; a gentle shading of something like pity stole across his regard, fixed and keen at first. He neither implored nor deprecated, but lifted my hand reverently to his lips, and said, in a tone of supreme calmness, "I can wait."

I should have combated the hope implied in those words. I was afterward angry with myself for enduring them; but at the moment uncertainty, shaped out of instinct and apprehension, closed my lips; I could not speak, and he left me. I went to my room more moved than I liked to acknowledge; and when he went away the next morning, though I felt the natural relief from embarrassment — knowing that I should not meet him as before — I still missed him, as a part of my daily life.

A month longer at the Beach protracted my stay into autumn; and then, with refreshed health and new strength, I returned home — home! whose chief charm lay in the prospect of seeing Eleanor.

It is true that this hope was not unalloyed. I am possessed of a nature singularly instinctive, and for some weeks past a certain shadow had crept into her letters that pained me. No word or phrase denoted change; but I perceived the uncertain aura, and was irrationally harassed by a trouble too vague for expression.

When I reached Bangor it lay waiting for me sufficiently tangible and legible in the shape of a note from Eleanor.

And here must I leave a blank. The forgiveness which stirs me to this record refuses to define for alien eyes what that trouble was. All that I can say to justify the extreme and piteous result which followed is, that Eleanor Wyse had utterly, cruelly, and deliberately deceived me; and when it was no longer possible to do so, had been obliged by circumstances to show me what she had done.

Of that day it is best to say but little: the world cracked and reeled under me; I returned from a brief stupor into one bitter, blind tempest of contempt; and in its strength I answered her note concisely and coldly. An hour's time brought me a rejoinder not worth answering, simply perfidious — a regret, "deep and true," that she had been compelled to grieve me, to "reserve" from me anything.

True! I had believed in truth, in goodness, in disinterested love, in principle; where now were such faiths swept? Verily, over the cliff into the sea! I was morally destroyed; I made shipwreck of myself and my life; my whole soul was a salt raging wave, tideless and foaming, without rest, without intent, without faith or hope in God — for he who loses faith in man loses faith in man's Maker — and this had Eleanor Wyse done for me.

Doubtless, to many, this emotion of mine will seem exaggerated. Let them remember that it was the loss of all that bound to life a lonely, morbid, intense, and excitable woman. Need I say more? If, after many years, with the kind help of nobler men and women, and the great patience of God, I have worn my way, inch by inch, back to some foothold of belief, I feel even yet — in some recoils of memory, some recurring habit of my soul — the reflex influence of those wretched days, months, years, when I suspected everyone — "hateful, and hating," of a truth.

Death is hard to bear when its angel breathes upon the face we love, and extinguishes therein the fiery spark of life; but what is death compared to such dissolution as treachery brings? If Eleanor Wyse had died when I loved her and trusted her, I should have gone mourning softly all my days, but not in pain; to find her untrue admitted no remedy, no palliation. Truth was the ruling passion of my mind; that, and nothing else, contented me. Its absence or its loss were the loss and absence of all in those whom I loved; and it was only within a brief time, as years go, that I had grown into the discovery that men are liars in spite of education or policy; what was it, then, to know this of my ideal — of Eleanor?

But let those helpless, miserable weeks go by. If I detail so much as I have, it is to show the reason of my righteous indignation — of my tenacious memory. After a time I supposed that I forgave Eleanor. I thought myself good, most Pharisaically good, to have forgiven such an injury. I made some little comedy of friendship for visible use; I visited her, though not as often as I had done before. I saw her try to supply, with the love of others, the lavish devotion and service I had given her; I saw her fail and suffer in the consciousness of want and dissatisfaction, and, self-righteously, I forgave again! Senseless that I was! — as if forgiveness rankled and grew bitter in one's heart — as if pardon, full and pure, rejoiced in the retributions of this life — fed itself with salt recollections of the past, and evil foreshadowings of the future; as if it could exist without love, without forgetfulness; as if good deeds were its pledge, or good words its seal!

No! I never forgave her. I never forgot one pang she inflicted on me, one untruth she uttered; I never trusted her word or her smile again. I gathered up every circumstance of the past, and hunted it to its source; I discovered that she had not simply deceived but deluded me, and laughed at me in the process.

How my blood boiled over these revelations! how my flesh failed with my heart! Slow, persistent fever gnawed me; my nights were without sleep or rest; my days laggard and delirious. Why I did not go crazy is yet unexplained to myself. I think I did, only that there was a method in my madness that won for it the milder name of nervousness. I was ill — I tottered on the very tempting brink of death, without awe or regret; I made no effort to live, nor any to die, except to pray that I might — the only prayer that ever passed my seared lips. I was sent away from home again; and while I was gone Eleanor married a certain Mr. Mason, of Bangor, and they removed to Illinois — in time, still further West. I was no better for this absence; and, impatient of strangers and intrusive acquaintance, I came home, and, strange as it may seem, I missed Eleanor! Habit is the anchor of half the love in this world, and my habit of loving her survived the love — or held it, perhaps — for I missed her sorrowfully.

I found Herman Van Alstyne at my uncle's when I came, and I was glad — glad of anything to break the desperate monotony of sorrow. He knew nothing more than everyone knew of this affair, except that he knew me, and from that gathered intuitively a part of the truth; and, by long patience, unwearied and delicate care — watching, waiting, forbearing, and enduring — he brought me nearer a certain degree of calm than I had believed possible, when a sudden summons called him away from Bangor; and it was during his absence that *It* began to come; as I said in the beginning, more than two years after I had lost Eleanor.

I lay still in my bed on that day of which I had spoken; the long stress of misery that I had undergone in the past years resulted in so much physical exhaustion as to have brought on the exquisite tortures of neuralgia, and it was a sudden access of this chronic rack that today held me prisoner. The draught I had taken was an anodyne, and under its influence I fell asleep. I must have slept an hour, when I woke abruptly with a renewed sense of something in the dusk beside me, at my pillow. I screamed as I woke into this terror, and instantly Aunt Mary came in. A cold sigh crossed my cheek; I shivered with a horror strange and unearthly. Aunt Mary asked if I had been asleep? I said yes. If I had been dreaming painfully? I did not answer that. I asked for some water, and getting it she forgot her question; but I could not bear to be alone. I begged her to sit beside me and to sleep with me, for I could not endure solitude; perpetual apprehension made me cringe in every nerve and fibre. I started at the slightest stir of leaf or insect upon the pane, and the repining autumn wind seemed to come over mile on mile of graves, bringing thence no mealy scent of white daisies — no infant-breathing violet odors — no frutescent perfume of sweet-briar, nor funereal smells of cypress, and plaintive whispers of fir and pine; but wave after wave of cries from half-free souls; sobbing with dull pain, and moans of deprecating anguish; a cry that neither heaven nor earth answered, but which crept — a live desolation — into the ear attent, and the brain morbidly excited.

Yet gradually this left me. I kept by some kindly human presence all day, and feared night no more till —

Let me say that all this time I was imperceptibly growing better than I had been. Hope, the very ministrant of Heaven, was by tiny crevice and unguarded postern stealing into my heart, though I knew it not, and softening all my hard thoughts of Eleanor, for I am moved to the outer world rather by my own moods than theirs; sorrow and pain make me selfish and unkind; peace, joy, even unconscious hope, expand my love for all mankind. I am better, more tender, more benevolent to others, when I receive some light and life within.

One night I was all alone; the low, unearthly glimmer of a waning moon lit the naked earth, a few leaves rustled on the fitful wind that lulled, and rose, and lulled again, with almost articulate meaning. I lay listening; a long pause came, of most significant quiet — a faint sigh crossed my brow. *It* was there beside me! — unseen, unheard, but felt in the secretest recesses of life and consciousness; a spirit, whereat my marrow curdled, my heart was constricted, my blood refused to run, my breath failed — fluttered — was it death? I sprung from my pillow; the presence drew farther away. I could see nothing, but I felt that something yearning, restless, pained, and sad regarded me. I began to gather courage. I began to pity a soul that had cast off life yet could not die to life; and now it drew nearer, as if some magnetism, born of my kindlier sympathies, melted the barrier between us, close — closer — till something rustled like a light touch the cover of my bed, stirred at my ear! Good Heaven! could I bear that? I could not shriek or cry, I fell forward upon my face. It went, and the wind began its wail; now reproachful sobs filled it: the moon sank, rain gathered overhead, and dripped with sullen persistence all night upon the roof, for all night I heard it.

It is tedious to recount each instance of this visitation. For weeks it stayed beside me. I felt it on my bed at night; I felt it by my chair in the day; it swept past me in the garden paths, a cold waft of air; it watched me through the window-blinds; it hung over me sleeping; yet never was I wonted to the presence; every day thrilled me with fresh surprise, and daily it grew, for daily it became more perceivable.

At first I felt only a sense of alien life in a room otherwise solitary; then a breath of air, air from some other sphere than this, penetrative, dark, chilling; then a sound, not of voice, or pulse, but of motion in some inanimate thing, the motion of contact; then came a touch, the gentlest, faintest approach of lips or fingers, I knew not which, to my brow; and last, a growing, gathering, flickering into sight. I saw nothing at first, directly; from the oblique glance that fear impelled I drew an impression of quivering air beside me; then of a shadow, frail and variant; then a shapeless shape of mist, a cloud, dark and portentous and significant; and next those sidelong glances revealed to me an expression; no face, no feature, but, believe it who can, an expression, earnest, melancholy, beseeching; a look that pierced me, that pleaded with my soul's depth, that entreated shelter, succor, consolation, which even in my terror I longed to give.

I might perhaps have suffered physically more than I did from this visiting, but the winged hope of which I spoke before upheld me still, daily, with stronger hands.

Herman had returned to Bangor after a brief absence, and was there still. I could not see him so constantly as I did and refuse my admiration to those traits that ever rule and satisfy me. Mr. Van Alstyne passed with some people for a philosopher, with some for a reformer: there were those who called him singular and self-opinionated; there were others who revered him for his devout nature and stainless life. He was more than any of these, he was a true man: and even in his plain exterior the eye that knew him found a charm peculiar and salient; the deep-sunken, clear, earnest eyes, kindled with a spark of profound depth and meaning; the thin, sharply cut, aquiline outline; the flexible, pure, refined mouth; the bronzed coloring; the overhanging brow — all these wore beauty indefinable, fired by the sweet and vivid smile of the irradiate soul within. In his presence, calm, restful, and strengthening, no subterfuge or evasion could live. He was just, direct, and tenderly strong; it was to him, to him it is, that I owed and owe a new and higher life than I had known before; he saw my sinking and lonely soul, but he saw its self-recuperative power, and with the most delicate and careful tenderness beguiled that motive force into action. He did far more than that; he recalled to me the higher motives that anguish had well-nigh scourged out from my horizon; he taught me as a father teaches his little child a newer trust in the Father of us all. I returned to those divine consolations that he laid before me with a pierced and penitent heart; and in knowing that I was prayed and cared for on earth, I learned anew that God is more tender and more patient than his creatures, and the logic of strong emotion made the truth living and potent. In all this was I drawn toward Herman by the strongest tie that can bind one heart to another — a tie that overarches and outlasts all the fleeting passions of time, for it is the adamantine link of eternity; and had I lost him then, I should have felt for all my life that there was a relation between us, undying and sure, to be renewed and acknowledged at length where such relations respire their native air, where there is neither marrying nor giving in marriage.

But it pleased God that I should live to receive my heart's desire; what began in gratitude ended in love. I might have shrunk from admitting so potent a guest again into my soul, had any other soul sent the messenger thither; but I trusted him when I disbelieved every other creature, and with this trust had crept back to me my faith in God, in good, in life and its ends. Truly, so far as man can do it, he saved my soul alive!

Now it was the early part of December. It was still haunting me. I could see more — eyes, deep and pleading, the outline of a head, pure lineaments, seemed hovering beside me, but if I turned for a direct look they were gone. I did not fear it; my happy faith and Herman shielded me.

The year drew on. The day before Christmas came, still, crisp, but yet warm for its season; no snow shrouded the earth; the far-off sun beamed out benign and pale; the few dry leaves lay quiet as they fell; the firs upon the lawn with curved boughs waited for their ermine, stately and dark. Herman asked me to walk with him. I cloaked and hooded myself, and we went away, away into the deep woods. What we said in that sweet silence of a leafless, sunny forest is known to us two: it is not for you, reader, friendly though you be; it is enough to tell you that I had promised to be his wife, that I was homesick no more.

It was well for me that this happened that day — should I not rather say God ordered it? — for as ever in this life sorrow tramples upon the foregoing footsteps of joy, so I found upon my return a household in tears. Mr. Mason, Eleanor's husband, had written, at last, two months after it happened, and another month had the letter been in coming — ah! however shall I say it? Eleanor was dead! her latest breath had gasped out a cry for me!

If Death is the Spoiler, so is he the Restorer; who shall dare to soil the shroud with anything but tears? I could do no more but weep; but I mourned for Eleanor again as I had never thought to do; evil, treachery, anguish, and distrust vanished — I remembered only love.

For hours I could not see or speak with Herman, the flood of misery overpowered me; and he too sorrowed, deeply, but serenely. It was late in the evening before I recovered any sort of composure. He sent to my chamber a brief penciled request, and

I went down; worn out with weeping, I obeyed like a child. I ate the food he brought me; I drank the restorative draught; quiet, but languid, I laid my head upon his breast, and, held by the firm grasp of his arm, I rested, and he consoled me; a deep and vital draught of peace slaked my soul's feverish thirst. Such peace had I never known, for it was the daughter of experience and trust.

You who, full of youth and its intact passion, give a careless hour to these pages, wonder not that I could find it just to give so noble a man a heart once given and wasted! Know that it is not the flower of any tropic palm that is fit to feed and sustain man, but the ripened clusters of its fruitage — the result of time, and sun, and storm. The first blush, the earliest kiss, the tender and timid glance are sweet indeed; but the true household fire, deep and abiding, is oftenest kindled in the heart matured by passion and by pain, tested in the stress of life, deepened and strengthened by manifold experience; and such a heart receives no unworthy guest, lights its altar-fire for no idol of wood or clay. I felt that I rendered Herman Van Alstyne far nobler and higher homage, that I did him purer justice in loving him now than it had ever been in my power to do before.

First love is a honeyed and dewy romance, fit for novels and school-girls; but of the myriad women who have lived to curse their marriage-day nine-tenths have been those who married in their ignorant girlhood, and married boys.

I have digressed to honor Herman, to vindicate myself. That Christmas-eve I lay sheltered and at rest on his arm, till the toll of midnight rang clear upon my ear. I could forever sing the angels' song now, that for years had been a blank repetition to my wretched and ungodly soul.

"Peace on earth!" was no more a chimera; I knew it at heart. "Good will to men!" that was spontaneous; I loved all in and for one. "Glory to God in the highest!" What did that ask to utter it but a full thankfulness that bore me upward like the flood-tide of a summer sea?

Blessed as I was, my common sense reminded me that it was far into the night, that I ought to sleep; so I said good-night to Herman, and crept with weak steps to my room. I fell asleep to dream of him, of Eleanor, of peace, and I woke into the deep silence that always preceded — *It*.

I woke knowing what stood beside me. Keen starlight pierced the pane, and shed a dim, obscure perception of place and outline over my room. A long, restful, sobbing sigh parted my lips; I perceived *It* was at hand; fear fled; terror died out; I turned my eyes — oh God! it was Eleanor!

Wan — frail — a flowing outline of shadow, but the face in every faultless line and vivid expression; now an expression of intense longing, of wistful prayer, of pleading that would never be denied.

I lifted my heavy arms toward the vision; it swayed and bent above me: the white lips parted; no murmur nor sound clave them, yet they spoke — "Forgive! forgive!"

"Eleanor! Yes love, darling! yes, forever, as I hope to be forgiven!" I cried out aloud. A gleam of rapture and rest relaxed the brow, the sad eyes; love ineffable glowed along each lineament, and transfused to splendor the frigid moulding of snow.

I closed my eyes to crush inward the painful tears, and a touch of lips sealed them with sacred and unearthly repose. I looked again; *It* had gone forever. The Christmas bells pealed loud and clear for dawn, and my thoughts rung their own joy bells beside the steeple chimes. Herman and Eleanor both loved me — I had forgiven; I was forgiven.

Yet must day and space echo that word once more. Hear me, Eleanor! hear me, from that mystic country where thou hast fled before!

I repeat that forgiveness again. So may Heaven pardon me in the hour of need; so may God look upon me with strong affection in the parting of soul and body, even as I pardon and love thee, Eleanor, with a truth and faith eternal! Thee, forever loved, but, ah! not now forever lost?

The Deserted Hut: A Ghost Story

Jane Goodwin Austin

I was lost; there could no longer be a doubt upon the subject. The forest road, which I had been following for the last hour, suddenly terminated in a tangled swamp, and the last rays of the sun were slowly sliding from the topmost twigs of the gloomy evergreens surrounding it.

I bitterly repented my own foolishness in rejecting the advice of mine host of the preceding night, who had advised me to wait until the following day, when his son would pilot me through the forest track I was forced to traverse, and when, beside, my poor horse might have sufficiently recovered from his fatigue to be able to proceed. But strong in self-confidence, and more than anxious to reach my destination, I insisted upon undertaking on foot, and without waiting for a guide, the fifteen miles of forest lying between my host's clearing and the small frontier town where he thought I might be able to procure another horse, either by purchase or loan.

I had, to be sure, received directions almost as minute as the cross-examination of a Philadelphia lawyer, and had drawn a rough chart of my course, and borrowed a pocket-compass, which I had frequently consulted through the day, with the comfortable conviction that I must be pursuing the direct course, and should arrive at my journey's end before night-fall. But now the path which should have continued well-trodden and direct, had dwindled to a mere track, such as might have been trodden by the wild creatures with which the wood abounded, and had finally disappeared altogether.

The situation was serious. The season was so far advanced as to render the prospect of a night beneath the open sky disagreeable, if not absolutely dangerous; and among the animals above-mentioned were a plentiful sprinkling of wolves, catamounts and bears, with an occasional panther or "Indian devil," as formidable an opponent, when enraged, as its congener of the Eastern jungle.

The sun's rays disappeared entirely, and a sullen gloom gathered beneath the arches of the wood, while the night wind stirred mournfully among the branches, and ominous rustlings of the underbrush suggested the idea of the approach of some crouching and hidden foe.

I looked about me with considerable anxiety. In the effort to retrace my steps, I had lost the path altogether, and now that the sun had set, was entirely at a loss to know in which direction to turn. To complete my misfortunes, I found that I had lost the compass, upon which I had principally relied.

All at once I perceived, through the gathering gloom, the approach of some moving object, which a brief scrutiny convinced me was a female figure, clothed in light, fluttering garments. Without pausing to consider the singularity of such an encounter in such a place and at such a time, I hastened toward her, shouting and waving my hand. To my great surprise, she neither paused, nor even turned her head, although I was quite sure that she must hear me, as the distance between us was not more than five or six rods.

"She must be deaf," muttered I, and attempted to run in order to overtake her, but found the under-brush so dense and tangled with vines, as to render haste impossible. "How the deuce does she get on so fast?" asked I, peevishly, as I found the attempt to diminish the distance between myself and the woman entirely useless. I stood still, and helloed at the top of my voice, but the woman, never pausing or looking round, moved on with a strange, irregular and waving motion, which struck me as peculiar, even through the dusk which was now deepening into night.

"At any rate," thought I, "she is going somewhere — she is not wandering aimlessly like myself, and by following her, I shall be more likely than in any other way, to extricate myself from this swamp."

Acting upon this plan, I hastened on as rapidly as possible, always keeping the fluttering garments of my guide in view, until we suddenly emerged from the forest into a small clearing, with a cabin in its midst.

"Thank Heaven!" said I, aloud. "Here is actually a house, and my deaf companion has probably already entered, as she is nowhere in sight. I hope she may prove more hospitable than she is quick of hearing."

Thus speaking, I approached the house, making a *detour*, that I might reach it from the front, for the point of my *debouchure* from the woods was at the rear of the cabin, and I naturally concluded that my singular guide had passed round to the door in the front, as I had lost sight of her while extricating myself from the last thicket upon the verge of the clearing. Judge then of my surprise, when, on arriving at the front of the cabin, I discovered it to be an uninhabited ruin, without door or window, or any sign of recent occupancy.

I entered, and looked about me. Upon the hearth, a little heap of pallid ashes showed where a fire had been, and beside it still stood a low wooden rocking-chair, that must once have been the family seat of the woman who had called this deserted house her home, but where now squatted a huge rat, so confident and so wonted in his right of inheritance, that he hardly retreated at my approach.

A bed, a table, and a few coarse articles of house-hold use stood about the walls; but all were weather-stained, covered with mould and dust, and dropping with decay. An air of gloom and desolation hung over all, deeper, to my mind, than even the obvious condition of the place would warrant. I looked about me with a shudder, and hastily retreated to the open air.

But the woman who had led me hither! Where was she? I peered earnestly into the forest, where now the night shadows gathered dense and close, and seemed creeping out on every side to invade the little clearing, and make headquarters of the deserted hut. Except the shadows, nothing was to be seen, although far in the wood something like a light garment seemed flitting from one dense covert to another, or it might have been but the waving of the poplar leaves, or the swaying branches of the silver birch, the "Lady of the Woods."

I called aloud, but except the mocking echo from the neighboring hillside, my wild cry remained unanswered, and died wearily into the rustle of the whispering wood, the wailing of the rising wind. I looked irresolutely about me; to attempt to proceed upon my journey was but sheer madness, and to choose a night beneath the open sky, exposed to the threatened storm, and to the attacks of the wild beasts infesting the forest, when I might have at least a roof over my head, and the defence of walls about me, would be absurd folly.

Clearly I must remain in the hut for the night, and fought hard to convince myself that the repugnance I felt to so doing was but an unreasonable whim, unworthy of the least attention.

"No, I will stay here, and I will make myself very comfortable, and even jolly, in spite of all the presentiments and will-o'-the-wisps in creation," said I, aloud; and throwing my knapsack upon the mouldy bed, I looked about me for the material of a fire. Kindling-stuff was soon obtained from some of the old chairs, which, at any rate, were too far gone to ever serve as seats again, and having broken one of them into suitable fragments, I went out, and soon collected from the edge of the wood a sufficient supply of branches and dead wood to keep a good fire all night.

As I returned toward the house, with my burden in my arms, I mechanically raised my eyes, and started so violently as to nearly throw down my whole load. In the doorway of the cabin, looking earnestly toward me, stood the figure of the woman, in her light fluttering dress, her pale and beautiful face distinctly visible against the dark background of the interior.

"This at least is no delusion," thought I; and, keeping my eyes steadily fixed upon the figure, I slowly approached the house, my forgotten fagot of wood closely clasped in my arms.

I had traversed perhaps half the distance, and was within two rods of the house, when the woman, whose eyes I could now plainly feel fixed upon my own with a mournful earnestness, slowly retreated backward into the house. Never removing my gaze from the doorway, I hurried on, and entered not a moment after. The place was as bare, as lonely, as utterly untenanted, as when I first set foot in it.

A heavy shudder ran through my frame, and the first impulse was to turn and fly to the wood, to the night — anywhere, away from this mystery, this mocking delusion. The next moment, however, a dogged determination to see the end of the affair seized upon me. I felt all my courage revive, mingled with a sort of angry contempt, both of myself, and the unknown agent of my discomfiture.

"If it is someone trying to frighten me, he or she will find it is not such an easy matter, and if it is —" So far I spoke, and then my voice died away, for, as truly as I breathe and speak at this moment, I felt a cold, soft hand gently laid across my mouth, as if to arrest the words already formed upon my lips. I staggered backward, but the next instant sprang forward, with both arms extended, and grasping for some substance in the direction whence the hand had seemed to come. They encountered nothing but the empty air, and, indeed, my own eyes sufficiently showed me that I was alone in the place. For a moment I stood as stupefied, but in the next I recovered myself, and proceeded in the line of action upon which I had previously resolved.

The heavy door of the cabin still lay upon the floor, where it had apparently fallen when time and damp had eaten through its hinges. This I raised into its place, and secured it there by dragging a high-backed settle across it. Next I closed the window, by hanging one of the bed-coverings upon two nails, driven into the logs just above it, and securing it at the bottom by setting an old chest, upon the end which lay upon the floor. Next I minutely examined the walls by the light of a pine torch, selected from among my supply of fuel, and kindled with the aid of some dried leaves, and my pocket matchbox. With this torch, I minutely examined the interior of the cabin in every direction. Nothing could be simpler than its construction. Above was the roof, formed of pine saplings, covered with bark; below was a floor of hard-beaten earth; around the sides four walls of logs, whole on three sides, and on the fourth pierced by the door and a small square window. Opposite the door, the fireplace, where, already, a merry blaze, curling up the chimney, closed that means either of entrance or egress. Clearly, nothing could now enter or leave the cabin, without my knowledge, and, if it were anything human, not without my consent.

As this thought defiantly shaped itself in my mind, a heavy sigh, close behind me, seemed to reply, and a breath of ice-cold air swept my cheek. I turned suddenly, and not only searched with my eyes through every corner of the now brilliantly-lighted cabin, but swept the air with my extended arms, in every direction. Nothing, nothing, either for sight or touch to seize upon, and again I shivered and slunk nearer to my fire, that most human and most sympathetic with man of all the elements. I sat beside my fire, then, and the fire renewed my courage, and my proud incredulity of danger.

"Sigh, now; put your hand upon my mouth; look at me with your great mournful dark eyes, or wave your white hand! I do not care — I am not afraid. This house is mine, tonight, and you shall not drive me from it," cried I, aloud, and looked defiantly about me.

Was it the wind, sweeping about the deserted hut — was it the blaze, crackling in the chimney — was it the rising storm, exulting in its mad glee? Heaven knows, not I; but no sound was ever plainer to me than the shout of derisive laughter which seemed to peal from a man's deep lungs, just outside the curtained window, and then die away in the sweep of the stormy wind.

I started to my feet, rushed to the window, and, tearing away the curtain, thrust my head and half my body out at the opening. As I did so, a flash of lightning spread through the heavens, throwing a vivid and ghostly light over the whole scene. I swept the clearing with a piercing gaze. Absolutely nothing, nothing but the brown grass, the stunted bushes, the forest tossing its myriad arms wildly against the ink-black sky. Above, the thunder pealed ominous as the war-cry of the infernal powers, whom I now believed let loose upon me.

"God help me!" muttered I, at last, and carefully readjusted the curtain; but had hardly done so, when around the edge of it crept the tips of four slender white fingers, which drew it gently aside, until, tearing from its hold at the top, it dropped, showing me, framed in the window opening, and thrown forward from the black night behind her, the figure of the woman, her dark hair, swept by the storm, about her pallid face, her dark eyes fixed mournfully upon my own.

With a final effort, I sprang forward, and grasped at the hand still holding the edge of the curtain. For an instant I felt it — a woman's cold, ice-cold hand, clasped within my own, but the next it was gone; not withdrawn, but melting within my grasp, as if suddenly resolved to the elements. At the same moment the figure disappeared — when, how, or by what process, I know not, although my staring eyes were fixed upon it, and my whole attention concentrated in the observation.

It was gone, and, half mechanically, I applied myself to replacing the curtain, which I did not accomplish without difficulty, for my right hand, which had grasped that of the apparition, as I now consented to call it, was numb, cold, and nearly useless.

Seating myself once more beside the fire, I took from my knapsack a flask of brandy, and some food, for I was faint with exhaustion and emotion, and a man accustomed to adventure and travel learns to systematically care for his body, whatever excitement may assail his mental powers.

I ate my supper, then, not, to be sure, with relish, but yet with a certain satisfaction, and the flask of brandy I drained to the last drop, and without the least effect upon my head, although I am ordinarily a temperate and abstemious man.

Then I arranged my knapsack as a pillow, piled my heaviest logs upon the fire, stretched myself before it, and, while listening to the wild roar of the storm, now at its height, and to the strange and unknown sounds mingling with it, I fell into a heavy sleep. How long this lasted, I cannot tell, but I was awakened by a sense of intolerable cold. It seemed as if the blood had frozen in my veins, my heart had ceased to beat, and all animation was suspended, save just sufficient to allow me to realize that I was suffering excessively.

My first conscious emotion was surprise at this terrible chill, for the fire still burned fiercely, and I lay not six feet distant from it. But the next moment I became conscious that I was not alone. A sound of whispering voices behind me, and the light rustle of a woman's garments, were plainly audible, and I slowly turned my head toward the sound.

There she stood, pale and beautiful, as I had before seen her, but with a look of intense love in the great eyes, now uplifted to the face of a young man, around whose neck her arms were tightly clasped, while his head was bent so closely over hers, as to quite conceal his features. They seemed in act of leave-taking, and the passionate embrace and kiss which I had surprised, was not yet done, when the door flew violently open, and a tall, middle-aged man, in hunter's dress, carrying a rifle, and followed by a hound, entered the hut.

In an instant all was confusion. A piercing shriek from the lips of the woman rang through the place; her lover, shaking her not ungently from her clinging hold about his neck, sought in his bosom for an instant, and then, obeying the gestures and frantic cries of the woman, he fled precipitately into the night, pursued by the dog. The hunter, who had stood for a moment as if stupefied, now uttered a horrible curse, and would have started in pursuit, but the woman had already closed the door, and now stood against it, her face set in a sort of terrified defiance, as she raised it to the fierce wrath of the hunter, who stood gazing at her a moment, with a frightful expression of rage, despair and love upon his rugged features, and then, drawing his hunting knife from his belt, slowly approached, and holding it upraised a moment, looked down into her eyes, which looked as steadily up to his.

God knows what question, too terrible for words, was asked and answered by those earnest eyes; nor can I tell whether any words were spoken, for all my senses were benumbed, my brain was oppressed, my whole being was more one of perception than of observation, but at the end of a moment, or an hour, I can hardly tell which, the hunter slowly raised his right hand still higher, and while the dilated eyes of the unresisting victim steadily watched its movement, the blade flashed in a sudden descending curve, and was sheathed within her heart.

The blow was followed by a short, gasping cry, not of terror, but of bodily anguish, and as the murderer withdrew his weapon, the body swayed sideways, and fell heavily to the ground, where it lay, with the wide-open black eyes staring up a dumb accusation, and the bright blood welling out and creeping slowly on in a little stream, until it reached and bathed the murderer's feet. He stood quite still, leaning on his rifle and looking down at his work — not carelessly or savagely, but with the air of a man who feels that he has taken a terrible justice into his own hands, and that his conscience acquits him of blame in the matter.

He still stood thus, and the life-blood of the beautiful woman whom he had slain lay a great red pool about his feet, when from the forest without was heard the voice of the great hound in furious outcry, mingled with the strangled cries and shouts of a man. The hunter listened for a moment, and smiled grimly.

"Venom has him, and won't leave him while there's life," muttered he.

The human cries grew weaker, those of the brute fiercer, until of a sudden both stopped, and, after an interval, a long, melancholy howl from the hound seemed to announce, and at the same time to lament, his victory.

"He's dead!" whispered the hunter; and a sudden tremor seized and shook his brawny frame.

Staggering to a seat, he leaned his elbows upon his knees, and covered his face with both hands, while from his broad chest broke a storm of terrible sobs and groans, and the great tears, forcing themselves between his fingers, fell plashing upon the ground, and mingled with the thread of blood which had followed him from the pool to where he sat.

A long, long time went over thus. The dead body of the woman, lying there so pale, so still, so lovely, the great eyes fixed relentlessly upon the face of the murderer — he, crouching there before it, his whole body racked with a fearful emotion, which was not sorrow, or remorse, or anger, but an insupportable anguish, the passion of a breaking heart — the wild storm howling about the house; the roll of the thunder, the hiss and glare of the lightning, — all made up a scene of such concentrated power that once to have seen it, makes all the minor effects of life seem weak and pale — only to remember it, destroys the interest of the romancist's most powerful efforts.

The emotion of the man exhausted itself at length, or rather changed its demonstration. He rose and went, with feeble steps, to kneel beside the terrible calm accuser, whose fixed eyes seemed to dwell forever upon his own. He tried to close them, but the stiffened lids refused to move. He smoothed the long, dark hair, he kissed the pale, still lips, he folded the hands upon the breast, and decently composed the limbs to rest. Kneeling there beside the dead, when all was done, and looking steadfastly down into the calm face, which looked as steadfastly back to his, it seemed to me that this man, at once so terribly injured and so terribly avenged, went over in his mind the history of his life, and as the events chronicled themselves in his memory, by some subtle process of sympathetic communication, they chronicled themselves in my consciousness, and there remained, when all was over, a clear and connected history, whose end lay at that moment before my eyes.

I knew, as if I had been told, that this hunter, a lonely, unloved and gloomy man, had set his strong heart and stronger will upon the winning of the woman who now lay dead before him, then a fresh and innocent girl in her father's distant home; that he had won her, half reluctant, and all untried in life or love as she was, at her father's hand, and had brought her here to the wilderness, where his lonely and savage tastes had led him to live. I knew that she had pined for home, for the gayety of her young companions, for the free and joyous life of her girlhood, not yet passed away; that she had grown at last to fear and shun, as far as she might, the stern and silent man whom she had married; that she shed in secret many a tear, until at last the beauty, that at first had glowed in the dusky cabin like the richest blossom of the summer time, waned and paled, until it was but that of the lily drooping upon its stem, and fading before its time. I knew, too — for I felt the pang with which his heart recalled it — I knew that as this change grew before his eyes, it hardened rather than softened the hunter's mood; that indifference became harshness, and silence was changed to taunts and upbraidings, in which he blindly sought to avenge upon her the cruel suffering that a disappointed love was working in his own heart.

Then came the gay young kinsman of the bride, who, on his return from a distant voyage, missed the pretty playmate of his boyhood, the half hoped-for bride of his manhood, and nothing could please or satisfy him, until he had seen her sweet face once more, and made sure that she was happy in her new home. He came, and she, poor innocent, thought it no harm to let the new life he brought with him beam from her once more blooming face, ring from her altered voice, shine in her dark, wonderful eyes. The kinsman marked it, and his heart beat high with the old love he had thought crushed and broken forever. The husband saw it, and all the gloom and ferociousness of his nature darkened into a terrible and relentless purpose. But he watched and waited, making no sign, giving no sign, willing that the unsuspecting children should stray blindly on, their eyes fixed upon each other, and the precipice before them so clothed in flowers at its edge that they should never see it, until they plunged wildly to the abyss beneath.

I knew, for I felt the memory tearing at his heart, that he had left them alone long summer days, while he went ostensibly to hunt in the forest, but soon returning, laid in wait, where he could watch the door of his own cabin, and the outgoings and the incomings, the long sweet hours of murmured talk beneath the forest shadows, the growing consciousness of something in either heart that should not, must not be spoken; the effort to control the rising passion, that in the end swept all before it; the wild love, that in itself was a despair; the temptation to flee together, the struggle that conquered that temptation, the resolve to part, to part forever, the anguish of the leave-taking — ah! I knew I felt it all, as he, kneeling there, went over the terrible tragedy, step by step, and saw for the first time many a thing in its true light, which before he had warped and twisted to a blacker meaning than it should have borne.

And now she lay before him dead, the woman whom he had loved with a passion as stern and strong as hatred; the woman whom he had so wholly loved, that it was easier to see her dead at his feet, dead by his own act, than to believe her false, and let her live, even out of his sight.

And his rival? I think the terrible strength of his love and of his vengeance toward that pale corpse at his feet, had crashed out all memory of him. He knew that the fierce brute, whom he had trained to share his hate and his love, had avenged both the one and the other, and he was content that it should be so, hardly spending a second thought upon the fate of dog or man. The end, the end of all had come, and the fierce excitement that for months had strung his whole existence, and given tone to his very being, had culminated in this, the first hour of a revulsion, which must be as terrible in its excess as had been the previous emotion.

Already he shuddered, as his foreboding soul pictured the days, the nights to come, the long vista of years down which his life should be pursued by those avenging phantoms of love and hate, the slow torture of memory, the keener pangs of apprehension! He felt them all, and I, through him, and to each fearful thought, each quivering pang of the soul, lashed to agony by remorse and terror, that pale, still face, with the shrinking eyes looking steadfastly up to his, said:

"Amen. It shall be so, and worse; for thus must my young life be avenged."

At last he rose, and as he uncovered his face, I shuddered to see the work the one hour had wrought upon it. Vengeance already had overtaken him, and marked him as her own.

Close to where she lay, he made her grave; fashioned it with care and skill, there in the midst of the home which now she should nevermore desert.

When all was ready, he raised her in his arms, kissed once more the cold lips, which now could neither reject nor return the caress, strained her in a wild embrace, until her heart's blood moistened his own breast, and then he laid her softly down, reverently covered the pale face, that to the last looked back his every look, whether of love or longing or wild regret, with the same stern, patient accusation, and heaped the earth upon the quiet form.

When all was done, he took his rifle in his hand, looked to see that it was in order, and, softly opening the door, went out into the night. A few moments later, a sharp report rung through the gray twilight of the morning, and then all was still save the low sobbing of the exhausted storm; as, moaning, it hid itself in the depths of the forest, while the drip of the raindrops from the roof of the cabin sounded like tears, or like the blood of the murdered girl, calling aloud to Heaven for vengeance.

The slow twilight broadened into day, and at last I rose, with the slow and cautious movement of one who fears to disturb a sleeper close at hand.

I was not surprised to find the door and window fast, as I had left them, although the hunter had passed out of the door, leaving it open behind him. I turned to the spot where I had seen him lay the body of the woman whom he had loved so well, and punished so terribly. A sunken grave was plainly visible by the dull morning light. I knelt beside it, and prayed for the peace of those three souls, gone to judgment, with all their sins upon their heads.

Then I crept softly from the house, and with the aid of the now risen sun, made my way to the point of my destination. But although I tried, I could not ask a question of those who might have given me the story of the deserted hut. Some inner impulse withheld me, and the words always died unspoken upon my lips. But, after all, what need? Did I not know it already, and know it as surely as if I had been an actor myself in the tragedy rehearsed before mine eyes?

Kentucky's Ghost

Elizabeth Stuart Phelps Ward

True? Every syllable.

That was a very fair yarn of yours, Tom Brown, very fair for a landsman, but I'll bet you a doughnut I can beat it; and all on the square too, as I say, — which is more, if I don't mistake, than you could take oath to. Not to say that I never stretched my yarn a little on the fo'castle in my younger days, like the rest of 'em; but what with living under roofs so long past, and a call from the parson regular in strawberry time, and having to do the flogging consequent on the inakkeracies of statement follering on the growing up of six boys, a man learns to trim his words a little, Tom, and no mistake. It's very much as it is with the talk of the sea growing strange to you from hearing nothing but lubbers who don't know a mizzen-mast from a church-steeple.

It was somewhere about twenty years ago last October, if I recollect fair, that we were laying in for that particular trip to Madagascar. I've done that little voyage to Madagascar when the sea was like so much burning oil, and the sky like so much burning brass, and the fo'castle as nigh a hell as ever fo'castle was in a calm; I've done it when we came sneaking into port with nigh about every spar gone and pumps going night and day; and I've done it with a drunken captain, on starvation rations, — duff that a dog on land wouldn't have touched and two teaspoonfuls of water to the day, — but someways or other, of all the times we headed for the East Shore I don't seem to remember any quite as distinct as this.

We cleared from Long Wharf in the ship Madonna, — which they tell me means, My Lady, and a pretty name it was; it was apt to give me that gentle kind of feeling when I spoke it, which is surprising when you consider what a dull old hull she was, never logging over ten knots, and uncertain at that. It may have been because of Moll's coming down once in a while in the days that we lay at dock, bringing the boy with her, and sitting up on deck in a little white apron, knitting. She was a very good-looking woman, was my wife in those days, and I felt proud of her, — natural, with the lads looking on.

"Molly," I used to say, sometimes, "Molly Madonna!"

"Nonsense!" says she, giving a clack to her needles, — pleased enough though, I warrant you, and turning a very pretty pink about the cheeks for a four-years' wife. Seeing as how she was always a lady to me, and a true one, and a gentle, though she wasn't much at manners or book-learning, and though I never gave her a silk gown in her life, she was quite content, you see, and so was I.

I used to speak my thought about the name sometimes, when the lads weren't particularly noisy, but they laughed at me mostly. I was rough enough and bad enough in those days; as rough as the rest, and as bad as the rest, I suppose, but yet I seemed to have my notions a little different from the others. "Jake's poetry," they called 'em.

We were loading for the East Shore trade, as I said, didn't I? There isn't much of the genuine, old-fashioned trade left in these days, except the whiskey branch, which will be brisk, I take it, till the Malagasy carry the prohibitory law by a large majority in both houses. We had a little whiskey in the hold, I remember, that trip, with a good stock of knives, red flannel, hand-saws, nails, and cotton. We were hoping to be at home again within the year. We were well provisioned, and Dodd, — he was the cook, — Dodd made about as fair coffee as you're likely to find in the galley of a trader. As for our officers, when I say the less said of them the better, it ain't so much that I mean to be disrespectful as that I mean to put it tenderly. Officers in the merchant service, especially if it happens to be the African service, are brutal men quite as often as they ain't. At least, that's my experience; and when some of your great ship-owners argue the case with me, — as I'm free to say they have done before now, — I say, "That's *my* experience, sir," which is all I've got to say; brutal men, and about as fit for their positions as if they'd been imported for the purpose a little indirect from Davy Jones's Locker. Though they do say that the flogging is pretty much done away with in these days, which makes a difference.

Sometimes on a sunshiny afternoon, when the muddy water showed a little muddier than usual, on account of the clouds being the color of silver, and all the air the color of gold, when the oily barrels were knocking about on the wharves, and the smells were strong from the fish-houses, and the men shouted and the mates swore, and our baby ran about deck a-play with everybody, — he was a cunning little chap with red stockings and bare knees, and the lads took quite a shine to him, — "Jake," his mother would say, with a little sigh, — low, so that the captain never heard, — "think if it was *him* gone away for a year in company the like of that!"

Then she would drop her shining needles, and call the little fellow back sharp, and catch him up into her arms.

Go into the keeping-room there, Tom, and ask her all about it. Bless you! she remembers those days at dock better than I do. She could tell you to this hour the color of my shirt, and how long my hair was, and what I ate, and how I looked, and what I said. I didn't generally swear so thick when she was about.

Well; we weighed, along the last of the month, in pretty good spirits. The Madonna was as stanch and seaworthy as any eight-hundred-tonner in the harbor, if she was clumsy; we turned in, some sixteen of us or thereabouts, into the fo'castle, — a jolly set, mostly old messmates, and well content with one another; and the breeze was stiff from the west, with a fair sky.

The night before we were off Molly and I took a walk upon the wharves after supper. I carried the baby. A boy, sitting on some boxes, pulled my sleeve as we went by, and asked me, pointing to the Madonna, if I would tell him the name of the ship.

"Find out for yourself," said I, not over-pleased to be interrupted.

"Don't be cross to him," says Molly. The baby threw a kiss at the boy, and Molly smiled at him through the dark. I don't suppose I should ever have remembered the lubber from that day to this, except that I liked the looks of Molly smiling at him through the dark.

My wife and I said goodbye the next morning in a little sheltered place among the lumber on the wharf; she was one of your women who never like to do their crying before folks.

She climbed on the pile of lumber and sat down, a little flushed and quivery, to watch us off. I remember seeing her there with the baby till we were well down the channel. I remember noticing the bay as it grew cleaner, and thinking that I would break off swearing; and I remember cursing Bob Smart like a pirate within an hour.

The breeze held steadier than we'd looked for, and we'd made a good offing and discharged the pilot by nightfall. Mr. Whitmarsh — he was the mate — was aft with the captain. The boys were singing a little; the smell of the coffee was coming up, hot and homelike, from the galley. I was up in the maintop, I forget what for, when all at once there came a cry and a shout; and, when I touched deck, I saw a crowd around the fore-hatch.

"What's all this noise for?" says Mr. Whitmarsh, coming up and scowling.

"A stow-away, sir! A boy stowed away!" said Bob, catching the officer's tone quick enough. Bob always tested the wind well, when a storm was brewing. He jerked the poor fellow out of the hold, and pushed him along to the mate's feet.

I say "poor fellow," and you'd never wonder why if you'd seen as much of stowing away as I have.

I'd as lief see a son of mine in a Carolina slave-gang as to see him lead the life of a stow-away. What with the officers from feeling that they've been taken in, and the men, who catch their cue from their superiors, and the spite of the lawful boy who hired in the proper way, he don't have what you may call a tender time.

This chap was a little fellow, slight for his years, which might have been fifteen, I take it. He was palish, with a jerk of thin hair on his forehead. He was hungry, and homesick, and frightened. He looked about on all our faces, and then he cowered a little, and lay still just as Bob had thrown him.

"We — ell," says Whitmarsh, very slow, "if you don't repent your bargain before you go ashore, my fine fellow, me, if I'm mate of the Madonna! and take that for your pains!"

Upon that he kicks the poor little lubber from quarter-deck to bowsprit, or nearly; and goes down to his supper. The men laugh a little, then they whistle a little, then they finish their song quite gay and well acquainted, with the coffee steaming away in the galley. Nobody has a word for the boy, — bless you, no!

I'll venture he wouldn't have had a mouthful that night if it had not been for me; and I can't say as I should have bothered myself about him, if it had not come across me sudden, while he sat there rubbing his eyes quite violent, with his face to the west'ard (the sun was setting reddish), that I had seen the lad before; then I remembered walking on the wharves, and him on the box, and Molly saying softly that I was cross to him.

Seeing that my wife had smiled at him, and my baby thrown a kiss at him, it went against me, you see, not to look after the little rascal a bit that night.

"But you've got no business here, you know," said I; "nobody wants you."

"I wish I was ashore!" said he, — "I wish I was ashore!"

With that he begins to rub his eyes so very violent that I stopped. There was good stuff in him too; for he choked and winked at me, and did it all up about the sun on the water and a cold in the head as well as I could myself just about.

I don't know whether it was on account of being taken a little notice of that night, but the lad always kind of hung about me afterwards; chased me round with his eyes in a way he had, and did odd jobs for me without the asking.

One night before the first week was out, he hauled alongside of me on the windlass. I was trying a new pipe (and a very good one, too), so I didn't give him much notice for a while.

"You did this job up shrewd, Kent," said I, by and by; "how did you steer in?" — for it did not often happen that the Madonna got fairly out of port with a boy unbeknown in her hold.

"Watch was drunk; I crawled down ahind the whiskey. It was hot, you bet, and dark. I lay and thought how hungry I was," says he.

"Friends at home?" says I.

Upon that he gives me a nod, very short, and gets up and walks off whistling.

The first Sunday out, that chap didn't know any more what to do with himself than a lobster just put on to boil. Sunday's cleaning day at sea, you know. The lads washed up, and sat round, little knots of them, mending their trousers. Bob got out his cards. Me and a few mates took it comfortable under the to'gallant fo'castle (I being on watch below), reeling off the stiffest yarns we had in tow. Kent looked on at euchre awhile, then listened to us awhile, then walked about uneasy.

By and by says Bob, "Look over there, spry!" and there was Kent, sitting curled away in a heap under the stern of the long-boat. He had a book. Bob crawls behind and snatches it up, unbeknown, out of his hands; then he falls to laughing as if he would strangle, and gives the book a toss to me. It was a bit of Testament, black and old. There was writing on the yellow leaf, this way: —

"Kentucky Hodge."
"from his Affecshunate mother
who prays, For you evry day, Amen."

The boy turned fust red, then white, and straightened up quite sudden, but he never said a word, only sat down again and let us laugh it out. I've lost my reckoning if he ever heard the last of it. He told me one day how he came by the name, but I forget exactly. Something about an old fellow — uncle, I believe — as died in Kentucky, and the name was moniment-like, you see. He used to seem cut up a bit about it at first, for the lads took to it famously; but he got used to it in a week or two, and, seeing as they meant him no unkindness, took it quite cheery.

One other thing I noticed was that he never had the book about after that. He fell into our ways next Sunday more easy.

They don't take the Bible just the way you would, Tom, — as a general thing, sailors don't; though I will say that I never saw the man at sea who didn't give it the credit of being an uncommon good yarn.

But I tell you, Tom Brown, I felt sorry for that boy. It's punishment bad enough for a little scamp like him leaving the honest shore, and folks to home that were a bit tender of him maybe, to rough it on a trader, learning how to slush down a back-stay, or tie reef-points with frozen fingers in a snow-squall.

But that's not the worst of it, by no means. If ever there was a cold-blooded, cruel man, with a wicked eye and a fist like a mallet, it was Job Whitmarsh, taken at his best. And I believe, of all the trips I've taken, him being mate of the Madonna, Kentucky found him at his worst. Bradley — that's the second mate — was none too gentle in his ways, you may be sure; but he never held a candle to Mr. Whitmarsh. He took a spite to the boy from the first, and he kept it on a steady strain to the last, right along, just about so.

I've seen him beat that boy till the blood ran down in little pools on deck; then send him up, all wet and red, to clear the to'sail halliards; and when, what with the pain and faintness, he dizzied a little, and clung to the rat-lines, half blind, he would have him down and flog him till the cap'n interfered, — which would happen occasionally on a fair day when he had taken just enough to be good-natured. He used to rack his brains for the words he slung at the boy working quiet enough beside him. It was odd, now, the talk he would get off. Bob Smart couldn't any more come up to it than I could: we used to try sometimes, but we had to give in always. If curses had been a marketable article, Whitmarsh would have taken out his patent and made his fortune by inventing of them, new and ingenious. Then he used to kick the lad down the fo'castle ladder; he used to work him, sick or well, as he wouldn't have worked a dray-horse; he used to chase him all about deck at the rope's end; he used to mast-head him for hours on the stretch; he used to starve him out in the hold. It didn't come in my line to be over-tender, but I turned sick at heart, Tom, more times than one, looking on helpless, and me a great stout fellow.

I remember now — don't know as I've thought of it for twenty years — a thing McCallum said one night; McCallum was Scotch, — an old fellow with gray hair; told the best yarns on the fo'castle always.

"Mark my words, shipmates," says he, "when Job Whitmarsh's time comes to go as straight to hell as Judas, that boy will bring his summons. Dead or alive, that boy will bring his summons."

One day I recollect especial that the lad was sick with fever on him, and took to his hammock. Whitmarsh drove him on deck, and ordered him aloft. I was standing nearby, trimming the spanker. Kentucky staggered for'ard a little and sat down. There was a rope's-end there, knotted three times. The mate struck him.

"I'm very weak, sir," says he.

He struck him again. He struck him twice more. The boy fell over a little, and lay where he fell.

I don't know what ailed me, but all of a sudden I seemed to be lying off Long Wharf, with the clouds the color of silver, and the air the color of gold, and Molly in a white apron with her shining needles, and the baby a-play in his red stockings about the deck.

"Think if it was him!" says she, or she seems to say, — "think if it was *him!*"

And the next I knew I'd let slip my tongue in a jiffy, and given it to the mate that furious and unrespectful as I'll wager Whitmarsh never got before. And the next I knew after that they had the irons on me.

"Sorry about that, eh?" said he, the day before they took 'em off.

"*No,* sir," says I. And I never was. Kentucky never forgot that. I had helped him occasional in the beginning, — learned him how to veer and haul a brace, let go or belay a sheet, — but let him alone generally speaking, and went about my own business. That week in irons I really believe the lad never forgot.

One time — it was on a Saturday night, and the mate had been uncommon furious that week — Kentucky turned on him, very pale and slow (I was up in the mizzen-top, and heard him quite distinct).

"Mr. Whitmarsh," says he, — "Mr. Whitmarsh," — he draws his breath in, — "Mr. Whitmarsh," — three times, — "you've got the power and you know it, and so do the gentlemen who put you here; and I'm only a stow-away boy, and things are all in a tangle, but *you'll be sorry yet for every time you've laid your hands on me!*"

He hadn't a pleasant look about the eyes either, when he said it.

Fact was, that first month on the Madonna had done the lad no good. He had a surly, sullen way with him, some'at like what I've seen about a chained dog. At the first, his talk had been clean as my baby's, and he would blush like any girl at Bob Smart's stories; but he got used to Bob, and pretty good, in time, at small swearing.

I don't think I should have noticed it so much if it had not been for seeming to see Molly, and the sun, and the knitting-needles, and the child upon the deck, and hearing of it over,

"Think if it was *him!*" Sometimes on a Sunday night I used to think it was a pity. Not that I was any better than the rest, except so far as the married men are always steadier. Go through any crew the sea over, and it is the lads who have homes of their own and little children in 'em as keep the straightest.

Sometimes, too, I used to take a fancy that I could have listened to a word from a parson, or a good brisk psalm-tune, and taken it in very good part. A year is a long pull for twenty-five men to be becalmed with each other and the devil. I don't set up to be pious myself, but I'm not a fool, and I know that if we'd had so much as one officer aboard who feared God and kept his commandments, we should have been the better men for it. It's very much with religion as it is with cayenne pepper, — if it's there, you know it.

If you had your ships on the sea by the dozen, you'd bethink you of that. Bless you, Tom! if you were in Rome you'd do as the Romans do. You'd have your ledgers, and your children, and your churches and Sunday schools, and freed niggers, and 'lections, and what not, and never stop to think whether the lads that sailed your ships across the world had souls, or not — and be a good sort of man too. That's the way of the world. Take it easy, Tom, — take it easy.

Well, things went along just about so with us till we neared the Cape. It's not a pretty place, the Cape, on a winter's voyage. I can't say as I ever was what you may call scar't after the first time rounding it, but it's not a pretty place.

I don't seem to remember much about Kent along there till there come a Friday at the first of December. It was a still day, with a little haze, like white sand sifted across a sunbeam on a kitchen table. The lad was quiet-like all day, chasing me about with his eyes.

"Sick?" says I.

"No," says he.

"Whitmarsh drunk?" says I.

"No," says he.

A little after dark I was lying on a coil of ropes, napping it. The boys were having the Bay of Biscay quite lively, and I waked up on the jump in the choruses. Kent came up while they were telling

"How she lay
On that day
In the Bay of Biscay O!"

He was not singing. He sat down beside me, and first I thought I wouldn't trouble myself about him, and then I thought I would.

So I opens one eye at him encouraging. He crawls up a little closer to me. It was rather dark where we sat, with a great greenish shadow dropping from the mainsail. The wind was up a little, and the light at helm looked flickery and red.

"Jake," says he all at once, "where's your mother?"

"In — heaven!" says I, all taken aback; and if ever I came nigh what you might call a little disrespect to your mother it was on that occasion, from being taken so aback.

"Oh!" said he. "Got any women-folks to home that miss you?" asks he, by and by.

Said I, "Shouldn't wonder."

After that he sits still a little with his elbows on his knees; then he speers at me sidewise awhile; then said he, "I s'pose I've got a mother to home. I ran away from her."

This, mind you, is the first time he has ever spoke about his folks since he came aboard.

"She was asleep down in the south chamber," says he. "I got out the window. There was one white shirt she'd made for meetin' and such. I've never worn it out here. I hadn't the heart. It has a collar and some cuffs, you know. She had a headache making of it. She's been follering me round all day, a sewing on that shirt. When I come in she would look up bright-like and smiling. Father's dead. There ain't anybody but me. All day long she's been follering of me round."

So then he gets up, and joins the lads, and tries to sing a little; but he comes back very still and sits down. We could see the flickery light upon the boys' faces, and on the rigging, and on the cap'n, who was damning the bo'sen a little aft.

"Jake," says he, quite low, "look here. I've been thinking. Do you reckon there's a chap here — just one, perhaps — who's said his prayers since he came aboard?"

"*No!*" said I, quite short: for I'd have bet my head on it.

I can remember, as if it was this morning, just how the question sounded, and the answer. I can't seem to put it into words how it came all over me. The wind was turning brisk, and we'd just eased her with few reefs; Bob Smart, out furling the flying jib, got soaked; me and the boy sitting silent, were spattered. I remember watching the curve of the great swells, mahogany color, with the tip of white, and thinking how like it was to a big creature hissing and foaming at the mouth, and thinking all at once something about Him holding of the sea in a balance, and not a word bespoke to beg his favor respectful since we weighed our anchor, and the cap'n yonder calling on Him just that minute to send the Madonna to the bottom, if the bo'sen hadn't disobeyed his orders about the squaring of the after-yards.

"From his Affecshunate mother who prays, For you evry day, Amen," whispers Kentucky, presently, very soft. "The book's tore up. Mr. Whitmarsh wadded his old gun with it. But I remember."

Then said he: "It's 'most bedtime to home. She's setting in a little rocking-chair, — a green one. There's a fire, and the dog. She sets all by herself."

Then he begins again: "She has to bring in her own wood now. There's a gray ribbon on her cap. When she goes to meetin' she wears a gray bunnet. She's drawed the curtains and the door is locked. But she thinks I'll be coming home sorry someday, — I'm sure she thinks I'll be coming home sorry."

Just then there comes the order: "Port watch ahoy! Tumble up there lively!" so I turns out, and the lad turns in, and the night settles down a little black, and my hands and head are full. Next day it blows a clean, all but a bank of gray, very thin and still, — about the size of that cloud you see through the side window, Tom, — which lay just abeam of us.

The sea, I thought, looked like a great purple pin-cushion, with a mast or two stuck in on the horizon for the pins. "Jake's poetry," the boys said that was.

By noon that little gray bank had grown up thick, like a wall. By sun-down the cap'n let his liquor alone, and kept the deck. By night we were in chop-seas, with a very ugly wind.

"Steer small, there!" cries Whitmarsh, growing hot about the face, — for we made a terribly crooked wake, with a broad sheer, and the old hull strained heavily, — "steer small there, I tell you! Mind your eye now, McCallum, with your foresail! Furl the royals! Send down the royals! Cheerily, men! Where's that lubber Kent? Up with you, lively now!"

Kentucky sprang for'ard at the order, then stopped short. Anybody as knows a royal from an anchor wouldn't have blamed the lad. I'll take oath to't it's no play for an old tar, stout and full in size, sending down the royals in a gale like that; let alone a boy of fifteen year on his first voyage.

But the mate takes to swearing (it would have turned a parson faint to hear him), and Kent shoots away up, — the great mast swinging like a pendulum to and fro, and the reef-points snapping, and the blocks creaking, and the sails flapping to that extent as you wouldn't consider possible unless you'd been before the mast yourself. It reminded me of evil birds I've read of, that stun a man with their wings; strike you to the bottom, Tom, before you could say Jack Robinson.

Kent stuck bravely as far as the cross-trees. There he slipped and struggled and clung in the dark and noise awhile, then comes sliding down the back-stay.

"I'm not afraid, sir," says he; "but I cannot do it."

For answer Whitmarsh takes to the rope's-end. So Kentucky is up again, and slips and struggles and clings again, and then lays down again.

At this the men begin to grumble a little, low.

"Will you kill the lad?" said I. I get a blow for my pains, that sends me off my feet none too easy; and when I rub the stars out of my eyes the boy is up again, and the mate behind him with the rope. Whitmarsh stopped when he'd gone far enough. The lad climbed on. Once he looked back. He never opened his lips; he just looked back. If I've seen him once since, in my thinking, I've seen him twenty times, — up in the shadow of the great gray wings, a looking back.

After that there was only a cry, and a splash, and the Madonna racing along with the gale twelve knots. If it had been the whole crew overboard, she could never have stopped for them that night.

"Well," said the cap'n, "you've done it now."

Whitmarsh turns his back.

By and by, when the wind fell, and the hurry was over, and I had the time to think a steady thought, being in the morning watch, I seemed to see the old lady in the gray bunnet setting by the fire. And the dog. And the green rocking-chair. And the front door, with the boy walking in on a sunny afternoon to take her by surprise.

Then I remember leaning over to look down, and wondering if the lad were thinking of it too, and what had happened to him now, these two hours back, and just about where he was, and how he liked his new quarters, and many other strange and curious things.

And while I sat there thinking, the Sunday-morning stars cut through the clouds, and the solemn Sunday-morning light began to break upon the sea.

We had a quiet run of it, after that, into port, where we lay about a couple of months or so, trading off for a fair stock of palm-oil, ivory, and hides. The days were hot and purple and still. We hadn't what you might call a blow, if I recollect accurate, till we rounded the Cape again, heading for home.

We were rounding that Cape again, heading for home, when that happened which you may believe me or not, as you take the notion, Tom; though why a man who can swallow Daniel and the lion's den, or take down t'other chap who lived three days comfortable into the inside of a whale, should make faces at what I've got to tell I can't see.

It was just about the spot that we lost the boy that we fell upon the worst gale of the trip. It struck us quite sudden. Whitmarsh was a little high. He wasn't apt to be drunk in a gale, if it gave him warning sufficient.

Well, you see, there must be somebody to furl the main-royal again, and he pitched onto McCallum. McCallum hadn't his beat for fighting out the royal in a blow.

So he piled away lively, up to the to'-sail yard. There, all of a sudden, he stopped. Next we knew he was down like heat-lightning.

His face had gone very white.

"What's to pay with *you?*" roared Whitmarsh.

Said McCallum, "*There's somebody up there, sir.*"

Screamed Whitmarsh, "You're gone an idiot!"

Said McCallum, very quiet and distinct: "There's somebody up there, sir. I saw him quite plain. He saw me. I called up. He called down; says he, *'Don't you come up!'* and hang me if I'll stir a step for you or any other man tonight!"

I never saw the face of any man alive go the turn that mate's face went. If he wouldn't have relished knocking the Scotchman dead before his eyes, I've lost my guess. Can't say what he would have done to the old fellow, if there'd been any time to lose.

He'd the sense left to see there wasn't overmuch, so he orders out Bob Smart direct.

Bob goes up steady, with a quid in his cheek and a cool eye. Half-way amid to'-sail and to'-gallant he stops, and down he comes, spinning.

"Be drowned if there ain't!" said he. "He's sitting square upon the yard. I never see the boy Kentucky, if he isn't sitting on that yard. *'Don't you come up!'* he cries out, — *'don't you come up!'*"

"Bob's drunk, and McCallum's a fool!" said Jim Welch, standing by. So Welch volunteers up, and takes Jaloffe with him. They were a couple of the coolest hands aboard, — Welch and Jaloffe. So up they goes, and down they comes like the rest, by the back-stays, by the run.

"He beckoned of me back!" says Welch. "He hollered not to come up! not to come up!"

After that there wasn't a man of us would stir aloft, not for love nor money.

Well, Whitmarsh he stamped, and he swore, and he knocked us about furious; but we sat and looked at one another's eyes, and never stirred. Something cold, like a frost-bite, seemed to crawl along from man to man, looking into one another's eyes.

"I'll shame ye all, then, for a set of cowardly lubbers!" cries the mate; and what with the anger and the drink he was as good as his word, and up the ratlines in a twinkle.

In a flash we were after him, — he was our officer, you see, and we felt ashamed, — me at the head, and the lads following after.

I got to the futtock shrouds, and there I stopped, for I saw him myself, — a palish boy, with a jerk of thin hair on his forehead; I'd have known him anywhere in this world or t'other. I saw him just as distinct as I see you, Tom Brown, sitting on that yard quite steady with the royal flapping like to flap him off.

I reckon I've had as much experience fore and aft, in the course of fifteen years aboard, as any man that ever tied a reef-point in a nor'easter; but I never saw a sight like that, not before nor since.

I won't say that I didn't wish myself well on deck; but I will say that I stuck to the shrouds, and looked on steady.

Whitmarsh, swearing that that royal should be furled, went on and went up.

It was after that I heard the voice. It came straight from the figure of the boy upon the upper yard.

But this time it says, "*Come up! Come up!*" And then, a little louder, "*Come up! Come up! Come up!*" So he goes up, and next I knew there was a cry, — and next a splash, — and then I saw the royal flapping from the empty yard, and the mate was gone, and the boy.

Job Whitmarsh was never seen again, alow or aloft, that night or ever after.

I was telling the tale to our parson this summer, — he's a fair-minded chap, the parson, in spite of a little natural leaning to strawberries, which I always take in very good part, — and he turned it about in his mind some time.

"If it was the boy," says he, — "and I can't say as I see any reason especial why it shouldn't have been, — I've been wondering what his spiritooal condition was. A soul in hell," — the parson believes in hell, I take it, because he can't help himself; but he has that solemn, tender way of preaching it as makes you feel he wouldn't have so much as a chicken get there if he could help it, — "a lost soul," says the parson (I don't know as I get the words exact), — "a soul that has gone and been and got there of its own free will and choosing would be as like as not to haul another soul alongside if he could. Then again, if the mate's time had come, you see, and his chances were over, why, that's the will of the Lord, and it's hell for him whichever side of death he is, and nobody's fault but him; and the boy might be in the good place, and do the errand all the same. That's just about it, Brown," says he. "A man goes his own gait, and, if he won't go to heaven, he *won't*; and the good God himself can't help it. He throws the shining gates all open wide, and he never shut them on any poor fellow as would have entered in, and he never, never will."

Which I thought was sensible of the parson, and very prettily put.

There's Molly frying flapjacks now, and flapjacks won't wait for no man, you know, no more than time and tide, else I should have talked till midnight, very like, to tell the time we made on that trip home, and how green the harbor looked a sailing up, and of Molly and the baby coming down to meet me in a little boat that danced about (for we cast a little down the channel), and how she climbed up a laughing and a crying all to once, about my neck, and how the boy had grown, and how when he ran about the deck (the little shaver had his first pair of boots on that very afternoon) I bethought me of the other time, and of Molly's words, and of the lad we'd left behind us in the purple days.

Just as we were hauling up, I says to my wife: "Who's that old lady setting there upon the lumber, with a gray bunnet, and a gray ribbon on her cap?"

For there was an old lady there, and I saw the sun all about her, and all on the blazing yellow boards, and I grew a little dazed and dazzled.

"I don't know," said Molly, catching onto me a little close. "She comes there every day. They say she sits and watches for her lad as ran away."

So then I seemed to know, as well as ever I knew afterwards, who it was. And I thought of the dog. And the green rocking-chair. And the book that Whitmarsh wadded his old gun with. And the front door, with the boy a walking in.

So we three went up the wharf, — Molly and the baby and me, — and sat down beside her on the yellow boards. I can't remember rightly what I said, but I remember her sitting silent in the sunshine till I had told her all there was to tell.

"*Don't* cry!" says Molly, when I got through, — which it was the more surprising of Molly, considering as she was doing the crying all to herself. The old lady never cried, you see. She sat with her eyes wide open under her gray bunnet, and her lips a moving. After a while I made it out what it was she said: "The only son — of his mother — and she —"

By and by she gets up, and goes her ways, and Molly and I walk home together, with our little boy between us.

The Strange Passengers

Harriet Prescott Spofford

"And heard the ghosts on Haley's Isle complain,
Speak him off shore, and beg a passage to old Spain!"

The schooner Unadilla, refitted and newly named, had shaken
all her linen to the gale, and was flying down the river's mouth,
a fruiter on her way to Malta for a cargo of red-hearted oranges.
Captain Deverard himself had named her after a twenty-dollar
bank-bill that once, in a critical moment of his finances, came
into his possession, and which in its clear blue and white
expanse had seemed to him the loveliest thing he had yet
beheld. It had been the most elastic piece of paper, too, that ever
was — what a quantity it covered! In the first place, a barrel of
flour — for wicked men did not just at that time make their
millions out of the flesh and blood of the poor, and flour was
cheap; there was enough of the bill remaining then for a pig — a
little one, to be sure — for a cloak for Em, and a pair of shoes for
Em's mother; and lastly, there was still a corner left that just
tucked over a steel-shod sled to delight the heart of little Jack.
Captain Deverard could see the boy now, in his great boots and
his cap tied down about such a rosy face, making plunges, with
his sled mounting and falling behind him, through the
snowdrifts that lined the yard that day like fortifications. There
had been another lastly, too, which it would seem like a breach
of confidence to mention, if it were not that Captain Deverard
held the remembrance of the night he spent with that bottle of
brandy — juicy old Cognac, he called it: it could never have
been anything in the world but Catawba, — if it were not, I say,
that the captain held the remembrance of that night, in spite of
his wife's tears, Em's dismay and Jack's fright, as one of the very
brightest ones of his experience. "Reg'lar blow-out," said the
captain with a chuckle. "Never was so happy in my life. By
George! I wouldn't lose the having had it for all the parsons
betwixt here and Georgy!"

He had prospered since then better than he deserved,
perhaps. And now he had bought a dismantled and nearly

worthless old schooner — "On her last legs," said the captain, "sea-legs" — had mortgaged her for new rigging and repairs, had named her for his friend in need, and having hugged his wife and kissed the children till they were red in the face indeed, was scorning a pilot and running before the wind across the bar and out to sea. Em was shaking her handkerchief in the front door when he ran down. "I'll have a house of my own when I come back," grumbled the captain, "and be beholden to nobody!" He took his glass and made out his wife standing behind the child and wiping her eyes with her apron, as one tear oozed after another so fast that she could not catch a glimpse of the Unadilla. He dipped his flag three times to salute them, fired his swivel, and when its echo had died out across the marshes and silver streams, heard Jack's little cannon give a puff of reply: then put sentiment and home behind him and turned to the business of the hour.

It was a November afternoon, but belonging to one of those delicious days that, bewildered in the order of their going, fall among us in doubt whether they are a part of opting or fall. Resinous odors from the pine forests swept over them on the fresh wind, soft blue hazes shrouded the horizon behind all the red and russet distances of shorn meadows and low hills; but when the Unadilla was once over the bar and rocking on the broad swells, the air thickened with a warm and pleasant vapor, into which the sudden twilight of that season fell with a cooling shock.

"Guess we'll give the shoals a little wider berth," said Captain Deverard to his mate. "There's that old Spanish craft that laid her bones there, they used to tell about, and the ten or eleven graves among the rocks: well, I don't care to make the twelfth. Shouldn't wonder if 'twas thickening up for foul weather. I'm afraid it's one of those false winds. If it holds, we'll get out into blue water and let it blow!"

The wind, however, not having that regard for persons which a well-conditioned wind should have, refused to hold, began to fall and began to veer, played various pranks of its own, and threatened to give him the lie in his teeth by turning about altogether, as if, now it had Captain Deverard out of reach of shore, it would just show him that there were two of them. The shoals were rising, on one hand, like faint purple phantoms in the less purple twilight as the captain spoke: the white lighthouse loomed like a ghost, with the air trembling all around it: suddenly its spark of fire struck out upon the gathering dimness, fluttered there on the fixed stone pinnacle a moment, and went wheeling on its way, laying long beams of light athwart the dark and purple sea. A trifling, baffling land-breeze blew out from the islands, and delayed them in the region of waters that Captain Deverard scarcely liked: there was something half supernatural in all the gloaming and glimmer and the long rise and fall of the dark wave with its white lips on the edges of the low islands not a mile away. "Hark, will ye?" said Captain Deverard. "What may that be?"

It was only a voice — a low, plaintive voice — to which one must listen ere distinguishing it from the murmur of the breeze through the cordage — a sound half complaining, half entreating, and as if spoken through the palms of hollowed hands that it might reach the farther.

"Well," said the captain, "if ever I heard the lingua Franca, that's it! — the identical gibberish they chatter round the ports where this Unadilla's bound. Shouldn't wonder — what'll you bet? It's those old Spanish ghosts I told you of! Always heard the place was haunted."

"Shouldn't wonder," said the mate, strengthening himself with some fresh tobacco.

"Here, you devil-too-whits," shouted the captain through his trumpet, "what do you want?"

If ever a mortal or immortal voice were heard, all hands on board the Unadilla heard the answer come: once in lingua Franca, again in broken Spanish speech, the third time in good English —

"A passage to old Spain!"

"Well, that's more'n I can give you," answered back the captain. "We didn't put up no bunks for ghosts, and we ain't laid in any glow-worms or that sort of provisions. To be sure, though, there's the dead-lights," added the captain.

Came back the cry again, forlorn and sad, as if with the wringing of hands —

"A passage to old Spain!"

"Well, it's sort of too bad," said Captain Deverard then. "They're buried up there in a foreign country, you see, just where the storm tossed them; while, if they'd been left to themselves in the furrer of the seas that drowned them, they'd have made a shift — who knows? — to get back to their own shore. I should myself; I know, if the case'd been mine. Come now! Dessay, they've left their sweethearts and wives, and a heap of little Marias and Jesuses, in that blasphemous country of theirs. I'll tell them. What do you want a passage home for?" shouted Captain Deverard, raising his trumpet again. "Don't you know your sweethearts are dead or married to other men? Your wives have played you false long ago. Your children —" But here the captain dropped his trumpet. "I d'no," said the captain. "It's kinder hard on 'em. I s'pose they were little red-cheeked rogues like Jack, them chaps of theirn, when they come away with the elf-locks hanging round their faces, just as you see 'em now swarming about the wharves like rats, and their eyes as black and bright. I reckon, now, if they could go back and see them children's grand-children, they'd take 'em for their onty-donty. But there! I wouldn't have a ghost aboard o' me for all — the oranges in Seville!"

"Do' no' what harm they'd do?" said the mate, in a superior way.

"D—— this wind!" said the captain, then at that. "Here we are creeping along like that old ivy-plant, when we should have put just twice our distance between us and Old Town hills. We'll have that wailing in our ears all night at this rate!"

"A passage to old Spain!" the cry told out again like a funeral bell.

"Blowed if they sha'n't have it!" exclaimed Captain Deverard, turning on the mate in good fighting trim, having been an atom nettled by that dignitary's latest remark. "What d'ye say?"

"Well, I don't mind, if the men don't," answered the other. "Fact is, I don't believe in 'em much."

"You ain't superstitious, be ye?" said the good captain, sneering as well as he knew how to do. "Some isn't. Maybe it's only the air singing through two rocks: I've heard say as much. But if you'll take the yawl and Turner and Janvrin, Mr. Coffin, we'll just make believe giving these Spanishers a lift. George! a man with your name's just the fellow to send for ghosts!" The captain chuckled with satisfaction, in spite of a certain creepiness that he experienced.

It is very likely that Mr. Coffin would have preferred another man to stand in his boots just at that minute of time, even if it hung a calf-skin on his recreant legs; but bravado goes a great way, and before Captain Deverard could make up his mind to countermand the imprudent order, he saw Mr. Coffin and his two subordinates already distant a half-dozen oars' lengths on their errand. They were Newburyport boys, brought up in the schools of that old town side by side with rich men's sons, possessing little awe and less fear, entirely disbelieving in the preternatural, and full enough of dash and daring to humor Captain Deverard's whim for the sake of the adventure. There was that absence of discipline on board the Unadilla, where crew and officers all messed together, which would have made it quite safe for them in the general free-and-easiness to have refused to stir an inch.

The mate did not exactly tell them what was the business in hand, and whether they divined it or overheard it, nobody knows.

"New branch of the business," said Janvrin, spitting in his palms and shipping his oars. "Hope it pays — doubloons, I s'pose."

"No you don't," said Turner. "Nothing but old Continental paper — spectralist kind."

"Better shut up!" growled the mate. "Them Spanish ghosts ain't none of your common cut. Run you through with their moustaches. Don't stand any joking. Wear sombreros and carry stilettos. Hope I may die if they don't strike you dead first time you see 'em!"

"Jes' so," said Turner — "first time."

"You be dashed," remarked Janvrin.

The boat had reached a distance of twice its length from the innumerable low rocks of the shore, when the captain, from the schooner's deck, signaled the rowers to pause just where the shallow water had not more than a foot's depth. "Come now," cried Captain Deverard to his shipwrecked Spaniards; here's your chance, unless you're too 'feard of salt water to wet your feet!"

The three men afterward averred to the captain that at that moment there was a rush and scurry in the air behind them, a sound like the skipping of stones over smooth water: looking down where their shadow was thrown on the brown, weed-imbedded bottom, that in the golden sunlight of day was always transmuted into such a wrought-work of splendor, but at this hour seemed only a place of darkness and mystery, they fancied that they saw it lessen and lessen, as a boat's shadow would be apt to do while the boat settled more deeply with fresh freight. When, at the word of return, they had measured half the way back to the schooner, Captain Deverard heard the familiar cry again — "A passage to old Spain!" — but coming from the boat itself and in such a different intonation, such a cry of hope and of surprise and joy, that he hardly believed his ears. The men heard it too, for it rose from among them: a cold chill shivered up their backs; and whether they pulled against an adverse current or they carried a weight no boat had ever borne before, the three men climbed their vessel's side, at length, with aching ribs and beaded brows, tired with toil and drenched to the skin, but not by sea-water.

"Guess he'll get his come-uppance," muttered Mr. Coffin, striding by the little captain, and discharging some double-barreled oaths on his underlings, who recognized them as mere safety-valves. As for the little captain, be declared, somewhat later, that he felt himself growing white about the gills, though, nevertheless, he kept a stiff upper lip. "Now my hearties," said he to his guests, addressing them, as one would say, by a slightly inappropriate term — "Now my hearties, you're passengers aboard this schooner, the Unadilla, bound for Malta. Behave yourselves respectably, and you're welcome; that is to say — well — no matter! But go to kicking up a bobbery and I'll pitch you everyone overboard again, just as true as Jonah swallowed the whale!"

"Don't think they'll stand much of that," said the mate surlily. "Papishers, you know. Their Bible's different sort of talk; all the stories there run t'other way. S'pose 'twould be as easy for Jonah as the whale, though."

"None o' yer lip!" said the captain.

There was a sound upon the deck — one of those sounds that set your teeth on edge and make the flesh crawl, as the sound of a slate pencil does in grating down a slate sometimes — as if every ghost of them all had scraped a foot and pulled a forelock: then there was nothing to be heard but the lapping of the water and the swelling of the wind.

"Now, Mr. Coffin," said the captain, "I'll leave the deck to you. We'll keep her as she is, I think. There's quite a little air of wind: shouldn't wonder if we made a run before the storm, after all."

So Captain Deverard, in his new dignity, went below for forty winks, while the mate took in his royals, the ship held on her course, and the "air of wind" went frolicking with the waves and whipping their caps white.

When the captain came on deck, as he did with the change of watch, every soul in sight was sound asleep. Who struck the bell then? who, indeed? Captain Deverard went aft as quickly as he could step: it was not a swift business, for the crank little Unadilla, leaning far over, carried one side almost under water. He seized the mate by the shoulder, shaking him till his teeth rattled. "What's this mean?" said he, as soon as the bewildered man had his blinking eyes open. "If ever I see a Yankee schooner turned into a Spanish brigantine, here she is! Where'd all this square rig come from?"

"Square rig be blowed!" exclaimed Mr. Coffin. "Nobody's touched a rope since you went below, except to shorten sail some when the wind got round into the north."

The captain rubbed his eyes, to the full as bewildered as the mate had been. He looked up the dim height of the great sail rising far and faint in the darkness very true, there was nothing but the usual gear of a foreign-going topsail schooner above him. "That beats all!" cried he: then falling back upon a more defensible position, "Well," said he, wetting his finger and holding it up for a weathercock, "I s'pose you see where the wind is now? As dead an east as ever whistled, and the Unadilla flying on it flaking. If 'twasn't too thick to see a star, I should say we'd been taken up in the air and set down the other way. What's that light on the bows? When I turned in I left one on the quarter — White Island light, or you may have my head for an orange! White Island light, as I'm a sinner! Hark a minute, will ye?" as a dull, low roar fell upon his ear — the awful sound of a breaker. "We're driving straight on destruction! We're turned completely round! That ought to be the spot where we took them fellers aboard. By George, sir!" as if an idea had struck him so that he staggered, "they're working their passage!"

"About ship!" thundered the mate into the instant's silence, while the captain's brain yet reeled. In a moment the mate had leaped into the ratlines and was trumpeting his orders to the hands, who, thoroughly awakened, sprang to the ropes like cats.

"Hard a-lee!" cried the captain, and threw his whole weight on the wheel as he spoke.

A momentary shudder, a throbbing of the hard waves beneath, and the Unadilla, minding her helm and helped by the men who worked the head-sails, moved about slowly and came up in the wind, gathered headway and left the white danger astern.

"Good for her!" said the captain then, wiping his forehead, something well pleased with his craft's fast tussle. "She'll ride it out. Butts at the sea like a little piece of cattle. I think we'll reduce the rag, though, Mr. Coffin — less muslin for this kind of tornadoes."

"Let go the flying jib!" cried the mate, the vessel careening under him with the force of the gale. "Let go fore and main sails! Stand by to lower the t'gallant halyards and clew them up!"

In a moment more, as it seemed, darkness had swallowed the sails: the schooner lay-to under her jib and a close-reefed topsail, and the tempest howled over her harmless.

"All's well that ends well!" said Captain Deverard. "Call the watch, Mr. Coffin!"

When everything was quiet again on board the Unadilla, her little skipper kept the helm still in his own hands, and seized the opportunity for reflecting on the situation, that he might discover, if possible, how all this rout came about.

But, do what he would, Captain Deverard could collect neither thought nor argument; there was as much confusion in his mind as there had been in the last ten minutes. He could not rid himself of the idea that not his own crew obeyed his commands, but a dozen swarming shadows. By what earthly or unearthly instrumentality they were here, when they ought to be thirty miles away, straight sailing; how, when he left the

Unadilla putting down her nose and running for the high seas, he had found her back again on these winter-curst shores, with her head toward her old wharf; who it could be on board, the mate and his watch asleep, that, in such a growing gale, knew how to wind a ship till her prow was in the place where her stern had been; through what kind of atmosphere, in what kind of glimmer, neither darkness nor light, he had seen his schooner spreading the sail of another sort of vessel, as if she had been the phantom of that other vessel long since wrecked and rotten, — as easily as those propositions he could have answered what material or immaterial souls were made of! It caused the captain to shiver from his crown to his heel. Had a decree gone out against the Unadilla? Was she never to make port again? Were they all imprisoned on a spectral ship for daring to make light of death and doom in trying to give respite to those sentenced souls? What had cast such a sleep upon the watch? Was it real thickness, real storm, or was it all some wild hallucination of the night — the night conjured up again in which that Spanish ship went down?

While he mused and marveled, and kept his place at the wheel, and the schooner drifted and still drifted, ever so slightly, in from sea, a singular effect of music stole toward him, whether rising over the halloo of the heavens and the piping of the cordage, or heard only in a lull of the boisterous wind — a soft, singing murmur, in spite of its power, swelling gently, till it seemed a chorus of voices far, far away — rough, male voices, it may be, but clarified and attuned by distance into a sweetness that was unutterable, a sadness that was unbearable, and yet nothing, as it were, but a hollow shell of sound. Captain Deverard was not skilled in foreign tongues, yet he heard the burden of these dead men's song as distinctly as ever it had been heard when, two hundred years ago, it was transferred from Calderon's old theatres to the streets, and descended thence in the hearts of that people whose religions and superstitions went with them to their play and sat down with them to their meat. The strain vibrated now round Captain Deverard's ears as if breathed from some æolian lyre:

"Pecador soy, tus favores
Pido por justicia yo,
Pues Dios en ti poderió
Solo por los pecadores,
A mí me debes tus loores,
Qui por mi solo muriera
Dios, si mas mundo no hubiera."

Though he could by no means give the words their literal
meaning, Captain Deverard knew as well what they signified as
if they had been his own speech: there was something in them,
words or voice, that belonged to the general language which all
men utter. Their melody seemed to come to him from every side
— from the forecastle, from the cross-tree, from the hold: it was
full of woe, and, with all its sweetness, seemed to emit horror as
a flame does smoke. He felt himself growing colder and colder
as he listened. From every side: they were all about him then.
The captain shouted to his men. A hoarse and dismal voice
replied — a Spanish hail. His own men slept — that he
understood — as those before them did, and in their turn, once
more the ghosts held the watch. From farther and farther away
the sound at length was floating, while it left dullness in his ears
and dimness in his eyes. By the broad daylight, with all his
powers in play, he had defied the might of any apparition: now
darkness robbed him and oppressed him even his flesh forgot
any longer to creep, and the spell of slumber was closing over
him. No! not while such a blast as that almost tore him from the
wheel — a good, real blast — a stinging, roaring buffet. Then, all
at once, a rending noise that the captain knew too well — a
sharp report, as of an exploding gun, and the topsail had torn
from its bolt-ropes and had whirled away through the night like
a flying ghost itself. A lifting of the Unadilla, as though she
would pierce heaven with her topmast — a sinking, a swooping:
she had broached-to and lay in the trough of the seas, billow on
billow beating her bows, a wall of waves rising on either side,
and one that, climbing over them in a towering cataract and
illumined for a moment by the rays of some light-house lantern,
in a great, blinding suffusion of spray and glory, leaned, with all
its vastness and weight and suffocating darkness, down, down,

and plunged and weltered and washed away; and the Unadilla rose like a cork, but with her bulwarks stove, her water-casks afloat and her deck-load swept from sight.

The wild cry of a drowning man cleft even the scream of the wave and overwhelmed all other terrors in its own. He might find a water-cask: there was no time nor place to help him — they might all be with him in a moment. For while Captain Deverard had questioned himself, and trusted his topsail, minding his helm the while, in order to escape the assault of such a sea, had listened and felt the glamour stealing over him, the gale had gathered and swelled and burst in its fury — a hurricane of snow and sleet, the air full of the driving flakes, stinging like needles and icing plank and rope as they fell — no light but the binnacle's, the blackness of death throughout the crippled little schooner.

"Hoist the mainsail!" roared the captain, putting the strength of ten men upon the wheel, and in a despair lest none were left on deck to hear him. "Hoist the mainsail and we'll work her out of this!" He could not see his hand before him. Whether it were his own men, or the shades and apparitions of the last hour, that slowly bent the great sail till it caught the wind, the captain dared not say; but it caught the wind, bellied forth, soared with them out of the abyss where they had been plunged, up, up, up, and suddenly bellowed and split from end to end, and with a shock, as of the meeting of the firmaments, the Unadilla was thrown on her beam-ends, the sea making a complete breach over her, while furious surge after surge rushed and raked her in a havoc of ruin.

"Cut away the weather lanyards!" cried out the captain, in tones firmer and clearer than a well-blown clarion, his courage rising with his need. He heard the men's familiar voices as they yelled reply, and a single stroke separated the ropes that were stretched as tense as harp-strings, and sent the whole quivering pile of rigging by the board. It hung there for one dreadful moment, hammering against the schooner's sides with mighty blows, that threatened in each fall to batter her to fragments. "Clear it away, for God's sake!" cried the captain.

The mate came dashing up the companion-way, echoing his superior's words; and then, as if remembering with Homer that "examples make excitements strong and sweeten a command," he himself clambered, axe in hand, swiftly along into the thick of the peril: the ponderous mass parted and fell astern. What was left of the Unadilla righted again, but Mr. Coffin was seen no more: he had gone with his work. And the schooner, rolling like a log, pounded by every sea, refused her helm and drifted toward the treacherous breakwater of Bar Island, a helpless wreck.

"Heaven save us!" groaned the captain; and he called out to them to lash themselves to what they could find.

The water piled itself in great polished masses of blackness: they could see it, colder than ice, yet outlined in fire, as it rose and swayed and shattered over them in a wild fierce way that had lost all semblance of frolic or play, and raged with a kind of malignity, as if the gaping jaws of every awful wave hungered for them. The light of the shoals wheeled upon its way on the one side: its flash shot up through the midnight every minute in a wide sheet that made only a visible horror: the Ipswich light shone steadily upon the other, while the fainter ray of the Plum Island light lit up the tumbling waste of roaring shadow behind them. "Wrecked in sight of three light-houses!" groaned the captain again, as he bound himself fast to his broken wheel. And he thought of his wife watching the storm through the darkened pane that night; of Jack leaving his restless bed to slip a hard little hand in hers for comfort; of Em's deep unconscious sleep, with the white ruffled nightcap that was the pride of her heart, making her pretty face look like a blushing flower. It was little likely he would ever see the three again — his clothes freezing on his back as fast as the last wave left him, his hands and feet mere lumps of grave-cold clay, save when they tingled with sharp hot pains as if they were on fire. The air was all one fluff of heavy snow, that made mere breathing a labor: now and then it parted, and he caught glimpses of those things, those strange passengers, now no longer shades, but moving flames, that would only leave him when the Unadilla quenched them by settling underneath the flood with her ungodly freight.

The hull of the little schooner could scarcely endure much more of this: these seas that brayed her in their mortar would soon finish her. She had sprung a leak, he fancied, already: it was impossible to man the pumps — a great plank came ripping off her side — she would go to pieces as she went down. Still, she drifted constantly to leeward. The waters on either hand were milk-white about her now: they spread themselves in broad and changing flourishes of silver on the black field of the night. It might be that the running sea had carried them faster than any wind could have done: this might be the bar at the river's mouth — it might be the white and spouting shafts of the North and South breaker that shot up here, it seemed to him, mast-high, as the Unadilla rolled in the depths. Now and then he hallooed to his men: now and then they called to one another. Drifting, drifting, they had left that tract of churned sea behind them: could he have clearly distinguished the first thing to mark his course, Captain Deverard would have thought himself on the way back to his own door-stone. "I know every drop of the river," said he to himself, "just let me get into still water: too black to see a b'y. Bump! Shouldn't wonder if 'twas the Gangway rocks — it's your last bump if it is. Off again? I'll be blest if 'twasn't the North flat. She's nothing but a log! a log! There's a sea for you! What's this? Bump — bump — the South flat? No? The Half-tide rocks then? Steady, you jade, and your own wharf two rods to looard! No, again? What? Great Havens!" shouted the captain, "we are going to pieces in the middle of Bar Island breaker!"

It was entirely true. The Unadilla would never see wharf or river-mouth, neither Gangway rocks, nor buoys, nor flats again: miles and miles away from them all, she was fixed fast and buried in the quicksand, and the waves had leaped on board and were tearing her apart with a thousand strokes and shocks and shivers. It seemed to Captain Deverard as if he saw them at their work in the shape of vast and awful spirits, as if he heard the hoarse and hollow shibboleth of their cries, as if he felt their icy breath blown full upon his forehead. Their great bards were upon him, were over him and under him: they lifted him, floated him, tore him free, tossed him on from one to another. Far and far away he heard them singing —

"Pecador soy, tus favores
Pido por justicia yo,

Pues Dios en ti poderió
Solo por los pecadores,
A mí me debes tus loores,
Qui por mi solo muriera
Dios, si mas mundo no hubiera."

Faintly and more faintly it came: then a blow as if from a thunderbolt, a blaze of light upon his brain, in which the rosy fare of Em flashed forth and burst in a myriad sparks — the solid earth rose to meet him, and he fell in blackness and oblivion.

Little Captain Deverard, made of iron and muscle, was the kind of man that dies hard.

When, by and by, he opened his eyes, it was all at once as wide and clear as he woke up every morning in his bed at home.

The wind had fallen a little, he fancied — had fallen very perceptibly: the roar of the waves on the beach was duller, the dark was being undershot with gray: he judged that the night had long since turned toward morning. He had been thrown in the hollow of two sand-hills: he was on a sort of dry land, if all the shifting ledges of Bar Island have any actual claim to land at all: he was alive and whole — so much was certain. Could it be possible that no others shared his safety?

"Halloo!" cried Captain Deverard, at the top of his voice.

"Halloo!" came back an answer from just below.

"That you, Mr. Coffin?"

"Ay, ay, sir!"

"Whereabouts?" cried the bewildered captain.

"Here — just come ashore on a water-cask I found as I went over. Lend a hand, I say, before the next big wave comes!"

The little captain sprang by instinct to the spot where the mate lay face downward and clutching the sand, and drew him up beside himself and out of the way of his howling pack of pursuers, but nearly spent with weariness and pain. If he did not perform a dervish's dance around this piece of real flesh and blood, which, at first, he had half doubted to be flesh and blood at all, so hollow and so muffled was the voice, it was because he was in no condition to do so. He did the next best thing.

"Had some mountain-dew in my pocket-flask," said he. "S'pose it's smashed? 'Tain't glass, though. Shouldn't wonder if 'twas all mixed with sea-water. Here it is, by all that's good! Sweet as a nut. That's a blessing I didn't look for. Here, Coffin, have a sip: now a swallow — another — drink it off: leave a drop and I'm blest if you sha'n't be tried for mutinying against superior orders!" The mate was never tried for mutiny.

"There's no more of us?" asked he.

"No more," answered the captain.

"By George!" said Mr. Coffin, in a tone that no words could have strengthened.

"Make out where we be?" he added, by and by.

"Well, as near as I can reckon — I've been looking about since it began to gray — the Unadilla's made her grave in the sand-bar yonder, and the currents, or something else, have tossed us here. If we can cross these hills, I've an idea we should find ourselves on the old Bluff road, nine miles from home. It'll be a tough pull. What do you say — find your legs?"

"Good as yourn," said the mate. And they started on their way without more ado. They wasted no words, nor uttered any regrets, but bent all their energies upon their travel, stumbling, falling, lying down to rest, dropping asleep, swearing out their groans, their feet frost-bitten, half dead at last, when the stars, that had one by one stolen out, melted into a warmer light, and the spires of the old town tipped themselves in sunshine and sparkled in the morning rays.

"It's surprisin'," said Captain Deverard then, "that there's no one hurrying to the beach this morning. There's more'n one wreck there by this time, I'll dare swear!"

"There's the tavern at last," said his companion, feebly, not being of the same indomitable stuff as his superior, and feeling utterly unequal to conjecture or remark upon conjecture.

"Guess we'll go in and rest a spell," replied the worthy captain. "'Morning, Remick! Little blow last night" — as if his news were so great that he must lead up to it by degrees, lest, if broken suddenly, it might prove too much for the hearer.

"Little," said Mr. Remick, casually, in response.

"Little?" repeated the insulted captain, with a rising voice. "You call a tempest that tears the Unadilla to chips a little blow?"

"You said it was, yourself," retorted the innkeeper. "As for me, I never opened an eye all night. How was it, Charlie? — much wind last night?"

"None that I heerd," said the hostler; "sea was smooth as a mill-pond."

"Well, that beats all!" exclaimed the captain and the mate together — the captain stentorian with indignation; the mate as if it certainly beat him.

"Have anything?" asked Mr. Remick.

It was of no use talking to such dunderheads as they. "Don't care if we do," answered Captain Deverard. "Got a team to set us home?" In ten minutes they were spinning up the turnpike, up the Water street, and had stopped before the cottage, where Jack was just filling the tea-kettle at the pump.

"What's that?" exclaimed the mate, suddenly.

"What's what?" answered the captain.

"The Unadilla, or I'll be —!"

"You've lost your wits!" cried Captain Deverard, seizing his arm and looking in his face.

It was something to look at, assuredly, that face of Mr. Coffin's: the jaw had fallen, the eyes were fixed and staring: it was as white and ghastly as a galvanized corpse; he shook as if struck by palsy.

"Don't look at me, man!" he continued to stammer between his chattering teeth. "Look at there!"

Captain Deverard followed then the mate's gaze with his own, alarmed for him and full of condescending pity; and there — beside the wharf — there she lay, the blue and white streamer at her mast-head, the signal for her captain flying — the Unadilla!

"Is she real?" gasped the mate.

"You may break her up for firewood!" cried the captain; "you may sell her for old iron. I'll never set my foot upon her waist again!"

"She's the devil's own darling," whispered the mate, below his breath.

But there lay the Unadilla, to all appearance as solid reality as she had ever been. There sat Turner on the side; there was Janvrin strolling down to meet him. Captain Deverard surveyed them with a long and leisurely survey, and his amazement crystallized into a scorn beyond expression. Turner and Janvrin! whom he had seen rolled into their restless graves! That these appearances were those men in the flesh, not all the power of all the gods could force him to believe: evil spirits in their guise it might be. He went into his own house and shut the door behind him, and, though it was broad daylight, went to bed. If his head ached for the next twenty-four hours as though it would roll together like a scroll, it was no more than might be expected, he said, after all he had gone through on the previous night. But from that day to this he has never exchanged a syllable with either of those unsubstantial beings — Spanish ghosts, it may be — who have stolen, to the best or worst of his belief, the bodies of other men to become visible in — beings never to have dealings with, never to be in any way countenanced by this honest captain, who absolutely looks through them and ignores their existence.

As for the Unadilla, — which lay there taut and trim, and positively inviting you with all her blue and white beauty, — set foot upon her planks again he had said he would not: to sell her would be like being in the receipt of blood-money. If anybody wanted her — if anybody dared be so foolhardy — let him take her!

When, then, a couple of weeks had rubbed away the sharp edge of the remembrances of that fearful night, Mr. Coffin, a trifle braver or more unbelieving, perhaps, than his superior officer, began to consider the matter of having a schooner for little more than the asking. It ended by his calling up all the reserved forces of his courage; and when he had obtained permission of the party holding her mortgage, he took the Unadilla down to Thomaston for lime, burnt her up and sunk her, and himself with her, on the homeward trip.

"Just as I expected!" said the captain. "The devil's own darling he said she was; and now she's proved it by fire and brimstone. Don't tell me!" he used to add, in reciting his adventures, at the time when, for a commission of five cents, he was in the habit of carrying to the dwellings of various purchasers their baskets from the fish-market — "Don't tell me! I might have been upon a spree, but how'd it happen that Mr. Coffin was on a spree too?

Nothing so remarkable in that? What? When it was the same sort of a spree, with the same identical visions and accidents and experiences to a tittle?" said the captain, warming himself with his wrath. "How'd it happen we both thought we took in the strange passengers off the shoals — both thought they worked the ship after their old ways to their old wreck, and both thought we were cast away together on Bar Island for flying in the face of Providence? How'd it happen I heard them singing that 'Pecador soy, tus favores,' when I don't know a word more Spanish than I do Japanese, if I *didn't* hear them? How'd it happen I got this crik in my back — that isn't moonshine, I can tell you — and he that scar on his hand, if we warn't cast away on board the Unadilla? How'd it happen we both brought up at Plum Island tavern in the morning, if we hadn't been cast away on board the Unadilla in the night?"

Ah! how, indeed, Captain Deverard?

Tom Toothacre's Ghost Story

Harriet Beecher Stowe

"What is it about that old house in Sherbourne?" said Aunt Nabby to Sam Lawson, as he sat drooping over the coals of a great fire one October evening.

Aunt Lois was gone to Boston on a visit; and, the smart spice of her scepticism being absent, we felt the more freedom to start our story-teller on one of his legends.

Aunt Nabby sat trotting her knitting-needles on a blue-mixed yarn stocking. Grandmamma was knitting in unison at the other side of the fire. Grandfather sat studying "The Boston Courier." The wind outside was sighing in fitful wails, creaking the pantry-doors, occasionally puffing in a vicious gust down the broad throat of the chimney. It was a drizzly, sleety evening; and the wet lilac-bushes now and then rattled and splashed against the window as the wind moaned and whispered through them.

We boys had made preparation for a comfortable evening. We had enticed Sam to the chimney-corner, and drawn him a mug of cider. We had set down a row of apples to roast on the hearth, which even now were giving faint sighs and sputters as their plump sides burst in the genial heat. The big oak back-log simmered and bubbled, and distilled large drops down amid the ashes; and the great hickory forestick had just burned out into solid bright coals, faintly skimmed over with white ashes. The whole area of the big chimney was full of a sleepy warmth and brightness just calculated to call forth fancies and visions. It only wanted somebody now to set Sam off; and Aunt Nabby broached the ever-interesting subject of haunted houses.

"Wal, now, Miss Badger," said Sam, "I ben over there, and walked round that are house consid'able; and I talked with Granny Hokum and Aunt Polly, and they've putty much come to the conclusion that they'll hev to move out on't. Ye see these 'ere noises, they keep 'em awake nights; and Aunt Polly, she gets 'stericky; and Hannah Jane, she says, ef they stay in the house, *she* can't live with 'em no longer. And what can them lone women do without Hannah Jane? Why, Hannah Jane, she says these two months past she's seen a woman, regular, walking up and down the front hall between twelve and one o'clock at night; and it's jist the image and body of old Ma'am Tillotson, Parson Hokum's mother, that everybody know'd was a thunderin' kind o' woman, that kep' everything in a muss while she was alive. What the old crittur's up to now there ain't no knowin'. Some folks seems to think it's a sign Granny Hokum's time's comin'. But Lordy massy! says she to me, says she, 'Why, Sam, I don't know nothin' what I've done, that Ma'am Tillotson should be set loose on me.' Anyway they've all got so narvy, that Jed Hokum has ben up from Needham, and is goin' to cart 'em all over to live with him. Jed, he's for hushin' on't up, 'cause he says it brings a bad name on the property.

"Wal, I talked with Jed about it; and says I to Jed, says I, 'Now, ef you'll take my advice, jist you give that are old house a regular overhaulin', and paint it over with tew coats o' paint, and that are'll clear 'em out, if anything will. Ghosts is like bedbugs, — they can't stan' fresh paint,' says I. 'They allers clear out. I've seen it tried on a ship that got haunted.'"

"Why, Sam, do ships get haunted?"

"To be sure they do! — haunted the wust kind. Why, I could tell ye a story'd make your har rise on e'end, only I'm 'fraid of frightening boys when they're jist going to bed."

"Oh! you can't frighten Horace," said my grandmother. "He will go and sit out there in the graveyard till nine o'clock nights, spite of all I tell him."

"Do tell, Sam!" we urged. "What was it about the ship?"

Sam lifted his mug of cider, deliberately turned it round and round in his hands, eyed it affectionately, took a long drink, and set it down in front of him on the hearth, and began: —

"Ye 'member I told you how I went to sea down East, when I was a boy, 'long with Tom Toothacre. Wal, Tom, he reeled off a yarn one night that was 'bout the toughest I ever hed the pullin' on. And it come all straight, too, from Tom. 'Twa'n't none o' yer hearsay: 'twas what he seen with his own eyes. Now, there wa'n't no nonsense 'bout Tom, not a bit on't; and he wa'n't afeard o' the divil himse'f; and he ginally saw through things about as straight as things could be seen through. This 'ere happened when Tom was mate o' 'The Albatross,' and they was a-runnin' up to the Banks for a fare o' fish. 'The Albatross' was as handsome a craft as ever ye see; and Cap'n Sim Witherspoon, he was skipper — a rail nice likely man he was. I heard Tom tell this 'ere one night to the boys on 'The Brilliant,' when they was all a-settin' round the stove in the cabin one foggy night that we was to anchor in Frenchman's Bay, and all kind o' layin' off loose.

"Tom, he said they was having a famous run up to the Banks. There was a spankin' southerly, that blew 'em along like all natur'; and they was hevin' the best kind of a time, when this 'ere southerly brought a pesky fog down on 'em, and it grew thicker than hasty-puddin'. Ye see, that are's the pester o' these 'ere southerlies: they's the biggest fog-breeders there is goin'. And so, putty soon, you couldn't see half ship's length afore you.

"Wal, they all was down to supper, except Dan Sawyer at the wheel, when there come sich a crash as if heaven and earth was a-splittin', and then a scrapin' and thump bumpin' under the ship, and gin 'em sich a h'ist that the pot o' beans went rollin', and brought up jam ag'in the bulk-head; and the fellers was keeled over, — men and pork and beans kinder permiscus.

"'The divil!' says Tom Toothacre, 'we've run down somebody. Look out, up there!'

"Dan, he shoved the helm hard down, and put her up to the wind, and sung out, 'Lordy massy! We've struck her right amidships!'

"'Struck what?' they all yelled, and tumbled up on deck.

"'Why, a little schooner,' says Dan. 'Didn't see her till we was right on her. She's gone down tack and sheet. Look! There's part o' the wreck a-floating off: don't ye see?'

"Wal, they didn't see, 'cause it was so thick you couldn't hardly see your hand afore your face. But they put about, and sent out a boat, and kind o' sarched round; but, Lordy massy! ye might as well looked for a drop of water in the Atlantic Ocean. Whoever they was, it was all done gone and over with 'em for this life, poor critturs!

"Tom says they felt confoundedly about it; but what could they do? Lordy massy! what can any on us do? There's places where folks jest lets go 'cause they hes to. Things ain't as they want 'em, and they can't alter 'em. Sailors ain't so rough as they look: they'z feelin' critturs, come to put things right to 'em. And there wasn't one on 'em who wouldn't 'a' worked all night for a chance o' saving some o' them poor fellows. But there 'twas, and 'twa'n't no use trying.

"Wal, so they sailed on; and by'm by the wind kind o' chopped round no'theast, and then come round east, and sot in for one of them regular east blows and drizzles that takes the starch out o' fellers more'n a regular storm. So they concluded they might as well put into a little bay there, and come to anchor.

"So they sot an anchor-watch, and all turned in.

"Wal, now comes the particular curus part o' Tom's story: and it more curus 'cause Tom was one that wouldn't 'a' believed no other man that had told it. Tom was one o' your sort of philosophers. He was fer lookin' into things, and wa'n't in no hurry 'bout believin'; so that this 'un was more 'markable on account of it's bein' Tom that seen it than ef it had ben others.

"Tom says that night he hed a pesky toothache that sort o' kep' grumblin' and jumpin' so he couldn't go to sleep; and he lay in his bunk, a-turnin' this way and that, till long past twelve o'clock.

"Tom had a 'thwart-ship bunk where he could see into every bunk on board, except Bob Coffin's; and Bob was on the anchor-watch. Wal, he lay there, tryin' to go to sleep, hearin' the men snorin' like bull-frogs in a swamp, and watchin' the lantern a-swingin' back and forward; and the sou'westers and pea-jackets were kinder throwin' their long shadders up and down as the vessel sort o' rolled and pitched, — for there was a heavy swell on, — and then he'd hear Bob Coffin tramp, tramp, trampin' overhead, — for Bob had a pretty heavy foot of his own, — and all sort o' mixed up together with Tom's toothache, so he couldn't get to sleep. Finally, Tom, he bit off a great chaw o' 'baccy, and got it well sot in his cheek, and kind o' turned over to lie on't, and ease the pain. Wal, he says he laid a spell, and dropped off in a sort o' doze, when he woke in sich a chill his teeth chattered, and the pain come on like a knife, and he bounced over, thinking the fire had gone out in the stove.

"Wal, sure enough, he see a man a-crouchin' over the stove, with his back to him, a-stretchin' out his hands to warm 'em. He had on a sou'wester and a pea-jacket, with a red tippet round his neck; and his clothes was drippin' as if he'd just come in from a rain.

"'What the divil!' says Tom. And he riz right up, and rubbed his eyes. 'Bill Bridges,' says he, 'what shine be you up to now?' For Bill was a master oneasy crittur, and allers a-getting' up and walkin' nights; and Tom, he thought it was Bill. But in a minute he looked over, and there, sure enough, was Bill, fast asleep in his bunk, mouth wide open, snoring like a Jericho ram's-horn. Tom looked round, and counted every man in his bunk, and then says he, 'Who the devil is this? for there's Bob Coffin on deck, and the rest is all here.'

"Wal, Tom wa'n't a man to be put under too easy. He hed his thoughts about him allers; and the fust he thought in every pinch was what to do. So he sot considerin' a minute, sort o' winkin' his eyes to be sure he saw straight, when, sure enough, there come another man backin' down the companion-way.

"'Wal, there's Bob Coffin, anyhow,' says Tom to himself. But no, the other man, he turned: Tom see his face; and, sure as you live, it was the face of a dead corpse. Its eyes was sot, and it jest came as still across the cabin, and sot down by the stove, and kind o' shivered, and put out its hands as if it was getting' warm.

"Tom said that there was a cold air round in the cabin, as if an iceberg was comin' near, and he felt cold chills running down his back; but he jumped out of his bunk, and took a step forward. 'Speak!' says he. 'Who be you? and what do you want?'

"They never spoke, nor looked up, but kept kind o' shivering and crouching over the stove.

"'Wal,' says Tom, 'I'll see who you be, anyhow.' And he walked right up to the last man that come in, and reached out to catch hold of his coat-collar; but his hand jest went through him like moonshine, and in a minute he all faded away; and when he turned round the other one was gone too. Tom stood there, looking this way and that; but there warn't nothing but the old stove, and the lantern swingin', and the men all snorin' round in their bunks. Tom, he sung out to Bob Coffin. 'Hullo, up there!' says he. But Bob never answered, and Tom, he went up, and found Bob down on his knees, his teeth a-chatterin' like a bag o' nails, trying to say his prayers; and all he could think of was, 'Now I lay me,' and he kep' going that over and over. Ye see, boys, Bob was a dreful wicked, swearin' crittur, and hadn't said no prayers since he was tew years old, and it didn't come natural to him. Tom give a grip on his collar, and shook him. 'Hold yer yawp,' said he. 'What you howlin' about? What's up?'

"'Oh, Lordy massy!' says Bob, 'we're sent for, — all on us, — there's been two on 'em: both on 'em went right by me!'

"Wal, Tom, he hed his own thoughts; but he was bound to get to the bottom of things, anyway. Ef 'twas the devil, well and good — he wanted to know it. Tom jest wanted to hev the matter settled one way or t'other: so he got Bob sort o' stroked down, and made him tell what he saw.

"Bob, he stood to it that he was a-standin' right for'ard, a-leanin' on the windlass, and kind o' hummin' a tune, when he looked down, and see a sort o' queer light in the fog; and he went and took a look over the bows, when up came a man's head in a sort of sou'wester, and then a pair of hands, and catched at the bob-stay; and then the hull figger of a man riz right out o' the water, and clim up on the martingale till he could reach the jib-stay with his hands, and then he swung himself right up onto the bowsprit, and stepped aboard, and went past Bob, right aft, and down into the cabin. And he hadn't more'n got down, afore he turned round, and there was another comin' in over the bowsprit, and he went by him, and down below: so there was two on 'em, jest as Tom had seen in the cabin.

"Tom he studied on it a spell, and finally says he, 'Bob, let you and me keep this 'ere to ourselves, and see ef it'll come again. Ef it don't, well and good: ef it does — why, we'll see about it.'

"But Tom he told Cap'n Witherspoon, and the Cap'n he agreed to keep an eye out the next night. But there warn't nothing said to the rest o' the men.

"Wal, the next night they put Bill Bridges on the watch. The fog had lifted, and they had a fair wind, and was going on steady. The men all turned in, and went fast asleep, except

Cap'n Witherspoon, Tom, and Bob Coffin. Wal, sure enough, 'twixt twelve and one o'clock, the same thing came over, only there war four men 'stead o' two. They come in jes' so over the bowsprit, and they looked neither to right nor left, but clim downstairs, and sot down, and crouched and shivered over the stove jist like the others. Wal, Bill Bridges, he came tearin' down like a wild-cat, frightened half out o' his wits, screechin' 'Lord, have mercy! We're all goin' to the devil!' And then they all vanished.

"'Now, Cap'n, what's to be done?' says Tom. 'Ef these 'ere fellows is to take passage, we can't do nothin' with the boys: that's clear.'

"Wal, so it turned out; for, come next night, there was six on 'em come in, and the story got round, and the boys was all on eend. There wa'n't no doin' nothin' with 'em. Ye see, it's allers jest so. Not but what dead folks is jest as 'spectable as they was afore they's dead. These might 'a' been as good fellers as any aboard; but it's human natur'. The minute a feller's dead, why, you sort o' don't know 'bout him; and it's kind o' skeery hevin' on him round; and so 'twan't no wonder the boys didn't feel as if they could go on with the vy'ge, ef these 'ere fellers was all to take passage. Come to look, too, there war consid'able of a leak stove in the vessel; and the boys, they all stood to it, ef they went farther, that they'd all go to the bottom. For, ye see, once the story got a-goin', everyone on 'em saw a new thing every night. One on 'em saw the bait-mill a-grindin', without no hands to grind it; and another saw fellers up aloft, workin' in the sails. Wal, the fact war, they jest had to put about, — run back to Castine.

"Wal, the owners, they hushed up things the best they could; and they put the vessel on the stocks, and worked her over, and put a new coat o' paint on her, and called her 'The Betsey Ann;' and she went a good vy'ge to the Banks, and brought home the biggest fare o' fish that had been for a long time; and she's made good vy'ges ever since; and that jest proves what I've been a-saying, — that there's nothin' to drive out ghosts like fresh paint."

The Story of a Shadow

Rebecca Harding Davis

The house stands in a quiet by-street in Philadelphia. After being vacant for many years it was bought by C. W. Knapp, a widower, and teacher of quiz-classes in one of the medical colleges, who took his mother and child there to live. A few months later his cousin, a Miss Demar, from Ohio, came to visit him, and soon perceived the singular hold the house had upon him.

"There are inexplicable passages in the Bible," she said, speaking of the matter afterward, "which refer to certain buildings as possessing life of their own. They had human diseases, and were blessed and cursed like men by the priesthood. This house reminded me of those Jewish buildings. It affected me from the day I entered it as an inferior grade of life would do; an animal's — a dog's, for instance. Of course, looking at it rationally, the impression became the merest absurdity; but it always came back, do what I would. It was not a disagreeable impression in itself."

She said nothing of this fancy to Mr. Knapp, accounting for his interest in his new possession on more rational grounds.

"To ordinary eyes it's an ordinary house enough," he used to say as they came home together in the evening twilight. "There it is: dull red brick, based and capped with brown stone; shutters dark and heavy; high stoop. Yet the moment my eye rested on it I said, 'There's a house could tell a story if it would.' I was on tenter-hooks until I found whether mother would like it. I think she's very comfortable in it, Mary, eh?" — anxiously.

"Very comfortable, Charley."

Knapp scans it complacently as they come up the street. The yellow sunset flames up behind it in the cold sky, throwing it into bold relief; in front the row of maples rustle cheerfully their few red, ragged leaves in the nipping air. Nobody but Mary Demar knew how that pile of dull red bricks had suddenly barred his life and absorbed all his hopes and plans. She looks curiously at the stout little man beside her, with his jaunty black dress and felt hat set on the back of his head, the broad rim making a frame for the fat, high-colored face, and twinkling blue eyes under their spectacles. They had been intimate as brothers all of their lives. She knew how the money had been saved, penny by penny, since he was a boy, on which he married. For since he was a boy there had been but one woman in the world for Charley Knapp, and when she was gone, even his most casual acquaintance knew that it was impossible he would ever marry again. Miss Demar had come to him a year ago, when she heard his wife was dead. She found him quiet and silent. "I am stifling here," he said to her. "I'll take what money I have and go out of the country with the boy. My only chance is to get away out of doors." Yet she had scarcely reached home when she heard that he had put all his savings into this house, and settled down for life.

"You changed your mind about going abroad, Charley?" she said now, gently.

He did not answer for a moment. "Yes. Well, mother was alone, and fancied I would be out of temptation if she had me in charge. Cain vagabondizing over the world was the only idea my journey suggested to her, so I gave it up."

His sorrow, then, was to be a sealed subject even to her. Mary was rebuffed, but the rebuff pleased her. She leaned more heavily upon his arm. Knapp's thinking, as usual, went on in his face, to be seen of all men, while he kept time to it by whistling under his breath and rattling his cane on the tree-boxes. He always carried a noise with him, like any other overgrown boy.

"It's curious, though," he broke out at last, "how that journey I did not take clings to me. Sometimes now, when I go into the halls, I think that here the sea was lost, and the nights on deck, the moon whitening the rim of water; and when we are at breakfast in the pretty dining-room I think how it swallowed up China and her wall and pagodas, and California cañons, Yosemite, and all. It's damnably selfish in me, but it makes me like the house. There are bits of the whole world built into the walls for me. Then," energetically, "it's such a home for her and Tom! When it's time for the boy to rough it at school, there's the garden to bring him back to Nature. Why, the smell of those bean-pods and grass after a rain would make the worst man choke in his wickedness! I've been thinking, too, as soon as he's old enough to want his friends about him, I'd run those side rooms into one, for dancing. He'll be a social fellow, Tom. I see that in his eye. When the dog marries there'll be plenty of room for him to bring his wife home — and their children, if God sends them any. Here we are, '130!'" glancing up over the door. "To think it's nothing but a pile of bricks and a number to people. Hey, Mary?"

"It would certainly be very inconsistent if the house were *not* numbered," said his mother, who was waiting inside. "The mat, Charles, my dear! Have some care for the carpets." Charley caught her in his arms and whisked her round. She began to laugh, but choked it off with a sigh. She was her son duplicated in caps and petticoats. Nature meant her to be dumpy and good-tempered, but her face had been twisted by some bastard notion of godliness into a perpetual penitence and woeful looking-for of judgment. She also protested against the sins of the world by a nasal twang — the ghost of a bagpipe. It was in play now. "Some of your boon companions are here for supper, as usual, Charles."

Knapp peeped through the open parlor door at a couple of half-fledged medical students guiltily conscious of their neckties and best coats. "All right, boys! I'll bring Tom and be with you in a moment!" He met Mary a moment afterward, with Tom astride of his shoulders. "They'll bore you horribly," anxiously. "But you'll not mind. There's such a lot of fellows like that in the college — strangers — got no mother here, nor friends, d'ye see — no place open for them but the theatres or rum-shops. I try to make it like home here. They're a little heavy, to be sure. But you'll like the boys, even the flashiest and most priggish among them."

"I'll come down and give you some music, Charley."

"All right."

Mrs. Knapp came into Mary's room and dumped herself with a wretched thud on a chair. "So it goes! Billiards, chess, pipes, night after night. They've not got to drinking yet, but what is tobacco but a mean makeshift for liquor? You'll say why don't I talk to Charles? But what does Charles care for *my* opinion? He has these men roystering with him for breakfast, dinner, and supper. He's introduced them to young girls, and says he hopes love affairs will come of it. Love affairs! Yes; and even with that the half's not told. Why, he has brought actors here. They wore their street clothes, to be sure, and did not play any of their fantastic tricks before me, I assure you. But to think it is not fifteen months since poor Sophy was laid to rest! Ah, child, now you see what man's love is worth!"

Miss Demar nodded, twisting her long hair about her head.

"Up from the ear, Mary — there. Not that Charles wasn't a sincere mourner at first. But I did hope Sophy's death would have been a call to his Master's service. I intended him always for a missionary, you know."

"Yes."

"Yes, Charles has been my cross. The Lord knows wherewith to try us," wiping her eyes. Miss Demar turned to speak, but changing her mind put on her collar. "Not but that he's a good son, Mary; but when I think of him as unregenerate, all his kindness to the poor but filthy rags — Now there's your aunt Johns. She gave up her son to carry the banner of the Cross to Africa. But when Charles wanted to leave me, it was to go gaping about at hills and sunsets and Papistical pictures —"

It was at this moment that Miss Demar, who had been standing motionless for a few seconds, turned on her with a startled face. "What is it that is in this house?" she said.

"You saw it?" Mrs. Knapp started up, looking from side to side. "I'm sure I don't know what you mean," petulantly. "There's a story that a child was killed here, or a bride — some ridiculous report that has hung about the house for years. You've heard the story and fancied you saw something."

"No, I never heard it; and I really saw nothing." Miss Demar, ashamed of having betrayed herself, tried to go on with her dressing, but her fingers shook and the blood burned in them.

Like most American women, Mary Demar's nerves lay on the surface, charged like the wires of an electric battery; but she had steady eyes and a broad chest, and usually managed to keep them in order. As soon as the dribble of talk behind her stopped, and she was left alone, she sat down to reason with herself. She had literally seen and heard nothing. In the midst of her annoyance with Charley's mother there had come upon her the sudden consciousness of a something present in the house, which was apart from its bricks and mortar and from its human inmates — some strength, vehement and kindly, which, as if for a whim, had turned her face to face with the poor old woman, showed her gray hairs, the honest love for her boy under her bigotry, the grave not far from her. It might have been Charley's self taking part with his mother.

"It certainly was not I," said Miss Demar with a shrug. "Such charity is not in me."

She began after that to ask questions carelessly about the house and its history, wondering herself at the hold the matter had taken upon her. Mary Demar had been betrothed for years to a man whom she loved with her whole heart. It was but a few days ago that she had discovered a fact in his early life which made him unfit to be her husband. It was not natural that idle vagaries about an old house should interest her now. Yet she could not shake them off; there was, too, an unaccountable feeling that this mystery concerned her personally.

"What do you know of this house?" she asked of Charley one evening as they were watching the sunset from the garden.

"Nothing. When the searches were made to establish a clear title, oddly enough it was impossible to find out when it was built or by whom. People had a vague dislike to living in it; it lay vacant for years in this crowded neighborhood. Old Seth — Kenyon's protégé, you know —"

Miss Demar's countenance changed suddenly. "Yes, I know Seth."

"He has some ancient ghost story about it. The vaguest nonsense! To my notion it's the most cheerful place I was ever in. This garden, for instance —"

Now the garden was a straight, long strip of ground, enclosed by a high, solid fence, which shaded the trim parterres of their neighbors — a strange, solitary place, which seemed to have brought its alien air into the city. The damp grass yielding to their feet was brown with the field clover; wild honeysuckles and grapes, such as tangle the hedges in unused lanes, grew along the borders; rows of hollyhocks stood like sentinels, turning their watchful faces toward the house; the common June roses, which all summer long sweeten and redden forgotten graves in country churchyards, sent their perfume up to it. Even the flowers had a friendly message for Knapp's home. The lighted windows shone coldly from garret to basement on one end of the dusky garden; beyond the other end a little way, the Schuylkill rolled, laden with craft, down to the bay; the tall masts of the clustered ships struck fine black lines up into the yellow evening sky. The air was damp but quiet; even the floating white ball of dandelion seed scarcely moved in it over their heads.

"I wish I could hear that ghost story," said Miss Demar.

"Very well. We'll go down to Seth," glancing at a little brick house beyond the garden. "By the by, Kenyon will be surprised to find us so near the old man."

Miss Demar stopped. "You don't mean — Is Mr. Kenyon coming here?"

"Now don't be vexed, Mary. 'Pon my soul, I never said come. I only wrote on business yesterday, and mentioned that you were here. Why not? One always thinks of you two as so nearly husband and wife that these petty formalities seem out of place to my notion. It's half a year to the wedding, and the poor devil's there, working night and day to be ready for it. Why shouldn't he have a glimpse of you to keep his heart up?"

"It was a kind thought of you, Charley," said Miss Demar after a pause. Her coldness irritated Knapp. He always had doubted whether she was quite competent to appreciate a man like Kenyon. Charley was very fond of Mary, but she was only a younger brother to him. He had knuckled with her at marbles and talked over his business to her ever since they were grown. Coming too close, he had grown blind to the beauty in her thin, singular face, and to the indescribable sway which she held over other men.

"Here she is, with her admirable sense, downright as a sledge-hammer," he thought, as they walked over the grass, "and Kenyon full of subtle delicate fancies. He'll be dashed to pieces against her admirable sense. It's the old story of the clay and porcelain pitcher again." The next minute, full of remorse at his own harsh judgment of her, he caught her hand and drew it affectionately through his arm.

"What is it, Moll?" He fancied she looked worn and tired.

"I was thinking of Seth." She stopped, hesitated. Knapp's instincts were keen; whatever question she was about to ask, he said, for some reason imported much to her. "What do you know of him, Charley?"

"Very little. Less than I ought, for Kenyon put him in a manner under my care, years ago. But the old fellow heeds no charity and keeps his affairs to himself. Scotch-Irish, you know. I used to look in on him now and then, until we moved into this house. Now of course I see him every day."

"You do not know then what — what connection there was between him and Mr. Kenyon? Would he be likely to know anything of John's early life?"

"No, certainly not. Kenyon, as you know, is from Carolina; his family dies out with him. High-blooded, high-handed old race, the Kenyons, I've heard. I've often told John both his virtues and his faults were those of civilization pushed too far. It's odd, isn't it, that American families won't bear high culture for several generations? The physical stock gives out unless inferior blood is brought in." Knapp began to stammer, remembering suddenly that Miss Demar could hardly claim to belong to her lover's Brahmin caste. "What could Seth know about him?" he added hurriedly. "Lived all his life in that shanty. Kenyon and I met him accidentally on the street here one day, and John mentioned him as a person who had done him a kindness." Miss Demar stopped at this, coming into the path before him in her breathless eagerness to hear. "A kindness — where was I? What the deuce can this matter to you Mary? He said, if I remember rightly, something about an annuity he paid him, and asked me to have an oversight of the old fellow, and if he were in want to send him word."

"Mr. Kenyon is charitable," bitterly.

"Why do you use that tone about him? What possible sinister motive could he have in his kindness to the old man?"

Miss Demar was silent. But Knapp noticed the glitter in her half-shut eye, and an unusual steadiness in her walk. With all her sense she had a temper of which Charley stood in wholesome awe. He quickened his pace, and began to talk with a sudden gust of cheerfulness. "Now I do suppose Kenyon did not dwell on the subject because it was a matter of charity, and for the same reason I never mentioned it to Seth. There he goes. Hello, Seth!"

"You need not call him. I've changed my mind. I'm going into the house."

"God bless me, these women! Don't hurt the old fellow's feelings, Moll."

Miss Demar turned at that and came back. She was miserable, and in a passion that she was miserable. Charley, manlike, only thought how lack of temper improved her looks. No doubt Kenyon would think her delicate face lovely with the hair rumpled about it, and her dark eyes full of unshed tears. The old sail-maker, meanwhile, came hobbling up with a broad smile, carrying a bucket of coals in either hand. He was generally watching the garden for Knapp in the evening, to "have a conference on the political sitooation," in which Seth doled out the views of his oracle, the "Review," of which he chewed the cud perpetually.

"We came to find you, Seth. I want you to raise the best ghost you can out of the house yonder for this young lady."

Seth bowed, but his mouth suddenly dropped at the corners. "You ben't afeard of sperrits then, Mr. Knapp?"

"Not much. But — what is it, Mary!"

Miss Demar drew up her shawl and stood erect. She, stooping forward, looking at Seth as he leaned on the gate, the low light bringing his short heavy body and square head into full relief, as if she would have dragged the secret of his life out. He nodded to her, smiling.

"Miss Demar were in my house the other evening, and we discussed different matters. But not sperrits."

She laughed and said "No," with a sudden light-heartedness. Now that she was face to face with the old man, the dread that haunted her appeared utterly fantastic and impossible. He was just at home from his day's work, and, instead of going to bed as the other workmen did, had washed and brushed himself. A scuffed black suit of Knapp's was stretched over his broad, rawboned body, the big wrists and ankles grinning bare with a grim sort of protest. A thin fringe of white hair and whisker was brushed with a soldierly air about his high-featured face, red and rasped with soap, on the top of which an old beaver hat of

Charley's was set jauntily. At every turn the body and brain of the old man betrayed, she fancied, the lifelong, dreadful drainage of poverty — betrayed it in nothing so much as in his aping the habits and gestures of gentlemen, and in the pitiful swagger with which he wore his begged clothes.

And this man she had believed to be John Kenyon's father.

Until Knapp told it to her a few moments ago, she had never heard this story of the family to which Kenyon belonged. But without it she recognized the absurdity of any connection between her lover and the sailmaker. Kenyon was a quiet homely man, thorough-bred as no other whom she had ever met. His enemies might question his intellect or kindliness; but whatever else he might be, that he was the product of generations of affluence and culture was a fact so patent that no one could doubt it — not the stranger who passed him on the street. His extravagance, his domineering temper, his morbid fastidiousness of taste, were all diseased outgrowths from that one cause, as Knapp had shrewdly noted.

Miss Demar forgot the proof which half an hour ago had seemed so inexorably sure to her. When she was in Seth's house the other evening a small photograph had fallen from one of his books into her lap. It was undoubtedly that of Kenyon as a much younger man. On the back a few lines were scrawled signed "Your son." There could be no question of the writing. She knew it better than her own. There was, too, the odd subtle likeness in the old man's face to the younger one, which came at times in an uneasy dropping of the eye or pose of the head. It was not there now. Miss Demar, when she missed it, blushed and trembled as though her lover had kissed her, and was unbelieving and happy.

When she turned to Charley and the old man she found them fully launched on the ghost story.

"You see, Miss Demar," said Seth, "it's an old neighborhood on the bank here, and them sort of stories hang around old houses like spiders' webs agen the wall. Yon's the room," pointing to a chamber on whose windows the rising moon began to glitter. "There's no figger seen there, howsoever, nor sound heard." So intent was he on his story that he spat deliberately on each of his palms as if he were moistening his thread, and rubbed them, while slowly eying his hearers.

"What is there, then?"

"A shadder, sir," solemnly. "To them as is left alone in that room there comes a shadder on the wall. Nothing more."

"The murdered man, I suppose," said Mary cheerfully. Seth did not relish her cheerfulness. "I've no knowledge of my own what it is, ma'am. But I've heerd say that every man has a ghost that follers him — the shadder of them that he has wronged. It comes into sight to him on that wall."

"By George!" laughed Knapp. "I'll put Kenyon there to sleep when he comes, Mary. He shall have a fair tug with his ghost."

"Kenyon?" said Seth, and then was quickly silent. Miss Demar watched him.

"You have no more to tell us of the ghost, then?" she said, to try him. He turned a countenance to her which might have been cut out of wood, it was so vacant.

"Miss Demar spoke to you, Seth."

"I beg your pardon ma'am. My wits was wool-gatherin'. Regardin' the ghost? No, I know nothin' more. I believe I'll be goin' now," taking up his bucket. But he lingered, fingering the gate-latch.

"I'll send you the morning's paper over, Seth."

"Much obleeged, sir. You said," in a forced deliberate tone, "that a gentleman was to sleep in that room — Mr. Kenyon. Is he with you now? You'll excuse me for askin'," he added hastily, "but I — I had some acquaintance with him fifteen years ago."

"To be sure you had! Why, you've no idea how kindly Mr. Kenyon spoke of you to me, Seth — charged me to have an oversight over you, and so on. You were able to oblige him once in some way, I think he mentioned?"

"Did he put it in that way?" with a queer flickering smile. "No, it was no obligation."

"Well, Mr. Kenyon is a warm-hearted man, and very likely to exaggerate any little service. You couldn't have a more generous friend in your old age. And you're well on to seventy now, Seth."

The old man straightened his back, and put his hand mechanically to his hips. "I'm quite able to work for the little I eat," he said quietly. "I'll not be likely to need money from Mr.

Kenyon. I'd be sorry if you gave him that impression. But when he comes, if you'll mention to him —" He stopped for a full minute. "If you'll mention to him that Seth Barnes is livin' yet, in the house where he used to know him, I'll be obleeged to you. You'll leave it to his own free will to come or not — if you please, sir?"

"Certainly, Seth, certainly. But Kenyon's the last man in the world to be uncivil to an old friend because he has not prospered like himself. You mistake him, Barnes."

Seth nodded gravely and, buckets in hand, limped away. "Well, really," said Knapp, "I thought Kenyon paid the old fellow an annuity. There must have been a mistake about it; I did not tell him John was coming tonight. I had a telegram from him; he'll be here in an hour. I thought I'd surprise you" — feeling with a certain pleasure that Miss Demar trembled and that her hand was cold. Her common sense was not so invincible, after all.

"We'll sit here and wait for him." He drew her to a bench, and remained silent. But Miss Demar was restless and impatient. She must keep off the one fact that filled the future for her. Tomorrow would prove whether Kenyon was a true man or the basest of frauds. She had but him in the world; she was an orphan, without kinsfolk.

Knapp sat smoking, nursing one foot on his knee, and glancing, she noticed, now and then, up at the two windows on which the moon cast a mysterious glitter.

"Confess that there is some reality in Seth's ghost story to you, after all, Charley," touching his arm.

"Nonsense! I never heard that story of the shadow. I did not even know it was to that room they had fastened the ghost. There is a curious fact about that room — a coincidence. Not that I believe in such rubbish as spirits, you know —"

"Of course not. But tell me the story."

"Two or three months after we moved into the house, I brought Russell Sands home one night. You remember him; don't you?"

"Very well. A slight fair-haired boy, with an innocent face, like a girl's?"

"Yes, that was Russell. Thorough mother's boy. Not a prig, or goodish either — as manly, spirited a little fellow as lived. That was four or five years ago. His mother was a widow, and she had but him." Knapp shifted his foot to the other knee, stroking it for a minute or two. "Well," hurriedly, "I lost sight of him for years, until I found him one night, as I was coming home, lying drunk on a market-house stall. He had grown out of all likeness to himself into a swollen bloated animal. He did not know me; I was glad of that. I brought him home and put him in that room to bed, and I went down below to smoke. About one o'clock (I was sitting quite quiet, somehow I couldn't sleep) I heard a noise overhead, a sadden gasp, as of fright or horror, and then there was a long silence. Presently the door of his chamber opened and Russell came down the stairs. He was perfectly sober, to my astonishment — quite master of himself. I shook hands with him and brought him in. He did not ask how he came there; sat down and talked in his usual self-possessed way on politics and the news of the day; but he was terribly shaken, and I saw there was some under-thought kept down, which now and then threatened to master him. I went down to the kitchen and broiled a bit of steak and made a strong cup of coffee for him, but he couldn't eat. He said, 'You'll sit up with me until morning, Uncle Charley? I would prefer not to be alone.' That was the only reference either of us made to his condition. The college boys have fallen into the way of calling me that, you see, and I like it; it makes them somehow free to ask help when they need it. But Russell is a man to whom you could not offer help. When the first streak of dawn came, he got up. I had brushed the mud off his overcoat without his knowledge. We stood in the front door together. The morning wind was keen. 'It will be a pleasant day,' he said, trying to be careless and easy. 'I thank you sincerely, Mr. Knapp, for your — your hospitality.' I looked up at the great broad-shouldered fellow, and thought how death was dragging him down, and not a soul to stretch a hand to him. But I had to be guarded. I took hold of one of the lappels of his coat. 'Can I do anything for you — in any way, Russell?' I said, 'I'm an old friend of your father's, you know, my lad.' 'No I thank you,' he said dryly; but he stood looking abstractedly down the street, and turned presently. 'A curious thing happened to me last night,' trying to bluff it off with a careless laugh, but I saw the poor boy wanted to open his heart to me if he knew how. 'Did you ever hear that that room of yours was an uncanny sort of place? I woke suddenly with my eyes on the blank wall, and do you know the picture that hangs there I could have sworn was myself? As I used to be five years ago — not *this*,' with a gesture of terrible meaning over his face and bloated figure — 'the Russell Sands now dead.' 'He's not dead,' I broke out, for I could keep quiet no longer. 'You can go back to your old self, dear boy, if you will.' 'O God! if I could believe that!' he cried, with a sort of sob. But in a moment or two he was cool and quiet again, buttoned up his coat, and talked of the weather until he bade me good-bye. He held my hand a minute. 'There is no use talking of these things,' he said, 'but if ever I can go back to the boy I once was, I'll come to you, Uncle Charley.'"

"Well, and then?" said Mary.

"He went away with that. For a long time I could find no trace of him; but I heard of him finally out West. Kenyon had secured a place for him where he could free himself from his old associates, and had seen him last July. He reported the poor boy as hard at work; thin as a rail, his jaws sunken like death's, but his eyes clear and steady. It had been a long battle, but Kenyon thought he had won it. 'See Mr. Knapp when you go back,' he said; 'tell him I'm not ready to meet him yet, but I mean to come. I'll come!' wrenching his hand with a nervous laugh."

"Don't put him in the haunted chamber when he comes. Don't let him see the picture again and find that his fancy was only a fancy."

Knapp laughed uneasily. "Now there is where the curious part of the story comes in. The wall is a blank wall. *There was no picture there.*"

"Then it was the shadow of the man he had wronged the most that he saw." Miss Demar rose.

"Tut, tut! Now, Molly, you don't pretend to believe that folly of Seth's?" She took a turn up the long path for lack of argument. But to Miss Demar the point of the story lay in the part Kenyon had taken in it. She thought she had looked at him on every side, as journalist, treasurer, clerk, *homme de société*, and lover; but doing good? a philanthropist? The *rôle* was a new one. She sat down to think it over.

"He went to John?" she said when Knapp came back.

"Yes. Men are very apt to go to Kenyon who are in scrapes. Especially lately. He was the first mover in that scheme for aiding discharged convicts, you know?"

Of course he was! Of course he was the one to whom all men would turn for aid. A gush of tears choked her throat and eyes. The idea of Kenyon's benevolence was new to her a minute ago, but it had sprouted up already, like Jack's scarlet beans, as high as heaven.

"No man," began Knapp, vehemently, "has a tenderer heart than — There he is!"

There he was: a sallow, thin man, carefully dressed in white linen, picking his steps down the walk to avoid the dust. Miss Demar tried to rise, but her knees shook under her, and a gusty heat went through her limbs. Charley was off like a flash, leading him down, wrenching his hand, watching him with any amount of inarticulate clucks and chuckles. How underbred and unmanly he always was beside Kenyon! Miss Demar also thought of the porcelain pitcher and the clay jug.

"Here she is! here she is! It's dark here, and your eyes are dulled coming out of the glare of the gas."

He brought Kenyon up to Miss Demar, and then was bolting off with a mumbled apology, when a second glance made him stay. He felt somehow that they would rather not be left alone. "A lover's quarrel, eh?" to himself. "There's a seat, Kenyon. Cursedly hot today, travelling, wasn't it? You're just off the cars?"

"No. I came in the afternoon train. I waited to shake off a little of the dust before I came up."

This was not the fiery, impulsive lover of a year ago. Knapp's face burned with the slight to Mary. There was, too, a certain uneasy guardedness about Kenyon which was utterly new in his usual simple, unaffected manner. Knapp, to cover it, rushed into the first subject that came to him.

"I was just giving Mary the account of Russell Sands. You think his reformation is complete?"

"I trust so. Sands can be of great use to our party in that part of Iowa. Just the magnetic sort of power about him that collects and leads weaker young men. I mean to make a lever of him out there as soon as I am sure he can be relied upon. I had that in view in sending him there."

"Politics is a bad field to put a man in who is trying to save himself from the devil of drink," said Knapp hastily.

"Yes. I suppose it is," carelessly. "But what would you do? Clever young fellows who choose that most disgusting mode of suicide are so common this winter in Washington that one grows hardened to them and their fate; while as to the importance of this next election there can be but one opinion."

"By the way, I hear, Kenyon, that if our party go in you are sure of an office here that pays — pays — 'pon my soul I forget what, but something stupendous. What's in it, eh?"

Kenyon, who had leaned forward and kept his eyes on Miss Demar's face, dimly seen through the darkness, during this speech, waited with a curious anxiety for her to speak. But when she did not, he replied in a dry business tone: "Some such offer was made to me, but I rejected it. I'm in a condition to set my own terms. They must give me an appointment abroad — one that pays equally well, too."

There was that malignant influence astir among them which sometimes makes each pause in the conversation appear significant and oppressive.

Knapp broke the silence each time with a more awkward effort.

"You did not use to care for the loaves and fishes, John," forcing a laugh.

"I've altered, then," dryly. "At my age one grows tired of giving the whole of life to grubbing for the means to sustain it. What a curious place you have *here*," changing his tone. "There's something unnatural in it; something — I hardly know what it is," looking about him. "The dust and dampness, probably. But this house always affected me strangely."

"Why, my dear fellow, I lived in Germantown when you were here last. You never saw this house before."

"I think I have," said Kenyon quietly, though cursing himself inwardly for his mistake; for he had come fully prepared to face and escape the danger of detection. Knapp's house he knew was near to his father's. What more likely than that Miss Demar should meet the old man and discover his secret?

Kenyon had thrown up all his engagements this morning, and started at a half-hour's notice, though it was the last day of Congress and the culmination of all his plots and wire-pulling for the year was at hand. What was success if this chance robbed him of her? What did she know? He was on guard as never before in his life — eye, ear, every nerve under control, and watching. He could see her face but indistinctly; she had spoken but once to him.

His ready tongue failed him; he sat silent.

"By the way," began Knapp again desperately, "I was talking to Mary just now of your winter's work — discharged convicts, you know."

"Pray do not induce Miss Demar to mistake me for a philanthropist, Charley."

"You did not mean to use them for 'levers,' eh?"

"Not precisely. But I went into the work to strengthen my popularity."

"I don't believe it! You shall not so wrong yourself!"

Miss Demar rose in a beat and walked hastily away. Kenyon rose also, and sat down again. The words thrilled him as with an electric fire.

"She knows nothing. She is safe," he thought. He gave a short, uncadenced laugh. "But it is true for all that," turning to Knapp. "I loathe demagogue-ism, but I am a demagogue. I hate work, yet I drudge harder than any man in Washington. I used to be honest, as men go, but now I cringe and fawn and lie — all for money."

Knapp looked at him in dismay.

"You did not use to care for it.'

"I care for her. I care to earn a few years in which to sit down with her, with money and ease to enjoy the world before I go out of it. I mean to wash my hands in innocency as soon as I have the appointment and sit down, as I said, to take 'mine ease in mine inn.'"

Knapp coughed uneasily, jerking at his waistcoat as if it did not fit him. He had keenness enough to see that Kenyon's life had been a fierce, breathless race for one end, and that some obstacle tonight was about to balk him. He knew him to be always a gusty, uncertain fellow, with a temperament either at high tide or dead low ebb, as anybody could see, but he was not used to talk about it to other people. The mental pang must have been extreme that wrenched this vehement egotism from him.

"What in God's name can I do for him?" Knapp repeated blankly to himself.

For ordinary men whose troubles grew out of broken bones or empty pockets he had cures enough, but he looked upon Kenyon as of a different order of being from himself. It was Pegasus, he thought, coming to a cow-doctor for help.

He stood rattling some pennies in his pockets, looking at Kenyon's thin face under the broad Panama hat, turned toward Miss Demar with a cynical, sad smile.

"We'd better join Molly, eh?"

"One minute. There's an old man, Barnes, lives hereabouts somewhere?"

"In the alley — not ten steps from the gate. I told them you'd not forget him — I told him and Mary both. I'm deucedly glad you asked for Seth, do you know, Kenyon?"

"Miss Demar has seen him, then?"

"Oh, of course. He comes to the gate every night for the 'Review.' He has just gone."

"Reads the 'Review' yet, does he?"

Kenyon stopped. For the moment he forgot Knapp, Miss Demar, himself. He only remembered how the old man used to sit waiting at night until he had learned his lesson for school from the "dog-eared" spelling-book, to take his turn at it while the boy played teacher. There was the little kitchen, ship-shape and neat as a man-of-war's deck, the crackling coal fire, the pot of mush simmering on one side for supper when they had finished. How anxious and red the old man's face was as he stammered dully over the unconquerable three syllables. How dull he always was! Kenyon remembered how his boy's heart used to ache and sicken when he first began to understand that his father was dull and poor, and all that it meant to be either. He had dashed the book down one day and caught the old man about the neck, crying out in his impotent rage:

"Why should other men be what they are, and you this, dad? How could God be so unjust as to make such a difference between men?"

"I don't see as He does," the sailmaker said gently. "However, you are to go beyond them all, Jack, and as soon as I can read I mean to take the paper and go through it reg'lar. I'll keep posted that way, so as I'll not shame you."

That was twenty long years ago. The old man was poring over it yet! Did he hope that his boy would come back to him, late as it was? He had sent back the money again and again without a word. He was waiting for something better than money. Kenyon glanced down to the low house, the red roof of which was just seen above the fence. If he ever went back it must be now. If he married under a false name, so it must stand; the old man must remain thrust aside until the end. What if he went now? What if he crossed the alley and went to the old man sitting alone by his fire? Although he had put this thing away from him for twenty years, so whimsical and perverse was the man, that his heart throbbed and his eyes were wet at the thought; the next, they had reached Miss Demar.

"I found them in the dark for you." She held out a branch of wet, fragrant roses toward him.

The night almost hid her from him. She seemed to belong to and to crown its passionate warmth, its strength, its solemn beauty. So set apart did she seem from all other women, that he thought how, if the whole world was lost in the night, he could straightway find her, as she had found the roses for him. He took her hand in his.

Charley sauntered up to the porch and smoked a cigar while the lovers passed slowly down the dusky alleys of the garden. A night-moth flapped its wet wings in Kenyon's face; the damp air was heavy with the scent of the roses she had given him; from one of the ships on the river came broken snatches of music which the distance softened into sweetness and sadness.

When they came back to the house and into the light of the gas, the politician's sallow face, which had warped lately into a shrewd cunning, glowed with a finer beauty than Miss Demar's. A word from the woman he loved caused his legs to tremble like a sensitive boy's; there was a fiery impatience in his eye which reminded Charley of a racer that is stayed within a stride of his goal.

"If you get this appointment, you can marry at once?" he said as he led Kenyon to his room.

"Yes. Nothing shall come between us now."

Charley wrung his hand, and bade him a hasty good-night. The next moment he was back. "I say, Kenyon, pardon me, but you never looked into this matter of spiritualism, did you?"

"I? No; it was always a repugnant subject to me. But did it never occur to you, old fellow, that your habit of hurling new ideas at a man was confusing?"

"I don't know," absently. "Repugnant? Now that's just what it is to me. But — you don't think it possible that disembodied spirits could manifest themselves in a room — in any way — by means of matter, then? Yet there are some things — things which those who are pure, you know, John, have worn or touched, which seem to me to be alive with their presence. Yet —"

He stopped, turned to the window, his double chin quivering. "Well, it's all a puzzle," turning presently and looking wistfully about the room. "When I think about the different lives in men and horses and vegetables, I get perplexed. How can I say, into this matter a soul has gone, and in that there is none? Why should not a human spirit linger in a house, for instance, and affect the matter in it, as it affected the matter in his body? Now, why not?" again looking about the dim chamber with the same curious hesitation.

"I can't tell you why not. I only know it never does."

Kenyon laughed good-humoredly, impatient as he was to be left alone.

"Of course it never does. Bless me, I forget what a bore this must all be to you. I only thought I'd warn you — but no matter. It's all trumpery gossip, no doubt." And still muttering to himself he burst out of the room and went stumbling down the stairs. Kenyon threw a quick glance about the room, as he threw off his coat and boots and sat down by the window. He had a vague impression when he came into it that there was someone in it besides Knapp and himself. He saw his mistake. It was a small, cheerful chamber, with no fireplace, its windows opening to the west. The walls were a pale green; a well-darned carpet on the floor, and a half-worn cottage suit of furniture of the same color ranged against the walls. Just the room one might look for in Knapp's house — commonplace, cheery, with the stamp of poverty on every part of it. Knapp knocked at the door that instant and dashed in with a fresh pitcher of water, went out with a final good night, came back again to thrust his hand into the bed and punch the pillows. "There. All right. I was afraid they hadn't put on the new mattress. Good night. God bless you."

Knapp's whole life and nature, with all their cheerfulness, Kenyon thought, were commonplace — bore the poverty stamp. For himself — it would be different! Another step, and he would have turned his back on poverty and self-denial forever. God, who made the man, only knew how he loathed them both; with what panting, breathless delight, as he sat there, he looked into the world he was about to enter, where love was the first blessing and money almost its equal; the world to which he had been climbing since he was a ragged boy in yonder alley; full of luxurious houses, art, music, delicate viands, rare wines, beautiful women delicately dressed. "There is no reason why she should not consent to an immediate marriage," he thought. "My appointment is sure: then for France or Italy. I'll shake the dust of the country off my feet forever."

What made him spring up suddenly and, going to the window, turn to the house in the alley where the old man's light still burned? Leaning with his knuckles on the sill, he looked down into it steadily. Men who knew him in the office of the "Age," or in caucus, would not have recognized this face that he wore. He recovered himself presently.

"Bah! It can never be. If she guessed the truth, she would spurn me under her feet." Yet he could not put away the fancy that the old man was sitting there, watching the windows of this room — waiting — waiting; that he would watch there all night believing that his boy would come to him.

"If a man sets himself a high aim in life, he must put all obstacles out of his way; it is unavoidable" — as he began to prepare for bed. But when he caught sight of his ghastly face in the glass, he started back, and did not go near it again. He did not care to know how much it cost him to put this obstacle out of his way.

The sounds on the streets had died into silence. In some room below he heard Knapp's mother grumbling and scolding, and Charley's unwearied, cheerful little cackle in reply; then Tom woke with the colic, and Charley trotted to and fro — to and fro, carrying him for hours, until all the house was asleep and quiet. Long afterward, Kenyon, standing by the darkened window, saw Knapp go out into the garden for a moment's coolness and rest before he slept. He walked up and down slowly. The stars had come out, and threw faintly the lines of the busby paths out from the darkness, massing into unbroken shadow the houses to the right. Beyond, a lamp at a mast-head here and there showed where the water flowed. The little man, thinking himself quite alone in the night, began to sing some old tune softly in his thin, chirrupy voice:

"Here in the body pent,
    Absent from thee I roam,
And nightly pitch my moving tent
    A day's march nearer home."

There was a slight pause, and he went on:

"I want a true regard,
    A single steady aim,
Unmoved by suffering and reward,
    To Thee and Thy great name."

Kenyon drew back. What dreadful Presence was this so near to commonplace Knapp, with his little body and little soul, of which he knew nothing? Kenyon's brain was feverish and strained. A new, vague idea entered readily among the thoughts that racked him: the something above the night — above him, his struggle, or his love — the infinite life before which his world of rare books, æsthetic dressing, and good eating sank into nothingness.

Knapp Went into the house, and the night sank back into silence.

In the door of the little house in the alley an old man stood looking up to the darkened windows of his son's room. "It is too late; he will never come now," he said.

Kenyon lay upon the bed, his eyes covered with his hand. But he did not sleep.

The sun was not up. There was no sign of morning beyond the cold wind that shook the wet trees to and fro, and a gray lightening of the banked clouds over the river. Of all his unhealthy, unquiet life, this night had been to Kenyon the most unhealthy and the fiercest in its struggle. That first cold wind of dawn came with a wholesome freshness. He sat up, rubbed his aching eyes. It was time to be done with shadows and to go down into the real world. He wiped the hot sweat from his forehead and looked about as a man does after a sleepless night, his eyes falling at last by chance on the opposite wall to his bed. He had not thought the light strong enough to throw a shadow, but the reflection of the drifting clouds made strange shimmering figures on the blank surface. The clouds — what else could they be? The shadows slowly moved, approached each other, grew compact. Kenyon leaned forward; one could almost fancy that they took human forms. The strange illusion annoyed him; he drew down the curtains over the windows; the wind waved them fitfully. It was their shadows that he saw now; or was it — Good God! what was this that faced him, beckoning to him with strange and solemn gestures, showing him —

The blood ebbed back to his heart; he stood stiffly erect, his hands behind him, as he was used to stand when he faced an enemy in debate whom he recognized as stronger than himself. There was silence over all the city in that last hour of the night. The silence was nowhere more profound than in this little chamber through which the strange wind blew violently, yet without sound.

What Kenyon saw in that room he never told. Whether his old boy's life came back to him, or the life yet to come, what truth was pressed home to his calloused scheming brain, no man ever knew.

Death and disaster meet a man sometimes on his journey, and bring him for a brief moment face to face with himself, his friend, and God. When Kenyon left his chamber at dawn his face wore the look of one who voluntarily had met them and wrenched their secret from them.

He went down the garden and crossed the alley. Seth was stooping over the fire warming his chilled hands. He was going to his work, and did not mean to come back until Kenyon was gone. "He'd have come last night if he meant ever to own me," he told himself again and again. "I'll think of the boy as dead now. Better we'd both died when he was a boy."

A shadow struck across the doorway. The next moment a man stood before him, put his hands on his shoulders.

"Father! It's I, father."

Seth was not strong. He staggered under the first touch of his boy. "Jack?" he cried — "Jack?"

His son led him to a bench. The old man covered his face with his hands, but in a little while he looked up and motioned Kenyon to a chair. "It's your old seat, my lad. I'm glad to see you in it agen," he said, quietly untying his gingham cravat. His high-featured face had strangely lost its color.

Kenyon sat cowed, humiliated. This twenty years of neglect rose before him; the more inexorably as Seth neither by word nor look recalled them. The delicacy which kept the old man silent from showing even the reproach of joy had different birth from his own fine taste in books and music and wine. He felt that with all the old man's passionate love for the boy he had lost, he would weigh and measure the man who had come back to him. He knew, too, having finer intuitions than Miss Demar, that the man who thus measured him was weightier than he, stood on firmer ground, was built up of larger, more liberal elements.

In the heat of his passionate contrition and old, awakened love, he felt all the sacrifices he must make for his father could be borne. "You will come to Washington to me at once," he said. "We will have our home alone together. Nothing shall part us again."

"I think you're wrong there, Jack," Seth said gently. "My ways are not your ways. You shall come to me when you will, but I'll live out my life as I've begun. Old trees grow best on their own rooting."

Kenyon was silent. He was not sure of his own rooting; he was not sure of himself, of the work he had done or the work he had planned to do. Was it all a sham? Had he grasped only shadows, while Knapp, with his mediocre brain, and this ignorant laborer, had laid hold on reality?

Today he would be done with shams, though it would cost all he had worked or cared for in life.

"Will you come with me a moment, father?" He led him quickly over to the garden, where Miss Demar stood gathering flowers for the breakfast table. He gave one passionate glance at the rare beauty in her face, at the fine soul that looked smiling from her eyes to welcome him, before he let the bar fall between them which could not be raised.

"Miss Demar, this is my father."

The smile deepened. She put out her hand cordially but calmly. "I knew he was your father long ago, Mr. Kenyon. Have you told him who I am?

"Mary?"

"Will you welcome a daughter as well as a son?" she said, all flushed and glowing. When the old man laid his hand on her head she, too, had a glimpse beneath the beggar's clothes and vulgar words.

They lingered long in the solitary garden. Apart from the morning light and dewy freshness there was a curious calm in it. The house had, as it still has, a strange trick of falling into silence in the midst of the busiest summer's day.

"What unaccountable stories hang about this old place," said Miss Demar to her lover. She could not restrain her curiosity as to his experiences of the night before.

But his face was inscrutable. "Where such a man as that lives," he said, glancing at Knapp, "no morbid shadows would linger long, I fancy. Yet I can believe that under his roof stronger men than he would be haunted by the ghosts of what they might have been. Their best selves would come to meet them."

But he never told her more than that.

The Walking Boy

Clara Florida Guernsey

I was spending my vacation at Dr. Leighton's house in Chester. Chester is a town in the lake country of New York, quiet, old-fashioned, sleepy, and pleasant. Dr. Leighton's was the oldest house in the place, and stood at the northern extremity of Main Street, just without the limits of the town. It was older than the village itself, and had been the first house of any pretensions in all that part of the country.

It had a pretty, old-fashioned garden running down in a succession of terraces to the water, very pleasant in summer, though rather bleak and frozen in winter, when the wind came shrieking down the hills and over the frozen lake. The house, however, was a solid, thick-walled erection, built to keep out the cold rather than for the sake of the picturesque, and was warm and bright upstairs and downstairs.

It was shaped a good deal like a brick set up on its longer edge, and was equally divided in the middle by a wide hall. It had a wing at the side, and what you might call a tail behind. The old roof was made of solid, immense timbers, framed into the wall in such a way that when they shook in the wind the whole house shook with them, and strange creaking, groaning noises came wandering down the garret stairs and through the halls.

The house had been built by a certain eccentric Mr. Williams. Mr. Williams had been disappointed in love — that is, he had offered himself to the beautiful Miss St. Valory, of Valory's Corners, and had been refused for the sake of a certain Mr. Lyndon, whom she afterward married. Upon this Mr. Williams conceived the idea of renouncing the world, and, by way of making the sacrifice as costly as possible, brought up workmen from New York at great expense, and built this house, then right in the woods, and a mile from the little hamlet that was growing up farther down the lake.

When the house was completed he furnished it expensively, and gave himself up to a comfortable state of misery and meditation on Miss St. Valory. But whether solitude was more solitary than he had expected, or whether he found that meditation was unprofitable, certain it is that at the end of three months he married the daughter of a raftsman, sold his house at a bargain to Dr. Leighton's father, and went back to Philadelphia.

Dr. Leighton had married Miss Priscilla Lyndon, a daughter of Mr. Williams's old love. There was a large family connection on both the Lyndon and the Leighton side, and Mrs. Leighton's brother, Mr. Lucian Lyndon, lived in Chester, but a quarter of a mile from his sister. At the time of my story Mr. Lyndon's house was undergoing extensive alterations, and its master, who was at that time a widower, was, with his daughter, spending some weeks with his brother-in-law.

One dark, rainy evening the young ladies of the family and myself were in the dining-room stoning raisins, blanching almonds, and cutting citron for the big cake intended to grace the coming birthday party of Posy and Rosy, the doctor's twin nieces, aged seventeen. If ever one soul animated two bodies, it was in the case of the Leighton twins. They were intelligent and rather precocious girls, but there was about them a certain simplicity and unconsciousness which made them seem younger than their age, and led their elders and equals to treat them as children.

There were also the doctor's two sons, Mark and Lewis, home from college in their Junior year, and there was Sharly, or Charlotte, Lyndon, Mr. Lucian Lyndon's only child.

Sharly was a nice girl; and having said that, I hardly know how else to describe her, or pay her any better compliment. I like "nice girls" myself better than I do some other varieties of the sex; better than young women who have "suffered," and make a terrible fuss about it, as the manner of some is; better than those glorious females who have a genius for everything but decency.

Sharly was a pretty girl, though not perhaps entitled to rank as a beauty if she had not been an heiress. She had soft clear blue eyes, a resolute little mouth and chin, light brown wavy hair, which was never in disorder; and everything about her was always smooth and spotless and speckless. Sharly was not brilliant, but she was agreeable, and she carried about her a certain atmosphere of pleasantness and serenity, though the legend ran that when a child she had been "a tartar." She was nineteen, and had been "in society" in New York, where the Lyndon connection saw a good deal of company in a fashion which might be described as conspicuously quiet. Sharly, though much liked, had made no great sensation in this circle. Her cousins said it was because she never cared to talk to anyone but old gentlemen, with whom she was a great favorite. Sharly had "faculty." She could cook and sew both with and without the machine to admiration. She could knit as fast as her grandmother, and she was great in the management and pacification of children. Sharly could sing, too, not loud enough for a concert hall, but in a way that was very pleasant at home, and she was always ready when asked for music.

This evening her slim fingers were flying through the rounds of a little red stocking destined for one of her aunt Elsie's numerous children.

Then there was David Van Epps, who was a teacher in the academy, and was said to be a young man of great talent. He was a handsome young fellow, fair-haired, gray-eyed, and very gentlemanly, though a good deal shy. David was of no particular family, and had nothing in the world but his salary of six hundred dollars a year. There was also in the room a young man who possessed the happy faculty of making himself universally detested. This was Mr. Cyrus Ford, who, because his father and Dr. Leighton were old friends, was oftener at the house than suited the ladies of the family. Even gracious Mrs. Leighton confessed that she could not bear Cyrus Ford, and Posy and Rosy, who did not mind being treated as children by anyone else, bridled and put on airs of dignity before this young man.

Mr. Cyrus Ford patronized everyone, his betters included. He was wont to proclaim openly that he never meant to marry any but a rich wife, lest some young woman who was not rich might fling away her affections, and it was evident that he paid court to Sharly Lyndon. He talked much about style, and gave it to be understood that when he was in New York, where he was an insurance clerk, he moved in the height of polite society. That evening he had given such mind as he possessed to impertinence toward David Van Epps. Cyrus was wont to say that David had much better have remained "in his original station."

It might have been difficult to define David's "original station." His first rise in life had been a situation with an eccentric old traveling tinman, whom much learning or some other cause had made not exactly mad, but a little cracked; and he had educated David to such good purpose that at eighteen he had been rather more than ready to enter the Sophomore Class in D—— College. His old friend dying, David had made his own way through college, with some little help from the Lyndons, and had taken a high place. He was a perfectly simple, straight-forward person, and would never have made any secret of his history, even if it had not been well known to the Leightons. He and Mr. Lyndon, who was a classical scholar, read Greek together, and he was reading Latin with Sharly, who had a liking for the language.

Mr. Van Epps had lately published, in a well-known review, an article which had attracted some little attention, and his friends had been pleased with this little triumph. I had not seen this essay myself; but I understood that it was anent the sacrifices offered by the ancients to the spirits of the dead, or some other equally abstruse subject. He had not only published it, which is something, but had been paid for it, which is more.

By-and-by Rupert, the mulatto waiter, looked into the dining-room and asked if Mr. Van Epps would please come into the drawing-room a minute to Mr. Lyndon. David was no sooner gone than Cyrus Ford remarked:

"How low birth will show! Now in spite of a sort of varnish and education, and the kind patronage of your family, that young fellow's real nature will come out. He'll never be a gentleman, nor have a bit of style."

"What do you call style?" asked Sharly, looking up with an air of gentle curiosity.

"Why, style is style. It can't be defined. That's its essence, you know. It's the way fellows have that have seen the world, you know;" and Cyrus looked at himself in the glass.

"You don't mean good-breeding, then?" said Sharly, smiling. "We are all rather old-fashioned people, and I think we have a preference for good manners, which are the result of natural refinement and intelligence, and cannot be bought, you know; but style, it always seems to me, is a thing one can get at the milliner's or the tailor's."

Mr. Cyrus Ford made no response, and shortly after left the room and went to the elders in the parlor.

"It takes your quiet people," said Mark.

"I don't like Mr. Ford," said Rosy. "He isn't nearly as nice as his father."

"But, you know, Rosy, boys never are," said Posy, from the treasures of her experience.

Mr. Van Epps returned at this moment, and Sharly asked him to hold her yarn. He seemed not ill pleased with the office, and it occurred to me that Mr. Lyndon was likely to find out that boys and girls grow into men and women. I wondered what he would say to such a discovery. To ask a young man of talent to read Greek with you is one thing; it is another to have him fall in love with your daughter, and it is even more another thing to have your daughter return the sentiment. Sharly was not a young woman to exhibit her feelings, but it struck me that her interest in David was more than friendly, and I had my doubts about the Latin lessons.

"What a night!" said Mark, as the wind screamed past the window and rattled the blinds. "It's just the weather for the Walking Boy."

"Do tell me," said Sharly, "who is he? I've always heard about him in a dim way; but I suppose they never told us the story when we were children for fear we should be afraid to go to bed."

"I only know that he's one of the family ghosts — there are several in the connection. He is in some way mixed up with Mr. Williams, grandma's old lover. Flora can tell you all about him, and here she comes."

Flora, the cook, a majestic old black woman, put her head in at the door.

"Now, young ladies," said she, "is them reasons done? 'cause I'm bound to begin that cake first thing in the morning."

We all looked conscience-stricken.

"Ah, young folks, young folks!" said Flora, shaking her red-turbaned head. "They never puts no rael, right-down sariousness into their work."

"Come in, Flora," said Mark, "and help us, and tell us the story of the Walking Boy. The girls want to hear it; and if they are afraid to go to bed afterward they won't dare to say so."

"Yes, Flora," said Sharly, finishing her skein, "do, and frighten the young gentlemen as well as ourselves."

"'Tain't no story, Miss Sharly," said Flora, gradually edging her portly person over the threshold. "It's a thing as is well known to all the colored folks ever was connected with the Lyndons or the Leightons. But as to the reasons, I see I've got to have a hand in the business, if that cake's going to be made;" and Flora sat down, and while she stoned the raisins she told her tale.

The substance of the legend which she gave us was as follows:

Mr. Williams, who built the house, had a sister who mortally offended him by marrying a young clergyman with nothing but his profession, and of no particular family.

The Rev. Mr. Merrion had a sore experience. Many olive-branches grew up around his table, which, unlike the literal article, could not provide their own leaves. There were sickness and death, and each succeeding year saw the parson's family more scantily clothed and fed. He was not popular as a preacher. He went from place to place, and was burdened with debt, while his brother-in-law grew richer every day, and was sent to Congress, which in those days was a distinction.

During all her care-worn married life Mr. Williams refused to hold the slightest intercourse with his sister or her husband. He was a man of bitter and relentless temper, and he did all that he could to add to his brother-in-law's heavy burden; and he it was who set on foot reports against Mr. Merrion's orthodoxy.

In those days theological bands were drawn tighter than at present. The Rev. Mr. Merrion was driven from his pulpit, and no other would receive him. Broken-hearted and with failing health, he gathered together the remnants of his property, and with his wife and children started for the new country in Western New York. He settled on the shore of the lake, at its southern extremity.

He gradually became a sort of missionary and doctor among the Indians, and they rewarded his services with presents of fish, game, and corn, and did not trouble themselves with his opinions on justification. His health improved with out-door life and the sense of freedom; and the harassed, weary man and his wife began to hope that they had found a resting-place.

It was no good news when they heard that Mr. Williams was coming into their neighborhood. Mr. Merrion's experience of his brother-in-law's temper had been bitter, and he dreaded fresh annoyance and persecution.

When Mr. Williams came up with the workmen his sister ventured to see him, and tried to bring about reconciliation. But it was quite useless. He would not speak to her for some time, and finally, passing from sullen silence to outrageous passion, he accused her, in the coarsest terms, of wishing to saddle her whole family upon him. The poor lady, driven past her patience, reminded him at last that there was another world where those who had dealt wickedly or cruelly must meet their victims face to face.

"I will take care that none of you ever come near me in this world, whatever may happen in the next," were his last words as he turned her from his door.

Among Mrs. Merrion's children was one boy who, though not exactly an idiot, was yet wholly different from the others. He was strange in a great many ways, and had an unconquerable love for long solitary wanderings. When a little child this propensity had caused his mother the greatest uneasiness; but if restrained by force he would fall into a state bordering on insanity; so that there seemed nothing for it but to let him have his own way. No harm ever happened to him, and the Indians, regarding him as one who held intercourse with the world of spirits, looked upon him with awe. He did not seem to wander aimlessly, but always went on his way like one with a set purpose, looking about him as though expecting to meet someone among the trees or on the shore. When asked the purpose of his expeditions, he would always reply that he was "looking for something," but what the something was he never told.

The great house in process of erection near his own home seemed to have a peculiar attraction for Elon Merrion. He went there day after day, followed the workmen, handled their tools, and as the house grew into shape, appeared to find singular pleasure in wandering from room to room, always, as he said, "looking for something."

Mr. Williams, who knew perfectly well that the strange boy was his sister's son, never took the slightest notice of Elon, and the boy seemed equally careless of him.

The summer had passed, September had come; the roof had been put on the house, and much done toward finishing the interior; for, with high wages and the personal superintendence of Mr. Williams, the work had gone rapidly forward.

The twilight was drawing in on the 25th of September. The day had been strangely close and oppressive for the season, and the sky had been hung with masses of gray cloud, which as the sun went down showed edges as of tarnished copper and brass. Below hardly a breath stirred, but in the upper air the ominous clouds were tossed and rolled as with a great wind. The lake lay almost unruffled, but now and then there ran along its surface a low moan — on that sheet of water the sure forerunner of a storm.

The workmen were about returning to their temporary shanty. One of them remarked that Mr. Williams, who was usually anxious to prolong the labor to the last moment, seemed in a hurry to leave the house. He waited, however, till the last man had crossed the threshold, and then locked the door himself. He took unusual pains to secure the lock, and tried it with his hand, as if to make sure.

"There will be a storm tonight, and the door might blow open," he remarked to a carpenter who stood by; and this little circumstance was afterward remembered, as it was quite contrary to Mr. Williams's usual habits to offer an explanation of any act of his whatever. Soon after dark the storm came on with great fury. There was little rain, but the thunder and lightning were wild and incessant, and the wind rose to a howling tempest which lashed the lake to foam, and roared through the woods like the surf on a rock-bound shore. Every now and then, through the continuous uproar, could be heard the crack and crash of a falling tree. The men were gathered around the fire in the shanty, hushed into silence, as the tempest increased from minute to minute.

Suddenly one of them spoke.

"Did anyone see that boy go home?"

Not one could remember seeing Elon leave the building, but he who had asked the question recollected that about four o'clock the child had climbed the unfinished staircase, and disappeared in a long dark passage which led from the upper part of the house into the wing.

"Can he be locked up there now?" said the carpenter who had first spoken. "Poor little innocent! I can't be easy unless I find out."

His companions laughed at him, but the carpenter, who was a spirited as well as kindly young man, lit his lantern, and went out into the storm. He struggled on against the wind until he was perhaps two rods from the shanty, and opposite the log-hut where Mr. Williams lived with his old black servant, Cuff.

To the surprise of the young carpenter, as he paused a moment to recover breath, the door of the hut was opened, and Mr. Williams's voice asked where he was going.

"We couldn't any of us remember whether the little boy left the house," said the carpenter. The young man declared afterward that as the light of the lantern fell upon Mr. Williams's face it was like that of a corpse; but this statement might easily have been one of those adornments added after the event from a sense of the fitness of things.

"Boy?" said Mr. Williams, hesitating. "What boy?"

"Your nephew, Sir," said the carpenter, suddenly inspired to speak out a fact hitherto ignored by all as far as possible.

"Oh, he!" said Mr. Williams, without the anger which might have been expected. "He went home about five o'clock; I saw him go myself."

The carpenter, glad to be spared further encounter with the tempest, went back to the shanty.

The storm raged all night, and only abated toward morning. When the men gathered to their work, somewhat later than usual, the young carpenter was the first to go upstairs. He had not been gone more than a minute when a sudden cry of horror summoned his companions. There, in the long passage, lay the boy — dead!

The eyes were wide open, the little hands clinched. Those who looked upon the sight covered their faces. Elon had probably fallen asleep, and so had not heard the workmen leave the house. There were traces which showed how he had gone to and fro seeking a way of escape; and when none could be found he had died apparently of sheer terror.

Mr. Williams, hearing what had happened, showed no particular emotion. He expressed his regret moderately enough, as it was thought. He said he supposed he must have been mistaken in thinking the boy had left the house, or that he must have come back again unobserved.

The young carpenter, however, always believed that Mr. Williams had purposely locked his little nephew into the deserted building, actuated by a double spite against the child and the mother. It was remarked, however, as singular that a child so fearless as Elon should have been literally frightened to death by finding himself alone at night, even in such weather.

Mr. Williams's persistent resentment against his sister was not softened by the child's death, and he took no notice of her in her trouble, which was soon doubled by the death of her husband, for poor Parson Merrion, then ill of a low fever, sank under the shock of Elon's tragical fate, and died in a few days, forgiving his enemy with his last breath. The widow sold the home where she had hoped to find a refuge, and went with her children to some other part of the country.

The new house was finished and furnished, and the owner took possession. But it was said there was one who had possession before him. There were whispers that the dead child, or something in its likeness, walked the house as the poor bewildered boy had walked during that long, lonely night. It was said that from dusk to dawn Mr. Williams heard a step pacing to and fro from room to room, and especially through the long passage, and that the doors at each end of this passage were opened and shut by no mortal hands.

This haunting presence, so ran the report, was the cause of Mr. Williams's marriage to the raftsman's daughter, as he dared not stay alone, and even old Cuff retreated from the ghostly walker. The constant persecution of the spirit forced Mr. Williams to sell the house and go back to Philadelphia, where he lived very unhappily with his wife, and finally died even poorer than his unfortunate brother-in-law.

"And ever since then," concluded Flora, "that boy walks, 'specially windy nights; and if anyone comes into the house that's to bring bad luck on the family, he goes past their door to and fro. And," continued Flora, sinking her voice to a mysterious whisper, "the very fust night that miserable Mr. Netherton, that married your poor aunt Rosalind that you was named for, Miss Rosy — the very fust night he staid in the house he heard it, and he asked next morning at the breakfast-table — 'Who's that,' says he, 'was walking past my door all night?' And your grandpa he turned it off, but he knew what it was and my mother was cook here, same's I am now. 'Depend upon it,' says she, 'won't no good come of this marriage;' and no more there didn't, for he broke Miss Rosalind's heart. And they do say — at least my mother had it from her mother, and she knew as much as most folks — that that boy's spirit'll never be quiet till some of Parson Merrion's folks gets good luck out of this house."

"My mother's maiden name was Merrion," said David, who had listened with great interest to Flora's legend.

"Now you don't say so!" said Flora, impressed. "Who was your grandfather, Mr. Van Epps?"

"Really that is more than I can tell you," said David, smiling, "except that his name was Merrion, and he was a farmer. I am afraid my ancestry were never important enough to have a hereditary ghost."

The raisins being finished with the story, we all went back into the parlor, talking over the tale, with which, I could see, the girls were a good deal impressed.

"Perhaps you are the Merrion who is to get good luck out of the house," I heard Sharly say to David.

"To hope for more than I have had would be presumption," said David, with some emotion in his tone.

"As to that," said Miss Lyndon, with remarkable indifference and composure of manner, "everyone is at liberty to hope, I suppose."

Mr. Cyrus Ford had been making himself agreeable to the doctor and Mrs. Leighton, and it seemed to me that the elders received us with an air of relief.

"What a wild night it is!" said the doctor, who had just come in from a late ride. "I thought the buggy would blow over before we could get home."

David Van Epps glanced up at the clock, and began to bid good-night.

"Don't go, David," said the doctor. "It is all of a mile to your house, and you will be drenched and blown away. Stay with us."

Mrs. Leighton seconded the invitation with great cordiality, and then, remembering that Cyrus Ford was also a long way from home, she extended the offer to him, though there was a difference in her manner toward the two young men. Both accepted the invitation, and as they did so Mr. Lyndon came in from the library, where he had been engaged with someone on business.

Mr. Lyndon was a handsome elderly gentleman, extremely courteous, rather stately, and much given to books. There was something in his manner which, if not French, at least reminded one of a Frenchman. "See here, doctor," he said: "Mr. Carr, after waiting all this time, has taken advantage of the storm to come and pay me Willy Maynard's two thousand dollars."

Willy Maynard was a little orphan, a ward of Mr. Lyndon's.

"Better late than never," said the doctor. "I hope it won't keep you awake tonight."

"Oh, I can lock it up in the old secretary in my room. It is a good solid piece of work; and whoever heard of a burglar here!"

It was late, and soon we separated for the night.

My room was on the second floor, a most comfortable chamber, opening from a little square "entry," as they called it. One door from this entry led into the main upper hall of the house, the other into the long passage where the ghost was supposed to walk.

It was after midnight when I finally composed myself to sleep; but I cannot say how long I had slept when I woke with a start, and with the impression that someone was in the room. A fire had been lighted on the hearth that damp, chilly evening. A clear glow from the red coals yet shone through the room, and I could see that its four walls contained no one but myself.

But what was the sound that went past my door through the entry? Who or what opened the door leading into the long passage? I had been through this passage often enough to know that perhaps two yards from the entry door was a board that always creaked beneath the foot. As the step, if such it was, passed on, I heard the accustomed noise. Another minute and there was a quick, sharp tap, as though the person or thing had knocked at a door in going by. I confess that a chill ran over me from head to foot; then I was ashamed of myself. Was I, an instructor of youth, a person whose mind had been fortified by the study of Latin and mathematics, to suffer myself to be startled by a noise at night and an old black woman's tale? The wind was still blowing, and fifty other strange noises were wandering in the air both within and without the old house. Nevertheless I listened.

Another instant and my ears, strained to discern that one sound among all the voices of the wind, caught the noise of the door at the further end of the passage opening with a slow creak.

Then I recollected that David Van Epps occupied a room opening into this passage, and that it must have been at his door that the tap had been made. Presently I heard another door open much more softly, and a second step go down the passage after the first. Either the person who had knocked had gone in, and was coming out again, or else Mr. Van Epps, braver or more credulous than myself, had risen "to see if he heard a noise or not."

I began to feel superior to that young gentleman, and once more nestled down among the pillows and prepared to go to sleep.

The next instant, however, I sprang up, for from the room below, Mr. Lyndon's, came the sound of a struggle and a heavy fall. As I hurried out of my room in my dressing-gown I saw that the whole house was alarmed. The doctor, Sharly, and myself were, I think, first on the ground.

When we entered the room this was what we saw: Mr. Lyndon sitting up in bed, looking somewhat bewildered; David

Van Epps in his shirt sleeves, leaning against the old secretary, and looking rather pale as the blood oozed through his right sleeve; Lewis Leighton, with a little sharp dirk in one hand, and a pocket-book in the other; and Mark, towering in wrath above Mr. Cyrus Ford, who was all in a heap in one corner of the sofa.

"What's the matter?" said the doctor.

"David and Uncle Lucian know best," said Lewis. "We heard the noise and came in, and David had Cyrus on the floor, and just that minute Cyrus got one hand free and stabbed David. The secretary was open, as you see, and we found Uncle Lucian's money in Cyrus's pocket."

Here Dr. Leighton faced about, and turned every one of those who had followed us out of the room, with the exception of his wife, Sharly, and myself. He was pleased to observe that we had some sense.

"Are you hurt, father?" said Sharly, holding him very tight.

"No, my darling, no; run away," said Mr. Lyndon, recovering himself.

"In one minute. Uncle George, David is hurt. You'll want some linen. Shall I take that sheet in the closet drawer in my room, aunt?"

"Yes, dear, certainly," said Mrs. Leighton; and Sharly went, came back with the linen, and vanished.

"Are you much hurt, Davy?" said the doctor, getting hold of him.

"Not very much, I think — only my shoulder."

"My dear boy," said Mr. Lyndon, "I would rather have lost the money twice over than that any harm should come to you."

"Would you, Sir?" said David, in an odd sort of voice.

"It's nothing very bad," said the doctor. "I'll have it in order for you in a few minutes, and then you can tell us the story. Don't go, Miss Lindsay," he said to me. "I fancy you know something about this business. Cyrus Ford, keep quiet. I don't mean to expose you if I can help it, for your father's sake."

David said that he had heard someone come out of the entry and into the long passage, and confessed that, having Flora's legend in his mind, he had been rather startled.

"He must have been very sure that everyone was sound asleep," said David, "for he seemed to take no particular pains to keep quiet; and I suppose he must have mistaken my door for the other, for he turned the lock, and by some accident gave a sharp little tap on the panel. I thought it might be Mark or Lewis, and said 'Come in,' and he passed on. Then I thought it might be something worse than a ghost, and naturally thought of the money. I must say that I had noticed Mr. Ford look at the bills in a strange, eager way. I happen to know that at the office where he is employed in New York he has taken money, been forgiven for his father's sake, and allowed another trial. I knew that he was in debt, and I could not help having a sort of suspicion. I felt inclined to follow the walker, whether it were a ghost or not, and I rose and went after the sound. Did you hear it too, Miss Lindsay?"

"I certainly did."

"As I went through the passage I heard the step go down the back stairs. I followed it to the foot of the stairs, and, listening a moment, heard a noise in Mr. Lyndon's room. I went to the door, which was ajar. The drawer was open, and Mr. Ford stood over Mr. Lyndon with the dirk. I sprang upon him, and then Lewis and Mark came in."

Mr. Lyndon had waked, seen Cyrus turning away from the open drawer, and had called him by name. Then Cyrus had threatened him with the dirk, and David had come in just in time to divert the attack to himself. The secretary keys Cyrus had taken from Mr. Lyndon's coat pocket.

Here Cyrus Ford broke silence for the first time, "not wisely, but too well."

"How could you or Miss Lindsay hear me," he said, "when I went down the front stairs?"

"If ever I heard a step in my life —" said David; and then he stopped and looked at me.

"But he must have come the other way," said Mark, "or you would have seen him come in here, and he would not have had time to find the keys and the money."

"It's very odd. Who went down stairs?"

No one could tell.

"It must have been the wind," I said; "and there are so many noises; and yet I suppose if it had not been for the story you would not have come to look after the sound."

"No, I suppose not. And you — you knew it belonged to that little orphan child!" added David, turning with sudden vehemence upon Cyrus.

"I knew Mr. Lyndon would make it good," said Cyrus, in a tone of apology.

"Upon my word, we are obliged to you for your good opinion," said Mr. Lyndon, with ironical courtesy.

"Go upstairs and go to bed, David," said the doctor, "and keep yourself quiet, or you may see trouble with that arm. Take care of him, Priscilla; he deserves it. And, Mark, take this — this *being* up to his room, and lock him in. I suppose we shall let him off, for his father's sake, and I shall have to tell the story in the morning," said the doctor, with a sort of groan.

Mr. Cyrus Ford disappeared early the next morning — summoned, it was said, by urgent business. The servants were supposed not to know the story, but I am certain they did. David's wound was not at all serious; but it made him quite a lion in Chester for a time, somewhat to his annoyance.

Perhaps two months after Posy, Rosy, and I had returned to school I had a letter from Mrs. Leighton.

"Do you know," wrote that lady, "that Sharly and David are engaged? My brother rather stood out against it at first. But who is there so worthy of Sharly? My mother, who has always liked the boy, put in her word; and Lucian filially consented to forget that his father was no one in particular. At first he said it must be a long engagement, but now we begin to talk about spring. Old Dr. Vernet retires from the academy, and we all think that David will be principal; so they would do very well even if Sharly were unprovided for. And then David begins to make a name for himself with his pen. But, after all, I think it was his conduct on the night of the robbery that influenced my brother more than anything else."

Of course I went to Sharly's wedding in May. It was to take place from her uncle's house, as her own home was still occupied by the painters, who, as usual, continued to haunt the place long after the time of their promised departure.

Just as I was getting ready for bed on the night after my arrival came a tap at the door, and Flora entered with a look of great satisfaction upon her shining face.

"I've got something to tell you, miss," said Flora, mysteriously.

"Let me hear it," said I, wondering.

Flora carefully closed the door.

"You 'member, don't you," said she, in a semi-whisper, "what I told you about the Walking Boy?"

"Of course," I answered, rather alarmed. "I hope he has no objections to this wedding."

"No, miss; quite contrary. Now jes let me tell you. When Mr. Van Epps said his mother was a Merrion it set me thinkin', 'cause I was int'rested in the young gentleman — 'cause he is a gentleman — and anyone could see that he and Miss Shady were fond of one another. Rupert and ole madam's Jim, they's dreadful disgusted 'cause he was a poor boy, and his father lived in Scrub Hollow, which *is* a most mizzable place as ever was. But, laws! look at young Ford, son of one of our fustest men, and our poor Miss Rosalind's husband, and Miss Elsie's won't never be worth his salt."

"But the ghost, Flora?"

"Well, I jes thought and thought, and finally I couldn't get no rest 'thout findin' out who was his grandfather on the mother's side so I jes abstracted myself for a day or two, and went over to Valory's Corners: I've got an aunt there — Lorendy's mother, that lives with ole madam. Ninety-six she is, but she's got all her faculties, and 'members everything ever happened round these parts. Well, I set Aunt Miny to thinkin', and presently it all come out, and sure enough his mother's father was Parson Merrion's son Jacob. He never came to much, and the daughter she married beneath her, Solon Van Epps, and by all accounts he was one of the shiftlessest critters ever was made, though he hadn't no harm in him. But David he's got the Williams streak in him for smartness, and he's got the Merrion streak in him for his book-learnin'."

"So that the Walking Boy is Mr. Van Epps's great-uncle?" said I, impressed.

"Yes, to be sure, miss. And now don't you tell anyone what I'm goin' to tell you; but as you heard the step, I take it for a kind of sign that you was to know.

"You couldn't expect Mr. Lucian to be pleased with the match, for, to tell you the truth, fust time any of our folks see David was in a little mission Sunday-school that ole madam's grandchildren started over in Scrub Hollow one summer all themselves — the Fentons and Miss Sharly and the Fitz Adam boys and David he was a little ragged fellow there in John Fitz Adam's class.

"Well, he kep' away from the house, and Miss Sharly she went round 'bout as usual, only she was wonderful quiet but it never would be her way to make a fuss. Mr. Lucian he wasn't easy, 'cause he couldn't bear to cross Miss Sharly, and he liked David, and everyone said the boy was as honorable as he could be about it.

"I didn't want to see two young folks made mizzable if I could help it, and I watched my chance, and jes mentioned to Master Lucian what I had heard over at Valory's Corners — 'cause *he* knew all about the Walking Boy, and he don't laugh at such things always neither. I didn't let on that it was anything particular, only jes a piece of news.

"'And so, Flora,' says he, when I'd told him, 'you think Mr. Van Epps is the man whom the ghost has chosen?'

"'Well,' says I, 'if you ask me, Sir, I do think so, and I'd be afraid that if he ever sets his heart on anything in this house and don't get it, it bring bad luck to us all,' and then I cleared out. And next day Master Lucian he gives his consent, and he thinks a sight of David. And, laws! they say it was this, that, and the other thing, but I tell you what, miss, it was me and the Walking Boy made that match — and now you'll see he'll never be heard again."

And though I have since passed many a night in the house, I have never again heard anything of the Walking Boy. But Mr. Van Epps and I have never been able to decide what was the sound which guided Parson Merrion's great-grandson on the night of that 25th of September.

The Haunted House by the Mill: A Texas Story

Clara Le Clerc

And when they talk of it, they shake their heads,
And whisper one another in the ear;
And he that speaks doth gripe the hearer's wrist,
And he that hears makes fearful action,
With wrinkled brow, with nods, with rolling eyes.
SHAKSPEARE

"Has someone really taken the *mill* house?" And the speaker, a tall athletic young man, gave his head a significant jerk in the direction of a long, low, weather-stained and rambling old house, while his eyes sought his companion's face.

"Yes, the house has been taken by a young man and his wife from the States. He has leased the mill, but it's my opinion he'll pack *out* of *that* house pretty quick, after stopping a night or two *inside*. Catch me spending a night in *that* place!" And this speaker tossed his head towards the low dark-looking house, and a kind of superstitious awe gathered upon his frank open face. "Why, man alive! I wouldn't do it for a hull hatful of these *yellow-shiners*." And he tossed up a couple of gold pieces, each marked "Five Dollars."

"Neither would I, Larry; but then, we had best say as little as possible before the new-comers. When will they be here?"

"Any hour, I suppose, as the wagons went to meet them yesterday for their traps and things. I don't think they have any children; that's one good thing, for they can hustle out o' there any minute."

"A dismal day to take possession of a home like that." And the younger of the couple again glanced significantly towards the really uncanny-looking house; then, turning their backs upon the object of their conversation, they entered the mill, and amid the dull roar and whirr of machinery inside, and the monotonous drip drip of the rain without, the day wore on.

"They have come, John!"

"Let me see! let me see!" And several eager faces peered through the gloom, and descried the mud-bespattered hack before the door of the house, and heard a clear young voice, through the rain and darkness, ask:

"Is this the place, Freddie?"

"Yes dear." The next moment a tall figure sprang to the ground, and reaching up his arms, soon placed a small woman on the wet ground beside him. "Run in now, before you get cold and damp."

As the small figure turned to enter the house, several willing hands offered to bring in trunks, and make a fire for the travellers.

"Thank you," replied the gentleman. "We are quite worn out, and will be glad of your assistance."

By ten o'clock the "traps and things" had been temporarily arranged, and with a hand-lamp the young wife explored the great barnlike rooms — only three in number — and peered into shadowy nooks; while the workmen gave each other knowing glances, and cast looks of pity upon the young couple.

"Eleven o'clock! Jiminy! I must be a gittin' from here, ef it's that late!" muttered one of the men, as the little timepiece rang out the hour. "Come, boys! 'Night, Mr. Greyson; 'night, marm, pleasant dreams to you!" And the crowd hustled out of the door, and each one seemed to give his feet an extra shake as he crossed the doorsill.

"Twelve o'clock!" The tones rang out clear and musical through the great room, and the young wife, turning restlessly on her pillow, reached over and passed her little hand over the face of her sleeping husband. "Fred! O Freddie! are you asleep? Somehow I *can't* go to sleep, tired as I am. I am all nerves — I have the *queerest* feelings, dear. Won't you talk to me just a little?"

"O Carrie, what *nonsense*, when I am so sleepy!" And one strong arm reached out and drew the little trembling figure to his side, and held it there. "Why, child, you are all of a tremble. What is the matter?"

"I don't know. Hush! What noise is that?"

A dull thud, thud, thud! The strokes were regular, and seemed as if someone was beating another.

"Do you hear it, Fred?"

"Rats!" muttered the sleepy Fred.

Again thud, thud, thud!

"O mercy! It seems to be in the next room!" murmured the nervous little woman.

"There! I certainly *did* hear a shriek and moan!"

"No, 'tis only the wind and rain sobbing and wailing around the house corners, I reckon."

"Now, what is that I hear upstairs?" And the excited little creature sat up in bed, and listened to the strange sounds overhead. Thipity-thump, thipity-thump! "Sounds like someone with a wooden leg or crutch. Queer rats in this old barn. I must make my little terrier clear them out." And with a shiver she crept back under the cover, and into the arms that were opened to receive her, though the owner was wrapped in sleep.

"Haint you 'ons heard strange noises o' nights since you 'ons got here?"

The speaker, a very old lady with many a wrinkle seaming her still comely face, peered into the eyes of the young stranger. This was Carrie Greyson's first visitor; and the old lady's voice sank into a low mysterious tone as she repeated the question.

"Yes, the rats are fearful!" answered the young wife.

"*Rats* indeed! Ef that aint a good un, my name aint Patty Harris! Honey," — and she placed one fat wrinkled hand on Mrs. Greyson's shoulder, while her voice seemed filled with awe and fear — "*this house is haunted!*"

And having delivered herself of this startling information, she gazed triumphantly at the young wife, expecting her to give vent to exclamations of wild alarm.

"Pshaw, Mrs. Harris! you certainly do not believe in such things?"

"Don't Mrs. Harris me, honey. I am Aunt Patty."

"Well, Aunt Patty, then."

"Of course I believe in it, for 'tis as true as the Gospel. Lud, honey, you see I was here that night when it all happened."

"When what happened, Aunt Patty?"

The look of amusement gave place to one of interest upon Mrs. Greyson's sunny face.

"Come here, I have something to show you first." And the old lady tottered across the floor, leading the younger. "There! do you see that?" she exclaimed, as they stood within the front room, and she pointed to a huge black spot upon the otherwise spotless floor.

"Of course I see it, and I have been at work on it ever since I got here, trying to rub it up. 'Tis a very unsightly stain of some kind."

"Yes, yes, honey, that's all true; an onsightly stain of *some kind*." And the old woman shook her head in a sad reflective manner.

"I'll be sixty-five year old, come Christmas-day, and all that happened when I was a little gel between thirteen and fourteen. Honey, I saw that spot flooded with *warm human blood!* Would you like to hear the story?"

"Yes, indeed I should, Aunt Patty; come, let me lead you back into the other room to the fire." For the old lady was trembling with cold and excitement.

"Well, when I was thirteen, just that day, 'cause it was on a Christmas, and my good mother always made me a cream-cake on that day," — this the old lady said as she seated herself in a large armchair, took off her glasses, and wiped them with the corner of her dark calico apron, and then put them again in place — "yes, that day father came in from the mill to dinner, and said, 'Well, old lady, we'll have strangers in the mill house afore long.' We always called it the mill house, as it had been built expressly for whoever might have the mill in charge; sometimes it was one man, and agin another. 'You don't say! Who is it?' asked mother.

"'A man by the name of George Hurst has leased the mill; he, his mother and cousin are to be here tomorrow.' 'How did you hear it, Henry?' 'Will Carter brung the news from town.'

"The next day, just afore dark, here they come, sure enough. I was playing about before the mill door, and had a good chance to see 'em. First the man, a great, tall, stout man clumb out, and got upon the ground; and as he did so, I saw with horror that he had only one leg. He placed a crutch under his left arm, and with the other hand helped out two ladies. The old lady looked sad and homesick; her hair was gray, and put back smoothlike beneath her bonnet.

"The young gel — well, she was the prettiest creatur' that I had ever seen in my life; she was tall and slim, had pretty feet and white hands; her eyes were large and dark, her skin dusky-like, with rosy cheeks and lips. But her hair was her greatest beauty. She had on a broad-brimmed hat with a scarlet ribbon round it, and a scarlet feather fastened in one side and hanging almost to her shoulder; and her hair had slipped out from the comb that held it in place, and fell from under her hat in great black curls, as big as my arm, way down to her knees. As soon as she touched the ground the man turned round fierce, like he was mad, and snapped, 'Come, Imogene! Don't stand there to be stared at. Come, mother, come into the house.' And he stumped on in front of them, and opened the door; while one and another of the crowd of workmen at the mill door exclaimed, 'Well, ef that's the boss, I don't think I shall like him. I wouldn't speak to my old mother, or cousin, either, for that matter, as *he* did, for all the money in Texas.'

"Yes, that was the boss, George Hurst, and he proved to be a strict harsh master. He was a good-looking man — or would have been but for an awful frown he always wore upon his otherwise handsome face. His hair was a reddish black, his beard also; his eyes large, and of a steely gray. I was always afraid of him, and very often when mother would send me to the mill with a message to father, he'd gaze at me hard with those great eyes of his'n, and snap out, 'What now; Patty!' as if it was any concern of his'n.

"It turned out that Imogene Dupree was his cousin, and he was her guardeen. Anybody could see with half an eye that he was very fond of her, in his savage way. And old Mrs. Hurst dropped a hint one day that Imogene would sometime be her daughter, and yet she always watched the young thing in a kind of sad pitying way whenever George was near.

"One night about six months later, when father came in to supper he brought a stranger with him; and, child as I was, I was struck with his fair handsome face; hair like curls of gold, and eyes as blue as wood violets. Ah, honey, he was as pretty as a picter; and as I sat on the doorstep after supper, and gazed up into his face while he talked with father, I thought, 'O my eye, don't I wish I was grown, so he could be my beau!' I heard them talkin' about gettin' work at the mill, and I wondered to myself ef that man, so finely dressed, with hands so soft and white, really wanted work. And then I listened, and heard Walter Wyman — that was the stranger's name — say that he had lost all of his property through the trickery of a purtended friend, and had tried in several places to get a situation, but had failed; that if he could get something to do for several months, he thought he would like to stay a while. I then heard father say that George Hurst was not much of a scribe, and that they needed someone at the mill to write down all the grain received and flour sent out; and that he heard the boss wishing for someone to attend to all that. 'So let me finish my smoke, and I'll step over to Hurst's with you, and see what can be done.'

"And so it was all arranged. Walter Wyman remained as George Hurst's secretary — he, Hurst, I mean, was fond of big dictionary words; and they took him to board at the mill house, and things went on very quietly for a time. But at last things began to look dark. I could hear George Hurst talking sharp and spiteful-like to his secretary; and once I heard Hurst tell father he 'didn't thank him for bringing that *meddler* and *interloper* into the concern;' to which father made no reply, for he knew, and we all knew, that Walter Wyman was a thousand times more of a gentleman than George Hurst ever dared to be.

"It got noised about at last that Imogene and her cousin George were to be married at Christmas. Mrs. Hurst was at work on pretty underclothes, and prettier dresses, but Imogene wandered about, seeming like one very unhappy. She often crossed the bridge, and strolled away off among the trees and bushes on the other side of the pond, where she would remain for hours. No one seemed to notice this at first — no one but me; child as I was, I often followed her at a distance, and when she imagined that she was hidden from everyone, I have seen her cast herself upon the ground and cry and sob, wring her hands and moan, and often have I heard her utter these words: 'My God, my God, why hast thou forsaken me?' I knew not at the time what she meant, but afterwards I knew.

"By-and-by George Hurst began to look at her in a savage way as she passed the mill, and would call out in a loud harsh voice, 'Where to now, my lady?' And she would reply in low trembling voice, while a frightened look crept over her pale sad face, 'Only across the millstream for a little walk, Cousin George.'

"'*Cousin George!* now that is a good one!' And he would laugh a short hateful laugh, while the wishful blue eyes of the secretary would follow the trim figure passing on the footbridge.

"Three weeks before Christmas came a heavy rain, lasting five or six days. The whole earth was flooded with water. The millstream seemed like a mighty river, a rushin' and foamin' along, a whirlin' limbs and dead logs like so many feathers adown stream. But on the sixth day the clouds lifted somewhat, and about three o'clock in the afternoon the sun peeped out, jest the least bit; and directly, who should come along the path before our door, but Miss Imogene, overshoes and wrappings on? going for her lonely walk, I knew.

"I saw Walter Wyman standing in the mill door, and heard him exclaim, 'You surely are not going to try to cross the pond this evening, Miss Imogene? The bridge is not very firm, at best, and it sways with the current now. The water is rising rapidly. In less than two hours that bridge will be floating down stream. Do not be so rash, I beg!'

"'I must go, Walter — Mr. Wyman. I want to think, and the house stifles me.'

"'Well, let me try the bridge first. If it should give way I can swim, you cannot.'

"He walked the whole length of the narrow bridge and back again; then taking Imogene by the hand, he led her safely over. When he reached the mill door again he turned and gazed after the form fast losing itself among the trees and stunted bushes. For over an hour Walter Wyman sat before the door of the mill, scarce taking his eyes from the heavin' and risin' waters, and the swayin' bridge whereon must cross Imogene on her return.

"'Why does she not come?' I heard him mutter, as I ran over to the mill for a pan of chicken-feed. 'If she does not soon come, I'll go after her.'

"Just then George Hurst put his head out of the mill house door and shouted, 'What are you doing at the mill this time of day, Wyman? I want you here to figure up some accounts for me.'

"The mill stopped at twelve every Wednesday for a half holiday, but George Hurst always kept his secretary at work, ef he could possibly find anything for him to do. With a deep moan Walter Wyman once more cast his eyes up the path across the water, then started for the house, stopping every two minutes to look back. He stopped on the doorstep and gazed eagerly up the path once more, but no Imogene was in sight.

"I stood before our door watching him, and saw him enter the mill house; then, child as I was, I determined to watch for Miss Imogene, and tell him when I saw her coming. So I seated myself on the door-step, cold and wet as it was, and gazed out upon the path beyond the bridge.

"Ten, twenty minutes went by, and then mother called, 'Come, Patty, set the table for supper afore it gits dark.' To hear was to obey, although I murmured something about watching for Miss Imogene.

"I had laid the cloth, had put on the cups and sassers, and was lifting a pile of plates from the corner shelf, when I heard a wild shrill scream. With a crash the plates fell to the floor, and I darted out of the house, but Walter Wyman was before me. Great heavens! that awful sight! The bridge was borne along by the rush of waters, a whirlin' round like a mere plank, and standing upon the whirlin' mass was Imogene Dupree, her pale face raised to heaven, her hands clasped, and one wild cry after another breaking from her ashen lips. Swift as thought Walter Wyman had rushed down the stream, and calling to Imogene, 'Be brave, and keep perfectly still, *my darling!*' he waited until the floatin' bridge reached a bend in the stream, then springing high in air, he gave a mighty leap and landed upon the bridge beside Imogene. And then we all witnessed a touchin' scene that we never forgot — one that caused George Hurst to gnash his teeth and curse like a madman; for Imogene, his intended bride, cast her arms about Walter Wyman's neck; while he clasped her close in his arms, and pressed kisses on her lips, cheeks and hair.

"'The cursed villain! he shall pay *dear* for those kisses!' I heard George Hurst mutter.

"By this time the workmen had gathered all the stout ropes they could find, and making fast a long hook to one end, they threw it on the bridge, and Walter made the hook fast by slippin' it over the beam of the bridge; then those on shore drove a large iron bar into the ground, and passin' the rope across it, began to haul in; but the bridge refused to come to shore. It was turned lengthwise, and they battled manfully, but it'would not start.

"'Just steady it as much as you can, boys, and I'll try to bring Miss Imogene ashore. There! steady now!' And, turning to Imogene, he spoke to her in a low voice, then pressed a long kiss upon her lips; and once again her two arms went up and clasped his neck, and remained there while he raised her in his arms; and calling out, 'Steady now!' walked to the edge of the bridge with his precious burden in his arms, and giving the spring, landed on the ground; but as he did so his foot caught upon a snag; he tottered, dropped Imogene as he fell, and struck his head against a large log that had been washed ashore.

"George Hurst caught Imogene as she fell, and givin' her a rough shake, cried, harshly, 'Go to the house now, my lady! You have created scene enough for one day; my turn comes next.'

"It was with difficulty that the men prevented him from striking Walter Wyman, as he lay so cold and lifeless upon the wet ground. Old Mrs. Hurst burst into tears and cried out, 'For shame, George Hurst! May God forgive me, but the time has come when I am ashamed of my child.' Then growing calmer, she went up to him, and placin' her hand upon his arm, while her pale sad face looked very stern, she said in a low voice, 'I think you had best get on your horse, and go to town for a few days; you are not needed here just now, and all will get on better for your absence. Go, lest I may live to curse the day that gave you birth!'

"Without a word George Hurst turned away from his mother; and as the crowd of workmen hastened to lift their favorite from the ground and bear him to the house, George Hurst passed them on his coal black horse, and, as he rode on, gave a low mocking laugh.

"On the third night after Walter Wyman had received his hurt, I came over to bring him some nice seedcake, jam and cream that mother had prepared for him. I came in just here at the back door, and found no one in this room but Mrs. Hurst. She was sitting before the fire, with her knittin' resting on her lap, while the strangest, scared look was on her face that I ever saw. 'What have you got there, Patty? Something nice for Mr. Wyman? Your mother is very kind, I am sure. Take it in the front room; they are in there.'

"Yes, Walter Wyman was lying on a cot near the right-hand corner, and Imogene was kneeling on a rug at his side, with her beautiful hair down; while he passed his long white fingers tenderly through the rich heavy mass, and now and then lifted a heavy curl to his lips. They were so wrapped up in each other that they did not notice me until I stood just before them.

"'Ah, little Patty, is it you?' And he lifted his handsome face to look at me, and makin' me stoop down, gave me a kiss on my cheek for bringin' him such a nice supper. How well I remember everything connected with that night!

"'I've had one supper, Patty, but I must try yours — that is' — and he glanced into Imogene's happy face — 'if my darling will feed me.'

"'Of course I shall; to hear is to obey!' And takin' the things out of my hands, she arranged them upon a little stand by the cot, tucked a napkin under his chin, took up the cream-jug and poured the cream over the jam, placed a seedcake between his white fingers, and laughingly said, 'Begin, sir!'

"I stood by and watched their merriment for a long time. Now he would make her taste, 'just to sweeten it,' he said, and then place the spoon to his lips. How happy they were! At last I sat down on a little low chair before the fire, and in watching them I must have dropped asleep; for by-and-by I heard the clock strike eleven, and, rubbing my eyes, I looked around, and if you'll believe me, there they were at their fun, Imogene makin' him beg and pay for each spoonful.

"'Now, sir, what will you give for this spoonful?' she merrily cried; and, catching at her hands, he drew her down and kissed her rosy red lips.

"'There, *that* is the currency I intend to pay you in always, my darling! Do you know' — and here his voice grew serious — 'I would be willing to die, almost, now that I *know* you love me? I would give my life freely in payment for the happiness of the last three days, rather than to have lived without the knowledge of your precious love.' And drawing her down again, he pressed loving kisses upon her sweet mouth.

166

"'What a pretty tableau! Am sorry that I shall have to spoil it!' spoke a harsh well-known voice at the door; and with a start the lovers turned, and saw George Hurst!

"Child as I was, I screamed in a low scared way when I saw his face. Turning the key in the lock, he then removed it and put it in his pocket. Then crossing the room to the other door, he did the same.

"'What is the meaning of that, Cousin George?' And Imogene turned her stricken face towards him.

"'*This* is your answer, my lady!' And standing over the low cot, he twisted his large fingers in the beautiful golden hair of Walter Wyman, and jerked him to a sitting posture.

"'Why, Hurst! Don't be so rough. Remember a fellow that has had his senses knocked out of him don't get well in a hurry.'

"'They don't, eh? Well, I have a little account to settle with you, and I had just as well begin.' And with that he jerked him off the cot, and commenced beating him with his crutch.

"'Aunt Mary! Aunt Mary! for Heaven's sake, call help! George is killing Walter!' And the voice but a few minutes before filled with laughter, rose to wild shrieks, as she flew at George Hurst and struck at him, with her puny arms. But alas! the murderer had done his work; the first or second blow upon the temple had sent the soul of Walter Wyman into the presence of his God; but the fiend, not satisfied, dropped upon the floor beside the lifeless body of his victim, and continued beating it until pools of blood covered the floor.

"'Ah! for every kiss you get a blow. I counted the kisses, now *you* count the blows!' And he chuckled in a most awful manner.

"Poor Imogene! She had sunk down on the floor by the body of her lover, tearin' her hair, beatin' her hands wildly until they were covered with blood; and all the while she screamed, 'O my love! my love! my dead, *dead* love!'

"At the first wild cry for help Mrs. Hurst had sprung to the door, but finding it fastened, I heard her run to the back door and scream 'Help! help! Murder! murder!' But it was late, everybody abed; and it was some time before that feeble voice could make itself heard. At last came a rush of feet towards the front door, and as they reached it George Hurst got up, took the key to the middle door from his pocket, and as the front door fell in with a crash, I heard him go thipity-thump up the stairs into his own room.

"O heavens! shall I ever shut out the picture! That pale handsome face looked very lifelike, with the exception of one spot on the temple; but the body was beaten into an awful mass. O, the sight was full of horror! And there that awfully mutilated body had to lie in that pool of blood until the coroner could be summoned. In the meantime, a guard had been placed at the foot of the stairs in this room to prevent George Hurst's escape. But it seemed as if he did not think of escape, for we heard the regular thipity-thump, thipity-thump through the long hours of the night.

"Mrs. Hurst and mother tried to get Imogene to leave the body; but no, she remained; and when the coroner and his jury arrived they found her thus.

"Their verdict was soon given — 'Wilful murder committed upon the person of Walter Wyman, by one George Hurst!' And with that, an officer with a warrant stepped softly up the stairs — where George Hurst's well-known steps were sounding — expecting to surprise him; but we soon heard his swift footsteps on the stairs, and his deathly pale face glared into the room, while he gasped, 'O Heaven! what a night of horrors!' and waved his hand in the direction of the stairs, towards which excited feet rushed — mine among the number. It seemed as if I *must* go; and when I got to the door and heard his regular thipity-thump, I was sure that I would see his angry face mocking at us. No form walked the room, but, extended on the bed, his throat cut from ear to ear, the razor still grasped in his right hand, and his bloody crutch pressed fondly to his breast with his left, lay George Hurst, the murderer and suicide!

"With a great cry I turned and fled, and never stopped until I had buried my head in the pillows of my own little bed at home. O, how I shook and quivered with fear! I could see the whole awful sight — pale, handsome, mutilated Walter Wyman lying in his pool of blood; the stricken form of Imogene Dupree as she knelt at his side, and hear her wild cry, 'O my love! my love! my dead, *dead* love!' and last, that awful hideous object with the blood pouring from his neck, as he lay upon his bed upstairs; while the queer strokes of his sound foot and his crutch kept pace upon the floor!

"Two days later the murdered and the murderer were buried side by side in a little graveyard not far from here. Imogene would not leave the coffin of her dead lover until kind hands bore her gently away; and when she heard the first clods of earth fall upon it, she screamed, 'O let me go! let me go to Walter!'

"Poor Mrs. Hurst! her grief found no expression. With lovin' care she watched over the wretched Imogene, and was makin' all haste to settle up her son's business, and leave this awful house, for she said she could not bear to stay here. Imogene's mind seemed perfectly crazed. She would sit for hours with her eyes closed, and hands locked on her breast; then starting up with a wild shriek, would cast herself upon that awful spot darkened with her lover's lifeblood, and moans and cries the most awful and heartrending would issue from her lips.

"One night — the one she was to have been the wife of her cousin — she awoke her aunt, in the dead of the night, with her wails and cries; and sitting up in bed, Mrs. Hurst saw her upon her knees by that spot, her head bowed to the floor, and heard her cry, 'Yes, Walter, my love, *my love*, I am coming!' And risin', she walked swiftly towards the door, and throwin' it open, rushed out into a storm of rain and wind, with no clothin' save her nightdress. With wild alarm Mrs. Hurst sprang from her bed, threw a wrapper around her, thrust her feet into her slippers, and followed out after her, calling my father to come to her aid. Soon dark forms with lanterns could be seen moving about in the storm. They shouted 'Imogene! Imogene!' until they were so hoarse they could not speak; no Imogene could be found! All the next day, and the next, the search went on, but all in vain; and at last it was concluded that poor Imogene had joined her lover in the spirit-land, but how and when they could not tell. Poor heartbroken Mrs. Hurst left the State, and returned to her old home in North Carolina.

"Years went by; the old mill house, with its now uncanny looks and haunted rooms, was an object of fear to us young folks. One after another tried to live here, but the dark crimson spot staring into their faces; the dull thud, thud, thud of blows, the faint moans of the dying man, the shrill screams of the bereft maiden, and the thipity-thump of the murderer overhead, forced them to leave the house.

"A few years later there came just such a storm of wind and rain as had caused the mill-house tragedy. The millstream was again a ragin' flood, castin' up boughs and broken bits of timber; and one morning after the storm had calmed, father came runnin' into the house, his face pale and voice tremblin', as he cried, 'Mother, the millstream has given up its secret! Come and see.'

"Yes, there cast up by the waters, and lying on the shore, was a skeleton; and full well we all knew that we looked upon all that was left of poor Imogene Dupree. We buried her beside her lover, and tried to forget the wild sad story of her and hers. But never a wild night comes but what I bury my head in the bedclothes and pray, 'O God, teach me to forget that awful scene!'"

Here the old lady paused, and wiped away the tears that coursed down her wrinkled cheeks. Carrie Greyson had carried her handkerchief to her eyes more than once during the old lady's pathetic story; and now she spoke for the first time since the commencement.

"O Aunt Patty, how very very sad! It must be trying to you, for she — poor Imogene — and her noble lover were known and loved by you all. Of course this house must, to you, seem to be accursed. But I am not afraid at all, Aunt Patty. 'Tis true your story will make me very sad at times; but the thought of fear will never enter my mind. Must you go? Come in often to see me."

"Yes, honey, 'tis gittin' dusk, and I wouldn't be here when *it* begins for all the gold in Texas. Good-by, honey. Come to see Aunt Patty." And with that the old lady made her way slowly down the steps, and out into the thickening winter twilight; while the young wife cast several sticks upon the fire, stirred it into a merry blaze, trimmed the lamp, and began to prepare her evening meal, listening with love's quick ears to the well-known steps that brought her Fred home to her, awaiting him there — all alone in the *haunted house.*

The American Ghost

Lucretia Peabody Hale

I would like to tell the story as an old friend told it to me in her garrulous way. She tried to write it down herself, indeed, at my request, but I shall have to give it as she read it to me, interspersed with her own interjections that came up at the moment, and that are needed to explain what she told.

I must begin, she said, with two young girls looking at each other, one evening, when we had all being sitting together, talking with those English ladies who had been visiting us, and they left the very next day quite disappointed that all the time they had been in the house they had heard no broad Yankee spoken, and my sister was quite put out about it, wondering that they should have expected it at our house, or thought to hear it in Boston. But they went on to say that, after all, the principal difference between us Americans and the English is that we have no faith in ghosts, or indeed that we have no ghosts to have faith in. Either because, if we have an old house we pull it down, or because our houses are all so new — and how could you expect a ghost on the Back Bay where the houses are only just built? And so, indeed, there is not a house for a ghost to go to, or to stay in, if there happened to be one.

Now in England, these ladies said, there is not a town but is old enough to have its traditions, and keep up its haunted house along with its old streets.

"I have not met one family ghost," said one of these ladies, "since I have been in America. And what is the worst, if there were one, nobody would believe in it. In England there's not a respectable family but has its ghost attached to it, — perhaps the ghost is gone, indeed, but it has been there, and the servants know all about it, and the nurse-maids, and they brought us up to believe in it. To be sure it is not every one of the family that can see a ghost, perhaps not one in a generation, but we would all of us be much disappointed if there had not been a ghost seen in the family sometime or other."

Then she went on to tell about one of her uncles. He was dead now, but he was one of that kind who had seen their family ghost — yes, more than once; and she made our blood curdle and our flesh cold, telling us about it, for it was late at night, and somebody had turned the gas down low, and there were only a few flickering embers in the fire round which we were sitting.

"But the noise?" asked a tall boy, breaking the silence that came after the story. He had been listening, with all the hairs, short as they were on his close-cut head, standing up on end. "What was the noise, after all — did you find out? Was it rats?"

"Just what I told you," exclaimed the English lady, quite angry; "you expect to have an explanation of everything and find out why it was so! It is enough to discourage any right-minded ghost! Of course, anyone who has really seen a ghost does not think to question. Rats, indeed! You don't deserve to have any ghosts!" And she would not say another word on the subject.

And the very next day these English ladies went back home to England, and I might have a great deal to tell about their letters, and what they thought about Americans, and what we thought about them, but that sort of thing comes into so many other stories that there is no need for it here.

But the two girls I was telling you of, sitting together on the sofa, who looked at each other that particular way, during this talk about ghosts — they had come from the country only the day before for the winter. We none of us knew them very well, and perhaps that is why they neither of them spoke, though they looked at each other as if they had something to say.

But, though they said nothing downstairs, they talked fast enough when they went up to their own room, and on this very subject. They were in the upper story of one of the houses in Beacon Street, by the side of the Atheneum, and they were looking across to the houses opposite.

Now, they had picked out this particular room for their winter home, because the place might seem something like home, for they knew that their mother was born in the house opposite. Of course, not in one of those very houses, for though they may begin to look old and weather-beaten now-a-days to the rising generation, we can many of us remember when they were new. And some of us can remember the house that was there before — a lonely old house that stood back, back on a hill, on a line with the State House — almost the top of Beacon Hill of those days, with a slope in front, and a garden behind. And if you should pass through one of these houses standing there now, you might see in the back yard a remnant of this old Beacon Hill, sloping the other way, as it used to slope up from the end of Somerset Court that was, and that now is Ashburton Place, which has cut through this hill. And you can still see remaining in this back yard a bit of slope, and on it the same grasses growing, and blue succory, if you look there in the spring, just such as we used to pick through the cracks in the boards on the bit of hill remaining at the end of Somerset Court in those days, long ago, when the mother of these girls lived in the old house. She left it when she was seven years old, for the house was pulled down; but her mother, and all her aunts and ancestors used to live there, and their great-grand-aunt, Dora, for whom one of these girls was named, must have visited there.

I am not going to stop and tell all these stories, because I hate stories within stories, and always did. Pilpay's Fables were always a disappointment to me when I was a child. I read all the fables, but I had to skip the between part. Of course I don't include the Arabian Nights, because there's no reason why one should ever stop reading on and on, in those stories, if only one had the leisure of the Arabs, smoking their nargiles, reclining on their Persian rugs, with their heads on foot-stools, in their garden, beneath their rose trees.

But, I would like to tell about Dora's mother, who was named Dora, too, after this same old great-grand-aunt, and how she used to tell of the days she played in the "mall" on Beacon Street when she was a school-girl — on the slope of Beacon Street — how there was a row of elms half-way down the bank, and a path worn along beneath the trees, making two gray banks where there is now one slope from the street. And there was one large tree, whose roots came out above the earth, and across into the path, and she used to play there with the other school-girls, — and such baby houses as they made among the twisted roots — they could push into deep holes way under the tree, making secret passages, and more than one doll they lost there, though of course they were careful with their most choice dolls; but they used to play as though the place were their own, and that nobody else would come there, and would leave their things, thinking to find them next day. But of course some other party of girls might come along that very afternoon, and carry away what they pleased, and when they came again everything would be gone, much to their surprise. They would take the loss as children take their loss, as they do their gains, as coming down upon them like breakfast, dinner or supper, not at any regular times, but just when the elders should choose.

But there came a more serious loss one day. This Dora, I mean my Dora's mother, had a queer old pin that came down to her from her great-grand-aunt Dora — a silver pin she called it, but it might have been lead, for it was no longer bright; some curious carvings on it were worn down, and whatever might be considered its value now, when all old things are raked up, and a high price set on them, it did not then rank much above a common pin, except that it had belonged to great-grand-aunt Dora. It had a round, heavy head, and was odd-looking anyhow. She had been using it to pin her favorite doll Janet's shawl with; and she knew she must have left it in the roots of the tree in a choice corner, called Janet's closet, which they always kept shut up close, with grass wedged in. But when she went to look for it, it was not there, and the grass all gone, and bits of cracker and orange-peel crammed into the closet instead. It could not be found, and very foolish all her aunts and uncles called her, for leaving it there, for by this time her own mother was dead, who might have been more careful for aunt Dora's pin.

Well, a long time passed on and Dora's mother was living no longer in Boston, but in that old house in the country from which these two girls had come this very winter, near Byfield, I believe, with a slope down to some river under its windows. And she went one day to a sleigh-ride, or some other party, when they stopped somewhere for a dance, and she had a great many partners; some of them she had never seen before, but there was one of these — there was one — and when he stood bowing before her, to ask if she would dance with him — that was, after she had been introduced — as he stood there, she could not but see he wore aunt Dora's pin — that same round-headed pin, with its worn carvings — it pinned his cravat! All confused as she went to dance, she could not keep her eyes off the pin, and as he could not help seeing how she looked at it, "There's an odd story about this pin!" he said; and he went on to tell how, when he was a boy, he and the schoolboys used to go to play by a tree in the mall by the common — the Beacon Street mall — and how they made fortifications among the twisted roots of the great old tree, and how they had barracks and bastions, and how it was in their "quarter-master's secret closet," one day, he found this queer pin. "But that was Janet's closet, my doll's," interrupted Dora's mother — only she was not married then, — but of course did afterward marry Dora's father, as he said there seemed no better way of restoring the pin that Dora inherits to this very day.

I ought not to have been so long telling this, except to show how it was that my Dora, this young Dora, felt a close connection with this old grand-aunt, and more so now, because she had just been going through a great sorrow that reminded her of great-grand-aunt Dora, and the story that was always told about her.

You see the two girls were looking out upon the very place, as I said, where their mother and grand-mother had lived before them, — only so different now, that row of brick houses, not so especially new either, and when their mother was a child the old house stood back from the street, and you went up to it by a succession of steps — first a few steps, then a landing place, then more steps, something like the front of the State House, with grassy banks each side, and the door in the middle of the house, and perhaps a lilac, or some other bush, either side of the door. This was the way it looked then. But now they were sitting up even with the upper windows of the row of brick homes close opposite them.

And Elsie, the older, said — she was the more cheerful one of the two: "Of course grand-aunt Dora used to come and visit her relations when they lived in the old house here, but it was not her home."

"No," answered Dora, "her home was in the part of Washington Street that used to be called Newbury Street, on this side of Essex Street."

"But, Dora," said Elsie, in a low tone, "our mother never saw her there — grand-aunt Dora, I mean."

For the story of grand-aunt Dora was that, far back in the olden days, living up there in what was Newbury Street — she was all dressed one day to go to Commencement — so always the family story went. For in those days "Commencement" at Harvard was considered a great event, and all the young girls (and grand-aunt Dora was a young girl then) had their hair dressed for the occasion high up on their head, as was the fashion, and the hairdressers were engaged to come the day before always, because they must go so early on Commencement day — no time for dressing beforehand, and because there were so many to have their hair dressed, and but one hairdresser of any great repute. And with all the rest grand-aunt Dora had her hair powdered and dressed, and a red poppy stuck in on one side, just above the cushion that puffed up her hair, and so she sat up all night that she might not tumble it by lying down (and many another young lady was doing the same), in a high easy-chair by the window. The high-cushioned side of the chair (these two girls still owned it in the old country house) could partly support her head — and there she sat all night — and not all that night only, but ever after — night after night.

So the story always went, but it does not tell when or how she died, but there she was still sitting, all that passing generation said, night after night at the window. When the dash and the clash of the carriages and horse-cars in front of the Globe and Park theatres dies away, and quiet comes over the midnight, and morning approaches, doubtless she might be seen in later days still in the front window of one of the upper stories, with her powdered hair, and the flower by the side of her head, waiting, still waiting, because the young lover that was to have taken her to Commencement — he never came.

So the story was always told, with never a reason why "he" did not come. Perhaps he went to Cambridge with another girl — or when it was she faded away in the easy-chair as she sat there — we never knew.

And so the tale was told, though there was one version, perhaps the true one, that the "strange lady" appeared only on Commencement morning; but the girls never knew if their mother, or her mother, had ever seen Aunt Dora sitting there, for the family had long ago given up the "Newbury Street" house.

But the night before — the very first night they had come to Boston — Elsie was waked up by her sister's restlessness, and she saw Dora get up in the middle of the night and go to the window, and draw the curtain — then, because Dora started and gave a little cry, Elsie got up too, and quietly stood by her side.

There, in the opposite window, was a lady sitting, but in a dress of the olden time. A soft light fell across her figure, and they could plainly see how she wore, not the dress of the present day, but a ruff about her neck, and her hair drawn up in high powdered rolls, and a flower in the side turned towards them. She seemed to be leaning back in an old-fashioned chair with high sides, and with her hands crossed over each other in her lap — waiting — waiting.

The two girls said nothing to each other. There was a noise in the street below. They looked down; when they looked back, the lady was gone. They could see no more, and went silently to bed. This was the very night they arrived; and all the next day, in the hurry of their first arrival, and seeing many people, they had not spoken to each other of it, perhaps had not thought much of it; but in the talk of the evening I have told you of, it had all come back. This was why they had looked at each other so, but had said nothing till now they were at the window again. But now Elsie went on:

"I do think, Dora, that must have been Aunt Dora we saw last night. Poor thing! I suppose the racket they make at the theatres frightened her away; and that opposite row must be about the height that the chamber story of the old house would have been, only it is all farther front, but perhaps that makes no difference to ghosts."

"Oh, don't joke about it," exclaimed Dora, whispering. "Do you know I trust it is she indeed, grand-aunt Dora, and that she came purposely to me, to me because it is all so much the same — my fate is so like hers. Oh, Elsie, I think it was truly she."

Elsie wanted to laugh, for they always used to laugh a little over grand-aunt Dora's story, but she knew what her sister meant and what her real sorrow was.

Only two months before Dora had sat waking, yes, waking — just that way — in the window of their old country home, where they had lived all their lives so happily — with her hat on, ready for a drive, laughing and joking with Elsie.

And then — and then — he had not come. She sat waiting, then wondering, took off her hat, put it on again, but sat there all the afternoon, then looked for some message, but none ever came. Richard did not come — he never came. She had heard of him in Boston, at the West; he was going to be married, somebody said. And how it made her cheeks redden, and how it pained her to the heart to think she had waited!

Since then, sad events had befallen. They were forced to leave the dear old home, and for the saddest of causes. Their only brother, much older than they, who should have cared for them, had wasted their little property — it seemed the old country house must be sold, and they must come to Boston, and "do something." They were very fortunate, so they thought, for Elsie found a place in the Public library, only a temporary place, but she was so quick and ready we felt they could never get along without her when once they had learned her value. For they came to the house where I was living, and that is how I learned to know them, being a connection, but never having met them before. With a little bit of their earnings Dora was to take lessons in singing, for with such a voice as she had she might command a place in any choir, if only it had more cultivation.

So the two were talking together, far into the night, with hushed voices, sitting by the window, when both started. Again the same light appeared as on the night before — and again the same figure at the opposite window, and the light seemed to gather about it, like the radiance that glows in some old pictures of saints. They sat silent for some minutes, till Elsie whispered, "They said, you know, those English ladies, that if two saw — it — together, if there were two that saw it, it really was — a ghost!"

"And do you remember," Dora said, scarcely above her breath, "how they said they got attached to their ghost; and would hate to have them go away, and that it seems natural to have them — a sort of protection? and I almost feel the same at seeing her now, only, Elsie, must it be my fate, mine — to sit waiting, waiting that way? Must I grow like that? See, she seems no longer young, as she must have been when she died, or did she fade away when she did die? She looks like a rose that has been put away in a book — withered and dry — the color all gone from that scarlet poppy they told us of, and her hands crossed so quietly, looking off, waiting still. Do you think she shows herself there to encourage me, because she knows my sorrow? She makes no sign; she sits there, sits there. Perhaps always has been sitting there these long years, as you say, because she has been disturbed from the old place. But must she sit there still? How dreadful to wait and wait all this life long, and then wait on and on, and on for how long, for generations and generations!"

"O, don't go on so," cried Elsie, breaking down, and bursting into tears, as she had never done before, she was always so strong. Dora leaned over to kiss and comfort her, for her sister was kneeling by her side, and when the two turned to look back all was dark opposite — no light, no figure in the window.

"We are in a bad state," said Dora; "we must go to bed."

And the next morning when they got up, even Elsie felt gloomy, and hated to leave her sister early as she must, she looked so sad. But Dora would not let her think of staying; she was to go to her lesson herself, and her practice always cheered her up.

But afterwards it was such a comforting day. The postman in the afternoon brought a long letter to Dora, that she was long in reading, and Elsie had unexpected visitors at the library. Dora's letter had been travelling round for two or three days, had been to the country post-office and been returned. Such a long letter, and it might just as well have been shorter, for all that Dora cared for in the letter was the news that Richard was coming — might be there, so she calculated from the date, that very afternoon! She had forgotten with this news all the agony of the last two months, and would have never remembered it at this moment, if it had lasted for years, and never would have asked an explanation, nor wanted one. Sometime or other they would laugh it all over together. He had missed his train that day, it seemed, two months ago, and there was no later train to connect. It was just such an absurd accident as that had kept him! But then he foolishly sent a telegram to explain his delay, and that he could not come the next day. It was foolish, for there was no telegraph office at the little branch station, and telegrams had to go to the junction, where nobody knew them, for they never used the telegraph. How foolish indeed!

All the rest was very confused, and perhaps she never rightly understood it. How that very afternoon of the day he missed the train, he, Richard, was summoned out West, on the death of an uncle. And how he did not write because he met her brother down in the depths of despair, and ready to kill himself with repentance and despondency, everything gone wrong. It was either in Montana or Arizona, Dora always mixed up the Western States. And then Richard's own affairs were changed, because the uncle had left him money or mines, or something, and he didn't want to write to Dora till he could write certainly, and explain and plan all things for their brother, for them, and mostly for Dora and himself, and would she see him as soon as he came?

That question was easily answered, for after reading the letter over and over — for there he was, and their brother with him; and they had picked up Elsie at the library; they had to wait for her, for she was way up on the top of some steps looking for 14-90-22, or some such, and when she came down had to wait and advise some boys on their way home from school what books they had better take out and find these books for them. She would not have cared after she had once seen them, Richard and her brother, and knew it was all right, but she wanted to send them to Dora. But they waited till her hours were over, and she could come too. And such a long happy talk they had together in the evening.

The next morning, before they went down to breakfast, the two sisters stood at the window, looking across to the opposite houses.

A housemaid stood in the window there, with a whisk in her hand, and a duster over her arm. She was brushing away on the sill of the window; chairs and furniture pushed back, a rug hanging from the other window, where the blinds were wide open.

"What cobwebs she is brushing away!" said Elsie; "do you know I think there must be some electric light below that gave that strange light on the window, and made us fancy what we saw."

"No, sister," said Dora, taking Elsie by the arm. "Let me tell you — last night I could not sleep — naturally — but I could only think of her in all my joy — and late in the night I got up and went to the window again and pulled the curtain —"

"She was there again?" asked Elsie.

"She sat there so quietly, just as before," answered Dora, "but presently she slowly turned — you know we have not seen her move before — and she looked across at me — and how the face changed! All that anxious look gone — and a smile came — for she saw me, and she seemed ready to speak, and I thought she had something to say to me, and I did not want to lose her words — and I opened the window, as if I could hear what she would say, but when I put out my head there was dampness in the air, a rain was falling between, and all was darkness there! I left the window open a little that I might be sure it was no dream, and I had really stood here. And you know you spoke of the damp air in the morning."

"Yes," said Elsie, "and I knew I shut it the last thing; but do you know we were so happy that last night I forgot all about Aunt Dora."

"I think she will not come again," said Dora. "I think perhaps she only came to console me — perhaps her waiting is really over — she came only for me."

"No, she cannot come again," exclaimed Elsie, "for see all those children trooping in — and a carriage at the door, and a new family come to the rooms. And there is the nursemaid — it is to be a nursery — with the gay clatter of children —"

Dora was called away by Richard's voice, as Elsie went on: "No more room for thee, poor old ghost! Poor Aunt Dora!"

That was what I found her saying, and she told me the rest.

On the Stroke of the Clock

Ellen Louise Chandler Moulton

"There's a time in the lives of most women and men,
    When all, I say, would go smooth and even,
If but only the dead could find out when
    To come back and be forgiven."

"Of course the very idea of a ghost's revisiting the glimpses of the moon is an absurdity on the face of it. Shakespeare himself couldn't make it seem possible. His choicest ghosts smack of melodrama, and suggest blue lights and the smell of brimstone."

I was rather young when I made this remark; and I think I felt a little proud of my strength of mind, and my superiority to benighted believers in the supernatural. At least, I expected the approval of the man to whom I was talking, — a hard-headed Canadian doctor, of French descent on one side and English on the other; the very last man to own to nerves or be subject to delusions. He listened to me with a somewhat singular smile; then he blew a meditative whiff from his pipe and said quietly, —

"You seem cock-sure about it. I suppose you never *saw* a ghost?"

"I'm inclined to think neither I nor anyone else ever saw one," I answered stoutly.

"So! Let me see. It's November, I think, — the 15th of November. How lonesomely the wind howls! I remember just such a night as this, twenty-two years ago. I'll tell you the story of it. I'm a tolerably sane man, — at least, I suppose that's your present opinion, eh?"

"Rather the sanest man I know, I should say."

"Very well. I'll take that statement at its present value. You'll probably want to change it by the time I get through."

After this point our dialogue ceased, and I listened to Dr. Gerrard's story without once interrupting him. I'll drop my quotation marks therefore, and let him tell the tale just as he told it to me on the 15th of November, A. D. 1888.

Twenty-two years and two weeks ago, I came home from my mother's funeral with a desperately sad heart. My father was an Englishman, as you know. He died when I was but a boy yet I remember his resolute though kindly nature, his strength of will, his conservatism, — all about him, in short, — as well as if he had died but yesterday. I had an unbounded reverence for him, which, indeed, he well deserved but my whole boyish heart was given to my mother. She was French, and she had all a Frenchwoman's charm. She was of stately height and splendid figure, and she had great dark eyes in which I could always read her thoughts. How tender those eyes could be, and also how proud and cold! She was notably beautiful in her young days, as I have been often told since by those who remembered her. I never thought whether she was beautiful or not; I only knew she was my mother, and that I adored her.

I can remember well the passionate grief with which she mourned for my father. I truly believe that she only went on living for my sake. For my sake, too, after the first few months, she did her best to hide her grief, and to share my life, and make herself my cheerful companion as before. She had one little trick which I always associate with her memory. I was a great sleeper. She, on the contrary, was naturally an early riser, and she believed in the morning hours as the best time for all mental work. If I slept beyond seven o'clock, she always used to wake me by scratching with her delicate nails upon my pillow. I used instantly to open my eyes at this sound, and sometimes was rewarded with roses, sometimes with the motherly kisses I was so unlike most boys as really to value. Forgive me. I am dwelling too long on the past; and it is not the story of those early days that I want to tell you.

They went by quickly enough. I entered college, got through creditably, took my degree, studied medicine, and at twenty-four began my practice in my native town, where my father had been for many years a successful physician. People seemed to believe in me from the first, for his sake, and I had none of the hard struggle that usually attends the beginning of a profession. I had a paying practice, even the first year, and by the time I was twenty-six I felt myself really well established. My mother was unreasonably proud of me, — that's a kind of delusion to which mothers are subject. Not one single shadow had ever come between us, and I did not suppose that one ever could.

I was sent for one day to attend a new case in a part of the town a little out of my usual beat. I found in my patient the most beautiful girl I had ever seen, — though even then, when I was twenty-six, and my mother was forty-four, *she* might safely have challenged comparison with this lovely young creature of eighteen. My mother was dark and stately and proud, — a woman to be worshipped. Lena Grey was slight, blue-eyed, sensitive, with a gentle, appealing manner, and a shy color that came and went on her cheeks at every breath. Her illness was not very serious, — merely a sort of slow fever, — but her parents were unduly alarmed about her.

They were such people as I had been accustomed to consider quite out of my sphere, having been brought up by my mother — who had a right to a *de* before her name — in all the absurd prejudices against trade which belonged to her race. I should never have expected to find anyone with the breeding of a lady under John Grey's roof , but my mother herself was no more exquisitely refined than this girl, who soon began to seem to me the one desirable object in the whole world.

I shrank weakly from speaking about her to my mother, for I foresaw a struggle. I never dreamed, however, but that in this struggle I should speedily triumph. I made sure that my mother loved me too well to hold out long against my wishes; but I thought I would wait before speaking to her, until I was sure of Lena's heart.

That time was not long in coming. Some magnetic attraction drew us together from the very first; and when I asked her one day if she loved me, she raised her appealing eyes to my face almost reproachfully, and said, —

"Don't you *know* I do, Arthur?"

I asked her of her parents, and they promised her to me gladly. And in that moment something like a first presentiment of trouble crossed my mind. What if my mother should *not* consent?

"You must understand," I said, "that I have not spoken on this matter to my mother. I hope she will approve; but whether she does or not, remember you have promised to give me Lena. I am twenty-six years old; besides my practice I have a comfortable fortune, inherited from my father, and I am quite able to please myself."

They made some weak remonstrances against thrusting their daughter upon a family where she was not wanted, but I overruled them.

"Lena is mine," I said resolutely, as I went away; and my heart grew strong, feeling that I had her happiness to care for as well as my own.

I went to my mother, and told her my love-story. She listened in ominous silence. When I ceased speaking she said, —

"I understand that you ask my permission to present to me as your betrothed, and afterward to make your wife, the daughter of John Grey, a tradesman?"

"Yes," I answered in tones as resolute as her own; "I ask just that." And then, my voice softening in spite of myself, I cried, "Only see her *once*, and you will understand. You will know she is as truly a lady as any Gerrard or de Brie of all my ancestors; and you love me, your own boy, too well to wish to break my heart."

She rose, and stood there in the clear light, — so tall, so proud, so beautiful that it seemed as if nothing on earth could resist her. Her voice when she spoke was resolute and strong. There was not one trace in tone or manner of indecision, — not one ray of hope for me.

"It is because you are my own boy, and because with all my heart and soul I love you, that I say No, no, no! ten thousand times, no! If you choose to lift this girl out of the mud and make her your wife, you are legally free to do so. Your fortune is your own. You can rush headlong on your fate if you please; but if you marry this low-born girl, so long as God spares my life on earth I will never willingly look upon her face. If you care to see me, you must come without her, and you will spare me all mention of her name."

"Good-by, mother," I said, and I went away, leaving her standing there in the sunlight, with her great eyes flashing and her cheeks and lips glowing.

Well, I married Lena. She understood perfectly the condition of things; but she was too childlike and trusting to be made unhappy by it. She believed me entirely when I told her that she could suffice for me, — that having *her* I should want nothing else. I even believed myself for a time; but after the first surprise of marriage was over, and when I had brought my wife back from her marriage journey and settled down at home in the house I had taken, I began to feel an intolerable yearning for the mother whose love, until I knew Lena, had been the one great joy and rest of my life. Would I have been unmarried again if I could? No, I think not. I loved Lena. She was as near to me as my own soul. If only we two, made one, could have had my mother's blessing!

I wrote letters in which I prayed for this; they were never answered. I went one day to the house — my mother's house — and sent up my card like a stranger. The old man-servant brought me back a pencilled message: —

"I will receive my son with pleasure, on the understanding that the person of whom he formerly spoke to me is not to be mentioned."

To see her on those conditions seemed a sort of treachery to Lena, and I went sadly home again.

Sometimes in my professional drives I met my mother driving her fast-trotting ponies in her little phaeton where I had so often sat beside her; and we exchanged civil bows, she and I, who was flesh of her flesh and bone of her bone.

When Lena and I had been married a year, our little girl was born; and from the first it seemed as if she should have been my mother's child, not ours. She resembled neither of us; for I was like my father, a fair-haired Saxon, and this child, born of our love and our sorrow, was the very image of my mother in miniature. There was something almost uncanny in her great dark eyes, so much too large for her baby face. Her little fringe of hair was jet black, and her cheeks and lips were as bright as my mother's own.

We named the little one Virginie, — my mother's name; and as time went on, it grew to seem to me a certainty that her grandmother, however she might scorn my wife, could not withhold her heart from this child, who was so utterly hers by all the signs of nature.

186

She was a wonderfully strong and forward little creature. When she was ten months old she could say various words; and every day I showed her a large picture of my mother, and taught her to say "Grandma!" when she saw it. By the time she was fourteen months she could walk, holding by my hand; and one day I took her to see my mother, leaving my wife at home. It was a brilliant May day. The roses were beginning to bloom in sheltered nooks where the sun shone warmly; and the fruit-trees were in flower. Some birds chattered as we crossed the lawn on our way to the well-known, dear old house, and Virginie pulled my hand to make me stop and look at them; and just then my mother came round a clump of trees, and stood suddenly confronting us. Virginie glanced at her, saw the face of the picture, and put out her little hands.

"Grandma!" she cried; "grandma!"

Oddly enough, this word, which in some blind way I had relied upon to move my mother's heart, seemed to repel and offend her. She evidently considered the whole scene as a carefully planned *coup de théâtre*, and scorned it accordingly. Her face was cold; her eyes were hard; her voice cut the air like steel.

"You make a mistake," she said, "in bringing here that person's child. I do not care to see her."

And with those words she turned her back on us, and walked off deliberately.

Virginie, unused to repulse, put up her piteous, quivering lips for my healing kiss, and I hurried her away.

That ended all hope or effort on my part to be reconciled to my mother. Ought I to have striven further? Sometimes I think so now; but I did not think so then. I used to see her at a distance, from time to time, as the summer went on, and she seemed to me to be changing strangely. Her bright color was gone; her face was growing thin. Some indefinable shadow of growing old age appeared to be settling down upon her.

On the morning of the 30th of October I heard a strenuous summons at my office door, and opened it. My mother I was told had been found dead in her bed. They had sent for the nearest doctor, and he had pronounced it heart disease.

"Yes," I said to myself, "it was disease of the heart in more ways than one."

I hurried to the old home. I walked up the path on which she had met the child and me and looked at us with scorn and repulsion. Had she ever been sorry since? I wondered. Was *she* wrong in not forgiving me, or was *I* wholly to blame because I had disobeyed her in the first place? I kept asking myself these questions in a dazed way; but I did not try to answer them. My brain seemed reeling. I felt like one clutching at some crazy plank amid the surge and toss of whelming seas.

I stood by the bed on which they had laid her. Was there something unutterably strange and sad on her face, at war with the accustomed peace of death? I thought so. I knelt beside her. I do not know whether my lips uttered any cry; but I know that with all the passion of my soul I prayed her to forgive me if the wrong had been mine, — to grant me some token that she loved me still. But the cold, beautiful face did not soften; the relentless lips held their secret.

The second day of November I followed her to the grave. I did not take my wife with me. She who had been undesired and unwelcomed in my mother's life had no place at her tomb. I think, had I taken her there, I should have expected the scornful lips to break their frozen death-silence and denounce me. I was half mad with grief and remorse, and I abandoned myself to fears and instincts, but had no power to reason.

Two weeks went on. I found myself unable to fulfil my usual duties. Few of my patients were seriously ill, and I made my recent bereavement an excuse for confiding them to the care of another physician. You see I do not conceal from you the disordered state of my own mind; but I have other testimony than my own of the truth and reality of the story to which all that I have already told you is but the preface.

On the night of the 15th of November I went to bed earlier than usual, utterly exhausted by my vigils since my mother's death, and I presently fell into a deep sleep; but before I dozed off, I remember listening to the wild wails of the wind. As I said, it was a night like tonight. The unquiet wind assailed the windows, and now and then uttered a low keen cry. It made me think of a spirit in pain, and I shuddered at it. The sleep that presently overcame me was merciful.

It must have been some time past midnight when I awoke suddenly, — so wide awake that I found myself sitting up in bed and listening intently to an approaching sound. It was the rumbling of my mother's phaeton that I heard — I never could have mistaken those wheels for any others — and the quick trot of her high-stepping ponies along the hard road. The carriage stopped at my gate. I did not awaken my wife, who was sleeping beside me; but I remember thinking with a sort of dull satisfaction how securely I had barred the front door. But in spite of bars, it seemed to me that I heard it open; and I know that I heard my mother's footsteps come up the stairs and along the hall and enter my very chamber. I sank back upon the pillow and shut my eyes and feigned to be asleep; and presently — doubt it as you will — I heard upon my pillow the same scratching of her slender fingers with which she used to wake me when a boy.

I opened my eyes and saw — for a night-lamp was burning as usual — the unutterable sadness of her look. Then she moved away, and walked to the crib, where at a little distance my child was sleeping; and I give you my word that as she stood there, as if under some strange compulsion, Virginie opened her eyes, fixed them for a moment or two on my mother's face, said "Grandma!" and then threw up her little hands over her head and seemed to go to sleep again. My mother stood there looking at her for some moments; then she slowly moved away and passed out of the room, and I remember that at that very moment the clock struck one. In a moment more I heard the rumble of her phaeton and the trotting feet of her ponies, and then I put on my dressing-gown and lit a candle at the night-lamp and went downstairs.

The door was bolted and barred just as I had left it, and there was no trace anywhere of the mysterious presence that had passed. I lay awake and pondered over what had happened. Surely she had heard my prayers for her forgiveness, and she had come to show me that she had accorded it to me; and I thought she had stood so long beside the child to show me that her old stern resolution not to see her was over now. I tried to feel satisfied and relieved, but I was haunted by the sadness of her look. There must be something she wanted to convey besides her forgiveness. What could it be?

Do you wonder that I remember well the 15th of November, — the first time I ever knew, believed, or even dreamed that the dead could come again? Before that I was as scornfully sceptical as you are now. As I lay there and thought, the teasing wind blew a branch of the leafless tree against the pane with a sort of scratching sound not unlike the one with which my mother had awakened me. It made me shiver. I drew the bedclothes over my head, and finally I went to sleep.

In the morning I kept silence about what had passed, and the next night I bolted and barred the doors as usual. I did not certainly anticipate another visit from my mother, for I thought she had come to make known her forgiveness, and that being done, would stay quietly in the grave where we had laid her. Still the hour between midnight and one o'clock found me very wide awake indeed. I was certainly in no less clear possession of my faculties than I am at this moment, when I heard again the rumble of that phaeton, the feet of those ponies. This time my mother had no need to waken me.

My eyes met hers as she entered the room. I had left the night-lamp a little higher than before. I saw that she was dressed as she was when we laid her in her coffin, in a rich, soft-falling gown of heavy black satin. I could see on her finger her wedding-ring, the only one we had buried with her.

This time she did not come to my bedside, but she went and bent over the child's; and again, as by some strange compulsion, the little one opened her eyes and murmured rather sleepily, "Grandma, come again!" and in a moment was once more asleep. But no smile came to the sad eyes that were watching her; the shadow of an immortal pain seemed on the face which death had given back. I longed to speak to her, but I could not. My throat was parched. My tongue would not move. I hardly breathed.

Suddenly the clock struck one, and on the stroke of it she vanished.

The next morning I told my wife. She was strongly impressed by my story, which she never thought of arguing away, or even of questioning. She begged me if our visitor ever came again to awaken her, which finally with some reluctance I promised to do.

The third night arrived, and I was mercifully able to go to sleep. I did not hear the rumble of the phaeton at the gate or the feet of the ponies. I heard nothing, indeed, until the sound of the delicate fingers I knew so well, scratching on my pillow as of old, awakened me. I opened my eyes, and the sad eyes of the dead met them; and then, as before, my mother moved away and stood over the bed of my little Virginie.

"Lena!" I whispered to my wife.

She slipped her hand into mine.

"I hear," she answered in a low whisper. "I am watching her. I think she wants something."

Low as her whisper was, evidently my mother heard it, for a look of unmistakable relief and hope crossed her face. My wife was observing her closely, and her woman's instinct supplied the interpretation of this look as my duller wits never could have done.

"I think," Lena said slowly, "that she wants us to forgive *her*."

These words seemed to me a sort of sacrilege. I would have thrown myself at my mother's feet and prayed anew for her forgiveness, but some power outside myself restrained me. And surely a look of relief, as of one who is understood at last after long endeavor, dawned upon her face, and yet she seemed not quite satisfied. Then Lena spoke, and her voice sounded to me like that of an angel whom love had made strong; and she said with gentle clearness of tone, —

"Yes, mother, we forgive you with all our hearts."

And as if constrained and almost against my will, I too said after her, as one says "amen" after a prayer, "With all our hearts."

And just at that moment Virginie opened her eyes and cried, "Grandma, come again!" and though my eyes were dim with a rush of sudden tears, it seemed to me that I saw my mother bend toward her, and the child's arms reach up for an instant to her neck.

And then my mother lifted her face, her happy face, and there was a light in her great eyes such as made me think of the days of her youth, when she used to welcome my father home. Her lips moved. I thought they formed the words, "Good-by, children!"

And at that moment the clock struck one, and she was gone. Then I heard for the last time the rumble of her departing wheels, and Lena heard it also, and cried softly and silently as she lay there with her head on my bosom.

One day, a week afterward, Virginie said, —

"Grandma never comes anymore;" and we knew that the child remembered.

No, I never saw any other ghost; why should I? I do not think they are visitors of every day; but I know — whether it be possible for the dead to return or not — that twenty-two years ago this night I saw my mother, who had been two weeks buried, stand at my bedside.

The Gray Man

Sarah Orne Jewett

High on the southern slope of Agamenticus there may still be seen the remnant of an old farm. Frost-shaken stone walls surround a fast-narrowing expanse of smooth turf which the forest is overgrowing on every side. The cellar is nearly filled up, never having been either wide or deep, and the fruit of a few mossy apple-trees drops ungathered to the ground. Along one side of the forsaken garden is a thicket of seedling cherry-trees to which the shouting robins come year after year in busy flights; the caterpillars' nests are unassailed and populous in this untended hedge. At night, perhaps, when summer twilights are late in drawing their brown curtain of dusk over the great rural scene, at night an owl may sit in the hemlocks nearby and hoot and shriek until the far echoes answer back again. As for the few men and women who pass this deserted spot, most will be repulsed by such loneliness, will even grow impatient with those mistaken fellow-beings who choose to live in solitude, away from neighbors and from schools, — yes, even from gossip and petty care of self or knowledge of the trivial fashions of a narrow life.

Now and then one looks out from this eyrie, across the wide-spread country, who turns to look at the sea or toward the shining foreheads of the mountains that guard the inland horizon, who will remember the place long afterward. A peaceful vision will come, full of rest and benediction into busy and troubled hours, to those who understand why someone came to live in this place so near the sky, so silent, so full of sweet air and woodland fragrance; so beaten and buffeted by winter storms and garlanded with summer greenery; where the birds are nearest neighbors and a clear spring the only wine-cellar, and trees of the forest a choir of singers who rejoice and sing aloud by day and night as the winds sweep over. Under the cherry thicket or at the edge of the woods you may find a stray-away blossom, some half-savage, slender grand-child of the old flower-plots, that you gather gladly to take away, and every year in June a red rose blooms toward which the wild pink roses and the pale sweet briars turn wondering faces as if a queen had shown her noble face suddenly at a peasant's festival.

There is everywhere a token of remembrance, of silence and secrecy. Some stronger nature once ruled these neglected trees and this fallow ground. They will wait the return of their master as long as roots can creep through mould, and the mould make way for them. The stories of strange lives have been whispered to the earth, their thoughts have burned themselves into the cold rocks. As one looks from the lower country toward the long slope of the great hillside, this old abiding-place marks the dark covering of trees like a scar. There is nothing to hide either the sunrise or the sunset. The low lands reach out of sight into the west and the sea fills all the east.

The first owner of the farm was a seafaring man who had through freak or fancy come ashore and cast himself upon the bounty of nature for support in his later years, though tradition keeps a suspicion of buried treasure and of a dark history. He cleared his land and built his house, but save the fact that he was a Scotsman no one knew to whom he belonged, and when he died the state inherited the unclaimed property. The only piece of woodland that was worth anything was sold and added to another farm, and the dwelling-place was left to the sunshine and the rain, to the birds that built their nests in the chimney or under the eaves. Sometimes a strolling company of country boys would find themselves near the house on a holiday afternoon, but the more dilapidated the small structure became, the more they believed that some uncanny existence possessed the lonely place, and the path that led toward the clearing at last became almost impassable.

Once a number of officers and men in the employ of the Coast Survey were encamped at the top of the mountain, and they smoothed the rough track that led down to the spring that bubbled from under a sheltering edge. One day a laughing fellow, not content with peering in at the small windows of the house, put his shoulder against the rain-blackened door and broke the simple fastening. He hardly knew that he was afraid as he first stood within the single spacious room, so complete a curiosity took possession of him. The place was clean and bare, the empty cupboard doors stood open, and yet the sound of his companions' voices outside seemed far away, and an awful sense that some unseen inhabitant followed his footsteps made him hurry out again pale and breathless to the fresh air and sunshine. Was this really a dwelling-place of spirits, as had been already hinted? The story grew more fearful, and spread quickly like a mist of terror among the lowland farms. For years the tale of the coast-surveyor's adventure in the haunted house was slowly magnified and told to strangers or to wide-eyed children by the dim firelight. The former owner was supposed to linger still about his old home, and was held accountable for deep offense in choosing for the scene of his unsuccessful husbandry a place that escaped the proprieties and restraints of life upon lower levels. His grave was concealed by the new growth of oaks and beeches, and many a lad and full-grown man beside has taken to his heels at the flicker of light from across a swamp or under a decaying tree in that neighborhood. As the world in some respects grew wiser, the good people near the mountain understood less and less the causes of these simple effects, and as they became familiar with the visible world, grew more shy of the unseen and more sensitive to unexplained foreboding.

One day a stranger was noticed in the town, as a stranger is sure to be who goes his way with quick, furtive steps straight through a small village or along a country road. This man was tall and had just passed middle age. He was well made and vigorous, but there was an unusual pallor in his face, a grayish look, as if he had been startled by bad news. His clothes were somewhat peculiar, as if they had been made in another country, yet they suited the chilly weather, being homespun of undyed wools, just the color of his hair, and only a little darker than his face or hands. Someone observed in one brief glance as he and this gray man met and passed each other, that his eyes had a strange faded look; they might, however, flash and be coal-black in a moment of rage. Two or three persons stepped forward to watch the wayfarer as he went along the road with long, even strides, like one taking a journey on foot, but he quickly reached a turn of the way and was out of sight. They wondered who he was; one recalled some recent advertisement of an escaped criminal, and another the appearance of a native of the town who was supposed to be long ago lost at sea, but one surmiser knew as little as the next. If they had followed fast enough they might have tracked the mysterious man straight across the country, threading the by-ways, the shorter paths that led across the fields where the road was roundabout and hindering. At last he disappeared in the leafless, trackless woods that skirted the mountain.

That night there was for the first time in many years a twinkling light in the window of the haunted house, high on the hill's great shoulder; one farmer's wife and another looked up curiously, while they wondered what daring human being had chosen that awesome spot of all others for his home or for even a transient shelter. The sky was already heavy with snow; he might be a fugitive from justice, and the startled people looked to the fastening of their doors unwontedly that night, and waked often from a troubled sleep.

An instinctive curiosity and alarm possessed the country men and women for a while, but soon faded out and disappeared. The newcomer was by no means a hermit; he tried to be friendly, and inclined toward a certain kindliness and familiarity. He bought a comfortable store of winter provisions from his new acquaintances, giving everyone his price, and spoke more at length, as time went on, of current events, of politics and the weather, and the town's own news and concerns. There was a sober cheerfulness about the man, as if he had known trouble and perplexity, and was fulfilling some mission that gave him pain; yet he saw some gain and reward beyond; therefore he could be contented with his life and such strange surroundings. He was more and more eager to form brotherly relations with the farmers near his home. There was almost a pleading look in his kind face at times, as if he feared the later prejudice of his associates. Surely this was no common or uneducated person, for in every way he left the stamp of his character and influence upon men and things. His reasonable words of advice and warning are current as sterling coins in that region yet; to one man he taught a new rotation of crops, to another he gave some priceless cures for devastating diseases of cattle. The lonely women of those remote country homes learned of him how to achieve their household toil with less labor and drudgery, and here and there he singled out promising children and kept watch of their growth, giving freely a most affectionate companionship, and a fair start in the journey of life. He taught those who were guardians of such children to recognize and further the true directions and purposes of existence; and the easily warped natures grew strong and well-established under his thoughtful care. No wonder that some people were filled with amazement, and thought his wisdom supernatural, from so many proofs that his horizon was wider than their own.

Perhaps some envious soul, or one aggrieved by being caught in treachery or deception, was the first to find fault with the stranger. The prejudice against his dwelling-place, and the superstition which had become linked to him in consequence, may have led back to the first vicious attitude of the community. The whisper of distrust soon started on an evil way. If he were not a criminal, his past was surely a hidden one, and shocking to his remembrance, but the true foundation of all dislike was the fact that the gray man who went to and fro, living his simple, harmless life among them, *never was seen to smile.* Persons who remember him speak of this with a shudder, for nothing is more evident than that his peculiarity became at length intolerable to those whose minds lent themselves readily to suspicion. At first, blinded by the gentle good fellowship of the stranger, the changeless expression of his face was scarcely observed, but as the winter wore away he was watched with renewed disbelief and dismay.

After the first few attempts at gayety nobody tried to tell a merry story in his presence. The most conspicuous of a joker's audience does a deep-rankling injustice if he sits with unconscious, unamused face at the receipt of raillery. What a chilling moment when the gray man softly opened the door of a farmhouse kitchen, and seated himself like a skeleton at the feast of walnuts and roasted apples beside the glowing fire! The children whom he treated so lovingly, to whom he ever gave his best, though they were won at first by his gentleness, when they began to prattle and play with him would raise their innocent eyes to his face and hush their voices and creep away out of his sight. Once only he was bidden to a wedding, but never afterward, for a gloom was quickly spread through the boisterous company; the man who never smiled had no place at such a festival. The wedding guests looked over their shoulders again and again in strange foreboding, while he was in the house, and were burdened with a sense of coming woe for the newly-married pair. As one caught sight of his, among the faces of the rural folk, the gray man was like a sombre mask, and at last the bridegroom flung open the door with a meaning gesture, and the stranger went out like a hunted creature, into the bitter coldness and silence of the winter night.

Through the long days of the next summer the outcast of the wedding, forbidden, at length, all the once-proffered hospitality, was hardly seen from one week's end to another's. He cultivated his poor estate with patient care, and the successive crops of his small garden, the fruits and berries of the wilderness, were food enough. He seemed unchangeable, and was always ready when he even guessed at a chance to be of use. If he were repulsed, he only turned away and went back to his solitary home. Those persons who by chance visited him there tell wonderful tales of the wild birds which had been tamed to come at his call and cluster about him, of the orderliness and delicacy of his simple life. The once-neglected house was covered with vines that he had brought from the woods, and planted about the splintering, decaying walls. There were three or four books in worn bindings on a shelf above the fire-place; one longs to know what volumes this mysterious exile had chosen to keep him company!

There may have been a deeper reason for the withdrawal of friendliness; there are vague rumors of the gray man's possession of strange powers. Some say that he was gifted with amazing strength, and once when some belated hunters found shelter at his fireside, they told eager listeners afterward that he did not sleep but sat by the fire reading gravely while they slumbered uneasily on his own bed of boughs. And in the dead of night an empty chair glided silently toward him across the floor as he softly turned his pages in the flickering light.

But such stories are too vague, and in that neighborhood too common to weigh against the true dignity and bravery of the man. At the beginning of the war of the rebellion he seemed strangely troubled and disturbed, and presently disappeared, leaving his house key with a neighbor as if for a few days' absence. He was last seen striding rapidly through the village a few miles away, going back along the road by which he had come a year or two before. No, not last seen either; for in one of the first battles of the war, as the smoke suddenly lifted, a farmer's boy, reared in the shadow of the mountain, opened his languid pain-dulled eyes as he lay among the wounded, and saw the gray man riding by on a tall horse. At that moment the poor lad thought in his faintness and fear that Death himself rode by in the gray man's likeness; unsmiling — Death who tries to teach and serve mankind so that he may at the last win welcome as a faithful friend!

The Giant Wistaria

Charlotte Perkins Gilman

"Meddle not with my new vine, child! See! Thou hast already broken the tender shoot! Never needle or distaff for thee, and yet thou wilt not be quiet!"

The nervous fingers wavered, clutched at a small carnelian cross that hung from her neck, then fell despairingly.

"Give me my child, mother, and then I will be quiet!"

"Hush! hush! thou fool — someone might be near! See — there is thy father coming, even now! Get in quickly!"

She raised her eyes to her mother's face, weary eyes that yet had a flickering, uncertain blaze in their shaded depths.

"Art thou a mother and hast no pity on me, a mother? Give me my child!"

Her voice rose in a strange, low cry, broken by her father's hand upon her mouth.

"Shameless!" said he, with set teeth. "Get to thy chamber, and be not seen again tonight, or I will have thee bound!"

She went at that, and a hard-faced serving woman followed, and presently returned, bringing a key to her mistress.

"Is all well with her — and the child also?"

"She is quiet, Mistress Dwining, well for the night, be sure. The child fretteth endlessly, but save for that it thriveth with me."

The parents were left alone together on the high square porch with its great pillars, and the rising moon began to make faint shadows of the young vine leaves that shot up luxuriantly around them; moving shadows, like little stretching fingers, on the broad and heavy planks of the oaken floor.

"It groweth well, this vine thou broughtest me in the ship, my husband."

"Aye," he broke in bitterly, "and so doth the shame I brought thee! Had I known of it I would sooner have had the ship founder beneath us, and have seen our child cleanly drowned, than live to this end!"

"Thou art very hard, Samuel, art thou not afeard for her life? She grieveth sore for the child, aye, and for the green fields to walk in!"

"Nay," said he grimly, "I fear not. She hath lost already what is more than life; and she shall have air enough soon. Tomorrow the ship is ready, and we return to England. None knoweth of our stain here, not one, and if the town hath a child unaccounted for to rear in decent ways — why, it is not the first, even here. It will be well enough cared for! And truly we have matter for thankfulness, that her cousin is yet willing to marry her."

"Hast thou told him?"

"Aye! Thinkest thou I would cast shame into another man's house, unknowing it? He hath always desired her, but she would none of him, the stubborn! She hath small choice now!"

"Will he be kind, Samuel? Can he —"

"Kind? What call'st thou it to take such as she to wife? Kind! How many men would take her, an' she had double the fortune? And being of the family already, he is glad to hide the blot forever."

"An' if she would not? He is but a coarse fellow, and she ever shunned him."

"Art thou mad, woman? She weddeth him ere we sail tomorrow, or she stayeth ever in that chamber. The girl is not so sheer a fool! He maketh an honest woman of her, and saveth our house from open shame. What other hope for her than a new life to cover the old? Let her have an honest child, an' she so longeth for one!"

He strode heavily across the porch, till the loose planks creaked again, strode back and forth, with his arms folded and his brows fiercely knit above his iron mouth.

Overhead the shadows flickered mockingly across a white face among the leaves, with eyes of wasted fire.

"O, George, what a house! What a lovely house! I am sure it's haunted! Let us get that house to live in this summer! We will have Kate and Jack and Susy and Jim of course, and a splendid time of it!"

Young husbands are indulgent, but still they have to recognize facts.

"My dear, the house may not be to rent; and it may also not be habitable."

"There is surely somebody in it. I am going to inquire!"

The great central gate was rusted off its hinges, and the long drive had trees in it, but a little footpath showed signs of steady usage, and up that Mrs. Jenny went, followed by her obedient George. The front windows of the old mansion were blank, but in a wing at the back they found white curtains and open doors. Outside, in the clear May sunshine, a woman was washing. She was polite and friendly, and evidently glad of visitors in that lonely place. She "guessed it could be rented — didn't know." The heirs were in Europe, but "there was a lawyer in New York had the lettin' of it." There had been folks there years ago, but not in her time. She and her husband had the rent of their part for taking care of the place. Not that they took much care on't either, "but keepin' robbers out." It was furnished throughout, old-fashioned enough, but good; and "if they took it she could do the work for 'em herself, she guessed — if *he* was willin'!"

Never was a crazy scheme more easily arranged. George knew that lawyer in New York; the rent was not alarming; and the nearness to a rising sea-shore resort made it a still pleasanter place to spend the summer.

Kate and Jack and Susy and Jim cheerfully accepted, and the June moon found them all sitting on the high front porch.

They had explored the house from top to bottom, from the great room in the garret, with nothing in it but a rickety cradle, to the well in the cellar without a curb and with a rusty chain going down to unknown blackness below. They had explored the grounds, once beautiful with rare trees and shrubs, but now a gloomy wilderness of tangled shade.

The old lilacs and laburnums, the spirea and syringa, nodded against the second-story windows. What garden plants survived were great ragged bushes or great shapeless beds. A huge wistaria vine covered the whole front of the house. The trunk, it was too large to call a stem, rose at the corner of the porch by the high steps, and had once climbed its pillars; but now the pillars were wrenched from their places and held rigid and helpless by the tightly wound and knotted arms.

It fenced in all the upper story of the porch with a knitted wall of stem and leaf; it ran along the eaves, holding up the gutter that had once supported it; it shaded every window with heavy green; and the drooping, fragrant blossoms made a waving sheet of purple from roof to ground.

"Did you ever see such a wistaria!" cried ecstatic Mrs. Jenny. "It is worth the rent just to sit under such a vine — a fig tree beside it would be sheer superfluity and wicked extravagance!"

"Jenny makes much of her wistaria," said George, "because she's so disappointed about the ghosts. She made up her mind at first sight to have ghosts in the house, and she can't find even a ghost story!"

"No," Jenny assented mournfully; "I pumped poor Mrs. Pepperill for three days, but could get nothing out of her. But I'm convinced there is a story, if we could only find it. You need not tell me that a house like this, with a garden like this, and a cellar like this, isn't haunted!"

"I agree with you," said Jack. Jack was a reporter on a New York daily, and engaged to Mrs. Jenny's pretty sister. "And if we don't find a real ghost, you may be very sure I shall make one. It's too good an opportunity to lose!"

The pretty sister, who sat next him, resented. "You shan't do anything of the sort, Jack! This is a *real* ghostly place, and I won't have you make fun of it! Look at that group of trees out there in the long grass — it looks for all the world like a crouching, hunted figure!"

"It looks to me like a woman picking huckleberries," said Jim, who was married to George's pretty sister.

"Be still, Jim!" said that fair young woman. "I believe in Jenny's ghost as much as she does. Such a place! Just look at this great wistaria trunk crawling up by the steps here! It looks for all the world like a writhing body — cringing — beseeching!"

"Yes," answered the subdued Jim, "it does, Susy. See its waist, — about two yards of it, and twisted at that! A waste of good material!"

"Don't be so horrid, boys! Go off and smoke somewhere if you can't be congenial!"

"We can! We will! We'll be as ghostly as you please." And forthwith they began to see bloodstains and crouching figures so plentifully that the most delightful shivers multiplied, and the fair enthusiasts started for bed, declaring they should never sleep a wink.

"We shall all surely dream," cried Mrs. Jenny, "and we must all tell our dreams in the morning!"

"There's another thing certain," said George, catching Susy as she tripped over a loose plank; "and that is that you frisky creatures must use the side door till I get this Eiffel tower of a portico fixed, or we shall have some fresh ghosts on our hands! We found a plank here that yawns like a trap-door — big enough to swallow you — and I believe the bottom of the thing is in China!"

The next morning found them all alive, and eating a substantial New England breakfast, to the accompaniment of saws and hammers on the porch, where carpenters of quite miraculous promptness were tearing things to pieces generally.

"It's got to come down mostly," they had said. "These timbers are clean rotted through, what ain't pulled out o' line by this great creeper. That's about all that holds the thing up."

There was clear reason in what they said, and with a caution from anxious Mrs. Jenny not to hurt the wistaria, they were left to demolish and repair at leisure.

"How about ghosts?" asked Jack after a fourth griddle cake. "I had one, and it's taken away my appetite!"

Mrs. Jenny gave a little shriek and dropped her knife and fork.

"Oh, so had I! I had the most awful — well, not dream exactly, but feeling. I had forgotten all about it!"

"Must have been awful," said Jack, taking another cake. "Do tell us about the feeling. My ghost will wait."

"It makes me creep to think of it even now," she said. "I woke up, all at once, with that dreadful feeling as if something were going to happen, you know! I was wide awake, and hearing every little sound for miles around, it seemed to me. There are so many strange little noises in the country for all it is so still. Millions of crickets and things outside, and all kinds of rustles in the trees! There wasn't much wind, and the moonlight came through in my three great windows in three white squares on the black old floor, and those fingery wistaria leaves we were talking of last night just seemed to crawl all over them. And — O, girls, you know that dreadful well in the cellar?"

A most gratifying impression was made by this, and Jenny proceeded cheerfully:

"Well, while it was so horridly still, and I lay there trying not to wake George, I heard as plainly as if it were right in the room, that old chain down there rattle and creak over the stones!"

"Bravo!" cried Jack. "That's fine! I'll put it in the Sunday edition!"

"Be still!" said Kate. "What was it, Jenny? Did you really see anything?"

"No, I didn't, I'm sorry to say. But just then I didn't want to. I woke George, and made such a fuss that he gave me bromide, and said he'd go and look, and that's the last I thought of it till Jack reminded me, — the bromide worked so well."

"Now, Jack, give us yours," said Jim. "Maybe, it will dovetail in somehow. Thirsty ghost, I imagine; maybe they had prohibition here even then!"

Jack folded his napkin, and leaned back in his most impressive manner.

"It was striking twelve by the great hall clock —" he began.

"There isn't any hall clock!"

"O hush, Jim, you spoil the current! It was just one o'clock then, by my old-fashioned repeater."

"Waterbury! Never mind what time it was!"

"Well, honestly, I woke up sharp, like our beloved hostess, and tried to go to sleep again, but couldn't. I experienced all those moonlight and grasshopper sensations, just like Jenny, and was wondering what could have been the matter with the supper, when in came my ghost, and I knew it was all a dream! It was a female ghost, and I imagine she was young and handsome, but all those crouching, hunted figures of last evening ran riot in my brain, and this poor creature looked just like them. She was all wrapped up in a shawl, and had a big bundle under her arm, — dear me, I am spoiling the story! With the air and gait of one in frantic haste and terror, the muffled figure glided to a dark old bureau, and seemed taking things from the drawers. As she turned, the moonlight shone full on a little red cross that hung from her neck by a thin gold chain — I saw it glitter as she crept noiselessly from the room! That's all."

"O Jack, don't be so horrid! Did you really? Is that all? What do you think it was?"

"I am not horrid by nature, only professionally. I really did. That was all. And I am fully convinced it was the genuine, legitimate ghost of an eloping chambermaid with kleptomania!"

"You are too bad, Jack!" cried Jenny. "You take all the horror out of it. There isn't a 'creep' left among us."

"It's no time for creeps at nine-thirty A.M., with sunlight and carpenters outside! However, if you can't wait till twilight for your creeps, I think I can furnish one or two," said George. "I went down cellar after Jenny's ghost!"

There was a delighted chorus of female voices, and Jenny cast upon her lord a glance of genuine gratitude.

"It's all very well to lie in bed and see ghosts, or hear them," he went on. "But the young householder suspecteth burglars, even though as a medical man he knoweth nerves, and after Jenny dropped off I started on a voyage of discovery. I never will again, I promise you!"

"Why, what *was* it?"

"Oh, George!"

"I got a candle —"

"Good mark for the burglars," murmured Jack.

"And went all over the house, gradually working down to the cellar and the well."

"Well?" said Jack.

"Now you can laugh; but that cellar is no joke by daylight, and a candle there at night is about as inspiring as a lightning-bug in the Mammoth Cave. I went along with the light, trying not to fall into the well prematurely; got to it all at once; held the light down and *then* I saw, right under my feet — (I nearly fell over her, or walked through her, perhaps), — a woman, hunched up under a shawl! She had hold of the chain, and the candle shone on her hands — white, thin hands, — on a little red cross that hung from her neck — *vide* Jack! I'm no believer in ghosts, and I firmly object to unknown parties in the house at night; so I spoke to her rather fiercely. She didn't seem to notice that, and I reached down to take hold of her, — then I came upstairs!"

"What for?"

"What happened?"

"What was the matter?"

"Well, nothing happened. Only she wasn't there! May have been indigestion, of course, but as a physician I don't advise anyone to court indigestion alone at midnight in a cellar!"

"This is the most interesting and peripatetic and evasive ghost I ever heard of!" said Jack. "It's my belief she has no end of silver tankards, and jewels galore, at the bottom of that well, and I move we go and see!"

"To the bottom of the well, Jack?"

"To the bottom of the mystery. Come on!"

There was unanimous assent, and the fresh cambrics and pretty boots were gallantly escorted below by gentlemen whose jokes were so frequent that many of them were a little forced.

The deep old cellar was so dark that they had to bring lights, and the well so gloomy in its blackness that the ladies recoiled.

"That well is enough to scare even a ghost. It's my opinion you'd better let well enough alone!" quoth Jim.

"Truth lies hid in a well, and we must get her out," said George. "Bear a hand with the chain?"

Jim pulled away on the chain, George turned the creaking windlass, and Jack was chorus.

"A wet sheet for this ghost, if not a flowing sea," said he. "Seems to be hard work raising spirits! I suppose he kicked the bucket when he went down!"

As the chain lightened and shortened there grew a strained silence among them; and when at length the bucket appeared, rising slowly through the dark water, there was an eager, half reluctant peering, and a natural drawing back. They poked the gloomy contents. "Only water."

"Nothing but mud."

"Something —"

They emptied the bucket up on the dark earth, and then the girls all went out into the air, into the bright warm sunshine in front of the house, where was the sound of saw and hammer, and the smell of new wood. There was nothing said until the men joined them, and then Jenny timidly asked:

"How old should you think it was, George?"

"All of a century," he answered. "That water is a preservative, — lime in it. Oh! — you mean? — Not more than a month; a very little baby!"

There was another silence at this, broken by a cry from the workmen. They had removed the floor and the side walls of the old porch, so that the sunshine poured down to the dark stones of the cellar bottom. And there, in the strangling grasp of the roots of the great wistaria, lay the bones of a woman, from whose neck still hung a tiny scarlet cross on a thin chain of gold.

The Soul of Rose Dédé

Mollie Evelyn Moore Davis

The child pushed his way through the tall weeds, which were dripping with the midsummer-eve midnight dew-melt. He was so little that the rough leaves met above his head. He wore a trailing white gown whose loose folds tripped him, so that he stumbled and fell over a sunken mound. But he laughed as he scrambled to his feet — a cooing baby laugh, taken up by the inward-blowing Gulf wind, and carried away to the soughing pines that made a black line against the dim sky.

His progress was slow, for he stopped — his forehead gravely puckered, his finger in his mouth to listen to the clear whistle of a mocking-bird in the live-oak above his head; he watched the heavy flight of a white night-moth from one jimson-weed trumpet to another; he strayed aside to pick a bit of shining punk from the sloughing bark of a rotten log; he held this in his closed palm as he came at last into the open space where the others were.

"Holà, 'Tit-Pierre!" said André, who was half reclining on a mildewed marble slab, with his long black cloak floating loosely from his shoulders, and his hands clasped about his knees. "Holà! Must thou needs be ever a-searching! Have I not told thee, little Hard-Head, that she hath long forgotten thee?"

His voice was mocking, but his dark eyes were quizzically kind.

The child's under-lip quivered, and he turned slowly about. But Père Lebas, sitting just across the narrow footway, laid a caressing hand on his curly head. "Nay, go thy way, 'Tit Pierre," he said, gently, "André does but tease. A mother hath never yet forgot her child."

"Do you indeed think he will find her?" asked André, arching his black brows incredulously.

"He will not find her," returned the priest. "Margot Caillion was in a far country when I saw her last, and even then her grandchildren were playing about her knees. But it harms not the child to seek her."

They spoke a soft provincial French, and the familiar *thou* betokened an unwonted intimacy between the hollow-cheeked old priest and his companion, whose forehead wore the frankness of early youth.

"I would the child could talk!" cried the young man, gayly. "Then might he tell us somewhat of the women that ever come and go in yonder great house."

The priest shuddered, crossing himself, and drew his cowl over his face.

'Tit-Pierre, his gown gathered in his arm, had gone on his way. Nathan Pilger, hunched up on a low, irregular hummock against the picket-fence, made a speaking-trumpet of his two horny hands, and pretended to hail him as he passed. 'Tit-Pierre nodded brightly at the old man, and waved his own chubby fist.

The gate sagged a little on its hinges, so that he had some difficulty in moving it. But he squeezed through a narrow opening, and passed between the prim flower-beds to the house.

It was a lofty mansion, with vast wings on either side, and wide galleries, which were upheld by fluted columns. It faced the bay, and a covered arcade ran from the entrance across the lawn to a gay little wooden kiosk, which hung on the bluff over the water's edge. A flight of stone steps led up to the house. 'Tit-Pierre climbed these laboriously. The great carved doors were closed, but a blind of one of the long French windows in the west wing stood slightly ajar. 'Tit-Pierre pushed this open. The bed-chamber into which he peered was large and luxuriously furnished. A lamp with a crimson shade burned on its claw-footed gilt pedestal in a corner; the low light diffused a rosy radiance about the room. The filmy curtains at the windows waved to and fro softly in the June night wind. The huge old-fashioned, four-posted bed, overhung by a baldachin of carved wood with satin linings, occupied a deep alcove. A woman was sleeping there beneath the lace netting. The snow-white bed-linen followed the contours of her rounded limbs, giving her the look of a recumbent marble statue. Her black hair, loosed from its heavy coil, spread over the pillow. One exquisite bare arm lay across her forehead, partly concealing her face. Her measured breathing rose and fell rhythmically on the air. A robe of pale silk that hung across a chair, dainty lace-edged garments tossed carelessly on an antique lounge — these seemed instinct still with the nameless, subtle grace of her who had but now put them off.

On a table by the window, upon whose threshold the child stood atiptoe, was set a large crystal bowl filled with water-lilies. Their white petals were folded; the round, red-lined green leaves glistened in the lamp-light. One long bud, rolled tightly in its green and brown sheath, hung over the fluted edge of the bowl, swaying gently on its flexible stem. 'Tit-Pierre gazed at it intently, frowning a little, then put out a small forefinger and touched it. A quick thrill ran along the stem; the bud moved lightly from side to side and burst suddenly into bloom; the slim white petals quivered; a tremulous, sighing, whispering sound issued from the heart of gold. The child listened, holding the fragrant disk to his pink ear, and laughed softly.

He moved about the room; examining with infantile curiosity the costly objects scattered upon small tables and ranged upon the low, many-shelved mantel.

Presently he pushed a chair against the foot of the bed, climbed upon it, lifted the netting, and crept cautiously to the sleeper's side. He sat for a moment regarding her. Her lips were parted in a half-smile; the long lashes which swept her cheeks were wet, as if a happy tear had just trembled there. 'Tit-Pierre laid his hand on her smooth wrist, and touched timidly the snowy globes that gleamed beneath the open-work of her night-dress. She threw up her arm, turning her face full upon him, unclosed her large, luminous eyes, smiled, and slept again.

With a sigh, which seemed rather of resignation than of disappointment, the child crept away and clambered again to the floor

... Outside the fog was thickening. The dark waters of the bay lapped the foot of the low bluff; their soft, monotonous moan was rising by imperceptible degrees to a higher key. The scrubby cedars, leaning at all angles over the water, were shaken at intervals by heavy puffs of wind, which drove the mist in white, ragged masses across the shelled road, over the weedy neutral ground, and out into the tops of the sombre pines. The red lights in a row of sloops at anchor over against

Cat Island had dwindled to faintly glimmering sparks. The watery flash of the revolving light in the light-house off the point of the island showed a black wedge-shaped cloud stretching up the seaward sky.

Nathan Pilger screwed up his eye and watched the cloud critically. André followed the direction of his gaze with idle interest, then turned to look again at the woman who sat on a grassy barrow a few paces beyond Père Lebas.

"She has never been here before," he said to himself, his heart stirring curiously. "I would I could see her face!"

Her back was towards the little group; her elbow was on her knee, her chin in her hand. Her figure was slight and girlish; her white gown gleamed ghostlike in the wan light.

"Naw, I bain't complainin', nor nothin'," said the old sailor, dropping the cloud, as it were, and taking up a broken thread of talk; "hows'ever, it's tarnation wearyin' a-settin' here so studdy year in an' year out. Leas'ways," he added, shifting his seat to another part of the low mound, "fer an old sailor sech as I be."

"If one could but quit his place and move about, like 'Tit-Pierre yonder," said André, musingly, it would not be so bad. For myself, I would not want —"

"The child is free to come and go because his soul is white. There is no stain upon 'Tit-Pierre. The child hath not sinned." It was the priest who spoke. His voice was harsh and forbidding. His deep-set eyes were fixed upon the tall spire of Our Lady of the Gulf, dimly outlined against the sky beyond an intervening reach of clustering roofs and shaded gardens.

André stared at him wonderingly, and glanced half furtively at the stranger, as if in her presence, perchance, might be found an explanation of the speaker's unwonted bitterness of tone. She had not moved. "I would I could see her face!" he muttered, under his breath. "For myself," he went on, lifting his voice, "I am sure I would not want to wander far. I fain would walk once more on the road along the curve of the bay; or under the pines, where little white patches of moonlight fall between the straight, tall tree-trunks. And I would go sometimes, if I might, and kneel before the altar of Our Lady of the Gulf."

Nathan Pilger grunted contemptuously. "What a lan'lubber ye be, Andry!" he said, his strong nasal English contrasting oddly with the smooth foreign speech of the others. "What a lan'lubber ye be! Ye bain't no sailor, like your father afore ye. Tony Dewdonny hed as good a pair o' sea-legs as ever I see. Lord! if there wa'n't no dif*fick*ulties in the way, Nathan Pilger'd ship fer some port a leetle more furrin than the shadder of Our Lady yunder! Many's the deck I've walked," he continued, his husky voice growing more and more animated, "an' many's the vi'ge I've made to outlandish places. Why, you'd oughter see Arkangel, Andry. Here's the north coast o' Rooshy" — he leaned over and traced with his forefinger the rude outlines of a map on the ground; the wind lifted his long, gray locks and tossed them over his wrinkled forehead; "here's the White Sea; and here, off the mouth of the Dewiny River, is Arkangel. The Rooshan men in that there town, Andry, wears petticoats like women; whilse down here, in the South Pacific, at Taheety, the folks don't wear no clo'es at all to speak of! You'd oughter see Taheety, Andry. An' here, off Guinea —"

"All those places are fine, no doubt," interrupted his listener, "Arkangel and Tahee*tee* and Guin*ee*" — his tongue tripped a little over the unfamiliar names — "but, for myself, I do not care to see them. I find it well on the bay shore here, where I can see the sloops come sailing in through the pass, with the sun on their white sails. And the little boats that rock on the water! Do you remember, Silvain," he cried, turning to the priest, "how we used to steal away before sunrise in my father's little fishing-boat, when we were boys, and come back at night with our backs blistered by the sun and our arms aching, hein? That was before you went away to France to study for the priesthood. Ah, but those were good times!" He threw back his head and laughed joyously. His dark hair, wet with the mist, lay in loose rings on his forehead; his fine young face, beardless but manly, seemed almost lustrous in the pale darkness. "Do you remember, Silvain? Right where the big house stands, there was Jacques Caillion's steep-roofed cottage, with the garden in front full of pinks and mignonette and sweet herbs; and the vine-hung porch where 'Tit-Pierre used to play, and where Margot Caillion used to stand shading her eyes with her arm, and looking out for her man to come home from sea."

"Jack Caillion," said Nathan Pilger, "was washed overboard from the *Suzanne* in a storm off Hatteras in '11 — him and Dune Cook and Ba'tist' Roux."

"The old church of Our Lady of the Gulf," the young man continued, "was just a stone's-throw this side of where the new one was built; back a little is our cottage, and your father's, Silvain; and in the hollow beyond Justin Roux has his blacksmith's forge."

He paused, his voice dying away almost to a whisper. The waves were beating more noisily against the bluff, filling the silence with a sort of hoarse plaint; the fog — gray, soft, impenetrable — rested on them like a cloud. The moisture fell in an audible drip-drop from the leaves and the long, pendent moss of the live-oaks. A mare, with her colt beside her, came trotting around the bend of the road. She approached within a few feet of the girl, reared violently, snorting, and dashed away, followed by the whinnying colt. The clatter of their feet echoed on the muffled air. The girl, in her white dress, sat rigidly motionless, with her face turned seaward.

André lifted his head and went on, dreamily: "I mind me, most of all, of one day when all the girls and boys of the village walked over to Bayou Galère to gather water-lilies. Margot Caillion, with 'Tit-Pierre in her hand, came along to mind the girls. You had but just come back from France in your priest's frock, Silvain. You were in the church door when we passed, with your book in your hand." A smothered groan escaped the priest, and he threw up his arm as if to ward off a blow. "And you were there when we came back at sunset. The smell of the pines that day was like balm. The lilies were white on the dark breast of the winding bayou. Rose Dédé's arms were heaped so full of lilies that you could only see her laughing black eyes above them. But Lorance would only take a few buds. She said it was a kind of sin to take them away from the water where they grew. Lorance was ever —"

The girl had dropped her hands in her lap, and was listening. At the sound of her own name she turned her face towards the speaker.

"*Lorance!*" gasped André. "Is it truly you, Lorance?"

"Yes, it is I, André Dieudonné," she replied, quietly. Her pale girlish face, with its delicate outlines, was crowned with an aureole of bright hair, which hung in two thick braids to her waist; her soft brown eyes were a little sunken, as if she had wept overmuch. But her voice was strangely cold and passionless.

"But... when did you... come, Lorance?" André demanded, breathlessly.

"I came," she said, in the same calm, measured tone, "but a little after you, André Dieudonné. First 'Tit-Pierre, then you, and then myself."

"Why, then —" he began. He rose abruptly, gathering his mantle about him, and leaned over the marble slab where he had been sitting. "'*Sacred to the memory of André Antoine Marie Dieudonné,*'" he read, slowly, slipping his finger along the mouldy French lettering, "'*who died at this place August 20th, 1809. In the 22nd year of his age.*' Eighty years and more ago I came!" he cried. "And you have been here all these years, Lorance, and I have not known! Why, then, did you never come up?"

She did not answer at once. "I was tired," she said, presently, "and I rested well down there in the cool, dark silence. And I was not lonely... at first, for I heard Margot Caillion passing about, putting flowers above 'Tit-Pierre and you and me. My mother and yours often came and wept with her for us all — and my father, and your little brothers. The sound of their weeping comforted me. Then... after a while... no one seemed to remember us anymore."

"Margot Caillion," said Nathan Pilger, "went back, when her man was drownded, to the place in France where she was born. The others be all layin' in the old church-yard yunder on the hill... all but Silvann Leebaw an' me."

She looked at the old man and smiled gravely. "A long time passed," she went on, slowly. "I could sometimes hear you speak to 'Tit-Pierre, André Dieudonné;... and at last some men came and dug quite near me; and as they pushed their spades through the moist turf they talked about the good Père Lebas; and then I knew that Silvain was coming." The priest's head fell upon his breast; he covered his face with his hands and rocked to and fro on his low seat. "Not long after, Nathan Pilger came. Down there in my narrow chamber I have heard above me, year after year, the murmur of your voices on St. John's eve, and ever the feet of 'Tit-Pierre, as he goes back and forth seeking his mother. But I cared not to leave my place. For why should I wish to look upon your face, André Dieudonné, and mark there the memory of your love for Rose Dédé?"

Her voice shook with a sudden passion as she uttered the last words. The hands lying in her lap were twisted together convulsively; a flush leaped into her pale cheeks.

"Rose Dédé!" echoed André, amazedly. "Nay, Lorance, but I never loved Rose Dédé! If she perchance cared for me —"

"Silence, fool!" cried the priest, sternly. He had thrown back his cowl; his eyes glowed like coals in his white face; he lifted his hand menacingly. "Thou wert ever a vain puppet, André Dieudonné. It was not for such as thou that Rose Dédé sinned away her soul! Was it *thou* she came at midnight to meet in the lone shadows of these very live-oaks? Hast *thou* ever worn the garments of a priest?... They shunned Rose Dédé in the village... but the priest said mass at the altar of Our Lady of the Gulf,... and the wail of the babe was sharp in the hut under the pines,... and it ceased to breathe,... and the mother turned her face to the wall and died,... and my heart was cold in my breast as I looked on the dead faces of the mother and the child... They lie under the pine-trees by Bayou Galère. But the priest lived to old age;... and when he died, he durst not sleep in consecrated ground, but fain would lie in the shadows of the live-oaks, where the dark eyes of Rose Dédé looked love into his."

His wild talk fell upon unheeding ears. 'Tit-Pierre had come out of the house. He was nestling against Nathan Pager's knee. He held a lily-bud in one hand, and with the other he caressed the sailor's weather-beaten cheek.

"'Tit-Pierre," whispered the old man, "that is Lorance Baudrot. Do you remember her, 'Tit-Pierre?" The child smiled intelligently. "Lorance was but a slip of a girl when I come down here from Cape Cod — cabin-boy aboard the *Mary Ann*. She was the pretties' lass on all the bay shore. An' I — I loved her, 'Tit-Pierre. But I wa'n't no match agin Andry Dewdonny; an' I know'd it from the fust. Andry was the likelies' lad hereabout, an' the harnsomes'. I see that Lorance loved him. An' when the yaller-fever took him, I see her a-droop-in' an' a-droopin' tell she died, an' she never even know'd I loved her.

Her an' Andry was laid here young, 'Tit - Pierre, 'longside o' you. I lived ter be pretty tol'able old; but when I hed made my last v'ige, an' was about fetchin' my las' breath, I give orders ter be laid in this here old buryin'-groun' some'er's clost ter the grave o' Lorance Baudrot."

His voice was overborne by André's exultant tones. "Lorance!" he cried, "did you indeed love me? — me!"

Her dark eyes met his frankly, and she smiled.

"Ah, if I had only known!" he sighed — "if I had only known, Lorance, I would surely have lived! We would have walked one morning to Our Lady of the Gulf, with all the village-folk about us, and Silvain — the good Père Lebas — would have joined our hands... My father would have given us a little plot of ground;... you would have planted flowers about the door of our cottage;... our children would have played in the sand under the bluff..."

A sudden gust of wind blew the fog aside, and a zigzag of flame tore the wedge-shaped cloud in two. A greenish light played for an instant over the weed-grown spot. The mocking-bird, long silent in the heart of the live-oak, began to sing.

"All these years you have been near me," he murmured, reproachfully, "and I did not know." Then, as if struck by a breathless thought, he stretched out his arms imploringly. "I love you, Lorance," he said. "I have always loved you. Will you not be my wife now? Silvain will say the words, and 'Tit-Pierre, who can go back and forth, will put this ring, which was my mother's, upon your finger, and he will bring me a curl of your soft hair to twist about mine. I cannot come to you, Lorance; I cannot even touch your hand. But when I go down into my dark place I can be content dreaming of you. And on the blessed St. John's eves I will know you are mine, as you sit there in your white gown."

As he ceased speaking, Père Lebas, with his head upon his breast, began murmuring, as if mechanically, the words which preface the holy sacrament of marriage. His voice faltered, he raised his head, and a cry of wonder burst from his lips. For André had moved away from the mouldy gravestone and stood just in front of him. Lorance, as if upborne on invisible wings, was floating lightly across the intervening space. Her shroud enveloped her like a cloud, her arms were extended, her lips were parted in a rapt smile. Nathan Pilger, with 'Tit-Pierre in his arms, had limped forward. He halted beside André, and as the young man folded the girl to his breast, the child reached over and laid an open lily on her down-drooped head.

The priest stared wildly at them, and struggled to rise, but could not. As he sank panting back upon the crumbling tomb, his anguish overcame him. "My God!" he groaned hoarsely, "I, only I, cannot move from my place. *The soul of Rose Dédé hangs like a millstone about my neck!*"

Even as he spoke, the cloud broke with a roar. The storm — black, heavy, thunderous — came rushing across the bay. It blotted out, in a lightning's flash, the mansion which stands on the site of Jacques Caillion's hut, and the weed-grown, ancient, forgotten graveyard in its shadow.

… And a bell in the steeple of Our Lady of the Gulf rang out the hour.

The Fear that Walks by Noonday

Willa Sibert Cather

I.

"Where is my shin guard? Horton, you lazy dog, get your duds off, won't you? Why didn't you dress at the hotel with the rest of us? There's got to be a stop to your blamed eccentricities someday," fumed Reggie, hunting wildly about in a pile of overcoats.

Horton began pulling off his coat with that air of disinterested deliberation he always assumed to hide any particular nervousness. He was to play two positions that day, both half and full, and he knew it meant stiff work.

"What do you think of the man who plays in Morrison's place, Strike?" he asked as he took off his shoes.

"I can tell you better in about half an hour; I suppose the 'Injuns' knew what they were about when they put him there."

"They probably put him there because they hadn't another man who could even look like a full back. He played quarter badly enough, if I remember him."

"I don't see where they get the face to play us at all. They would never have scored last month if it hadn't been for Morrison's punting. That fellow played a great game, but the rest of them are light men, and their coach is an idiot. That man would have made his mark if he'd lived. He could play different positions just as easily as Chum-Chum plays different roles — pardon the liberty, Fred — and then there was that awful stone wall strength of his to back it; he was a mighty man."

"If you are palpitating to know why the 'Injuns' insist on playing us, I'll tell you; it's for blood. Exhibition game be damned! It's to break our bones they're playing. We were surprised when they didn't let down on us harder as soon as the fellow died, but they have been cherishing their wrath, they haven't lost an ounce of it, and they are going into us today for vengeance."

"Well, their sentiments are worthy, but they haven't got the players."

"Let up on Morrison there, Horton," shouted Reggie, "we sent flowers and sympathies at the time, but we are not going to lose this game out of respect to his memory: shut up and get your shin guard on. I say, Nelson, if you don't get out of here with that cigarette I'll kick you out. I'll get so hungry I'll break training rules. Besides, the coach will be in here in a minute going around smelling our breaths like our mammas used to do, if he catches a scent of it. I'm humming glad it's the last week of training; I couldn't stand another day of it. I brought a whole pocket full of cigars, and I'll have one well underway before the cheering is over. Won't we see the town tonight, Freddy?"

Horton nodded and laughed one of his wicked laughs. "Training has gone a shade too far this season. It's all nonsense to say that nobody but hermits and anchorites can play football. A Methodist parson don't have to practice half such rigid abstinence as a man on the eleven." And he kicked viciously at the straw on the floor as he remembered the supper parties he had renounced, the invitations he had declined, and the pretty faces he had avoided in the last three months.

"Five minutes to three!" said the coach, as he entered, pounding on the door with his cane. Strike began to hunt frantically for the inflater, one of the tackles went striding around the room seeking his nose protector with lamentations and profanity, and the rest of the men got on their knees and began burrowing in the pile of coats for things they had forgotten to take out of their pockets. Reggie began to hurry his men and make the usual encouraging remarks to the effect that the universe was not created to the especial end that they should win that football game, that the game was going to the men who kept the coolest heads and played the hardest ball. The coach rapped impatiently again, and Horton and Reggie stepped out together, the rest following them. As soon as Horton heard the shouts which greeted their appearance, his eyes flashed, and he threw his head back like a cavalry horse that hears the bugle sound a charge. He jumped over the ropes and ran swiftly across the field, leaving Reggie to saunter along at his leisure, bowing to the ladies in the grand stand and on the tally-hos as he passed.

When he reached the lower part of the field he found a hundred Marathon college men around the team yelling and shouting their encouragement. Reggie promptly directed the policemen to clear the field, and, taking his favorite attitude, his feet wide apart and his body very straight, he carelessly tossed the quarter into the air.

"Line 'em up, Reggie, line 'em up. Let us into it while the divine afflatus lasts," whispered Horton.

The men sprang to their places, and Reggie forgot the ladies on the tally-hos; the color came to his face, and he drew himself up and threw every sinew of his little body on a tension. The crowd outside began to cheer again, as the wedge started off for north goal. The western men were poor on defensive work, and the Marathon wedge gained ground on the first play. The first impetus of success was broken by Horton fumbling and losing the ball. The eleven looked rather dazed at this, and Horton was the most dazed looking man of them all, for he did not indulge in that kind of thing often. Reggie could scarcely believe his senses, and stood staring at Horton in unspeakable amazement, but Horton only spread out his hands and stared at them as though to see if they were still there. There was little time for reflection or conjecture. The western men gave their Indian yell and prepared to play; their captain sang out his signals, and the rushing began. In spite of the desperate resistance on the part of Reggie's men, the ball went steadily south, and in twelve minutes the 'Injuns' had scored. No one quite knew how they did it, least of all their bewildered opponents. They did some bad fumbling on the five-yard line, but though Reggie's men fell all over the ball, they did not seem to be able to take hold of it.

"Call in a doctor," shouted Reggie; "they're paralyzed in the arms, every one of 'em."

Time was given to bandage a hurt, and half a dozen men jumped over the ropes and shot past the policemen and rushed up to Reggie, pitifully asking what the matter was.

"Matter! I don't know! They're all asleep or drunk. Go kick them, pound them, anything to get them awake." And the little captain threw his sweater over his shoulder and swore long and loud at all mankind in general and Frederick Horton in particular. Horton turned away without looking at him. He was a younger man than Reggie, and, although he had had more experiences, they were not of the kind that counted much with the men of the eleven. He was very proud of being the captain's right-hand man, and it cut him hard to fail him.

"I believe I've been drugged, Black," he said, turning to the right tackle. "I am as cold as ice all over and I can't use my arms at all; I've a notion to ask Reggie to call in a sub."

"Don't, for heaven's sake, Horton; he is almost frantic now; believe it would completely demoralize the team; you have never laid off since you were on the eleven, and if you should now when you have no visible hurt it would frighten them to death."

"I feel awful, I am so horribly cold."

"So am I, so are all the fellows; see how the 'Injuns' are shivering over there, will you? There must be a cold wave; see how Strike's hair is blowing down in his eyes."

"The cold wave seems to be confined to our locality," remarked Horton in a matter-of-fact way; but in somewhat strained tones. "The girls out there are all in their summer dresses without wraps, and the wind which is cutting our faces all up don't even stir the ribbon on their hats."

"Y-a-s, horribly draughty place, this," said Black blankly.

"Horribly, draughty as all out doors," said Horton with a grim laugh.

"Bur-r-r!" said Strike, as he handed his sweater over to a substitute and took his last pull at a lemon, "this wind is awful; I never felt anything so cold; it's a raw, wet cold that goes clear into the marrow of a fellow's bones. I don't see where it comes from; there is no wind outside the ropes apparently."

"The winds blow in such strange directions here," said Horton, picking up a straw and dropping it. "It goes straight down with force enough to break several camels' backs."

"Ugh! it's as though the firmament had sprung a leak and the winds were sucking in from the other side."

"Shut your mouths, both of you," said Reggie, with an emphatic oath. "You will have them all scared to death; there's a panic now, that's what's the matter, one of those quiet, stupid panics that are the worst to manage. Laugh, Freddie, laugh hard; get up some enthusiasm; come you, shut up, if you can't do any better than that. Start the yell, Strike, perhaps that will fetch them."

A weak yell that sounded like an echo rose from the field and the Marathon men outside the ropes caught it up and cheered till the air rang. This seemed to rouse the men on the field, and they got to their places with considerable energy. Reggie gave an exultant cry, as the western men soon lost the ball, and his men started it north and kept steadily gaining. They were within ten yards of the goal, when suddenly the ball rose serenely out of a mass of struggling humanity and flew back twenty, forty, sixty, eighty yards toward the southern goal! But the half was versed in his occupation; he ran across and stood under the ball, waiting for it with outstretched arms. It seemed to Horton that the ball was all day in falling; it was right over him and yet it seemed to hang back from him, like Chum-Chum when she was playing with him. With an impatient oath he ground his teeth together and bowed his body forward to hold it with his breast, and even his knees if need be, waiting with strength and eagerness enough in his arm to burst the ball to shreds. The crowd shouted with delight, but suddenly caught its breath; the ball fell into his arms, between them, through them, and rolled on the ground at his feet. Still he stood there with his face raised and his arms stretched upward in an attitude ridiculously suggestive of prayer. The men rushed fiercely around him shouting and reviling; his arms dropped like lead to his side, and he stood without moving a muscle, and in his face there was a look that a man might have who had seen what he loved best go down to death through his very arms, and had not been able to close them and save. Reggie came up with his longest oaths on his lip, but when he saw Horton's face he checked himself and said with that sweetness of temper that always came to him when he saw the black bottom of despair,

"Keep quiet, fellows, Horton's all right, only he is a bit nervous." Horton moved for the first time and turned on the little captain, "You can say anything else you like, Reggie, but if you say I am scared I'll knock you down."

"No, Fred, I don't mean that; we must hang together, man, every one of us, there are powers enough against us," said Reggie, sadly. The men looked at each other with startled faces. So long as Reggie swore there was hope, but when he became gentle all was lost.

In another part of the field another captain fell on his fullback's neck and cried, "Thomas, my son, how did you do it? Morrison in his palmiest days never made a better lift than that."

"I — I didn't do it, I guess; some of the other fellows did; Towmen, I think."

"Not much I didn't," said Towmen, "you were so excited you didn't know what you were doing. You did it, though; I saw it go right up from your foot."

"Well, it may be," growled the 'Injun' half, "but when I make plays like that I'd really like to be conscious of them. I must be getting to be a darned excitable individual if I can punt eighty yards and never know it."

"Heavens! how cold it is. This is a great game, though; I don't believe they'll score."

"I don't; they act like dead men; I would say their man Horton was sick or drunk if all the others didn't act just like him."

The 'Injuns' lost the ball again, but when Reggie's men were working it north the same old punting scheme was worked somewhere by someone in the 'Injuns'' ranks. This time Amack, the right half, ran bravely for it; but when he was almost beneath it he fell violently to the ground, for no visible reason, and lay there struggling like a man in a fit. As they were taking him off the field, time was called for the first half. Reggie's friends and several of his professors broke through the gang of policemen and rushed up to him. Reggie stepped in front of his men and spoke to the first man who came up, "If you say one word or ask one question I'll quit the field. Keep away from me and from my men. Let us alone." The paleness that showed through the dirt on Reggie's face alarmed the visitors, and they went away as quickly as they had come. Reggie and his men lay down and covered themselves with their overcoats, and lay there shuddering under that icy wind that sucked down upon them. The men were perfectly quiet and each one crept off by himself. Even the substitutes who brought them lemons and water did not talk much; they had neither disparagement nor encouragement to offer; they sat around and shivered like the rest. Horton hid his face on his arm and lay like one stunned. He muttered the score, 18 to 0, but he did not feel the words his lips spoke, nor comprehend them. Like most dreamy, imaginative men, Horton was not very much at home in college. Sometimes in his loneliness he tried to draw near to the average man, and be on a level with him, and in so doing made a consummate fool of himself, as dreamers always do when they try to get themselves awake. He was awkward and shy among women, silent and morose among men. He was tolerated in the societies because he could write good poetry, and in the clubs because he could play football. He was very proud of his accomplishments as a halfback, for they made him seem like other men. However ornamental and useful a large imagination and sensitive temperament may be to a man of mature years, to a young man they are often very like a deformity which he longs to hide. He wondered what the captain would think of him and groaned. He feared Reggie as much as he adored him. Reggie was one of those men who, by the very practicality of their intellects, astonish the world. He was a glorious man for a college. He was brilliant, adaptable, and successful; yet all his brains he managed to cover up by a pate of tow hair, parted very carefully in the middle, and his iron strength was generally very successfully disguised by a very dudish exterior. In short, he possessed the one thing which is greater than genius, the faculty of clothing genius in such boundless good nature that it is offensive to nobody. Horton felt to a painful degree his inferiority to him in most things, and it was not pleasant to him to lose ground in the one thing in which he felt they could meet on an equal footing. Horton turned over and looked up at the leaden sky, feeling the wind sweep into his eyes and nostrils. He looked about him and saw the other men all lying down with their heads covered, as though they were trying to get away from the awful cold and the sense of Reggie's reproach. He wondered what was the matter with them; whether they had been drugged or mesmerized. He tried to remember something in all the books he had read that would fit the case, but his memory seemed as cold and dazed as the rest of him; he only remembered some hazy Greek, which read to the effect that the gods sometimes bring madness upon those they wish to destroy. And here was another proof that the world was going wrong — it was not a normal thing for him to remember any Greek.

He was glad when at last he heard Reggie's voice calling the men together; he went slowly up to him and said rather feebly,

"I say, a little brandy wouldn't hurt us, would it? I am so awfully cold I don't know what the devil is the matter with me. Reggie, my arms are so stiff I can't use 'em at all."

Reggie handed him a bottle from his grip, saying briefly, "It can't make things any worse."

In the second half the Marathon men went about as though they were walking in their sleep. They seldom said anything, and the captain was beyond coaxing or swearing; he only gave his signals in a voice as hollow as if it came from an empty church. His men got the ball a dozen times, but they always lost it as soon as they got it, or, when they had worked it down to one goal the 'Injuns' would punt it back to the other. The very spectators sat still and silent, feeling that they were seeing something strange and unnatural. Every now and then some 'Injun' would make a run, and a Marathon man would dash up and run beside him for a long distance without ever catching him, but with his hands hanging at his side. People asked the physicians in the audience what was the matter; but they shook their heads.

It was at this juncture that Freddie Horton awoke and bestirred himself. Horton was a peculiar player; he was either passive or brilliant. He could not do good line work; he could not help other men play. If he did anything he must take matters into his own hands, and he generally did; no one in the northwest had ever made such nervy, dashing plays as he; he seemed to have the faculty of making sensational and romantic situations in football just as he did in poetry. He played with his imagination. The second half was half over, and as yet he had done nothing but blunder. His honor and the honor of the team had been trampled on. As he thought of it the big veins stood out in his forehead and he set his teeth hard together. At last his opportunity came, or rather he made it. In a general scramble for the ball he caught it in his arms and ran. He held the ball tight against his breast until he could feel his heart knocking against the hard skin; he was conscious of nothing but the wind whistling in his ears and the ground flying under his feet, and the fact that he had ninety yards to run. Both teams followed him as fast as they could, but Horton was running for his honor, and his feet scarcely touched the earth. The spectators, who had waited all afternoon for a chance to shout, now rose to their feet and all the lungs full of pent-up enthusiasm burst forth. But the gods are not to be frustrated for a man's honor or his dishonor, and when Freddie Horton was within ten yards of the goal he threw his arms over his head and leaped into the air and fell. When the crowd reached him they found no marks of injury except the blood and foam at his mouth where his teeth had bitten into his lip. But when they looked at him the men of both teams turned away shuddering. His knees were drawn up to his chin; his hands were dug into the ground on either side of him; his face was the livid, bruised blue of a man who dies with apoplexy; his eyes were wide open and full of unspeakable horror and fear, glassy as ice, and still as though they had been frozen fast in their sockets.

It was an hour before they brought him to, and then he lay perfectly silent and would answer no questions. When he was stretched obliquely across the seats of a carriage going home he spoke for the first time.

"Give me your hand, Reggie; for God's sake let me feel something warm and human. I am awful sorry, Reggie; I tried for all my life was worth to make that goal, but —" he drew the captain's head down to his lips and whispered something that made Reggie's face turn white and the sweat break out on his forehead. He drew big Horton's head upon his breast and stroked it as tenderly as a woman.

II.

There was silence in the dining room of the Exeter House that night when the waiters brought in the last course. The evening had not been a lively one. The defeated men were tired with that heavy weariness which follows defeat, and the victors seemed strained and uneasy in their manners. They all avoided speaking of the game and forced themselves to speak of things they could not fix their minds upon. Reggie sat at the head of the table correct and faultless. Reggie was always correct, but tonight there was very little of festal cheer about him. He was cleanly shaved, his hair was parted with the usual mathematical accuracy. A little strip of black court plaster covered the only external wound defeat had left. But his face was as white as the spotless expanse of his shirt bosom, and his eyes had big black circles under them like those of a man coming down with the fever. All evening he had been nervous and excited; he had not eaten anything and was evidently keeping something under. Everyone wondered what it was, and yet feared to hear it. When asked about Horton he simply shuddered, mumbled something, and had his wine glass filled again.

Laughter or fear are contagious, and by the time the last course was on the table everyone was as nervous as Reggie. The talk started up fitfully now and then but it soon died down, and the weakly attempts at wit were received in silence.

Suddenly everyone became conscious of the awful cold and inexplicable downward draught that they had felt that afternoon. Everyone was determined not to show it. No one pretended to even notice the flicker of the gas jets, and the fact that their breath curled upward from their mouths in little wreaths of vapor. Everyone turned his attention to his plate and his glass stood full beside him. Black made some remarks about politics, but his teeth chattered so he gave it up. Reggie's face was working nervously, and he suddenly rose to his feet and said in a harsh, strained voice,

"Gentlemen, you had one man on your side this afternoon who came a long journey to beat us. I mean the man who did that wonderful punting and who stood before the goal when Mr. Horton made his run. I propose the first toast of the evening to the twelfth man, who won the game. Need I name him?"

The silence was as heavy as before. Reggie extended his glass to the captain beside him, but suddenly his arm changed direction; he held the glass out over the table and tipped it in empty air as though touching glasses with someone. The sweat broke out on Reggie's face; he put his glass to his lips and tried to drink, but only succeeded in biting out a big piece of the rim of his wine glass. He spat the glass out quickly upon his plate and began to laugh, with the wine oozing out between his white lips. Then everyone laughed; leaning upon each other's shoulders, they gave way to volleys and shrieks of laughter, waving their glasses in hands that could scarcely hold them. The negro waiter, who had been leaning against the wall asleep, came forward rubbing his eyes to see what was the matter. As he approached the end of the table he felt that chilling wind, with its damp, wet smell like the air from a vault, and the unnatural cold that drove to the heart's center like a knife blade.

"My Gawd!" he shrieked, dropping his tray, and with an inarticulate gurgling cry he fled out of the door and down the stairway with the banqueters after him, all but Reggie, who fell to the floor, cursing and struggling and grappling with the powers of darkness. When the men reached the lower hall they stood without speaking, holding tightly to each other's hands like frightened children. At last Reggie came down the stairs, steadying himself against the banister. His dress coat was torn, his hair was rumpled down over his forehead, his shirt front was stained with wine, and the ends of his tie were hanging to his waist. He stood looking at the men and they looked at him, and no one spoke.

Presently a man rushed into the hall from the office and shouted "McKinley has carried Ohio by eighty-one thousand majority!" and Regiland Ashton, the product of centuries of democratic faith and tradition, leaped down the six remaining stairs and shouted, "Hurrah for Bill McKinley."

In a few minutes the men were looking for a carriage to take Regiland Ashton home.

A Transient

Annie Trumbull Slosson

'Twas when I was keeping the Banks House, over to Bentley Centre, more'n thirty year ago. Mr. Harris had been dead quite a spell, and I was running the house alone, and doing well. Mother lived with me, but she was too old to do much, and feeble anyway. 'Twas the only tavern in the Centre, and open all the year round, but we didn't have many folks except in summer. But from the last of June 'way into September I had a nice lot of summer boarders every year, and we had a good many transients, stopping over for dinner and often all night too, with supper and breakfast. There wasn't much to bring business people. You've been there, haven't you? It's just a quiet little place, but it's got the mountains all round it, making it sightly and nice, and plenty of green, cool, woodsy spots to walk or sit in. And that's what summer boarders like.

The transients was most generally folks that was travelling for pleasure, through the mountains and on their way to the Gorge or back. Sometimes farmers come along on their way to Westboro to 'tend the county fair, or horse men for the races, and then again there'd be a runner or two travelling for some city store or other.

But the transient you asked me to tell you about — put up to it, as you said, by Dr. Little — was another sort. The first time I saw him — I remember it as well as if 'twas last week — was the summer Mis' Haskins's folks boarded with me. You know they're among the first families, as to standing, in the State, and 'twas a great thing for my house, and for the whole town, for that matter, to have them put up there. Mis' Haskins wasn't well that year, and was dreadful nervous and whimsy. So they thought they'd go to some real quiet kind of place, instead of a big hotel, as they'd generally done. She was pretty hard to please, but I did my best, and she got along well enough, considering.

But one day everything appeared to go wrong, seem' 'sif. There wasn't any other boarders that time — 'twas toward the last of June — but the Haskins folks and the Sperrys from Derby. And they set all together at meals to the long table by the south windows, where 'twas light and airy. There was twelve of 'em, five each side and one to each end, and 'twould have held sixteen comfortable. Well, that day the whole party'd been out driving in two wagons, over to the east village and Wells Pond. They'd had dinner put back to half past one, and 'twas all ready when they come in. They'd called at Miss Leonard's on their way home, and brought a young lady that was boarding there, a friend of Miss Ellen Sperry's, back with them. I was in the kitchen, dishing up, when I heerd 'em all trooping in together to the table, and then the chairs scraping as they pulled 'em out to set down. Then I heerd a kind of loud speaking out, and some talking back, and a sort of fuss, and next moment Sarah Willett, the table girl, came running out. And she says, a little flustered, "Mis' Haskins won't set down and won't let nobody else set down, 'cause there's too many folks to the table."

I knew she'd got it wrong some way, for, as I said before, the table would accommodate sixteen easy, and I went right in. They was all standing up by their chairs, looking real hungry and cross, and Mis' Haskins was talking in a kind of scolding, upset way. "No, I won't do it," she says; "it's a-tempting Providence; it's as much as my life's worth. No, no, no!" and she begun to sort of cry.

"Why, what's the matter?" says I. "Is anything wrong, Mis' Haskins?" And then two or three of them spoke up all to once, and I got to understand that there was thirteen to set at that table, and that was bad luck. I don't recollect that I'd ever heerd of that sign before, though I've often read about it late years, and seen a few folks that held by it. But it wasn't one of our sayings there in Bentley. Thirteen wasn't any worse than any other number there; a little better, maybe, for it went by the name of a baker's dozen, and generally meant something thrown in, which is always satisfying in this world.

But I see at once 'twas a sign Mis' Haskins believed in, and that she was terrible upset. But what in the world could I do? They was all one party and all hungry, and I couldn't ask anyone of them to leave the table, and there wasn't another boarder in the house to call in. I was at my wits' end, and didn't know what I'd better do, when all of a sudden, but very quiet, a man come into the door that led out to the front hall and walked right up to the table. He was an under-size, homely-looking man, but he had a real pleasant kind of face, a mite freckled, and slick, thinnish red hair — a perfect stranger to me.

Everybody stopped talking directly, and turned to look at him. He sort of bowed to us all, and says, in a bashful kind of way but real friendly, "Don't let me put you to any trouble," he says; "I'm only a transient for dinner." Well, I never was so glad to see anyone in all my life. And all the folks was tickled to death, and showed it. You'd have thought he'd been a bit surprised at the way they give him a welcome and made room for him, but he took it as calm as you please, and dropped right into the chair Sarah Willett set for him, without a word.

Sarah said afterwards that he didn't hardly say anything through the meal, but eat hearty, as if he enjoyed his victuals. Only once when young Mr. Sperry spoke to him direct and told him what a fix he'd helped 'em out of, and how much they was obleeged to him for happening in, he says. "Don't speak of it; 'tain't anything," and went on with his dinner. I meant to speek to him myself before he got away, but I was kept by one thing and another, and when I got into the office at last, he'd gone. He paid his half-dollar to Parker Smith, who was clerking for us that season, and went off. "Did he have a team," I says to Parker, "or was he afoot?" And Parker didn't know, hadn't took notice. Well, of course there isn't anything wonderful in that part of the story. 'Twas lucky he happened along just that minute, that's all. And I never should have thought of the man again but for what come after.

'Twas two or three weeks after that, one hot day in July, that I had the biggest scare of my whole life, I believe. Some ways or other I'd turned my ankle, and 'twas swelled up and stiff so's I couldn't put my foot to the floor. I was up in my bedroom, setting in my rocking-chair, with my foot all wrapped up with cloths wet with opedildoc and up on a cricket. All the boarders was off one way or other, except Mis' Skinner. She was in her room with Janie, her little girl. After a spell she come over to my room with her bonnet on and hold of Janie's hand, and asked me if she could leave the child there with me for a few minutes while she went over to the post-office. "She don't need any looking after, Mis' Harris," she says. "She'll play round the room real good and quiet, only I don't exactly like to leave her all alone." I always liked children, and Janie was a favorite of mine, so of course I said let her stay. Well, she trotted around and looked at my things and played with her dolly. I was knitting, hard at work on a new kind of bed-spread with a real mixed-up pattern Miss Lee had been learning me. I got to the most ticklish place in it, where the holes come in, and I was looking close at it and saying over to myself, "Put your thread over and knit one, put your thread over and narrer, knit three plain," when I heerd a little noise.

I looked up quick, recollecting the child — oh, dear, dear, dear! My south window was wide open, and there was a morning-glory vine climbing up on some strings just outside. There was pink and blue and white flowers on it, all shut up and twisted, of course, at that time o' day, but they looked bright and pretty to Janie. So she'd climbed up in a chair and tried to reach 'em. The chair'd tipped, and she'd slipped out, and — oh! there she was hanging with her little white frock catched on the thing the green blinds fasten to.

Before the dress give way, before I could holler out, before — oh, anything, I see someone right in my room step up quick behind the child, catch her up in his arms, unhitch her frock, and put her down on the carpet close up to me. For a spell I didn't think of anything but Janie and her being safe and sound. I kept stroking her yellow head as she leaned it up agin' my dress, and I felt sort of sick and head-swimmy. Then I heerd the door creak, and when I looked up there was a man going out. He was an under-size, homely-looking man, with a real pleasant freckly face and thin reddish hair, and I see he was the transient that helped us out at the table that day I was telling about. I called out to him to stop, and begun to pour it all out how thankful and obleeged I was and all, but he only says, very quiet, "Don't speak of it; 'tain't anything," he says. Then he mumbles out sort of quick and bashful something about how he was passing, and see I needed a little help, and come in. I couldn't hear him very plain, and then he was gone.

I couldn't follow after him, 'count of my lame foot, and he didn't appear to hear when I called out to him again. So off he went without any more thanks from me or anybody.

Well, that time I did ask a heap of questions about him, but nobody seemed to know a thing. Folks had seen him coming along the street, and Mary Willey see him running like a streak through our front gate and into the house that afternoon. But nobody knew who he was, nor which way he come from or went to.

I disremember just what was the next time I saw him. Mebbe 'twas the day Hiram Merrit's cows broke into our corn-field. There wasn't any men folks about, but Aleck Brace, a little fellow not more'n twelve year old, was in the barn, and he run out to see if he could drive 'em out. I knew be couldn't do it alone, and I was just starting out myself, though my ankle wasn't strong yet awhile, when I see the cows was all running out o' the field, and there was a man helping Aleck drive 'em.

I didn't get a chance to speak to the boy till 'most night, and then I asked him who it was helped him get the cows out. He said 'twas a stranger to him, a man that was going by and see the trouble. Said he was a smallish man, with slinky red hair and freckled as a turkey egg, but a real friendly way with him. I guessed in a minute 'twas that transient again.

I don't know but 'twas afore that, after all, that he turned up just at the very minute the keeping-room chimney got afire. I was out myself, and there wasn't anybody downstairs but Sarah Willett and old Aunty Mills that was turning and sewing over the breadths of the carpet, and upstairs there wasn't any gentlemen, only two or three of the ladies. I heerd about it as I was coming up the street, and I run home as fast as I could.

But when I got there 'twas all out, and Sarah was sweeping up the soot. She said they'd had a dreadful scare, but just's they was 'most distracted somebody run in and emptied a bag of salt on the fire — 'twas only a blaze of papers Sarah'd been burning to get 'em out of the way — and it put it right out. Neither she nor Aunty Mills had noticed who done it. But Parker Smith, the clerk, come in a spell afterwards, and he says, "I see that sandy-haired man just now, that was here to dinner the day Mis' Haskins had the tantrums." So I felt certain sure that transient had helped me out again.

'Twas the queerest thing. He never went anywhere else, never give assistance to any of the neighbors, and nobody knew who or what he was. But he was always and forever turning up in the very nick; yes, the nickest of time, when I needed help or got into any scrape or mess. They wasn't all big things he done, some was little; they wasn't all solemn things, some was real comical. Why, once I'd gone over to Petersville with Mis' Bryan to have a pictur' took of her baby. It was fretty with its teeth, and wouldn't look pleasant, all the pictur' man and the rest of us could do. 'Twas getting late, and I'd got to be home to make tea rusk for supper. I was real nervous, but just then a man come in, or was in, for I didn't see him open the door. He stepped up in front of the baby, just where the pictur' thing couldn't take him, and he begun to move his hand up and down, and wiggle his feet, and shake his head all covered with smooth stringy red hair, and twist his homely, freckled face in such a ridic'lous way that the baby, let alone the rest of us, just laughed right out, and I've got the pictur' of it with the laugh all sot on his little countenance. 'Course 'twas that transient. But he wouldn't stop to any a single word, and was off before we could thank him.

Another time I'd been out in the rain and got wet, and I catched cold. I felt sick all over, and that night I thought I'd take some hot peppermint tea. I went to the closet for the peppermint, and there was the bottle all empty; not a single drop left. Now if there's a thing I pride myself on, it's my never being out of peppermint. It's the one thing that every respectable family should keep in the house. Aunt Nancy Bartlett used to say that to be without peppermint in the house overnight was temptin' Providence, and I guess she was about right. It's the one thing I know that's hot and cold to the same time. So, nat'rally, good for folks that's hot-blooded and feverish, and for people that's peaked and shivery. But there I was without a drop in the house, and late in the evening too. Just then I thought I heerd a noise at the back of the house.

I went to my bedroom window and listened, but I couldn't hear anything. Pretty soon I felt sure there was steps in the yard, and all of a sudden I recollected I hadn't bolted the side door. I took a candle and run down stairs. I looked about a little, and see there wa'n't nothing wrong; then I fastened the door and started to go upstairs. I don't know what 'twas made me turn round and look at the clock that stood on a little shelf in the entry. Just as I done it I see a bottle standing there by the box of matches, and I reached up and took hold of it. It was a middlin'-size bottle, and 'twas brimful of peppermint right up to the cork, as if it had just come out of Deacon Hubbard's store.

Do you s'pose I didn't know, just as well as if I'd seen him, that 'twas that friendly transient done that?

But I tell you there was another kind of help that man fetched me once, and I'll never forget it to my dying day. I told you mother was living with me then. She was most eighty, and she failed up fast that summer. The hot weather was too much for her, and she grew weaker, and one day in August — 'twas the 25th — we see plain she was a-dying. Dr. More had been and gone, saying she wouldn't last many hours, and there wasn't anything he could do. She hadn't sensed anything all day, and her eyes was shut.

I was setting close beside her, and Libby States, my niece-in-law, nigh by. There wasn't anybody else in the room. All of a sudden I see ma move her lips as if she was trying to speak, but she didn't open her eyes. I leaned over her and says, "What is it, ma?" She sort of whispers, "Sing 'How — firm — a — foundation,'" and I knew she wanted her favorite hymn. Now I never could sing a note in my life, hadn't any ear or voice or idee of tune, besides being all choky with sorrow now. Libby was crying so hard she couldn't raise a note. I tried to say the hymn over, instead of singing it, but I see that didn't satisfy ma. She'd always been fond of music, sung in the choir when she was young. Her poor dry lips moved again, and she says, "Sing, sing!" Oh dear, what wouldn't I've given to do what she wanted; Just then I heerd a voice begin the old hymn to the old tune, the very one ma wanted.

The door was on a jar, and somebody was singing outside in the entry. 'Twasn't much of a voice; it flatted terribly, and it cracked on every single high note, but it satisfied mother. She sort of smiled, and she kept her thin, wrinkled old hands — is there anything on this whole earth like your mother's hands? — moving a little on the sheet to keep time. The voice went right through the whole hymn — a real long one, you know; and just as it come to

"He'll never, no, never, no, never forsake,"

ma stopped moving her hands, and sort of whispers, "Never — forsake —" and then, "Ann" (that's my name), and a second after she says, very softly, "Nathan," and she was gone.

Nathan was my only brother, a little fellow dead and buried twenty year before, but mother'd never forgot him. I could just remember him — a cute, homely little fellow, with sandy hair that never would curl, and a pleasant little face tanned and freckled with being outdoors.

But ma thought there never was such a child, said he was too good to live, always doing things for folks, so helpful and self-denying. She said he was always talking of how he was going to spend his whole life just helping folks and getting 'em out of trouble, partic'lar his own folks. He died, poor young one, when he was nine year old; so he never had much chance to show what a helper he could be. But here was ma thinking of him, and saying his name over the very last thing.

I mustn't make this story too long and tire you all out, so I won't tell you how I felt to lose my mother, and the lonesome time that come afterwards. I found out what I'd felt pretty sure of all the time — that 'twas my friend the transient that had come in just the very minute he was needed and sung that hymn for ma. I didn't see him myself, but Sarah Willett met him on the stairs, and knew him right away. I didn't think of anything for a spell but mother and the last things I could do for her. But after the funeral I begun to remember what a comfort the hymn had been to her, and I was bound to find out something about that man.

But 'twasn't any good, all my questions and searching out. Nobody knew who he was, or'd ever had any talk with him, though a lot of folks had seen him one time or another, and always pretty close to my house.

'Twas a few weeks after that time, one day in September, that Dr. More stopped at my door in his buggy. He said he was going to see a sick woman over to North Bentley, and as he should have to pass right by the Red Hill burying-ground, where ma was, he thought maybe I'd like to go out there with him. I was glad of the chance, for I hadn't been there since the funeral, and I went upstairs to put on my things. As I was hurrying, so's not to keep the doctor waiting, I thought to myself that I wished I had some flowers to put on mother's grave. She was a master hand for flowers, could always make them grow and bloom. And she set a great deal by the wild flowers round Bentley, and knew 'em all apart. "It's just the time," I says to myself, "for blind gentian that ma always liked so, and the twisted-stalk, and everlastings. And golden-rod and blue daisies is out a plenty. But the doctor'll be in a hurry, and I can't ask him to stop for me to pick any."

I run down stairs and out to the buggy. Just as I got in, Dr. More handed me a big bunch of posies, and says: "Here's your flowers. I'm glad you had them ready."

"Why, what in the world!" I says. "Where did these come from?"

Dr. More looked real surprised, and says, "Why, I thought you sent them out! A man fetched them here to me just now, and says, 'Here's some flowers for Mis' Harris.'"

"What man?" I says.

"He was a stranger to me," says the doctor, "and I didn't take partic'lar notice of him."

But I knew who 'twas well enough. There wasn't but one person on the whole airth that would 'a' happened along with just them posies at just that minute. 'Twas that transient again. I looked at the flowers as we rode along. There was blind gentians, purply blue, with their green leaves a mite streaky and spotty. Mother she was from Vermont, and she called them dumb foxgloves. You know what I mean — them flowers that's always buds and never open. And there was a lot of twisted-stalk, the big kind that comes late, with a spike of frosty-looking white flowers that smell just the way a peach pit tastes. And there was ever-lastings and golden-rod and blue daisies — all the things ma'd been fond of and I'd been wishing for.

Well, then I just had to tell Dr. More all about it. This last thing had somehow stirred me all up, and I begun to think there was something a good deal out of the common about this man and his doings. I was dreadful excited, and I let the doctor have the whole story. I told him all about it, all the things that had happened to me, and all the times this man had helped me out, and how I couldn't find out anything about him, and couldn't get a word with him, and nobody could, and all that. But, some ways or other, it didn't seem to make much impression on the doctor. He didn't appear to think 'twas no great of a myst'ry, nothing very amazing, after all. I guess I didn't tell it just right, mebbe. 'Tany rate, he said things only'd happened so; he dare say the man was all right, and we'd find out all about him sometime. Said he was a respectable-looking man, and pleasant spoken, and he'd surmised at first he was some relative of mine that was staying to my house. I suppose he meant the man favored my family. He said women folks was given to imaginings and such. Dr. More was a single man, and they said he'd been disappointed when he was young.

I disremember how long 'twas before I see the man again, or whether I ever did see him more'n once after that time. But, any ways, I recollect the last time, and everything that happened then, as well as if 'twas last week. 'Twas in October, the very beginning of the month. All my boarders had been gone some time. I was doing my own work, for I didn't need any help when I was alone, except Wells Sanford for out-door chores. 'Twas after five o'clock one afternoon I see a team drive up to my door and stop, and there was a wagonful of folks come visiting.

They was my relations from Danby, Cousin Levi Bourne's folks — him and his wife and her mother, and Joshua and his wife and little Abigail. They'd come to have supper and spend the night. I was dreadful glad to see 'em, and made 'em real welcome. I had plenty of things in the house to do with, and I knew I could get 'em up a good supper in no time. But who was going to wait on them at table while I was cooking, frying their griddle-cakes and all? 'Twas kind of chilly that day, and I made 'em all set up to the wood fire in the keeping-room, and I went out to the kitchen to see what I could do.

I set to work beating up biscuit and making my batter for the cakes, and chopping up the cold beef and potatoes for hash, when I heerd a man's step in the back entry. Then someone come to the door and looked in. 'Twas kind of dark, and I couldn't see at first, but I heerd a man's voice say, "Don't put yourself out any, Mis' Harris; it's only a transient for supper," and I knew in one minute 'twas that man.

I was in such a hurry, and as nervy and flustered, that somehow I didn't think of how I'd wanted to see him, and all I wanted to say. But I just says, "Deary me, another for supper, and me with not a soul in the house to help me!"

He come in real quiet, set his hat down on the table, and says, very pleasant and soft: "Let me help ye, Mis' Harris. I'm quite a hand to help, I am."

And if you'll believe me, before I could say a word he set to work. He set the table, getting out the crockery without asking me a thing, going in and out very quick and still, laying the napkins around, and putting on the plates and knives and forks, He fixed it real nice, but in a kind of an old-fashioned way. When I went in to take a look at it, I declare it looked for all the world like my mother's tea table when I was a young one; all the more because he'd used the old blue and white crockery and some other odd dishes ma'd left to me. He helped me about every single thing; he was real handy for a man, and saved me lots of steps and trouble. Pretty soon he says, still just as easy and quiet: "I suppose you'd like to have me wait on table," he says. "I'm used to waitin', and there ain't nothin' I like so much as helpin' folks to things."

I tell you I was pleased. Seems queer now that I took it so easy and let a man that had come for his own supper work around so, but it seemed to come real nat'ral then. Well, he waited on table, and I never see anyone do better, and so they all said. Levi told me afterwards that he waited on them more's if he was a friend doing for 'em than like paid help. He put a big book in one of the chairs for little Abigail to set on, and he lifted her up on it as if he was her pa, and pinned her napkin round her neck just as nice. Old Mis' Fish, Levi's wife's mother, was getting old and sort of childish, and when he passed the biscuit to her she looked up at him, and she says: "How air ye, sir? Your face is real familiar, but I disremember your name. How do you call yourself?" she says. "You can call me Nathan," he says, very pleasant and soft.

I didn't hear nor know anything about it till they told me afterwards. He was real attentive to the old lady, wrapping her knit shawl around her every time it slipped off, and picking up her specs when she dropped 'em. They said he had a real friendly way with him, urging 'em to eat, pressing the victuals on 'em, and doing a good deal more'n there was any call for.

Bime-by they finished, and I heerd their chairs scrape, and then they went into the keeping-room again. I run in for a minute to tell 'em I'd be ready pretty soon to visit with 'em, and they begun to ask me about the man that waited on table. Levi said he thought first he might be a relation — he had a kind of family look — and when he told 'em his name was Nathan, he was pretty sure of it, because that had been a great name among the Bourneses for generations. But I told him 'twa'n't so; the man was 'most a stranger, and I didn't even know till that minute his name was Nathan. But I said that bime-by I'd come in and tell 'em something remarkable about this transient and the time I'd had with him.

Then I went back into the dining-room. The man was there waiting for me, though I'd been dreadful afraid he'd go off in his aggravating way before I come back. He'd seemed real taken with my old chiny, and he was standing by the table with a piece of it in his hand. 'Twas a queer, old-fashioned thing — a mug — sort of yellowish-white, with a black pictur' on it, and it had been my little brother Nathan's; he'd always drunk his milk out of it. He set it down real careful's I come in and I says: "Now you and me, we must have our supper. I'll run out and put the griddle on and fry some hot cakes, and I'll be back in a jiffy. But first," I says, "I must know what to call you, for I 'ain't an idea what your name is."

He says, kind of bashful like, "You might call me Nathan."

"But that's your first name, I suppose," I says.

"Yes, ma'am," he says, with a real pleasant look on his face, "that's my very first name."

"And might I ask your last one," I says, "so's to call you by it?"

He waited a minute, and then he says, "You wouldn't know any better if I was to tell you; you wouldn't understand it; but Nathan's my first name."

I thought that was kind of queer, but I only said, "Well, when I bring in your supper we must have a little talk. For you know well enough," I says, smiling, and nodding my head at him, "that there's a good many things to be gone over betwixt you and me, and there's a sight of things I'm beholden to you for, and never a chance before to say obleeged to ye."

"'Tain't worth speaking of, Mis' Harris," he says, in his softly way. "I was dreadful glad to help ye. There ain't nothin' I set by more'n helpin' people, partic'lar my own folks."

"What did he mean by that?" I asks myself, as I fried the griddle-cakes and drawed some fresh tea. "I ain't his folks as I know; mebbe he means his fellow-bein's or his neighbors. I mean to ask him."

But I never done it. He was gone when I went back into the dining-room, and, sure's I live and breathe, from that day to this I've never catched a sight of that man — never, never, never. Nobody see him go, but Levi heerd the side door shut, and then steps going down the walk. All my looking and asking and wondering and guessing come to nothing. All I ever knew about him you know yourself now.

Dr. Little, that told you to ask me about it, hasn't been here long. He's dreadful interested in folks' minds and heads — the inside of 'em — and what they believe, and why they believe it, and all that. They've got some name for that sort, but I disremember it; but, 'tany rate, he's one. He's made me tell him that story twenty times if he has once, and he goes over 'n' over it with me. He uses pretty big words, but I've got so I can follow him, after a fashion. He'll ask me what I really think about it myself. Well, I tell him I don't know; sometimes I think one thing and sometimes another, and then again I don't think anything at all. Then he asks me if I ever thought that maybe this man was my little brother Nathan come back in this form, and carrying out his idee of helping folks. Yes, I had thought of it, and the doctor knew I had, and more'n a little, too. But it don't seem a satisfyin' sort of the'ry. Seems 's if folks, if they're let to come back at all, would come lookin' kind of different from us poor folks that's never had their opportunities; they'd be more like angels or heavenly bein's, appears to me. But this man was just a real Bentley-lookin' kind of man, plain and homely, and dreadful bashful.

Then, if 'twas Nathan, why, he'd growed up. I wonder if they do grow up in that place. This man seemed just about as old as Nathan would have been if he'd lived. And he'd got the same ideas as Nathan about helping folks and getting 'em out of trouble. And it was just me, his own sister, he helped. But then it don't stand to reason that a soul would come back to do such common kind of helping jobs as making a baby look pleasant to have its pictur' took, or fetching peppermint, or driving cows out of the corn, and all that. To be sure, it might come down to sing a favorite hymn to a dying woman, or to save a little child's life, but — no, I can't tell what I do think, and so I always tell Dr. Little.

"But," he says, in his solemn, book-word kind o' way that I've got by heart now — "but, Mrs. Harris, do you consider this visitant a supernat'ral being? Do you call it a spirit or ghost?"

And I always answer, "No, Dr. Little, I don't dast to say I hold that."

"Well, then, my dear Mrs. Harris," he says again, "what do you call this apparition?"

And I always answer, "Why, I just call him a transient."

The Shape of Fear

Elia Wilkinson Peattie

Tim O'Connor — who was descended from the O'Conors with one N — started life as a poet and an enthusiast. His mother had designed him for the priesthood, and at the age of fifteen, most of his verses had an ecclesiastical tinge, but, somehow or other, he got into the newspaper business instead, and became a pessimistic gentleman, with a literary style of great beauty and an income of modest proportions. He fell in with men who talked of art for art's sake, — though what right they had to speak of art at all nobody knew, — and little by little his view of life and love became more or less profane. He met a woman who sucked his heart's blood, and he knew it and made no protest; nay, to the great amusement of the fellows who talked of art for art's sake, he went the length of marrying her. He could not in decency explain that he had the traditions of fine gentlemen behind him and so had to do as he did, because his friends might not have understood. He laughed at the days when he had thought of the priesthood, blushed when he ran across any of those tender and exquisite old verses he had written in his youth, and became addicted to absinthe and other less peculiar drinks, and to gaming a little to escape a madness of *ennui*.

As the years went by he avoided, with more and more scorn, that part of the world which he denominated Philistine, and consorted only with the fellows who flocked about Jim O'Malley's saloon. He was pleased with solitude, or with these convivial wits, and with not very much else beside. Jim O'Malley was a sort of Irish poem, set to inspiring measure. He was, in fact, a Hibernian Mæcenas, who knew better than to put bad whiskey before a man of talent, or tell a trite tale in the presence of a wit. The recountal of his disquisitions on politics and other current matters had enabled no less than three men to acquire national reputations; and a number of wretches, having gone the way of men who talk of art for art's sake, and dying in foreign lands, or hospitals, or asylums, having no one else to be homesick for, had been homesick for Jim O'Malley, and wept for the sound of his voice and the grasp of his hearty hand.

When Tim O'Connor turned his back upon most of the things he was born to and took up with the life which he consistently lived till the unspeakable end, he was unable to get rid of certain peculiarities. For example, in spite of all his debauchery, he continued to look like the Beloved Apostle. Notwithstanding abject friendships he wrote limpid and noble English. Purity seemed to dog his heels, no matter how violently he attempted to escape from her. He was never so drunk that he was not an exquisite, and even his creditors, who had become inured to his deceptions, confessed it was a privilege to meet so perfect a gentleman. The creature who held him in bondage, body and soul, actually came to love him for his gentleness, and for some quality which baffled her, and made her ache with a strange longing which she could not define. Not that she ever defined anything, poor little beast! She had skin the color of pale gold, and yellow eyes with brown lights in them, and great plaits of straw-colored hair. About her lips was a fatal and sensuous smile, which, when it got hold of a man's imagination, would not let it go, but held to it, and mocked it till the day of his death. She was the incarnation of the Eternal Feminine, with all the wifeliness and the maternity left out — she was ancient, yet ever young, and familiar as joy or tears or sin.

She took good care of Tim in some ways: fed him well, nursed him back to reason after a period of hard drinking, saw that he put on overshoes when the walks were wet, and looked after his money. She even prized his brain, for she discovered that it was a delicate little machine which produced gold. By association with him and his friends, she learned that a number of apparently useless things had value in the eyes of certain convenient fools, and so she treasured the autographs of distinguished persons who wrote to him — autographs which he disdainfully tossed in the waste basket. She was careful with presentation copies from authors, and she went the length of urging Tim to write a book himself. But at that he balked.

"Write a book!" he cried to her, his gentle face suddenly white with passion. "Who am I to commit such a profanation?"

She didn't know what he meant, but she had a theory that it was dangerous to excite him, and so she sat up till midnight to cook a chop for him when he came home that night.

He preferred to have her sitting up for him, and he wanted every electric light in their apartments turned to the full. If, by any chance, they returned together to a dark house, he would not enter till she touched the button in the hall, and illuminated the room. Or if it so happened that the lights were turned off in the night time, and he awoke to find himself in darkness, he shrieked till the woman came running to his relief, and, with derisive laughter, turned them on again. But when she found that after these frights he lay trembling and white in his bed, she began to be alarmed for the clever, gold-making little machine, and to renew her assiduities, and to horde more tenaciously than ever, those valuable curios on which she someday expected to realize when he was out of the way, and no longer in a position to object to their barter.

O'Connor's idiosyncrasy of fear was a source of much amusement among the boys at the office where he worked. They made open sport of it, and yet, recognizing him for a sensitive plant, and granting that genius was entitled to whimsicalities, it was their custom when they called for him after work hours, to permit him to reach the lighted corridor before they turned out the gas over his desk. This, they reasoned, was but a slight service to perform for the most enchanting beggar in the world.

"Dear fellow," said Rick Dodson, who loved him, "is it the Devil you expect to see? And if so, why are you averse? Surely the Devil is not such a bad old chap."

"You haven't found him so?"

"Tim, by heaven, you know, you ought to explain to me. A citizen of the world and a student of its purlieus, like myself, ought to know what there is to know! Now you're a man of sense, in spite of a few bad habits — such as myself, for example. Is this fad of yours madness? — which would be quite to your credit, — for gadzooks, I like a lunatic! Or is it the complaint of a man who has gathered too much data on the subject of Old Rye? Or is it, as I suspect, something more occult, and therefore more interesting?"

"Rick, boy," said Tim, "you're too — inquiring!" And he turned to his desk with a look of delicate hauteur.

It was the very next night that these two tippling pessimists spent together talking about certain disgruntled but immortal gentlemen, who, having said their say and made the world quite uncomfortable, had now journeyed on to inquire into the nothingness which they postulated. The dawn was breaking in the muggy east; the bottles were empty, the cigars burnt out. Tim turned toward his friend with a sharp breaking of sociable silence.

"Rick," he said, "do you know that Fear has a Shape?"

"And so has my nose!"

"You asked me the other night what I feared. Holy father, I make my confession to you. What I fear is Fear."

"That's because you've drunk too much — or not enough.

> "'Come, fill the cup, and in the fire of Spring
> Your winter garment of repentance fling —'"

"My costume then would be too nebulous for this weather, dear boy. But it's true what I was saying. I am afraid of ghosts."

"For an agnostic that seems a bit —"

"Agnostic! Yes, so completely an agnostic that I do not even know that I do not know! God, man, do you mean you have no ghosts — no — no things which shape themselves? Why, there are things I have done —"

"Don't think of them, my boy! See, 'night's candles are burnt out, and jocund day stands tiptoe on the misty mountain top.'"

Tim looked about him with a sickly smile. He looked behind him and there was nothing there; stared at the blank window, where the smoky dawn showed its offensive face, and there was nothing there. He pushed away the moist hair from his haggard face — that face which would look like the blessed St. John, and leaned heavily back in his chair.

"'Yon light is not daylight, I know it, I,'" he murmured drowsily, "'it is some meteor which the sun exhales, to be to thee this night —'"

The words floated off in languid nothingness, and he slept. Dodson arose preparatory to stretching himself on his couch.

But first he bent over his friend with a sense of tragic appreciation.

"Damned by the skin of his teeth!" he muttered. A little more, and he would have gone right, and the Devil would have lost a good fellow. As it is" — he smiled with his usual conceited delight in his own sayings, even when they were uttered in soliloquy — "he is merely one of those splendid gentlemen one will meet with in hell." Then Dodson had a momentary nostalgia for goodness himself, but he soon overcame it, and stretching himself on his sofa, he, too, slept.

That night he and O'Connor went together to hear "Faust" sung, and returning to the office, Dodson prepared to write his criticism. Except for the distant clatter of telegraph instruments, or the peremptory cries of "copy" from an upper room, the office was still. Dodson wrote and smoked his interminable cigarettes; O'Connor rested his head in his hands on the desk, and sat in perfect silence. He did not know when Dodson finished, or when, arising, and absent-mindedly extinguishing the lights, he moved to the door with his copy in his hands. Dodson gathered up the hats and coats as he passed them where they lay on a chair, and called:

"It is done, Tim. Come, let's get out of this."

There was no answer, and he thought Tim was following, but after he had handed his criticism to the city editor, he saw he was still alone, and returned to the room for his friend. He advanced no further than the doorway, for, as he stood in the dusky corridor and looked within the darkened room, he saw before his friend a Shape, white, of perfect loveliness, divinely delicate and pure and ethereal, which seemed as the embodiment of all goodness. From it came a soft radiance and a perfume softer than the wind when "it breathes upon a bank of violets stealing and giving odor." Staring at it, with eyes immovable, sat his friend.

It was strange that at sight of a thing so unspeakably fair, a coldness like that which comes from the jewel-blue lips of a Muir crevasse should have fallen upon Dodson, or that it was only by summoning all the manhood that was left in him, that he was able to restore light to the room, and to rush to his friend. When he reached poor Tim he was stone-still with paralysis. They took him home to the woman, who nursed him out of that attack — and later on worried him into another.

When he was able to sit up and jeer at things a little again, and help himself to the quail the woman broiled for him, Dodson, sitting beside him, said:

"Did you call that little exhibition of yours legerdemain, Tim, you sweep? Or are you really the Devil's bairn?"

"It was the Shape of Fear," said Tim, quite seriously.

"But it seemed mild as mother's milk."

"It was compounded of the good I might have done. It is that which I fear."

He would explain no more. Later — many months later — he died patiently and sweetly in the madhouse, praying for rest. The little beast with the yellow eyes had high mass celebrated for him, which, all things considered, was almost as pathetic as it was amusing.

Dodson was in Vienna when he heard of it.

"Sa, sa!" cried he. "I wish it wasn't so dark in the tomb! What do you suppose Tim is looking at?"

As for Jim O'Malley, he was with difficulty kept from illuminating the grave with electricity.

The Path of the Storm

Marie van Vorst

There are people who will remember how a certain dingy rockaway, drawn by a stout gray horse, passed through streets piled high with mountains of snow; how it passed where no wagon had been seen for twenty-four hours, hailed by those whom profit and loss, life and death, called from one part of the great city to another. They will remember how the occupants — an old man and an old woman — muffled up to the ears, remained deaf to the prayers of the people who would have bought for fabulous price the plain country conveyance. The harness was rusty, and mended here and there with rope; the flapping curtains of cracked leather were lacquered with dust and mud spots; but the vehicle rolled smoothly along; the gray horse never slackened speed. Through a glistening world, under brilliant skies, the object moved like a shadow. But there are those who will remember! And it has passed into my story, as records of disturbed traffic, arrested commerce, buried roadways, and marvels of disasters and of death have passed with the great blizzard of 1888 into history.

Chapter I.

The cold wind blew the rain against the houses, and then flung it like a tattered garment across the street. The drops fell with a force that broke them into a thousand more. They splashed up from the pavement, and when they touched the stones a second time they froze. The sidewalks were covered with ice and water; the gutters streamed rivers that poured in violent torrents until they were dammed by a wall of slush. The wind blew the rain across the North River in a trembling sheet that wavered and palpitated. Here and there were distinguishable the dark hulls of anchored vessels, their masts covered with ice, their decks washed with a freezing flood. Between Jersey City and New York the hideous ferry-boats, with a monotonous b-r-r-r and swash, plied through the storm.

On the after-deck of a ferry-boat that was still fast to the Jersey City side stood a man, his coat buttoned up to his chin. Every now and then, as a whip of wind slashed under the shelter and swirled around him, he shivered like a trembling dog. Among the last of the oncoming passengers was a young woman. The man started forward, went up to her side, pushed in the swinging-door of the cabin, and followed her into the reeking atmosphere of the interior. Little fogs arose from the streaming garments of those who had been unsheltered from the rain. Umbrellas, dripping from handles to ferrules, sent out rivulets that streamed toward the centre of the muddy floor. The heat, the steaming clothes and mingled breaths, soon covered the windows with mist. The man and woman, who had exchanged no form of greeting save a look of recognition, took the first vacant places, and he turned to her eagerly:

"Well?"

"They gave me two dollars and a half. Just think of it, Stephen! Two dollars and a half. I went from the Charity-Work Commissioners to this address in Jersey City. It was a mile from the boat. I walked, and when I got there I was so faint that I could hardly speak. I was afraid the woman would think me too weak to work, and that kept me up."

She sank into her seat in a little huddled heap like an old woman, her chin on her breast, a frayed veil lifted above her eyes wrinkled on her forehead. But little by little she straightened herself; her face brightened. She unwound the veil, and the hair under her small hat gleamed a halo of light. The blood stirred and glowed under the drawn skin of her cheeks, her lips lost their pinched expression and looked fuller and redder.

"Go on," he said. "Go on. What did they give you to do?"

She leaned toward him closer. "On my bended knees I scrubbed the back stairs, the kitchen, and the great veranda that runs all the way around the house. It took me five hours! I carried out buckets of hot water and washed the floors with washing- soda and yellow soap."

He made a low exclamation. "*You* did that — *you?* Let me see your hands!"

"No! no!" She had hidden them under her coat and she drew away a little from him.

"Let me see them, Esther!"

Reluctantly she showed them, swollen to twice their size, mottled and red where the cold had chilblained them, white where the soap and soda had changed the color of the flesh, that stood up in ridges against the nails. From the palm of her hand on which she had leaned all day the flesh was worn; and the man took his breath in hard, and clinched his own hands until the nails went into the palms. He looked at her, the hot tears burning in his eyes.

"Don't, please, Stephen. Think of the money!"

"Curse them!"

"No! no! They gave me money and food. I was their machine! How could they know that I was anything more than that?"

Around her face were the tendrils of her glowing hair. Through the skin the veins in her temples showed too plainly. Her luminous eyes were intensified by the blue rings under them, and she personified misery; but to the man she was the light of the world, to him she shone from head to feet.

"Then it was dinner-time," Esther went on: "and what do you think I had to eat? A whole dinner — a real hot dinner!"

He felt sick and faint. Just before he had met her he had tasted food for the first time during the day. He broke his fast on a sandwich at the ferry-house restaurant on the Jersey City side, and now he was alive with hunger.

"What did you have to eat, Esther?"

"Soup, and beef, and boiled potatoes, and good bread and butter — all we could eat!"

"I am so glad!" he said — "so glad!"

"At first, when I thought of you, I could not touch a thing; but, then — isn't it dreadful? — I was just like an animal; I forgot everything but myself. I don't know what they thought of me. I must have eaten like a beast!"

They were silent a moment; then he said, almost timidly,

"I have a little news for you, dearest."

"Wait!" She put out her disfigured hand warningly. "Don't tell me anything that isn't sure. It seems to me as though I couldn't live through another *perhaps* that ended on the wrong side." Then she was all repentance. "Forgive me! Tell me everything, of course. I don't know what makes me so cowardly. Isn't it the first time? Don't I always want to share the uncertainty?"

"Yes, yes! I don't blame you, God knows. There is only this: I have made a lot of sketches of street life and have taken them to the —— today. I am to know tomorrow if they can use them. It will mean more work of the same kind — perhaps something permanent," he said, without enthusiasm, without hope.

She sank back, and they were silent, and slowly through her crept benumbing fatigue. She was keenly conscious of her exhausted body, in which every bone seemed to have been first beaten and then broken. People were rising and walking slowly toward the narrow passage between the cabins. Esther rose with difficulty, and Stephen encircled her with his arm; she leaned on him heavily. As they stepped out into the night, the wind went down their very throats, closed their eyes, and tried to take away breath and life; but they bent their heads against it. It tore off Esther's shabby veil, which clung desperately to her hat by one pin and waved out a long floating streamer behind. They went on as swiftly as they could to a crowded cross-town car. The girl looked about her helplessly. The blood seemed to surge up within her and fill her eyes. A West Twenty-third Street dandy was adjusting himself comfortably, when Stephen touched him on the arm.

"Would you be so good as to give my wife your seat? I'm afraid she is going to faint."

"W'y, cert'n'y," said the man, rising at once, and staring at the girl, who sank down almost unconscious. From the cars, through the driving rain, to the door of the tenement on the fifth floor of which they lived, Stephen carried her. She could not protest; her head lay heavily on his shoulder; the loosened veil, soaked to limpness, fluttered no longer; on her face, on the white lids of her closed eyes, the rain fell; and, goaded by a frenzy against all powers and all the world to a strength superhuman, Stephen carried her up four flights of stairs to their room.

Chapter II.

There are certain people who possess a wand of destruction, and all that they touch turns to ashes. So it was with the man to whom Esther Dunstable had given her life. Whatever prospects he had when they married faded away as sun-flecked clouds swallowed by the storm. One after another Esther saw scheme and project fail and promising efforts come to a standstill, as clever mechanical toys that rush with every semblance of perpetual motion across a platform for a few yards, and then come to a deathlike stop. There were many who had confidence in Stephen's ability. He had not been lacking in friends, and he had used them all, until the time came when there was not a human soul to whom he could return holding out his empty hands of failure. His monumental mistakes swept away all his personal means and left him some thousands of dollars in debt. But even in the blackness of this night new schemes, new projects, shone out for him like stars. The misfortune which to others appeared a wanton blow of fate, striking him down by caprice, opened the hands of one or two who still looked to Stephen for success. One by one he put forth his fragile essays, that, like children's balloons sent out into the vast and let free, fluttered a moment aggravatingly near, then melted away into the thin air and were lost. It is easy to exhaust our own resources; it is still easier to exhaust those of our friends, and Stephen stood finally absolutely alone, want and ruin staring him grimly in the face. Then it was that Esther wrote to her father. She received a letter over which she wept her heart out, her tears falling on the cruel words and on the head of the child she nursed at her breast.

A faith, a belief such as hers in her husband might have breathed over a valley of dead bones and made them alive. It never wavered, it never changed. "I believe," she said —

"I believe you have great talents, great powers. If you fail steadily on to the end, Stephen, and all the world mocks at you, if you die on the eve of a great mistake, a great failure, I shall believe 'if he had lived until tomorrow, he would have succeeded!'"

At moments when his discouragement was as great as his most sanguine hopes had been brilliant, this light shone into his soul. Belief and confidence are the wings of a love such as hers, and she had awakened the best in Stephen. Her deeper, more balanced nature he reverenced and admired, and in their close relationship he began to reflect it, until finally two things stood out for him clear and distinct — Esther's belief in him, and his own failure. Scales fell from his eyes, and he saw these two to be incompatible. Toward the one he stretched out his hands. From the other he shrank as we shrink from a spectre no less horrible because we have ourselves invoked it.

In the interstices of the web of circumstance that surrounds us it is hard to say how much we have entangled with our own fingers. Certain it is there are those who seize their threads and wind them straight; others stand helplessly held in the mesh. Stephen had eagerly seized every loose end that presented itself, and wound until he came to an inextricable knot.

With a letter of introduction to the editor of a daily paper just starting in New York, Esther and Stephen came to that city, and took a room at the top of a house little better than a tenement. Stephen entered upon his duties as night reporter with enthusiasm. In a short time he had proved more than ability. In a month he had become invaluable. One night in January he came in at eleven o'clock with a chattering chill, and for days lay between life and death. When he was again able to leave the house they had not a cent in the world. Then it had been that Esther had gone to take, with her rough-handed sisters, what work she could get from the Board of Charity Commissioners.

Chapter III.

For three days after her unaccustomed labor she had not left her bed, and the third day she lay back on her pillow a shadow of a once strong and beautiful womanhood.

"You should not have come for me, Stephen. You were not well enough. It was dreadful to have carried me upstairs! But, after all, what difference does it make?"

"None," he said, shortly, after a pause — "none."

"Stephen," and she fixed on him her eyes and seemed to look from another world, "are you afraid to die?"

"No," he said, half speaking to himself. "No world hereafter could treat me worse."

"Listen," she said. "We have striven and failed; it is not our fault — not our fault. We ought not to have married, perhaps; but then we ought not to have cared as we did. To have turned away from that voice of our natures would have been a greater sin."

Stephen listened, without grasping the import of her words. He thought with a terrible pang how wasted she was, how changed, how she had given her very life for him to this end.

"I am not strong enough to do the work I can get, and you are ill. There remains for us the charity hospital — apart from one another; for our children, the public asylum. Have we not, I ask you, a right to choose between these horrors and to go quietly out of life?"

Stephen rose, and leaning over his wife, felt her hands and her forehead. She divined his thought at once.

"I am not ill; I am more at peace than I have been in months. I am weak and half crushed out of existence, yes — and as for the miserable remnant of life that remains to me, I am simply taking it in my own hands."

"You speak as though you were a supreme power," he said, with thick, trembling voice, "and not under God."

She smiled slightly. "That is a great field into which I cannot go. I have failed, and I shall sever the web."

"What right?" he faltered; "what right?"

"How do we know, we who know so little? It may have been given to us to take, if we will. A good, a wise man said, 'There is always the open door.' Think of what the days have been for years — of the agony of the yesterdays, and the dreadful tomorrows! Think, Stephen, think what it would be to be still and to be at rest!"

He covered his face with his hands.

"Did you mail the letter I gave you on Friday?" she asked, suddenly.

"Yes. Why did you write your people again?"

"To bid them good-by."

Stephen leaned over her; taking her face between his hands, he looked steadily into her eyes.

"You must stop this, Esther; you don't know what you are saying. Lack of food and fatigue have used you all up. We will forget forever what you have said."

If Esther had hoped to make her husband see with her eyes, if she had hoped that with her he was ready to break the chain that held body and soul together, she saw that she was wrong. She saw, too, that he regarded her as ill, as mentally unbalanced, and it gave her a sense of absolute desolations; out of the small circle which, in spite of misery and want, had been full of love and complete understanding, Esther slipped now and stood alone.

"Yes," she said, returning his steady look, and she even smiled — "yes, we will forget it forever."

She folded her hands together — the disfigurement that had wrung his heart was passing away, and they were taking again something of their old beautiful lines. His eyes filled with burning tears that scalded under the lids; he was suffocated with a grief that, like a swollen stream, dashes all obstacles away and will not be kept back. Unable to control himself, he rose abruptly and hurried out of the room.

Chapter IV.

Back from the road that runs from the village of B—— to Tarrytown stands a brown house. It is surrounded by a country garden, where the beds are brilliant with dahlias and hollyhocks and sweet-pease part of the year, and in winter are a succession of snowy hillocks. The place is called the Dunstable Homestead. Here Thomas Dunstable and his wife, with two servants, lived summer and winter. It was rumored that Thomas Dunstable put by every year more than most men made; it was rumored that he was very rich and sordid; it was rumored that appearances were kept up with difficulty, and that the servants were never paid. But rumors of all kinds died out slowly, for where there is no youth about the house, its annals and ghosts cease after a while to awaken lively interest. And Mr. and Mrs. Dunstable pursued the even tenor of their way, drove in to town and out behind the stout gray horse, and whether or not they paid their servants, they kept them.

On the evening of March 11, 1888, Mr. and Mrs. Dunstable sat together in the room they called the library. Mr. Dunstable in his Sunday clothes, his waist coat unbuttoned, his slippers kicked off, and his feet in white stockings propped up on a footstool before the stove, in which a fire glowed and reddened through the isinglass. Mrs. Dunstable rocked comfortably to and fro, her eyes closed behind her spectacles, her book open on her lap. Thus the two sat, scarcely speaking, for an hour after the noon dinner. Every now and then the isinglass cracked a little. Mr. Dunstable's watch ticked loudly in his pocket. Save for that there was an unbroken silence. It was a gray day, and a few flakes of snow fell gently past the window. Mr. Dunstable did not seem inclined to nap — indeed, he was keenly alive, his eyes wide open and brilliant. From time to time he shifted his position uneasily. Finally, turning around abruptly, so that his movements awakened his wife with a start, he said:

"Mary, I have got a letter upstairs from Esther. I'm going to get it and read it."

Mrs. Dunstable was quite awake now. Her healthy cheek grew pale, her eyes eager.

"Oh, father!" she said; her tone was trembling and eager, but he was gone and back again, the thick envelope in his hand, and all this before her eyes had lost their startled surprise.

"When did you get it?" she asked.

"Last night when I went to the post-office" said Mr. Dunstable, shortly.

She made no comment, but her lip was quivering.

Sitting in his arm-chair near the window, Mr. Dunstable broke the envelope and read the letter. He read it through to himself. Mrs. Dunstable sat forward in her chair, waiting. He did not read it aloud, but handed it over to her without a word.

"Why don't you read it to me, father?" and she adjusted her spectacles and bent closely over the paper. Mr. Dunstable did not reply. He had risen and stood before his wife, his jaw hanging down, his eyes fixed, a stiff, rigid figure, as though smitten to stone by a terrible image. With no change of expression on her mild old face, Mrs. Dunstable read the letter to its close. Then, as though there were only herself and the piece of paper in the world, clutching it fast in her hands, she rose from her chair with a sharp cry and rushed toward the door that led into the garden.

"Mother!" cried the old man, starting from his stupor and seizing her by the arm. "Mother, where are you going?"

"Let me be! Don't touch me!" The gentle voice was high and shrill. "My Lord! Lord of Heaven! I'm going to my child!" She was struggling to free her arm; with her other hand she stretched toward the door —

"God tells me I shall be in time! You can't stop me now, Thomas! Let me be! Let me go!"

"Wait, mother," he said, soothingly. "Wait! there ain't any trains Sunday."

"*Trains!*" She laughed a laugh that was a scream. "There are roads, ain't there, and I'm a-goin' to hitch the horse and drive to town."

She spoke of New York as though it was a village at her garden's foot, and not a great city thirty miles away.

"Mary," said the old man, authoritatively, "you go upstairs and get your warm clothes and the mufflers and rugs, and heat the bricks and get some whiskey, and I will go out and hitch up."

Mrs. Dunstable suddenly became what she had never been in her life until then — a personality. But even in this supreme moment of her first assertion of self the habit of obedience and yielding to her husband was strong. The arm stretched toward the door fell slowly, and she turned her twitching, agonized face toward his, scarcely less inured than her own.

"I'm afraid you can't get along alone, Thomas; you can't hurry enough. I had better help you. I am afraid you will keep us back, and I'm going to town if I walk; if I crawl through the snow, I'm going to see my child!" Again she moved toward the door; she grasped the knob; it rattled in her trembling hand.

Mr. Dunstable put his hands on both her shoulders. "You go straight upstairs and get them things. We'll need them all. You'll help that way. I'll be here with the team before you're ready. If you don't go and get them you'll hinder us, and you don't want to hinder us, do you?"

"Lord, no!" wailed the old woman, wringing her hands. "I'll get them. I'll do as you say, but I'll be ready before you. Go, Thomas, go!" She would have sent him out hatless and coatless in the storm. He passed through the kitchen, where in the stove was a red fire, and the teakettle sang and hummed.

"It is so long since we had any fire, that the world must have frozen since then." That was what part of the letter said. As for the rest, its import chilled the blood in his veins. He took his hat and coat from where they hung, lit a lantern, and went out across the garden, over the lightly falling snow, to the barn.

Thomas Dunstable had been a stern, unbending husband, and a stern, unbending father, and the wayward, capricious girl, impatient of correction, with feelings as strange as they were indifferent to his own, had been an enigma, more of a pain to him than a pleasure. He had, however, done his duty by her, so far as worldly advantage goes. He sent her to New York to a fashionable school, supplied her generously with clothes and pocket-money, sent her abroad to travel for a year. When she returned, matured in thought and beauty, he looked at her as one might regard a plant of an unknown species. The narrowness and crudeness of her home settled around Esther Dunstable as a frost around the roots of a flower. Finally, after months of opposition to her father's will, she ran away, as they call it, and married a man whom Mr. Dunstable disliked and despised. Then he shut the doors of her home against her, and for him she was as one dead. The mother, whose will had long since become part of her husband, yielded to this tyranny, and to it she yielded her soul. She had existed ever since in a lethargy which her husband took to be wifely submission. It was in reality a stupor of grief and impotence in which she had no power to think or greatly feel. But tonight the chains were struck from her and she was a free woman. Everywhere she went, in her eager gathering together of things for her journey, she saw Esther. In the parlor, a slender girl figure stole from the garden door, her hands full of flowers, and it was summer-time. In the kitchen, as Mrs. Dunstable put the bricks in the oven, Esther was there, a child, her hair falling about her red cheeks as she bent to shove in the oven her little play pans of dough. Mrs. Dunstable stood in her bed-room, before her mirror, putting on the little black bonnet, wrapping a veil around her head, getting her mittens from the bureau, and Mr. Dunstable's fur gloves. There all the while was Esther in her bright plaid dress, with her school-books, by the work-table, under the lamp; and there, as she went to the bed, was the baby Esther, with wide, sweet eyes that smiled at her. Mrs. Dunstable was a young mother again, leaning over her child. Here she wept, and with the tears came a great relief.

260

And the same presence was with the father, as in the cold barn, with feverish haste, he harnessed the horse. There came to the old man a sudden realization of what he had been, what he had failed to be, to his child, and as he bent to fasten the straps and to buckle the traces, over and over again accusing voices within him called with cruel persistence — "Her blood be on thy head." He put up his arm and wiped the perspiration from his forehead, and once he was so dizzy that he leaned against the shafts and the gray horse until his senses reeled into place again. Then he piled what blankets he could find into the rockaway, and drove out of the stable into the little driveway up to the door. On the sill, with the light and warmth from the house behind her, the snow blowing about her and settling on her bonnet, cloak, and veil, stood the mother, waiting.

"Are you ready?" she called in a clear voice which sounded to the father like the full, assured tones of the girl whose will was ever against his.

"Yes, Mary." He got out and helped her to lift in rugs, two heavy blankets, and the hot bricks.

"The baskets are full of food *for them*," said the old woman, significantly, as she climbed up on to the front seat.

"Hadn't you better sit back, Mary?" asked her husband.

"No. I want to see the road and watch with you."

He tucked her in as warmly as he could, and took his place beside her. She had left a note on the table for the servants, when they should return, and the key was under the mat, which the snow was fast covering. The father took up the reins.

"Wait!" she said, putting her hand on his arm. "Your will, Thomas?"

He looked at her in astonishment. She, who had never asked a question of him, was suddenly a stern catechiser.

"It is changed," he said, quickly. "I went down yesterday and had it witnessed in Tarrytown, and I have left her everything."

"Go on, then," said his wife. "Let us go on as fast as we can!"

They were out of the gate by this; the snow was falling and the wind rising.

"It's a good road all the way," said Mr. Dunstable, "and I know it like a book. We turn by Stern's meadow and strike the post-road, and then it's plain sailing to New York."

Chapter V.

All night the wind, as though let loose from an imprisonment of ages, went mad with freedom, and rioted with the white softly falling thing, the snow, embracing it, carrying it hither and thither in a fearful course. If death and desolation should lie in the morning under the beautiful covering, the wind cared not. Child of the cyclone and tornado, it lived one night of madness, and leaving the land still and white as a tomb, went rushing out to sea. And the great white storm that folded its wings over village and city, shutting in the rich in their warm dwellings, shut the poor and the destitute in their empty homes, and with them Esther, Stephen, and their little children. From high up through their window they could look over trafficless streets and watch the efforts of pygmy men to overcome the obstacles of the dazzling element. For them there was neither food nor warmth; but through the hours of this day Esther was conscious of neither hunger nor cold. She was walking on the borders of another world, and though her hands were stretched out to the three she loved, already she seemed to feel the wind from a strange country stir her hair, already these faces, which had held heaven and earth for her, were growing dim and indistinct.

"It is my last day with Stephen; it is my last day with my little children!" She was already seeing them through a mist, and their voices were far away. She had always been to Stephen a tower of strength. But he dimly remembered her words of the day before. The weakness was so foreign to her character that he could not associate it with her, and was far from knowing, that every touch, that every caress, was a farewell. During the afternoon the four sat together, the children wrapped in the bed-covering, and the strange bright day that stands alone in the history of storms in the Eastern States slipped into shadow. Then Esther put the children to bed that they might get warm, and forget, if possible, to be hungry. She had turned, and was standing in the middle of the floor, when someone knocked at the door. Before she could speak it was opened, and to Esther's eyes revealed a burst and radiance of light, for her mother stood on the threshold, and she entered with open arms, her face all smiles, all tenderness. Her father, too, muffled up to his ears, snow on his cap and coat, was close behind; he was smiling at her — a smile she had looked all her life to see. With a cry that brought up from the depths of her soul the misery borne in silence for years, that brought it all forth and sent it ringing from her lips and freed her soul forever, she rushed into her mother's arms. The two women clung together.

"Esther, my child, my child!"

The mother held her closely, then put her away a little, and with hands exquisite with love touched the girl's brow, her hair, her eyes. "Dear Heaven! those cruel, cruel lines! How you have suffered! Poor child! poor child!"

And the father stood watching, listening, his lips twitching, his breast heaving, until over his smile crept tears that rolled down his cheeks like summer rain.

"Will you forgive me, Esther?" He held out his arms. She was in them, her frail body leaning against his strength as a loosened vine, torn and battered by the wind, is blown against an oak.

"Stephen, will you take my hand?"

"Yes!" in both his thin hands, and he raised his wan look to the old man with a forgiveness that was holy to see.

"The children, Esther?"

"They are asleep; I will wake them."

"No, no," murmured the grandmother, bending over the sleeping children, "not for the world. Don't waken them. Let us see them this way. Come, father." She beckoned to her husband, and he drew near, looking down at the small faces scarcely seen in the shadow. "How pretty! how pretty! Like you, Esther, only not so round and rosy; but they shall grow strong and well soon — soon." Her tears were falling over them. "Forgive us, forgive us!" she murmured.

"How do you call them, Esther?" asked the father.

"Mary and Esther; for you, mother, and for me." The mother's arm was always around the girl, who clung to her like a little child.

"How did you get here in this terrible storm?" asked Stephen.

"In the old rockaway, with Jock, the gray horse. You remember Jock, Esther?"

Did she remember him! She laughed and cried together. She had ridden him, harnessed him, fed him many a time.

"Remember," said the father, "that all your cares, all your troubles are over, my girl. The years of famine have become years of plenty — a new life — remember!"

Stephen was still holding the old man's hand. From the warm, strong clasp health and vigor went out into his exhausted body, and a new strength, a new courage, rose up within him.

"Take off your things, father and mother," said Esther, eagerly. "You must stay; indeed we will not let you go!"

"First," said the old man, gently freeing his hands, "we must go down to the carriage and bring up what we have brought you children."

Mrs. Dunstable was disengaging herself from Esther's close embrace. "No, no, not mother too," pleaded the girl. "Let Stephen go; I can't spare mother."

A light such as fills the heavens from horizon to horizon on a summer evening after the sun has gone down flashed across the old woman's face. "I have brought some things for you all and for the children, my dear," she said, gently; "it is my fancy to get them myself." The two guests were going towards the door. Through it the father had already passed.

"I will go and help you bring up the things. It is nothing less than a miracle for you to have come in such a storm. Why, they told me no carriage could pass through the streets!" said Stephen, following the two figures down the long flights of stairs. They reached the hall door, and the wind came sucking in the key-hole with a sharp note of pain.

"When I opened this door this morning there was a block of snow in front of it like a wall," he said. He unfastened the door. It blew open violently in his hand, and a gust of wind whirled the snow up from the steps into his eyes and all around him, one fine feathery wraith after another, until he was enveloped in a shroud of snow. He caught his breath and staggered back a little, shut the door after him — *and he was alone!* For a moment he stood leaning against the wall; flakes of melting snow were on his wrist, on his hair, on his shoulders. What was he doing here at the foot of the stairs, by the door, *alone!* He shook himself, and again he opened the door. The wind must have subsided with strange suddenness, for now no snow wreaths covered him. Most of the barricading snow block had been cut away; there was a passage down the steps to the street. He peered out. In the gutters were drifts six feet high. There was no sign of any life astir. He passed his hand over his forehead, dazed, bewildered; then he shut the door again, moistened his lips, held the palms of his hands over his eyes for a few moments. He was alone, alone! What did it mean? Was he going mad? Before him wound the narrow, dirty stairs, straight up into the dark. From rooms at the side came voices coarse and loud. He began a slow ascent, holding fast to the banister; when at last he reached his own room, from under the door streamed a fine line of light; Esther must have lighted a candle. He entered gently. The light seemed to come not alone from the candle on the mantel, but from the little group on the floor; Esther knelt there, her arms about her two children, who, half awake, clung to her. She was kissing them, straining them to her; her hair fell over her face and over her shoulders, a glory of light, and on the three fair heads the candle's pale light and the shadows swept and passed.

"Stephen! Stephen!" Her voice rang out to him with a freshness, a joy that made his heart thrill. How dull had been his ears that he had not missed that clear, sweet note! "Stephen: Stephen! put your arms around us and hold us close!" His arms were around the children, and hers were about his neck, her cheek close against his face.

"How little they are! how helpless! We gave them life, and we will keep it for them and help them to be good; and they will, they will. Listen! I would have committed a great sin, but God put out His hand. I have been selfish, wickedly selfish, and a coward; but it is all over forever, forever. Can you ever forgive me, Stephen? Some terrible thing had come to me. I had ceased to care. I would have left you and them to bear it alone, and tried to go to sleep forever to find peace. What peace would have come to me? Wherever I awakened, I should have awakened in sin!"

"Hush, hush, Esther! You will be ill! Hush, darling!"

"Let me go on, Stephen, let me go on; it will do me good." She was shaken with sobs through which she found her voice in broken sentences, and every now and then she touched his hair and his face with her hand, then touched the heads of the children in his arms.

"Hunger and cold and misery can waste our bodies and drag us down to a grave, but unless we will, it cannot touch our souls; and we have had what many another has gone to the grave rich, and lacking — love. Do you think that God will ever forgive me? Do you think He will let me live *now?*"

"Esther, Esther, dearest!"

"Hush!" she said. "Listen! I say now before Him, cold and weak and needing every good of life, for you, for my children, and for myself, that life is worth living. I count it good to suffer for you, Stephen, and for your children. I am glad to have lived. Do you hear? Do you know? Do you understand?"

"Yes, I know, I know."

What had she seen? Had the spirit passed before her face?

"No," she said, more calmly, and with infinite solemnity, "you do not know. I have been close to death and to the grave. Tomorrow! There would have been no tomorrow for me — *but — God put out His hand!*" For the first time she held to Stephen for protection. Hitherto, unconsciously, he had leaned on her; now he felt himself the stronger and possessed of a new manhood, a new force that had been slowly becoming his for years. As he held her closely, kissing her, her sobs subsided. Over and over to himself he asked, "*What* has Esther seen?" He said nothing, however, nor did she.

There are people who will remember reading of a strange thing when at last in the newspapers the story of the great blizzard was made known.

About four miles from Tarrytown, on a hill-slope between a meadow and the high-road, was found an old rockaway buried under great drifts of snow. The stout gray horse and the two occupants of the carriage, an old man and an old woman, were frozen to death. They had evidently lost track of the road, and in the hurricane of wind and drifting snow must have been soon overcome.

This one incident among many fatal casualties was not so remarkable. But one or two, who recalled the passage through New York of a certain dingy rockaway on the day when no other vehicles passed through the streets, felt a thrill as of having seen that which unveiled vision does not often discern. To them the names of Mr. and Mrs. Thomas Dunstable meant nothing, and with the unexplained things of life this memory was put away after a while until it became as the shadow of a dream.

Back from the high-road that runs between the village of B—— and Tarrytown stands an old-fashioned house. You may see it as you turn up the hilly road past Stern's meadow. The country garden is ablaze with bloom in summer; in the autumn, brown and soft with falling leaves; but all the year round brown and golden heads are at the windows, and little white figures are blown hither and thither in the garden like tiny drifts of snow.

Drifts of snow! Dear Heaven! The sadness that followed in the path of the great white storm! But that is long ago, and rumor again stirs about the old Dunstable homestead. It says that the present occupants are very rich, but it murmurs of past years of misery and hardship, whose traces ease and luxury can never efface. But for those who know Esther Dunstable, and for Stephen above all, the marks in her hands and the lines in her face are part of her loveliness; for they give to her a beauty that is only seen in those who, bending over their task of life, no matter how bitter it may be, look up and take courage.

The Ordeal of Sister Cuthbert

Elizabeth Garver Jordan

Sister Philomene, mistress of novices at St. Mary's, fingered nervously the letter she held in her hand. The envelope, addressed to Sister M. Cuthbert, lay face upward on the table before her. She looked at the firm, clear writing and smiled ironically when she realized that she was studying the characteristic slope of the letters in an absent-minded endeavor to read from them something of the writer's personality. This interest in chirography was the nearest approach to a hobby in the life of the self-contained nun. It seemed singular, however, to her that it could encroach ever so slightly on her attention when her mind was engrossed by a painful problem.

She frowned reflectingly and opened the drawer of her desk. Another letter, addressed to herself, lay in it. She took it out, drew it from its envelope, and spread it open on the table beside the first. Then, with a deepening of the line between her severe, straight brows, she carefully reread them both. The second was written in the stiff, angular hand of age. It exhibited no elegance of style, but the cry of a human heart was in it:

"DEAR CHILD, — You will grieve to hear that your father cannot remain with us much longer. He gets weaker all the time, and the doctor says he cannot live more than a few days. He is conscious, and knows us all. He knows he is going to die, but he will not talk about it, or let us say a word about the salvation of his soul. You know how much I want him to die a Catholic. I have hoped and prayed for fifty years that he would be converted, and you have hoped it, too, ever since you were old enough to know what it meant. But he says he will die in the Protestant faith his mother taught him.

"It breaks my heart. Even Father Murphy is almost discouraged. He thinks there is just one hope for your father, and that is you. If you come and talk to him, he may listen. He loves you, and you might be able to do something with him. I cannot bear to think of his death unless he changes. How can I live alone without any hope of meeting him in heaven? He keeps asking for you all the time. Come home and see him. The Superior will send you home, I know, if you tell her this. Write and let me know when to expect you. There is no time to be lost. MOTHER."

"If I go, Sister Rodriguez is the only one who could take charge of my duties," reflected Sister Philomene. "That would mean that Sister Cuthbert would have to take her place in the infirmary."

She read again, slowly, the letter addressed to the novice:

"Sister M. Cuthbert.

"DEAR MADAM, — You will pardon the intrusion of a friend who writes in your interest. I feel it my duty to inform you of the very alarming condition of your mother. Yesterday at the request of the family I and several other physicians held a consultation over her case. There was only one opinion. Unless a marked change for the better comes within forty-eight hours, we must look for the end. I regret to say there is little probability of such a change, but there is one chance for her, and that, it seems to me, rests with you.

"A pathetic feature of your mother's illness, and one which, as an old friend of the family as well as its physician, has moved me deeply, is the fact that in her delirium she constantly calls for you. In her conscious moments she insists with the unselfishness you know so well that you be not summoned to her, as such a call at this time might interfere with your duties in the cloister. She has made the family promise not to send for you. I, however, am free to follow the dictates of heart and reason, and I refuse to see her agonizing for her daughter, whose presence at this juncture might afford the one chance of her mother's recovery, without doing what I can to secure her that boon. Now you have the facts. You will do as you think best — and in any event you will pardon the interference of a friend who has known you from your childhood.

"Respectfully yours,

"HENRY C. SEDGWICK."

"Sister Cuthbert must take as much of Sister Rodriguez's work as she can while I am away," reflected Sister Philomene, slowly. "Her mother is a good Catholic, and will die happily in the Church. She herself realizes that her daughter's duty lies here. The case is clear to me: I hope it will be to Sister Cuthbert. And yet — it is hard, for she must be told of it, and her love for her mother is the strongest I have ever seen."

She quietly returned the letters to their envelopes after this brief summing-up of the question. It was part of her routine work to read the correspondence that came to the nuns under her care, and the duty frequently brought in its train harassing problems and responsibilities. It had never brought her a harder one than this. Before her rose the face of the young novice, at work in happy unconsciousness of the clouds that hung over the dear home she had forsaken. She was in the infirmary assisting Sister Rodriguez, the convent infirmarian, and had proved a tower of strength to the fragile nun whose health had failed sadly during the year. In fact, it was a question whether Sister Rodriguez herself would not soon be forced to swell the list of invalids under Sister Cuthbert's zealous care. She had to hurry from the wing of the convent where the sick nuns lay to the dormitory that held the ailing pupils, and her days knew little rest. The pupils submitted to her tender ministrations with touching docility. In fact, it was whispered that the presence of this popular novice in the infirmary had brought about an alarming increase in the list of applicants for its shelter.

Only Sister Philomene fully understood the far-reaching influence of the ascetic novice in whose deep eyes burned the light of intense religious fervor. Sister Philomene knew why the other novices went to Sister Cuthbert in their trouble, rather than to her. It was Sister Cuthbert who soothed them, who quieted their fears, who prayed for them and with them when doubt or trials assailed them. It was Sister Cuthbert's simple piety, so deep and so moving, which, by the mere fact of its holiness, had brought many to a realization of their religion as the most important element in their lives.

"She can do more with them than I can," Sister Philomene had reported to the Superior. She recalled the remark now as she waited for Sister Cuthbert to respond to the summons she had sent.

"I wonder how she will take it?" she thought. "She will do her duty — there is no doubt of that. But will this experience do her good or harm?" She started almost guiltily at the sound of Sister Cuthbert's gentle tap on the door, and when the young nun had entered and stood awaiting orders with respectful, downcast eyes, her superior found it oddly difficult to speak. When she spoke, the words came slowly.

"We have both had bad news, Sister," she said. "We must pray for each other, that God may give us strength to bear it rightly."

She handed the two letters to her and bade her read them. Sitting in her big chair, she noted with her steady, clear eyes every change of expression on the other's face. There were many. Sister Cuthbert had unfolded her own letter first and glanced at the signature. Then, with a quick flush and a word of apology, she laid it down and read the other slowly and carefully. She looked up when she finished, with a sweet, modest sympathy in her glance. Her reverence for her superior had something of awe in it. She was about to speak, when Sister Philomene said, quietly:

"Read your letter, Sister Cuthbert."

There was silence in the little office, broken only by the ticking of the clock, marking off the slow, precious moments of the cloister. Sister Cuthbert hurried through her letter, growing white as she read. At the end, she raised her eyes quickly to meet the grave gaze fixed on her.

"I must go," she said, breathlessly. "I ought to go. Reverend Mother has promised that I may obey a call like this from my mother." Her voice was choked and her features looked ghastly in the dim light of the little room. "I may start at once, may I not?" she added, turning towards the door.

Sister Philomene rose and laid a lightly detaining hand upon her arm. This was one of the crises to which she was accustomed, and she knew how to meet it. Sister Cuthbert was very human, she reflected, after all.

"Wait," she said, gently. "You have forgotten something. Your mother is dying a good Catholic, with all the consolations of religion. My father is at the point of death, and is not a Catholic. I shall submit both these letters to Reverend Mother. If I go, there is no one to take my place but Sister Rodriguez; there is no one but you to take hers. It will have to be for both of us what Reverend Mother decides, but I should be glad to have your own heart select now what later may be imposed as obedience."

Sister Cuthbert sank upon her knees and laid her forehead against the carved arm of the chair from which her superior had risen. Tears poured from her eyes.

"Forgive me," she said, chokingly. "Forgive me — and may God forgive me. I was selfish; I thought only of myself. I must stay. And I will pray for my dear mother here —" she stopped.

The older woman slipped a strong hand under her arm and helped her to her feet.

"You have chosen wisely," she said. "It is well that you made this sacrifice voluntarily — well, indeed. But your ordeal may come later. Go to the chapel and pray for strength to bear it."

She heard the door close and the soft steps of the novice recede in the distance. There was an unusually mild expression in her keen gray eyes as she went to the Mother Superior with the two letters. She submitted them without a word.

In the dim chapel of the convent Sister Cuthbert knelt before the altar and prayed chokingly. In her short, serene life no such grief as this had come to her before, and the anguish of it rolled over her like a great wave. Yes, she would do her duty — with all her soul would she do it. But could she bear the pain? Could she live through the next few days, hearing in her ears the voice of her mother calling to her in her delirium — as she heard it now, as she would hear it day and night — until the end? Seeing her mother's face, the soft brown eyes looking for her so eagerly — looking for her whom they would never see again. She would not go — no. She would stay, as duty and her own will dictated. But could mind and body stand the strain? Could she listen to that voice, that dearly loved voice, calling, calling — and calling in vain? It was in her ears now, in the silent chapel. Would she ever cease to hear it if she did not obey it? Only one short half-hour had passed since she read that letter, and already she seemed to have gone through the suffering of a long life. Could she bear it? Or was it some awful dream, some hideous fantasy of the night from which she would mercifully awake? If that was it — Oh, God, for daylight! She felt as if she might shriek aloud. Never had she been conscious of the restraint of convent walls till now. Was she losing her mind? Was she going to succumb to the assault of one great affliction?

Ah, but such a grief — and such a mother! True, she had left her mother. She had given her up when she heard the call to the cloister, and they had both realized, the two who loved each other so fondly, all that separation meant. But her mother had been well and strong and happy in the love of her husband and her other daughter. At the stipulated intervals her letters had come to the convent without the maternal tenderness and the home atmosphere they breathed ever causing a regret in the nun's breast. But now, in sickness, in sorrow, in death — oh, if she could be there, with her mother!

Sister Cuthbert sank lower before the altar. She had forgotten where she was; almost forgotten what she was. She drooped, a huddled mass of black, under the white veil that told of her probation.

Yes, she reflected stanchly, her place was here, and here she would remain. Was it only yesterday she had been so happy? Now she felt like a prisoner, for her mother lay dying outside the walls within which, by her own act, she had shut herself away. She had come, and her mother had wished her to come. Were they both wrong in feeling that here her life-work lay? Never! A thrill of the old ecstasy in her choice filled the nun. Across the black of her horizon a blue line appeared dimly. She straightened herself, buried her face in her hands, and prayed again. And as she prayed the clouds that had obscured her soul were dissipated and peace came to her.

Thank God, it was only a passing storm that had struck her. Through all she had not really wavered in her choice. This was her life — this the ideal life — she, one of those gloriously privileged to share it. If she had seemed to waver, it was because the strongest human love she knew was threatened. She had been weak, she would be strong; she had rebelled, she would be submissive. Tears rolled down her cheeks, but they were those that fall when the storm has spent itself. After their soothing flow, the young nun raised her head as a flower straightens itself under an April shower.

She was alone in the chapel. That was fortunate, she thought. No other eye had seen her struggle, no one but her Maker knew how far she had fallen below the standard she had set herself. But she would go on from this point unfalteringly. The dear mother would understand — she who always understood. Even here, she would see — and how much more beyond! What was this little life, this little world, that one should mourn over a few years of separation? After it came the enduring peace of perfect union. Sister Cuthbert looked up at the altar; in her eyes burned their habitual look of exaltation. The suffering of the hour had left few traces on her serene face. It was over. She had struggled;

she had conquered; she could endure. She leaned her head against the low railing with a parting prayer of resignation and faith.

"Into Thy dear hands, O Lord, I place myself utterly; and there, too, I place the dear mother whom I love more than anything save Thee. Be Thou the more with her, now that Thy will keeps me from her."

Her eyes were wide open, but she no longer saw the altar and the familiar surroundings of the chapel. Instead there came before her vividly an old Colonial house, towards the entrance of which she seemed to be walking up a garden path. The door opened. She entered the house, passed through the wide hall, and up the broad steps that led to the second floor. At the head of them she turned to the right and entered a large, square room. She moved with accustomed steps, for she knew every inch of the way, and all the objects on which her eyes rested were the familiar surroundings of her early years. It was her home.

The room she entered was full, but no one heeded her. She walked its length to the bed between the windows opposite the door, and took her station at its head. In the bed lay her mother, with closed eyes; she seemed to breathe, but that was all. Dr. Sedgwick held the sick woman's hand in his, counting the pulse. Beside him stood a strange man with a professional air whom the nun had never seen before. At the foot of the bed knelt her father, his face hidden in the counterpane, and her sister Edith sat in a large chair near him, her head buried in her hands. The physicians talked softly, but the nun could not hear what they said. This did not surprise her, nor the fact that no one observed her entrance. She looked steadily at her mother's face and saw the eyelids flicker. The physicians bent over their patient. They worked rapidly. Something was done; something that looked like a battery was applied. There was a quantity of apparatus near the bed, unfamiliar to her. At last the mother's eyes opened. She alone of those in the room saw the black-robed novice at the head of the bed. Over her face flashed a look of recognition and delight.

"Katherine," she gasped. "You have come — how good — dear child — now I can die content."

She smiled the old familiar smile, and closed her eyes. Over her face a gray shadow fell. Even as the nun looked the features seemed to stiffen. The doctors stepped back, and Dr. Sedgwick, going to the man at the foot of the bed, put a sympathetic hand under his arm and helped him to rise. Edith, who had sprung to her feet, sank down again with a bitter cry. The strange doctor drew the sheet gently over the still face on the pillow.

And now there were tapers burning about that placid face. — No! — This was the convent chapel, and the tapers were those that burned dimly on the altar. It had grown dark and cold. She was still upon her knees. She heard the sound of the vesper bell.

Oh, the tender mercifulness of God! She had given up seeing her mother after the long, rebellious outcry of her weak, human heart. And then He had taken her to her mother, who had seen her and had died in peace. She seemed not to touch the floor as she walked down the long aisle and out of the chapel to the main hall beyond.

One of the nuns met her and spoke as she passed. Sister Cuthbert replied with her usual sweet dignity, but her expression, in the white light of the electric globe overhead, breathed such exaltation that the nun stopped and looked after her with reverent wonder. Sister Cuthbert went directly to the room of the Mother Superior and told her experience.

In the days that followed, the influence of Sister Cuthbert, always benign, had in it in the sick-room a new element which even the most careless of the girls felt strongly. In the past she had helped, strengthened, and comforted. Now she seemed to uplift as well — to bear others upward by the gentle force of her own spiritual ascent. If there had been any criticism of her in the old days, among those most severe of critics, the school-girls, it was that she was visionary.

"She is not human enough; she is not one of us," they had said. "She lives in a rarefied atmosphere. Her sympathy is not the sympathy of understanding; it is sympathy in the abstract — a regret over something she has never known and only half gets."

Groping around now in their puzzled minds for an explanation of the change in her, they decided that the new element was a human one — the sympathy of perfect understanding. But with it was an increase of the spiritual quality which had always characterized the young nun.

"She is more ecstatic in her moods than ever," said May Iverson, slowly, "and yet, somehow, she is more of us. What an atmosphere she gives out! Her mere presence is like a prayer. The expression is not new, but how it fits! — how well it fits! She is going through some experience, take my word for it; something we know nothing about."

Sister Philomene returned a week from the day she had left. Her father had passed away, but one look at her face made Sister Cuthbert feel that her mission had been successful. There was no time for conversation between the two on the subjects so near to both. Sister Cuthbert made her verbal report with her usual sweet conciseness, and, though Sister Philomene felt the subtle change in her, she could ask no questions.

The afternoon of her return the portress brought Sister Philomene a message and a card. The card read:

HENRY C. SEDGWICK, M.D.

The message, conscientiously delivered by the little portress, was rather a lengthy one. The gentleman, she said, was the physician of Sister Cuthbert's family. Sister Cuthbert's mother had died a week ago, and the doctor wished to tell the young nun of her affliction and give her some details concerning the last hours of her mother's life. He had not made the journey for that purpose; professional business had brought him to the city near the convent, and he had driven there on the chance that an interview might be granted him. And because he was to come, her family had not yet written her of their great loss. Sister Philomene made her decision promptly.

"Ask him to be so kind as to wait," she said to the portress, "and tell Sister Cuthbert I would like to see her." She glanced sympathetically at the young nun when she responded to the summons.

"Dr. Sedgwick is here to see you," she said, "and to tell you the details of your dear mother's — death. We will go to him together, if you would like it." She straightened the papers on her desk very carefully as she spoke, and listened, with a little quickening of her steady heart-beats, for some sound from the other woman. There was none. Sister Cuthbert was silently moving towards the door. She stepped back as she reached it, and stood aside for her superior to precede her. Sister Philomene looked at her as she passed, and something in the nun's expression made her catch her breath. Sister Cuthbert was almost smiling.

The doctor, awaiting them in the prim little reception-room at the right of the convent entrance, was stalking up and down the highly polished floor, bending his shaggy head over the wax pieces on the small tables, and scrutinizing with his near-sighted eyes the paintings and embroideries on the wall. He dreaded the fifteen minutes before him with his keener realization of the cost of the kindly impulse that had made him come. But the sense of personal tax faded away as he turned to greet the young nun he had known since she was a child. He held out both hands, and she laid her own in them. Then he bowed gravely to the Sister who accompanied her, and placed chairs for them both with punctilious courtesy. Not a word had been spoken, but his quick eyes had already taken in every detail of the novice's expression, and he, too, wondered.

"You can surmise my melancholy errand, Sister," he said, gently. "Your dear mother died a week ago today — the day you must have received the letter I wrote telling you of her illness. You could hardly have reached her in time, you see, even had you started at once. I thought there might be some comfort to you in hearing of her last hours, and so I have ventured to make this call."

"You are very kind," said the nun, softly.

Dr. Sedgwick rubbed his glasses. He was conscious of a sensation touching on irritability. Was this the warm-hearted girl he had known — this woman who had not one tear for her mother's death? Or was it another illustration of the drying-up of all human impulse which he believed convent life entailed? He unconsciously took on his most professional manner as he continued.

"There was no pain or suffering at the last. But one rather extraordinary thing happened. Your mother, as I wrote you, had been calling for you constantly. Just at the end she became conscious, and she thought she saw you. She spoke to you and died happy in the belief that you were with her."

"I was," said Sister Cuthbert, quietly; "I was there." She lifted her eyes as she spoke and fixed them on the doctor's face. He regarded her with professional calm.

"Sister Cuthbert means," interrupted Sister Philomene, gently, "that she was there in spirit and sympathy. Her duties kept her here. It was unfortunate, but we could not permit her to go."

"I was there," repeated Sister Cuthbert, with quiet conviction. She seemed not to have heard the other woman's words. She spoke slowly, as one who describes a picture and wishes to overlook no detail.

"She died between four and five o'clock," she continued, "in her own room. The bed had been moved between the two large windows. You were there, and another man I had never seen before, who seemed to be a doctor, too — both standing at the left side of the bed. You held my mother's hand and counted her pulse. Father knelt at the foot of the bed, with his face buried in the bedclothes. My sister Edith sat on a chair near him. When you were giving my mother some stimulant she revived and saw me. She said, 'Katherine — you have come — how good — dear child. Now I can die content.' Then she — fell asleep, and you helped my dear old stricken father to his feet."

Comprehension dawned on the doctor's face. "Oh, you have heard from your father or sister, after all," he said, more briskly and with an air of relief. "They said they would not write, as I was to tell you personally. But I see they have given you minute details."

"No one has written," said the novice, simply. "I have not heard one word." She was very erect, and her pure tones had the throbbing quality of a cello string.

"I saw it all — the whole scene — as I knelt before the altar in our chapel, where I had been praying God for strength to do my duty here. He gave it — and more. He took me there, my mother saw me, and I saw her die. I told Reverend Mother of it that night — just as I have told it now. Oh — the glory of it, the goodness of it, the miracle of it! Do you wonder that I can endure her death after that? Do you wonder that I can smile, though she has gone?"

Sister Philomene started to her feet. Her serene face was transfigured by a reflection of the light that shone from the face of the novice. She crossed herself. Without doubt or question she accepted the experience, as Sister Cuthbert had done, as a manifestation of the divine love and mercy. Her lips moved as she prayed silently. Sister Cuthbert, too, was praying. Both seemed to have forgotten that they were not alone.

Dr. Sedgwick took his hat and turned it doubtfully in his hands. He looked at the inspired faces of the nuns and his eyes dropped as he bowed his farewell. Here was something new in his experience. Give him time and he could explain the thing, he thought. In fact, half a dozen explanations suggested themselves as he went slowly down the steps that led from the convent entrance to the street. The novice was in an overwrought, nervous state at the time of the — er — vision, he reflected. She knew the house and the room, and some telepathic signal might have come to her at the hour of her mother's death. But she had described the scene so accurately! How could she know the mother's very words, and that little incident of his helping the broken husband to rise?

Dr. Sedgwick stopped a passing cab and jumped in. His nerves were on edge. He did not like to meet these supernatural experiences on a bright, warm day in the beginning of the scientific twentieth century. The clang of the cable-car was in his ears, the shouts of quarrelsome cabmen rising above it, yet in these most prosaic surroundings that strange experience kept obtruding itself. Dr. Sedgwick put it away at last by a strong effort of will.

"Too much work, not enough nourishment, I'm afraid," he reflected, practically. "What she needs is a change of air, rest, and good food." This was satisfactory as far as it went. But no sooner had the doctor nicely adjusted his point of view than he recalled, with surprising vividness, that scene in the death-room.

Oh, the radiance of the dying face as the woman had looked up at that empty corner: *"Katherine — you have come — how good — dear child. Now I can die content."*

What had she seen? Dr. Sedgwick brusquely turned away from the answer.

Made in the USA
Las Vegas, NV
08 August 2024